# Contemporary African Literature in English

# Contemporary African Literature in English

## Global Locations, Postcolonial Identifications

Madhu Krishnan
*Department of English, University of Bristol, UK*

First published 2014 by
PALGRAVE MACMILLAN

Palgrave Macmillan in the UK is an imprint of Macmillan Publishers Limited, registered in England, company number 785998, of Houndmills, Basingstoke, Hampshire RG21 6XS.

Palgrave Macmillan in the US is a division of St Martin's Press LLC, 175 Fifth Avenue, New York, NY 10010.

Palgrave Macmillan is the global academic imprint of the above companies and has companies and representatives throughout the world.

Palgrave® and Macmillan® are registered trademarks in the United States, the United Kingdom, Europe and other countries.

ISBN 978–1–137–37832–3

This book is printed on paper suitable for recycling and made from fully managed and sustained forest sources. Logging, pulping and manufacturing processes are expected to conform to the environmental regulations of the country of origin.

A catalogue record for this book is available from the British Library.

A catalog record for this book is available from the Library of Congress.

Typeset by MPS Limited, Chennai, India.

# Contents

# Acknowledgements

This project began as an idea which came at the end of my doctoral studies and has since developed across three institutions and with the generous input of countless colleagues, friends and practitioners working in African literary studies and postcolonial studies, more broadly. I am grateful to Máire Ní Fhlathúin who, while acting as my doctoral supervisor in the School of English at the University of Nottingham, was both a sage advisor and meticulous reader of the papers and presentations which formed the earliest kernels of this study. I owe Máire a particular debt of gratitude for encouraging me to think beyond the literary text to the circuits of production which define its appearance in the world and for her encouragement in the development of my academic career. Equally, I would be remiss not to acknowledge my doctoral examiners, Matthew Green, at the University of Nottingham, and Patrick Williams, at Nottingham Trent University, for their insightful comments on my work, ideas for future avenues of inquiry and continued support.

This monograph was largely drafted and revised while I spent a year working in the School of English Literature, Language and Linguistics at Newcastle University. I am enormously grateful to all of my colleagues in the School for the warm and convivial atmosphere in which this book was written. I'd like to particularly thank Kate Chedzgoy for her mentorship and interest in my professional advancement and James Procter and Neelam Srivastava for being inspiring role models, providing constant intellectual stimulation and showing me the ways in which academic research can come alive in our postcolonial present. My thanks also go to James Annesley and Anne Whitehead, who both provided me with invaluable guidance in navigating the waters of academic publishing and who offered much needed perspective beyond the world of the postcolonial. While at Newcastle, I was extraordinarily fortunate to be a part of the Newcastle Postcolonial Research Group. My thanks go to Janelle Rodriques, Tom Langley, Claire Irving, Marie Stern-Peltz, Joe Barton, Alex Adams and Laura Routley for the conversations, debates and drinks which sustained this project.

The editing and final stages of this project took place during my first months at the University of Bristol. My thanks to all of my colleagues in the Department of English for their support, encouragement and commiseration. I have been fortunate to be a part of a lively and always-interesting cohort of colleagues working in African literatures on four continents. My thanks go to Hamish Dalley, Christopher Ouma, Steph Newell, Shauna Morgan Kirlew and Louis Chude-Sokei for their generosity of spirit in reading and thoughtfully commenting on draft sections of this monograph.

I am especially grateful to Palgrave Macmillan for the ease with which this project was developed and progressed through the publication process. Particular thanks go to the anonymous reader, whose comments were both thoughtful and thorough and have helped shape this monograph into its current form, Ben Doyle, who has been unfailingly insightful and encouraging as my commissioning editor, and Sophie Ainscough, who has patiently guided me through the murky fields of editing and production. I would also like to thank all of the editors with whom I have been fortunate to work in the process of developing this study. Parts of Chapter 3 concerning exoticism in *Half of a Yellow Sun* have been published in a different form as 'Abjection and the Fetish: Reconsidering the Construction of the Postcolonial Exotic in Chimamanda Ngozi Adichie's *Half of a Yellow Sun*', *Journal of Postcolonial Writing*, 48.1 (2012), 26–38, <http://www.tandfonline.com/loi/rjpw20>, reproduced here with the permission of Taylor & Francis. Chapter 4's discussion of *GraceLand* and the *ogbanje* previously appeared as 'Beyond Tradition and Progress: Re-imagining Nigeria in Chris Abani's Graceland', *Re-imagining Africa: Creative Crossings*, edited by Simon Gikandi and Jane Wilkinson, *Anglistica*, 15.2 (2011), 97–106, <http://www.anglistica.unior.it>, reprinted by permission of Università degli Studi di Napoli 'L'Orientale'. Sections of Chapter 5, discussing the trope of the book within the book in *GraceLand* and *Half of a Yellow Sun*, have been published in an extended form as 'On National Culture and the Projective Past: Mythology, Nationalism, and the Heritage of Biafra in Contemporary Nigerian Narrative', *CLIO: A Journal of Literature, History, and the Philosophy of History*, 42.2 (2013), 187–208, <http://www.ipfw.edu/clio/>, reprinted by permission of Indiana University-Purdue University Fort Wayne.

Special thanks go to my family, Krishnaswamy, Durgalakshmi, Sriram, Lori and Sathvika Krishnan, for always and unfailingly encouraging me in all of my pursuits and their tireless support, both material and emotional. Last, but by no means least, I am more grateful than words can convey to Jason Ellis, my partner in life and everything that goes with it, without whom none of this would have been possible and whose love has sustained me beyond all things.

# Introduction: Writing Africa in a Global Marketplace

In his 2005 essay, 'How to Write About Africa', Binyavanga Wainaina counsels the aspiring writer of African literature to

> Always use the word 'Africa' or 'Darkness' or 'Safari' in your title. Subtitles may include the words 'Zanzibar', 'Masai', 'Zulu', 'Zambezi', 'Congo', 'Nile', 'Big', 'Sky', 'Shadow', 'Drum', 'Sun' or 'Bygone'. Also useful are words such as 'Guerrillas', 'Timeless', 'Primordial' and 'Tribal'. Note that 'People' means Africans who are not black, while 'The People' means black Africans.[1]

Africa, Wainaina reminds the would-be scribe, is a homogeneous space in crisis. Faced with increasing sectarian violence and governmental mismanagement, the continent which has only emerged into independence in the last fifty years is once again on the brink of collapse as ethnic, religious and cultural identities go to war, dictatorial regimes flourish and humanitarian intervention goes unheeded. This is the popular image of Africa outside of the continent, a common-sense vision circulated across Europe and North America through film, television, the news media and popular culture. Yet, within the realm of African literature, a far different picture of the continent has developed. This Africa is one of promise, hope and struggle, where individual lives and collective fates strive towards an open future; it is this Africa which has held the interest of literary critics over the past sixty years. This book focuses on the ways in which this vision of Africa has been negotiated in contemporary writing. In order to analyse the nexus of factors which impel a literary image

1

of the continent, I draw upon close textual analysis, socio-historical contextualization and an exploration of the material circuits of pro- duction, dissemination and reception that contribute to the global image of Africa. Through a close examination of representation at the intersection of the aesthetic and the political in contemporary Anglophone African writing, this book considers the extent to which imaginative literature is able to pose a response to the dominant view of the continent perpetuated by the popular media, opening avenues for subjectivities—individual and collective—unchained from the deterministic absolutes of stereotype while remaining, through its selection and constriction by the demands of an international audi- ence of consumers, perpetually in peril of reverting to the same.

To meet these aims, this book focuses primarily on those award- winning and internationally-published texts and authors most often put forward as representative of contemporary African literature in Europe and North America. To explore how these globally- published authors and their works have become representative of Africa and African fiction, I read Brian Chikwava's *Harare North* (2009), Nuruddin Farah's *Links* (2005), Tsitsi Dangarembga's *The Book of Not* (2006), Chimamanda Ngozi Adichie's *Half of a Yellow Sun* (2006), Aminatta Forna's *Ancestor Stones* (2006), Yvonne Vera's *The Stone Virgins* (2002), Chris Abani's *GraceLand* (2004) and Ngũgĩ wa Thiong'o's *Wizard of the Crow* (2004/2006). Originally published in serialized form in Ngũgĩ's native Gĩkũyũ, the last text, at first, may seem out of place in a study on Anglophone African literature. A product of 'auto-translation',[2] *Wizard of the Crow* is only Anglophone in the sense of having been translated by its author from its original Gĩkũyũ form. However, despite its origins in Gĩkũyũ, the novel has nonetheless entered the landscape of Anglophone African writing. This is for a variety of reasons but most notably Ngũgĩ's own canoni- cal status as an author of African literature in English, conferred by earlier works like *The River Between* (1965) and *A Grain of Wheat* (1967). Regardless of his own wishes Ngũgĩ remains interpellated into the category of English-language African literature, both in the dissemination of his texts and in his international reputation.

The relative reception of the two versions of his novel provides an apt study of the ways in which the African literary text is always received as more than just a text. More broadly, it could be argued that each of the aforementioned writers is equally non-African, despite his or her status as a high-profile writer of African literature: Abani resides in Los Angeles, Chikwava in London; Adichie and Dangarembga both spend much of their time in Europe and North America; Vera resided in Canada for much of her adulthood and at the time of her death; Ngũgĩ lives and works in California and Farah in Cape Town which, while in Africa, remains remote from his native Somalia. How does this geographic dissonance impact upon the image of Africa circulated in each author's work? Why has this decidedly migratory African identity become representative of African literature, writ large? To better understand the stakes at issue in these questions, the final chapter of this study places these works in a critical dialogue with fellow contemporary works which have not found a similar international audience, reading Valerie Tagwira's *The Uncertainty of Hope* (2006), G. A. Agambila's *Journey* (2006) and Francis B. Nyamnjoh's *The Disillusioned African* (1995/2007), all published by independent continental African presses, to interrogate the contours of the local and the global in the construction of a literary Africa.

Timothy Brennan writes that

> the public stance of the writer (and critic) from the imperialized formations—negating the variety that first brought him or her into the public eye—exhibits a homogenization, although a complex one. Here is developed, passively, a set of doctrinal demands for the 'third-world' writer, whose features coalesce in what then appears as an appropriate cosmopolitanism. Together, these features form a geopolitical aesthetic, first with the requisites of metropolitan assumptions in mind (or at least at hand), but then, in its full articulation, with matters of taste left untouched while it seems to reorient them.[3]

At the same time, as Sarah Brouillette demonstrates, authors, as figures with agency, may attempt with varying degrees of success to contest these conventions and sanctioned aesthetics: 'self-constructing gestures are challenged by the same circumstances that encourage their emergence, as writers will themselves readily admit, and so a cycle of critique and response typically ensues'.[4] In other words, writers in a global literary marketplace both challenge and are constrained by the conventions of representation mediating the reception of postcolonial literatures. By placing these global texts against works marked by their conditions of production and reception as local, then, this study aims to draw out the particularities of the 'geopolitical aesthetic' that describes Africa abroad and its larger ideological and socio-political import.

African literary studies have proven to be a fast-growing subfield of postcolonial studies, one of the largest emerging disciplines in cultural and literary studies over the last thirty years. Based in no small part on the global popularity and celebrity status of the founders of the African literary canon, particularly Chinua Achebe, Wole Soyinka and Ngũgĩ wa Thiong'o, the study of African literature has remained an integral aspect of postcolonial studies' literary programme of inquiry. Despite this critical focus, however, current scholarship on literary writing associated with the continent remains limited by an inability to adequately address the contours of that work deemed 'African' on a global stage. The idea of Africa in these works, in other words, remains caught in a critical schism between authenticity and cosmopolitan detachment. Based in this conceptual opposition, studies of African writing largely revert to a split method which relies upon an allegiance either to the political value of African literature, writing back to imperial formations, or to its aesthetic value in recuperating a lost heritage. In both cases, the question of the will-to-knowledge in the transnational construction and circulation of an African literary canon in the context of a 'continuous history' of the postcolonial,[5] along with the related question of truth-value in representation, remains obscured through a cleaving of the aesthetic from the political. This is evidenced in the range of studies which focus alternatively on magical realism, orality and pre-colonial tradition, on the one hand,[6] and those which focus on anti-colonial nationalism, Marxism and historical determinism, on the other.[7] Even those works which foreground the construction of African literature as a global category remain hesitant to address the text as a specifically literary work, favouring instead what has been called the sociology of the text in their approaches.[8] While these studies represent important contributions to the on-going study of African literature, the current schism in studies of African writing nonetheless reflects a critical lacuna in approaching the African literary text in its totality. Unlike scholars of South African literature, a context of writing directly influenced by the immediacy of the ethical imperatives created by apartheid, criticism of continental African literature, writ large, has remained largely unable to address the narrative space where aesthetic and political imperatives overlap with the constraints of material culture in the transmission of the image of Africa dispersed across the globe today. As Simon Gikandi notes, 'More often than not, key African novels are either read as social documents which utilize the resources of fictionalization only superficially, or simply as decorative forms which seem to exist for their own sake'.[9] Gikandi calls for a heightened attentiveness to the relationship between form and content as a corrective to this critical neglect; in this book I take this plea further, suggesting that not only is the relationship between form (aesthetics), content (the political) and context (socio-historical and material) essential to the study of African literature, but that these aspects of the text are in fact co-constitutive and irrevocably intertwined in the creation and dissemination of a global Africa such that the study of one necessitates the study of the others.

Certainly, the split between the aesthetic and the political in critical inquiry is not unique to African literary studies; indeed, this condition of literary criticism in African letters reflects a larger split within postcolonial studies itself, between the discursive branch aligned with poststructuralism (including Gayatri Chakravorty Spivak and Homi K. Bhabha, two of postcolonial studies' 'holy trinity' of scholars) and its Marxist division (represented in the work of Neil Lazarus, Benita Parry, Aijaz Ahmad and Arif Dirlik). While certain practical advantages to this theoretical schism persist, neither of these approaches has fully addressed the mechanisms of representation evident in African literature and the bearing these mechanisms maintain on the image of Africa disseminated across the globe today. Indeed, this theoretical separation of the aesthetic and the political has resulted in critical readings which demand the elevation of a single discourse within the text and a repression of its alternate and multiple valuations. African literature must either be 'mostly sociopolitical',[10] where, in Chidi Amuta's terms, 'the immediacy of historical experience collectively felt becomes the real litmus test on the matter of creative genius',[11] or else it must 'capture and recreate the tone, flavor and texture of life in our society' through a return to the poetics of orality.[12] In each case, the literary text is taken to function within an already-decided system of meaning, based upon whether literary worth is encoded through the aesthetic form of the text or its political function. The result has been a reification of the aesthetic/political split through the proliferation of critical schools, territorial disputes across the academy and the perpetual debate surrounding authenticity and representation in African literature. Mired in these conflicts, African literary study remains locked in partial and often-antiquated views of what it means to represent Africa within a transnational world system which, ironically, often fall prey to the stereotypical image of an Africa in crisis.

This book address this critical lacuna through an extended study of the intersection of the aesthetic and the political in contemporary African writing, situating close readings of primary texts against both the material cultures which dictate their production, circulation and reception, and the socio-historical contexts towards which they gesture and within which they are embedded. Throughout, I argue that it is in this interstitial space that the ethical imperative of postcolonial literatures, both as representative and re-presentative, comes to the fore. At the place where the aesthetic opens to the world, in other words, the literary text becomes subject to a series of positions related to its roles as speaking-for and speaking-of which relate directly to the larger valuations and ideologies which drive the global construction of borders, boundaries and identities. Considered in this light, textuality, cultural materiality and historical/social context will not be presented as discrete categories for analysis, but rather as mutually-implicated aspects of literary production, together creating what has been called 'the localized conditions of knowledge production' which impel understanding.[13] Over the course of this study, I consider the ways in which contemporary African literary narratives, as examples of imaginative literature, demonstrate the complex and often contradictory workings of identification, as they both shape and are shaped by the larger discourses surrounding Africa across the globe. This book focuses, in particular, on the construction of race, gender, mythopoetics and the question of address, progressing from a study of individual, character-based identity-formation to collective forms of identification which occur at the site of reading. Certainly, this book does not purport to give a definitive answer to the question of how identities and communities are represented in narrative. It does, however, set out to illuminate some of the ways in which identities are challenged, created, mired and shifted within the complex web of interacting discourses and material constraints which marks the contemporary postcolony.

## Postcolonial Studies and Representation: Contexts and Criticism

When the field of postcolonial studies was unofficially inaugurated with the 1978 publication of Edward W. Said's *Orientalism*, a main concern of the field was how cultural representations were legitimized.[14] Said demonstrated how, through the circulation of discourse, the Orient was authenticated in both the Western imaginary and, crucially, in the Orient itself, thereby exposing the textual mechanisms behind colonial control. As Said writes in that work:

> The Orient and Islam have a kind of extrareal, phenomenologically reduced status that puts them out of reach of everyone except the Western expert. From the beginning of Western speculation about the Orient, the one thing the Orient could not do was to represent itself. Evidence of the Orient was credible only after it had passed through and been made firm by the refining fire of the Orientalist's work.[15]

The Orient, metonymically standing in for the non-Western world, cannot know itself. It can only become known through the expertise of Western scholarship, creating and fixing its image in time and space. Moreover, as Kojin Karatani has explained, '"Orientalism" sees people of the non-West as convenient objects of analysis for the social sciences but ignores their intellectual and ethical existences'.[16] Under this view, artistic reproductions of the Orient, particularly, were taken to buttress an already-read system of representation and meaning, where the pleasure of the exotic or the otherworldly artefact emerged not from a quest for understanding, but from the enforcement of an already-known ontological essence. Central to the production of the Orient, then, was the devaluation of the non-West as less than human, a condition that persists today through what Judith Butler has characterized as 'the extent that a "Western" civilization defines itself over and against a population understood as, by definition, illegitimate, if not dubiously human'.[17]

In the African context, numerous scholars have noted what Spivak has called the 'epistemic violence'[18] of the colonial project as it forced misappropriations of African belief, rendering Africa the 'primitive' and 'tribal' foil against which Europe could feel its superiority.[19] V. Y. Mudimbe describes this process as Europe's 'ordering of otherness',[20] where '[outsiders] were nonetheless imagined and rejected as the intimate and other side of the European-thinking subject'.[21] Indeed, Mudimbe's two studies, *The Invention of Africa* and *The Idea of Africa*, provide a corollary to Said's *Orientalism* in the African context in which the present study is situated by outlining the difficulties of translating what Mudimbe terms African gnosis, 'by definition a kind of secret knowledge',[22] to a Western idiom. As Mudimbe explains:

> Although in African history the colonial experience represents but a brief moment from the perspective of today, this moment is still charged and controversial since, to say the least, it signified a new historical form and the possibility of radically new types of discourses on African traditions and cultures.[23]

More directly speaking, colonialism irrevocably altered the image of Africa which persists to the present day, including the means through which the continent is thought, theorized and represented on a world stage. This is perhaps most clearly seen in the preponderance of binary oppositions in defining Africa against the West: 'traditional versus modern; oral versus written and printed; agrarian and customary communities versus urban and industrialized civilization; subsistence economies versus highly productive economies'.[24] In short, 'The African has become not only the Other who is everyone else except me, but rather the key which, in its abnormal differences, specifies the identity of the Same'.[25] Crucially, this image of Africa is one which has been interiorized, both through a positive assimilation and an oppositional resistance, a double bind captured in Ezekiel Mphahlele's lament that 'We [Africans] must stop placing ourselves on show to the outside world and begin teaching our own people'.[26]

In the contemporary context, this vision of Africa as a place of exotic fascination and unspeakable suffering has persisted across a variety of forms and media. American and British news coverage of recent events in African history provides one example of this lingering and catastrophic rhetoric. An op-ed in the *New York Times*, looking at the run-up to the 2012 Somali presidential elections, for instance, features the headline 'Getting Somalia Right This Time', while another editorial essay, this time describing bureaucratic stagnancy in Zimbabwe, declares that the nation-state has become 'Where Citizenship Went to Die'. Similar coverage appears in reports detailing the 2008 Kenyan elections ('Kenya, Known for Its Stability, Topples Into Post-Election Chaos', a title which neglects to mention the inconvenient fact that the aforementioned stability came at the price of dictatorship) and 2011 Nigerian elections ('Election Fuels Deadly Clashes in Nigeria'). Meanwhile, on the other side of the Atlantic, the *Guardian* features headlines like 'Scores Hacked to Death in Nigerian Sectarian Clash' and the *Times* ones such as 'Sierra Leone: a Tale of Post-colonial Disaster: How Prosperity Declined into Bloody Revolution'.[27] Beyond the headlines, a recent profile featured in *The Boston Globe* details the travails of Abubakar 'Bubbles' Suleiman, a Nigerian immigrant and a recent middle school graduate who joyfully discusses the opportunities life in America has given him after a childhood spent 'hunting zebras with spears and trying to avoid antagonizing cheetahs'.[28] Never mind that northern Nigeria, Suleiman's place of birth, features little by way of savannahs and no known cheetahs or zebras. Equally, the image of Africa portrayed in fashion and cultural publications displays a similar preoccupation with foregrounding the wild, exotic, yet somehow homogeneous, nature of the continent. In the September 2009 issue of American *Harper's Bazaar*, supermodel Naomi Campbell dashes across the plains in a playful race with a cheetah, whose skin is replicated in the fabric of her dress. Later, in the same layout, clad in zebra skins and fur she frolics under a jump rope twirled by two monkeys. In the June 2007 issue of *Vogue* USA, actress Keira Knightley stands proud, surveying the empty distance, surrounded by a group of silent Masai warriors, clad in bright colours and utterly interchangeable in their passivity. More recently, a fashion spread in the May 2011 issue of British *Vogue* heralds its title, 'White Mischief', with a photo of an ethereal Agyness Deyn, millennial It girl, staring vacantly down at a young man in full tribal drag with what is presumably his pet cheetah, all against the picturesque backdrop of the Namib Desert. This is the Africa of Hollywood, that place depicted in recent films like *Blood Diamond* and *The Constant Gardener*. This is an Africa which cannot function on its own, always in need of the Western gaze to admire its wonders or Western intervention to save it from itself. Across these examples, even the most nuanced reportage is packaged under headlines and images which recall Africa as that savage place, incapable of democracy and independent leadership and still in need of the firm guidance of a wiser and more just West. Africa may be exotic in its primal beauty, but it remains remote, empty of humanity and open to the ministrations of the adventurous Western traveller-cum-humanitarian.

Of course, this idea of Africa does not represent the full complexity of colonial intervention on the African continent and its lasting legacy in the representation of Africa today. As these examples highlight, the Orientalist/Africanist vision of Said and Mudimbe results in a view in which the African continent, along with its inhabitants, functions in entirely passive terms. Colonial violence is done to the continent, and the image of Africa is imposed upon its peoples. Without downplaying the immensity of colonial violence and its violation of the African continent, however, there still remains room to enliven moments of resistance to and appropriation of the discourses and material legacies of colonialism by the diverse populations of Africa. This may be reflected in the characterization of colonial conquest and subjugation as 'an enabling violation',[29] constitutive of contemporary African thought, and a focus on agency within the colonial frame. As Gikandi reminds us, the issue is less what has been done to the African continent, staged as a passive repository for imposed values, than the ways in which actors and agents from the continent worked and continue to work within an evolving system of representation to create visions of self, world and community.[30] Without removing the asymmetric system of violence which defined colonial conquest on the continent, it remains imperative to recall the extent to which these discourses, systems and functions have become part of Africa's own history through what Spivak calls 'a wrenching coupling of epistemes'.[31] Colonization, in other words, was not passively accepted by the African continent and its populations; instead, the colonial encounter became the site of radical appropriations and reinscriptions,[32] an epistemological realignment which is of particular relevance to contemporary imaginings of Africa. Rather than functioning through oppositions, Africa and the West may be viewed as nodes in a complex, unevenly-loaded and ever-shifting network of influence and interaction, both acting upon and within a transnational cultural and socio-political world system. Throughout the body of theoretical work associated with postcolonial studies, the control of narratives of self, other and society has been cited as a central means through which colonial intervention operated and continues to operate, with ramifications in both the symbolic reproduction of violence and its material effects. In his study of colonial 'states of emergency', for instance, Stephen Morton interrogates the extent through which legal, literary and military rhetoric served to reinforce an image of the colonies as lawless spaces in need of the civilizing discipline of the metropole, a justification for brutality which elides the foundational violence of colonialism, in which 'European colonial governments mobilised a repository of narratives and metaphors to mask and obfuscate the terror and violence of colonial sovereignty'.[33] The deployment and control of narratives casting the colonized as savage and the colonizers as benevolent patrons, Morton explains, served to undergird and legitimize the normalization of terror and use of force to maintain colonial order. More broadly, Said, in the preface to *Culture and Imperialism*, explains that 'nations themselves *are* narrations. The power to narrate, or to block other narratives from forming and emerging, is very important to culture and imperialism, and constitutes one of the main connections between them'.[34] Narrative is thus seen as 'central to the representation of identity, in personal memory and self-representation or in collective identity of groups such as regions, nations, race and gender'.[35] As Kwame Anthony Appiah has noted, 'evaluating stories together is one of the central human ways of learning to align our responses to the world. And that alignment of responses is [...] one of the ways we maintain the social fabric, the texture of our relationships'.[36] Because of the potency of narrative as a means of ordering the world and creating meaning, then, a central facet of colonial expansion functioned through its investment in a negative image of the colonized. 'If you are going to enslave or to colonise somebody', Achebe reminds us, 'you are not going to write a glowing report about him either before or after'.[37]

Most relevantly for this study, this focus on narrative extends to the literary; as Brennan notes, '*cultural* study, and specifically the study of imaginative literature, is in many ways a profitable one for understanding the nation-centredness of the post-colonial world'.[38] Indeed, as my opening discussion of Said implies, the manipulation of racial and cultural representation in imaginative literature has remained one of the primary ways in which imperialist and colonialist powers maintained themselves.[39] The non-Western individual, rather than existing as a subject in her or his own right, becomes an invention of Western discourse through the West 'inseminating itself globally, after having properly tilled, turned over and reduced to compost the once lived actualities of the historicity of the non-European world'.[40] At the same time, it is important to recall that this constructed representation is not mere caricature. Rather, it accounts for 'a complex ignorance' which functions 'actively as a form of *positive* knowledge'.[41] The resulting internalization of externally-produced discourse repeats and perpetuates dominance and oppression with devastating psycho-social effects on the colonized subject, in the terms of Frantz Fanon's theorization in 1952's *Black Skin, White Masks* and 1961's *The Wretched of the Earth*. It has also inspired a more contemporary body of work outlining the importance of narrative-as-testimony to combat this, including notable contributions from bell hooks, Paul Gilroy and Kelly Oliver.[42] By attempting to destabilize colonial appropriations of the narratives of nation and individual, however, postcolonial studies implicitly questions the very basis of narrative representations. With its emphasis on how 'we' understand 'our' world explicitly interrogated, postcolonial readings may thus attempt to expose the constructed and Eurocentric nature of the 'us' who defines the world through narrative control and, in the process, imposes its viewpoint on 'them' through a system of binary oppositions. Rather than passively accepting narrative as a means of self-production and world-creation, a postcolonial critique may thus question the construction of narrative and the tacit assumptions about self, others and the world which are encoded within it. Certainly, in Africa, a continent of nations fabricated through colonial imposition, the notion that colonial power works to 'transform non-European areas into fundamentally European constructs' is relevant.[43] Yet, equally central is the means through which these avenues of control were appropriated and transfigured into something else entirely, refusing this single-minded and Manichean imposition of value. Even the nation, that imaginary structure so neatly imposed upon the map of the continent, has become a lived construct, often in direct opposition to its colonial founders' interests. This mutability is a point to which I will return throughout the course of this study, as the re-presentation and representation of individuals and events will show the fragility of this process as well as its complexity.

It is my argument in this book that current debate surrounding African literature has strayed too far from this nuanced view of the complexity of representation, favouring instead often-polemic posturing on the relative value of authenticity, cosmopolitanism or recuperation, as discrete textual functions. Certainly, work of this nature is crucial to the advancement of African literary studies; at the same time, the inability of criticism to not only concern itself with what has become global African literature but why, and through what means, has marked a gap in the potential for a deeper understanding of how and why Africa has come to mean in its contemporary context. Echoing the concerns of critics of postcolonial studies more broadly, this reification of critical approaches led to a certain fossilization of scholarship. Lazarus, for example, has commented that 'postcolonialist readings often have a quality of appropriativeness'.[44] This statement captures the sentiment that the range of studies put forth by postcolonial scholars has become constrained by the discipline's early affiliation with French theory, celebrating ideas of hybridity, difference and dislocation, what John C. Hawley has called 'traditional postcolonial interests',[45] over ideals of resistance or social realism, essentially complaining that the aesthetic has overtaken the political. Conversely, Eli Park Sorensen argues, this same preference has resulted in a critical paradigm that overlooks texts which fail to function as studies in the interstitial, dismissing them as reactionary and elevating the political over the aesthetic.[46] Regardless of perspective, the preference for readings of a certain sort in postcolonial studies has resulted in a sense of neglect in critical inquiry. In African literature, Mudimbe echoes this notion with his observation that

> when one speaks of African literature one is referring both to a body of texts whose authors are known and to anonymous discourses which carry on successive deposits of supposedly unknown imaginations. This is already a problem, and it has, so far, not been addressed in a convincing way by specialists of African studies.[47]

Africa, in short, becomes a place that is already-read and already-known and yet is simultaneously and paradoxically alien. Set in this context, then, the image of Africa becomes a negative exposure of the accepted normativity of late capitalism and contemporary developmentalist narratives of world progression, which it is contemporary criticism's task to combat.

In considering these questions of identity and representation in African literature, this study progresses thematically, rather than geographically or chronologically, focusing on the means through which the aesthetic and political valuations of African literature produce space for representing-otherwise. While this structure bears the advantage of allowing for considerable scope for comparativism and the drawing of transnational connections, it also means that concepts and debates brought up in one chapter may be revisited, expanded upon or refined in subsequent chapters. Additionally, because of its thematic focus, geographical, historical and political contextualization will be spread across the study as relevant to a particular section. The first chapter of this study sets the theoretical and broad cultural context for the remainder of the monograph, introducing the notions of representation and ethics. The question of narrative representation will be linked to the intersection of the aesthetic and the political, and this, in turn, will be drawn out to debates on the anthropological exotic, the writer in an African state and the worldliness of the literary text.

The next chapters consider the textual work of representation and identification by looking at the construction of individual subjectivities in contemporary African writing. Chapter 2 focuses on the construction of racial and ethnic identities through readings of Brian Chikwava's *Harare North*, Nuruddin Farah's *Links* and Tsitsi Dangarembga's *The Book of Not*. This chapter dwells particularly on the tension between performativity in identification and fixity in subject position in all three works, highlighting the contingency and perpetual variability of ethnic and raced identities. It argues against a Manichean worldview, instead presenting the notion of racial and ethnic coming-into-being as a multi-valenced and constantly-dispersed process of becoming, refracted through aesthetic innovation in narrative form. The following chapter turns to the construction of gendered identities through readings of Chimamanda Ngozi Adichie's *Half of a Yellow Sun*, Aminatta Forna's *Ancestor Stones* and Yvonne Vera's *The Stone Virgins*, focusing particularly on the intersection of gender and conflict in contemporary African literature. This chapter highlights the multiple and often-conflictual processes of gendered becoming in these texts, arguing that the aesthetic decision to present alternative modes of gendered becoming through contrapuntal writing serves a political purpose of destabilization and recuperation whose promise cannot be entirely fulfilled within the boundaries of the novel.

The final chapters of this book move away from close readings to consider collective identifications as enacted at the site of reading, through the construction of readerships and demands for a reading-otherwise in approaching contemporary African literature. Chapter 4 focuses on case studies of Chris Abani's *GraceLand* and Ngũgĩ wa Thiong'o's *Wizard of the Crow* to explore the re-constitution of mythology and subversion of the oft-used narrative technique of magical realism as rhetorical strategies. By reconfiguring mythological narratives and resisting a collapse into the surreal or arcane in their narrative forms, each novel presents a vision for contemporary Africa which resists totalities and absolutes in favour of an ever-vigilant sense of multiplicity. The final chapter of this monograph focuses on the question of address. This chapter will first examine the ways in which globally-published African literature has both been positioned as authentically African to its largely-Western readership, while remaining under the auspices of Euro-American systems of production, valuation and dissemination, and then, through readings of three locally-published African texts, seeks to position the contours of this global literary vision of Africa. The monograph ends with a brief conclusion which notes trajectories for African literature today and evaluates the interconnectedness of the aesthetic and the political as African literature emerges into the twenty-first century.

Throughout this study, I focus on the complicated relationship between address, context, publication, readership and text which contemporary African literature presents, seeing in this nexus of factors an explicit call for attention to the intersection of the aesthetic and the political in this body of writing. It is in this space, this study asserts, that the ethical imperatives of representation most keenly feel their strength and urgency. Rather than dismissing contemporary African literature as written by and for an elite and largely Euro-American readership by a class of estranged and alienated transnational and diasporic native informants, then, this study focuses on the extent through which the aesthetic act of re-presentation attempts to surpass its limitations as representative through the manipulation of identification and the encoding of address in these novels. Citing a 2000 interview with contemporary Nigerian writer Helon Habila, Elleke Boehmer writes that 'as African novelists in the 2000s turn increasingly towards local audiences and narrative traditions, and away from the implied European reader, they become ever more independent interpreters of their own internal conflicts and identities'.[48] It is the relative efficacy of this turn of address, away from an implied collusion with essentialisms in identity and representation, that this study focuses upon in considering the works of contemporary African literature. In so doing, this study seeks a form of reading somewhat akin to what Robert Spencer has called 'cosmopolitan criticism' and Spivak 'reading as translation',[49] a cry for 'a reader who responds to the call of the text, surrenders to it, and finds there all the risky mutual solicitations of love and politics'.[50] Unlike these formulations, however, this study does not highlight the affective response of the text; rather, it seeks to situate the moment of responsibility in reading at the site where the aesthetic and the political come into contact with the material, staging the act of reading as a perpetual play within the dual senses of representation. Taken together, the novels considered in this book represent Nigeria, Zimbabwe, Sierra Leone, Kenya, Somalia, Cameroon and Ghana. Some of these texts, along with their authors, have found international acclaim, earning the Orange Prize for Fiction (Adichie), the Hurston-Wright Legacy Award (Forna, Abani), the Neustadt Prize (Farah), the Commonwealth Writers' Prize (Dangarembga), the Macmillan Writers' Prize for Africa (Vera), the Lotus Prize for Literature (Ngũgĩ), amongst many others, and readerships numbering well into the millions. Others (Tagwira, Agambila, Nyamnjoh) remain relatively unknown. Through the prominence of some, as eminent literary authorities playing a critical role in the shaping of our global imagining of Africa today, and the neglect of others, as parochial or peripheral, these texts demonstrate the stakes, contours and valuations at play in the creation of a contemporary African literary canon. Throughout the chapters which follow, this work of representation, one encompassing resistance, identification, appropriation and destabilization, will be interrogated, questioned and ultimately mapped in all of its functions.

# 1
# Ethics, Conflict and Re(-)presentation

## Representation and Re-presentation

The impetus to view the African literary text at the intersection of the aesthetic and the political gives rise to an ethical imperative at the site of representation.[1] As Gilroy reminds us, in approaching discursive constructions of the black Atlantic it is essential that 'we reread and rethink this expressive counterculture not simply as a succession of literary tropes and genres but as a philosophical discourse which refuses the modern, occidental separation of ethics and aesthetics, culture and politics'.[2] These arenas of meaning, so often received in isolation, remain intimately intertwined, blocking the efficacy of partial perspectives which give pride of place to one above the other. The literary work cannot, with this understanding, be seen in fragments or by slices. Rather, the totality of value for the literary text comes from its articulation of the political and the aesthetic, and the ethical meanings which arise from this articulated approach. Because the literary work operates through what may be seen as a doubling of representation, both in the 'aesthetic appropriation of reality in the work and the appropriation of the work's aesthetic reality by the recipient',[3] the aesthetic object plays a central role in linking cultural re-presentation with the construction of ideological horizons. As Tobin Siebers has noted, aesthetics, like ethics and politics, represents 'the repetition of experience' through which communities and value systems are formed,[4] a crucial aspect of what Terry Eagleton refers to as the 'project of reconstructing the human subject from the inside, informing its subtlest affections and bodily responses with this law

17

which is not a law'.[5] Framed as such, the aesthetic and the political become deeply intertwined in the negotiation of meaning and representation in the text.

Of course, asserting a link between the aesthetic, the political and the work of ethical judgement is not a new endeavour. Indeed, the role of aesthetic re-presentation in the development of social, political and moral evaluations has been a central concern of theory since Kant's conception of aesthetic judgement and moral perfection. In this chapter, however, I consider the ethical imperative of literary practice in a slightly different manner, through a focus on the implications of the slippage between aesthetic re-presentation and political representation. This discussion draws considerably on Spivak's 'Can the Subaltern Speak?' and the significantly-rewritten version of that same essay published in *A Critique of Postcolonial Reason*.[6] As one of the most widely-cited essays circulating within postcolonial studies today, and, at the same time, one of the most widely misunderstood, the concerns and questions which Spivak raises both in the original essay and subsequent revision are of a central importance to the focus of inquiry in this study, evoking the delicate balance of the aesthetic and the political in a call to vigilance for the producers of postcolonial intellectual histories. In these texts, Spivak addresses the question of representation through an extended reading of Marx's *Eighteenth Brumaire of Louis Napoleon*, dwelling in particular on the distinction between *vertreten* (speaking-for or sociopolitical representation) and *darstellen* (speaking of, or aesthetic re-presentation), glossed as 'proxy' and 'portrait' or 'representation or rhetoric as tropology and as persuasion'.[7] Put simply, *darstellen* acts as re-presentation in the rhetorical or aesthetic sense, while *vertreten*, by contrast, refers to a literal 'standing-in-for', as social or political representation. Focusing on this dual sense of the term, Spivak considers the elision of these two senses of representation as a type of appropriation of the Third World woman, the subaltern *par excellence* and a figure she describes as caught within the discourses of imperialism and patriarchy to her ultimate erasure.

As the introduction to this study indicated, a predominant tension surrounding the development of postcolonial studies as a discipline has centred on the question of representation. As Lazarus aptly notes, '"Representation" is perhaps the single most fraught and contentious term within postcolonial studies'.[8] Who, precisely, does the work of postcolonial criticism? To whom do they address themselves and of whom are they attempting to speak? Which voices are heard and which are lost in the shuffle? Based in these concerns, a primary criticism of postcolonial literary studies has been its celebration of certain highly-educated, middle-class and transnational intellectuals operating from within the Euro-American academy. Again, to invoke Lazarus, 'representation is taken to be a game of high stakes; the danger is thought to rest in the fact that in speaking of or for others [...] we might unintentionally and unwittingly find ourselves both objectifying "them" and superimposing our own elite cognitive maps on "them"'.[9] The chasm between the subject positioning of these scholars and the unspeaking masses whom they represent has been cited as a critical blind spot of the discipline, reflected in literary practice by the 'representative status' of the writers of decoloniza-tion.[10] For Spivak, the problem arises precisely when the represen-tational status of the postcolonial intellectual elides the two very different senses of *vertreten* and *darstellen* into a single term. As Spivak puts it, while these two meanings of representation are related, 'running them together, especially in order to say that beyond both is where oppressed subjects speak, act, and know *for themselves*, leads to an essentialist, utopian politics'.[11] This has been further explained by Dina Al-Kassim, who states that:

> The representative intellectual, in wanting to/attempting to speak for the other, inevitably rebounds into a descriptive and represen-tation depiction of that other's speech and interest because the subaltern is denied the right of entry. To demand or make room for the subaltern's speech is equivalent to demanding that the subaltern adopt the discourse of political agency and enter into that enlightenment space of self-representation. This demand effec-tively censors those others who cannot assume their own 'image' in the space cleared for an enlightenment politics by perversely asking that the subaltern cease to be 'herself' as the price of becoming a modern subject.[12]

By doing the work of *vertreten* through *darstellen*, the subaltern is spoken for and assumed, as a totemic figure, to attend to a certain narrative and intellectual appropriation which suppresses the play of difference in favour of a continued assimilation of the already-known and the overdetermined. Writing on the problems of working-class representations, Peter Hitchcock has stated that 'the challenge [...] is to resist both the idealism that *darstellen* can simply do the work of *vertreten* and the defeatism that brackets the cultural as some kind of bourgeois fib'.[13] At the same time, recognizing that '"speaking the truth about" and "acquiring the authority to speak for" implicate one another' does not require that we 'choose between attention to truth [...] and attention to rhetoric'.[14] Instead, this doubling of representation creates the very situation under which narrative, in its representational thrust, defines a space for perceiving-otherwise, whose importance remains central to the task of recuperation and regeneration. In the context of contemporary African literature the challenge, then, becomes that of resisting the urge to turn re-presentation into a straightforward representation, while maintaining the text's position in articulating an other voice, through an attention to the play of representation in both senses. This form of representational responsibility would thus signal, as Thomas Keenan aptly states, 'the acknowledgement of and response to complicity, implication, an acknowledgement that by definition can never be complete'.[15] Particularly because, as R. Radhakrishnan notes, 'the dominant ideology denies those different subject-positions their histories and their perspectival productions of their own agendas',[16] the notion that any single perspective may occupy the role of representative for what is, as Spivak phrases it, 'the heterogeneous collection of subjects in the space of difference'[17] becomes the site of an ethical instability, one which both interacts with the materiality of the text and impedes its resistant qualities, and which calls for a perpetual vigilance towards its formations.

The tension surrounding representation and its dual force is perhaps best exemplified in the controversy surrounding Fredric Jameson's postulation of Third World literature as 'necessarily' national allegory, a concept outlined in his 'Third World Literature in the Era of Multinational Capitalism',[18] which will be discussed at greater length in the next chapter. In what has become the canonical response, Aijaz Ahmad writes that, in this move, Jameson flattens the complexity of Third World literary production, homogenizes what is a vastly heterogeneous landscape and engages in a binary-formulation of 'us and them' rhetoric which relies on a falsely-inflated notion of nationalism in the once-colonized world.[19] Since the publication of that response, Ahmad's reading of Jameson has in many ways become the de facto means through which the notion of national allegory has been focalized.[20] Yet, despite the vitriol with which it has been received, Jameson's text provides an insightful account of the dynamics of representation in postcolonial, or Third World, literature. For Jameson, the construction of Third World literature as national allegory appears as a necessity not through its production by the Third World writer, but as a central aspect of its reception by the First World reader. As Julie McGonegal writes, 'at the core of Jameson's thesis is a recognition that "Third World" texts are a priori interpreted as Third World: there is and can be no possibility of unmediated access to the Other'.[21] In other words, Third World texts are received as national allegory not so much because of their content as their conditions of circulation. Interpellated as 'Other', the Third World text 'arrive[s] belatedly, always already mediated by prior interpretations and carrying the inscriptions of readings that went before'.[22] This sense of the 'always already mediated', in turn, hinges upon the ways in which these texts exist '*within* the global economic and political system that produces the third world *as* the third world'.[23] As commodities circulated within a global market of readers, publishers and writers, Third World literature, a category into which African literature has certainly been interpellated, is subject to a cultural framework of exchange that, as Arjun Appadurai, in his exposition of commoditization and value, notes, 'lies at the complex intersection of temporal, cultural, and social factors' in which 'the very definition of what constitutes singularities as opposed to classes is a cultural question'.[24] In creating a class through its network of circulation, African literature, as a unified, global commodity, remains subject to the always a priori mediation of a global marketplace in which writers and their texts are positioned as representing a certain sanctioned vision of the continent, despite the multiplicity of re-presentations depicted within that body of work. In this sense, then, Jameson's notion of the national allegory becomes less an indictment of 'other' literatures and more a means through which to process the complexities of global production, circulation and reception against the background of an overdetermined sense of that which is other.

In the realm of postcolonial literary studies, this elision of re-presentation with representation, or the aesthetic and the political work of the text, is of central importance. In engaging in the act of creating a work of narrative fiction, all of the writers under examination in this study can be said to engage in an act of re-presentation. At the same time, by virtue of their celebrity status, numerous accolades and wide readerships in North America and Europe, those authors feted internationally may equally become drawn into a discourse of representation, in which he or she functions as a stand-in of sorts for the numerous and diverse populations presented within their literary writing. Indeed, for certain authors this role as representative is a desirable corrective to the historical circulation of negative images of the African continent. In discussing her role as a representative of the continent, Chimamanda Ngozi Adichie, for instance, has stated that she 'hate[s] the image of Africa as simply a continent of starving people and warring people and, behind that, the notion of a continent of stupid people', citing Western tendencies to forget that Africa, like anywhere else, is a continent rife with varied classes.[25] As Stephen Moss has explained, with her novels Adichie 'is determined to show an Africa that isn't one huge refugee camp—a continent with many diverse stories, not a single story of suffering and dependency'.[26] For Adichie, then, the work of cultural re-presentation takes on a distinctly political edge, directly confronting decades of negative stereotyping as a much-needed counter-discourse. Likewise, Aminatta Forna's work has been located as part of the effort to advocate for the war-torn populations of Sierra Leone. As John Marx explains, 'Forna's name is on the byline of journalistic commentary about international justice and on the cover of both a memoir of political turmoil in Sierra Leone and the 2006 novel "of how it was to live as a woman in our country's past" called *Ancestor Stones*'.[27] Certainly, both of these perspectives, and others like them, are laudable in their ultimate aim to destabilize hegemonic views of the African continent and find a venue for its diverse voices. At the same time, such authorial self-positionings open the possibility of further appropriation and reductionism at the site of reception, regardless of intention. Faced with this dilemma, others of these authors take a different approach to their role as representatives of African culture and society. Chris Abani, for example, has stated that, in literary inquiry, 'the problem is we're looking for something that doesn't exist. We're looking for authenticity. There is no such thing as authenticity. [...] Art is never about its content it's always about its scaffolding', mocking the notion that art may be cathartic or provide a moment of total closure in its representative function.[28] At the same time, however, Abani's own status as an artist is not so straightforwardly held. According to Abani's publicity materials, following the publication of his first novel, *Masters of the Board* (1984), the then-teenaged author was sentenced to prison for allegedly providing the blueprint, with the novel, for a failed coup against the Babangida government. Later, having been released from prison, the author would become involved in protest and political theatre, leading to a series of additional periods of imprisonment, including a stint in Nigeria's notorious Kiri Kiri maximum security prison, and culminating in a death sentence for treason. Yet, this very tale, rarely told by the man himself but widely circulated as part of his biography, was severely challenged by Ikhide R. Ikheloa in a November 2011 blog posting that claimed these details to be largely fabricated.[29] Linking what he claims to be the curious lack of official documentation of these events to a broader charge of authorial exploitation of the African continent in the name of international literary prestige, Ikheloa's criticisms of Abani, along with the often-vitriolic debate they have sparked within the African literature community, indicate the level of unease and suspicion with which an attempt at a conscious separation of artistic re-presentation and social representation is met. The truth of Ikheloa's allegations and the details of Abani's early biography will likely be known by no one but the author himself. Nonetheless, the attacks against Abani illustrate the ways in which the demand for some level of verifiable proof of the author's status, and therefore legitimacy, as a representative of African conflict emerges as a central concern tied directly to the literary value of his work. Reverting to a polemicism that demands a singly-determined politicization of the text, the controversy surrounding Abani's biography points towards the continual lack of ease with which the transnational circulation of African artistic formations is met.

Of no small significance in all of the above cases is the fact of location, the notion that texts are produced in a particular geography. For Adichie, Forna and Abani, this fact of location leads to a tension in the positioning of these authors as 'African', given each author's status as either part of the diaspora (in Abani's and Forna's cases) or as only partially-resident (Adichie). Largely residing and working outside of Africa, that is to say, the positioning of these writers as representative of a larger African reality is one which necessarily troubles. At the same time, a wholesale castigation of any representative function remains equally problematic, given the ways in which African writing, like postcolonial writing more broadly, 'has also sought to recover and transmit or provide access to modes of life, forms of culture, and ways of thinking that have been obliterated, destabilised, or rendered invisible by the systematic operations of power',[30] a task for which a certain level of representation remains necessary. Complicating this situation further lies the very status of the artist/intellectual as a public figure in the world, one who, as Said reminds us, is 'endowed with a faculty for representing, embodying, articulating a message, a view, an attitude, philosophy or opinion to, as well as for, a public';[31] in other words, the dual play of representation cannot be outright avoided because the writer, as a public presence, is specifically tasked with both of its senses. As the Abani controversy indicates, moreover, no attempt to divest oneself from a representative role is so easily undertaken and indeed the very success of these authors, as artists, feeds directly into a sense of responsibility on the socio-political front. Thus, while such a collapse of the two notions of representation in literary writing appears to be nearly inevitable, following Spivak, the work of the literary critic remains to attend to the shifting occlusions of representation and re-presentation, teasing out from the interstices of these two senses of the word a space for ethical responsibility through the acts of contrapuntal reading and writing or, alternatively, what has been called a 'reading otherwise'.[32] It is only by attending to the mutual implication of these senses of representation, rooted within the aesthetic and the political, that literary study may uncover the fuller picture of what it means to write from and read of Africa today.

As these comments indicate, beyond its aesthetic form, much of the ascribed value of the postcolonial literary text comes from external factors. In considering these external factors, however, the reader of African literature need not revert to a simplified socio-political determinism, though such an imperative may continually assert itself through the material production of the text. If, as I have suggested, the ethical value of the text operates at the hinge between representation, a political stance, and re-presentation, an aesthetic rendering of culture, then this hinge, in turn, calls directly upon what Said has called the worldliness of the text. Said has written that, in the realm of literary criticism and critical theory, two distinct but interrelated academic pursuits,

> We tell our students and our general constituency that we defend the classics, the virtues of a liberal education, and the precious pleasures of literature even as we also show ourselves to be silent (perhaps incompetent) about the historical and social world in which all these things take place.[33]

This is a silence particularly felt in the realm of postcolonial criticism where, as Park Sorensen has noted, readings promoting a sense of interstitial liminality in what Said, in a different context, once referred to as the labyrinth of textuality have taken precedence over those deemed conventional or orthodox.[34] It is this tendency which has led to the often-cited quality of appropriation and repetition within postcolonial readings of texts which I highlighted in the introduction of this study. Put differently, we may consider Hitchcock's claim that 'the challenge of cultural transnationalism is to scale up the world of the text while scaling down the eponymous world out there, not in the interest of homology (or simply inflated culturalism), but to bring difference sharply into view'.[35] In order to claim this space of difference, readings, like their readers, are challenged to maintain their public dimension through a rigorous sense of commitment. Crucially, for the work of postcolonial cultural and intellectual production, this issue of worldliness may be traced in Butler's remark that 'there is no "I" that can fully stand apart from the social conditions of its emergence, no "I" that is not implicated in a set of conditioning moral norms, which, being norms, have a social character that exceeds a purely personal or idiosyncratic meaning'.[36] The very myth of the individual subject, like the individual work of art, remains tied to a set of social and mutually-constitutive conditions of being. In attending to the worldliness of the text, then, we attend to the limits and fault lines within the work itself and its conditions of possibility. Recalling that 'We have access in the west to a tiny proportion of the literary output of the rest of the world' and that 'we are often subliminally encouraged to read texts that do reach us in ways that flatter rather than challenge our preconceptions',[37] the challenge of foregrounding worldliness thus becomes one of recognizing when re-presentation becomes representation as a means only of confirming the already-known.

Said elaborates on his remarks on worldliness by saying that each text, through its 'reproducible material existence'[38] and its status as a means of communication between the author and medium, presents limits to criticism:

> This means that a text has a specific situation, placing restraints upon the interpreter and his interpretation not because the situation is hidden within the text as a mystery, but rather because the situation exists at the same level of surface particularity as the textual object itself. [...] Such texts can thereafter be construed as having need at most of complementary, as opposed to supplementary, readings.[39]

Placed next to Mudimbe's observation that, within African letters and philosophy, there exist 'signs of a major contradiction [that] are manifest in the increasing gap between social classes, and within each class, of the conflict between those who are culturally Westernized Africans and the others', this is of particular importance to the dissemination and reception of African literature. Because of this division between populations, Mudimbe continues, 'The conceptual framework of African thinking has been both a mirror and a consequence of the experience of European hegemony'.[40] The temptation to divest with worldliness and responsibility in reading is tacitly endorsed by intellectual practices which uncritically embrace the elision of meaning in representation's function. In an effort to combat this tendency, then, in this study I repeatedly highlight the dual existence of each novel as textual, on the one hand, and equally, on the other, as an attempt at re-presentation by and of a people, with consequences for the representation of African realities on a global scale. It is this doubling of value which, for the African literary text, produces its imperative towards responsibility.

## Authenticity and Exoticism

As the comments above imply, the elision of a work of literature's representative and re-presentative functions is of central importance because of its complicity in the construction of a totalized vision of what are, in reality, dynamic, variable and multifaceted realities. By ascribing a representative function to a particular piece of work, in other words, its re-presentational aspects become reified into icons of 'authentic' or 'true' experience which, ironically, often serve only to undergird our pre-existing assumptions about the already-known. In the case of Africa, in particular, this is a fraught issue, given its complicity in the global transmission of what Graham Huggan has called the 'anthropological exotic', or the assignment, to the African literary text, of an ethnographic and anthropological valuation of authenticity and primitivism which only serves to buttress the sense of selfhood of the West.[41] Through the function of the anthropological exotic, Africa becomes that alien other which confirms the West's own humanity, playing out an already-staged set of stereotypes whose purpose is to conform what is already felt to be true under the guise of neutral, scientific interest. At the same time, this 'making-known' of Africa operates on the assumption of a requited interest, a belief that in establishing an identity for and image of Africa, the West is responding to an unspoken desire, by the alien other, to be known. The exotic 'reflects the simultaneous repulsion and attraction toward the other', using the veil of fascination to mask 'the need to tame it, to control it, and ultimately to neutralize and destroy it'.[42] Thus, exoticism remains 'a contradictory structure articulated according to fetishism's irreconcilable logic. Its mastery is always asserted, but is also always slipping, ceaselessly displaced, never complete'.[43] The exotic functions through a simultaneous process of disgust and fascination as an encounter with that which is both strange and familiar, where the alien other may authenticate the metropolitan subject's superiority. In embracing the exotic, European culture displaces the historical context of the other, 'creating a distorted picture that conform[s] more with the expectations and fears of Europeans than with reality'.[44] Culturally-exotic motifs are assimilated through appropriation to erase the presence of the irreducibly other from circulation,[45] because in exoticism 'what is valorised is not a stable content but a country and a culture defined exclusively by their relation to the observer'.[46] The African other, that is to say, is defined under parameters that take Western culture as the universal norm and enforce the use of external categories to make sense of it. This same desire for the exotic represents a danger which must be destroyed, a stance particularly complicated in its deployment in postcolonial histories where 'exoticism describes [...] a particular mode of aesthetic *perception*—one which renders people, objects and places strange even as it domesticates them, and which effectively manufactures otherness even as it claims to surrender to its immanent mystery',[47] thereby turning the exotic other into an object of commoditization falsely valorized for an imposed authenticity.

This quality of exoticism becomes foregrounded in the realm of African letters, where the implied distance and repulsion are exacerbated by stereotypes of the 'dark continent' and all of its savagery. As Lyn Innes reminds us, 'Africa has been "read" by outsiders for many centuries, all too often as unreadable, a blank, a dark continent'.[48] Amplifying this conundrum is the construction and deployment of authenticity and tradition as markers of value in African literature. Through the reification of the exotic, both authenticity and tradition are transfigured into anthropological essences, stripped of their discursive instability.[49] In the process, these terms are falsely neutralized, stripped of their complicity with power. Yet, as David Scott recalls:

> A tradition [...] is never neutral with respect to the values it embodies. Rather a tradition operates *in and through* the stakes it constructs—what is to count and what is not to count among its satisfactions, what the goods and excellencies and virtues are that ought to be valued, preserved, and inculcated, and what the practices and institutions are that will enable (or disable) the achievement of its preferred mode of human flourishing.[50]

Thus, by erasing the discursivity of tradition and authenticity under the anthropological exotic's guise of disinterested observation, exoticism tacitly reproduces its own conditions of domination. Unsurprisingly, set in this context, as Huggan points out, '"African literature" [...] already conveys a fiction of homogeneity that smacks of "sanctioned ignorance" (Spivak 1993a: 279); as if the vast literary and cultural diversity of one of the world's largest continents could be arrogantly reduced to a single classificatory term'.[51] This, he continues, is due in large part to African literature's implication within a system of global capitalism and its attendant knowledge industry. This politics of representation, then, leads to a system in which

> the perceptual framework of the anthropological exotic allows for a reading of African literature as the more or less transparent window

onto a richly detailed and culturally specific, but still somehow homogeneous—and of course readily marketable—African world. Anthropology is the watchword here, not for empirical documental, but for the elaboration of a world of difference that conforms to often crudely stereotypical Western exoticist paradigms and myths ('primitive culture', 'unbounded nature', 'magical practices', 'noble savagery', and so on).[52]

The status of the work of African literature, in this scenario, is precarious. On the one hand, authors and writers may be seen to unconsciously (or not) conform to the expectations of a Western readership of 'How to Write About Africa', internalizing and reproducing the exotic mythologies of the former colonizing powers. As Soyinka has written, castigating this state of affairs, 'The curiosity of the outside world far exceeded their critical faculties and publishers hovered like benevolent vultures on the still foetus of the African Muse'.[53] Faced with this proposition, the African writer responds by mistaking 'his own personal and temporary cultural predicament for the predicament of his entire society and turn[ing] attention from what was really happening within that society'.[54] Re-presentation becomes representative, as the African writer momentarily 'den[ies] himself' to serve the material demands of postcolonial literary publishing.[55] Even where the inevitable turn described by Soyinka is conscientiously avoided, the reception of African literature nonetheless runs the risk of such a collapse into the anthropological exotic. This latter tendency is perhaps best illustrated through the reception and worldwide celebration of Chinua Achebe's landmark *Things Fall Apart* (1958). A literary text, the novel has nonetheless been frequently read as an ethnographic or sociological study of pre-colonial Igbo culture. Indeed, the novel appears with as great frequency on the syllabi of courses in anthropology and ethnography as it does in literary studies, marking the institutionalization of this view. The acritical ascription of anthropological significance in Achebe's text, a by-product of early Anglophone African publishing practices, overlooks the strategies of address which Achebe himself encodes within the novel, most felt in the ways in which the novel plays with the notion of a pre-colonial Igbo tradition.[56] The result is a critical stance, mired in the anthropological exotic, that neglects the complexities of the work and extrapolates, from a singular work of aesthetic fiction, a totalizing and (mis)represented notion of African culture and society.

Yet, literature may, too, encode a resistant function, destabilizing and appropriating these vestiges of exoticism. Indeed, the moment of exoticism is itself a moment of destabilization, mired in the notion of the stereotype which, as Bhabha reminds us, is both fixed and contradictory, confirming our subject positions while simultaneously unveiling the deep anxiety around which they fluctuate. As Bhabha aptly notes, 'The subjects of the discourse are constructed within an apparatus of power which *contains*, in both senses of the word, an "other" knowledge—a knowledge that is arrested and fetishistic and circulates through colonial discourse as that limited form of otherness [...] called the stereotype'.[57] Faced with this precarious position, the African literary text is left

> as having both a recuperative and a deconstructive dimension: recuperative insofar as it conscripts the literary text into the service of a continually refashioned cultural identity; deconstructive insofar as it plays on and challenges Western readerly expectation, and in so doing works toward dismantling self-privileging Western modes of vision and thought.[58]

Through this double movement and occlusion, then, the African literary text unsettles and exposes the workings of the anthropological exotic, unveiling the traces of alternative discourses and unsettled foundations. Yet, taken uncritically, the interstitial space where representation and re-presentation meet runs the risk of collapsing into a totalizing sense of exoticism which suppresses its internal contradictions in favour of its holistic mythologies. This risk is complicated by practices of publishing and dissemination which leave the work of African literature in the perpetual danger of a collapse into the anthropological exotic regardless of textual encodings, narrative frames or resistant strategies. The question, with contemporary writing, remains to interrogate the extent to which, through a series of narrative and rhetorical moves which demand a readerly engagement which remains attentive to the contradictory workings of stereotype and exoticism, this seemingly-inevitable collapse may be deferred.

## Publishing Africa: Who Writes and Who Reads?

That the question of address is central to the dissemination of African literature and the transnational circulation of an image of Africa created through these literatures should be of no great surprise. Indeed, the question of address is at the heart of many debates surrounding African literature, particularly contemporary African literature, and remains highly relevant for critical discussion. Central to this question of address, then, has been the history of publishing practices and the construction of readerships for African literature. The construction of an African literary canon has been, from its inception, deeply linked with the neo-imperialism of postcolonial policy and the commodification of an image of Africa which operates alongside of it. As Gail Low has noted, the creation of a market for early Europhone African literature 'fostered cultural connections at a time when political independence might have spelt the dissolution of colonial ties', positioning African literature under what she likens to a second scramble for Africa.[59] As alluded to above, early examples of African literature, notably Achebe's *Things Fall Apart* and Amos Tutuola's *The Palm-Wine Drinkard* (1952), were marketed largely as ethnographic and folkloric texts, rather than literary writing, transforming their cultural valuations in order to conform to external socio-political pressures. As Low has written with respect to the latter's dissemination as 'primitive' art, Tutuola's 'originality as a signifier of literary value is transformed into authenticity as a signifier of anthropological and cultural value. Framed as an exotic artefact, the manuscript's value was, of course, directly linked to its genuineness as naïve art'.[60] The anthropological significance of the text, regardless of its grounding, would overtake the text's value as a literary work and the African writer would be positioned as whispering his secrets for a Western audience.

More pertinently, the example of *The Palm-Wine Drinkard* raises a number of questions regarding the reception of African literature and assumptions surrounding authenticity and representation. Published by Faber and Faber in 1952, the work stands as the first major African novel published internationally in English, gaining notoriety both for Tutuola and as a marker of the shift from orality to writing in African letters.[61] Yet, in current scholarship, Tutuola is rarely recognized as the father of African literature. Rather, it is his countryman,

Achebe, whose *Things Fall Apart* is today generally regarded as having borne the African literary tradition with its 1958 publication. This historical neglect of Tutuola's work has been explained with reference to several factors. For certain critics, Tutuola engaged in an act of plagiarism, transcribing the Yoruba folktales of his heritage in a disjointed form of English, leading to a critical tendency, Ato Quayson describes, 'to undervalue Tutuola's own role as a creative imagination, making him a slave of totalizations deriving either from his culture or from universal mythic paradigms'.[62] For others, the episodic quality of the novel, which follows the largely-unconnected exploits of the eponymous character, leads to its categorization as epic or myth, rather than narrative.[63] Still other critics view Tutuola's re-configuration of the English language as a prime example of writing against the dominant cultural forces of postcoloniality.[64] Critically, as Low has reported, Tutuola's novel was largely well-received outside of Africa, positioned as an example of 'authentic' and 'primitive' writing, while, within Africa, critics 'objected to what they saw as very poor writing and expressed dismay at the uncritical promotion of the book'.[65] *The Palm-Wine Drinkard* was thereby transfigured from a literary text and aesthetic artefact to an object in the midst of an ideological and political struggle over what it might mean to represent Africa and how an image of the continent might be circulated transnationally. Moving beyond the text's literary value, criticism would place its greatest emphasis on its sociological import, hinging upon the wider reverberations the novel represented for the image of Africa across the globe. These differing perspectives highlight the mechanisms through which Tutuola's novel has been appropriated in critical discourse on African literature, transforming the text from a cultural artefact to a site of valuation and contestation in a way which bears considerably on the writing of contemporary African authors; though these writers work outside of Tutuola's Yoruba tradition, their literary production nonetheless functions in tension with the same issues of ascribed authorship, cultural ownership and authenticity in narrative as seen in *The Palm-Wine Drinkard*.

These questions are more explicitly raised in the theoretical and reflective writings of Ngũgĩ wa Thiong'o, who, published first as James Ngũgĩ, abandoned both the name and the English idiom of his early writing in order to embrace his native Gĩkũyũ as a literary language. Ngũgĩ's turn away from English can be directly linked to his Marxist interpretation of Obi Wali's claim that, by writing in European languages, African writers betray their continent, relegating African literature to 'a minor appendage in the main stream of European literature'.[66] Ngũgĩ's reasoning behind this break draws upon two aims: first, to restore a sense of dignity to indigenous languages devalued under colonialism, and second, to engage directly with his intended readership, the peasants, rural population and working citizens of Kenya. While interrelated, it is important in any discussion of the politics of language in African literature to avoid conflating these two ends. The first, which Ngũgĩ describes as his desire 'to prove and show that when one writes in an African language, one is not invisible for other communities such as the English-speaking communities',[67] points directly to the vectors of power which, operating globally, define certain languages and cultures as literary and others as lacking. The second, linked to Ngũgĩ's involvement in the Kamĩrĩĩthũ Community Education and Cultural Centre in the 1970s, relates more to the efficacy of literary expression as a means of cultivating social and political engagement from the bottom-up. While the latter goal is complicated by the economic realities of publishing literature in Africa, as well as the intricacies involved in the choice of a single vernacular to read a multilingual population, the former goal is perhaps more relevant to the development of African literature as a global institution.

In a discussion of his early writing in English, Ngũgĩ explains that, 'what I'm doing in reality is taking away from the Gĩkũyũ language to enrich English. So when I'm writing in Gĩkũyũ, I'm really exploiting the possibilities of that language and I have found it very, very liberating for me in expressing my environment',[68] a comment which highlights the issue of structural inequality realized in the use of language. Reflecting on his early education in English letters, Ngũgĩ writes that 'language and literature were taking [Africans] further and further from ourselves to other selves, from our world to other worlds'.[69] Expanding upon these formative experiences to his status as a celebrated writer of Anglophone African literature, Ngũgĩ wonders whether 'by our continuing to write in foreign languages, paying homage to them, are we not on the cultural level continuing that neo-colonial slavish and cringing spirit?'[70] More recently, Ngũgĩ has explained how 'Each language has its own capacity, its own possibilities. [...] it was colonialism which gave us this hierarchical arrangement of languages where some languages seemed higher than the others or some languages seemed lower than the others',[71] directly referencing the need to recuperate a sense of dignity, power and possibility through a return to indigenous language writing. In other words, Ngũgĩ posits that a continued writing in English would result in a continued orientation of address towards the West, in contrast to a writing aimed at one's locality. This, in turn, marks a sense of continually and perpetually re-colonizing the mind, so to speak, which tacitly reproduces the structures of inequality driven by colonialism. The individual and symbolic choice of language thus feeds back into large-scale material systems of global domination. Coextensively, the hesitancy to embrace a local language, for fear of limiting one's audience, points to the concomitant factors of translatability and literary value, where some languages remain central and others marginal. To combat this perpetuation of colonial structures of meaning, for Ngũgĩ, entails a process of writing in the local Gĩkũyũ language of his ethnic group, followed by a process of (self-)translation of his works from Gĩkũyũ to English, as well as the serialization of his novels into newspapers and other periodicals, to widen access at the local level. Of course, writing in Gĩkũyũ is not an inherently liberatory act, nor is writing in English hopelessly relegated to the realm of false consciousness. Instead, Ngũgĩ argues, 'If you chose to produce knowledge in one language rather than another, you are making a very fundamental choice. But, of course, once you make that choice, it does not mean that you are going to invent your own history or a new world, so to speak'.[72] More than providing a simple solution for the language question, then, Ngũgĩ's comments point to the extent to which the very necessity of such a choice is one which requires investigation. Rather than simply assume that an African writer must work in English, that is to say, the workings of power which shape such assumptions need questioning.

The strategies adopted by Ngũgĩ, while heartening, are not necessarily a prescriptive answer to the problem of publication and dissemination across African literature. For one, Ngũgĩ's status as an already-celebrated writer and public intellectual has allowed his writing greater scope for variation from dominant publishing practices than would be possible for an unknown or emerging writer. At the same time, this is not an entirely negative observation. Indeed, as a high-profile author and international spokesman, Ngũgĩ's choice is particularly potent in the message it sends both to aspiring African writers and to his readership as a whole. If a writer of Ngũgĩ's stature can turn away from English and remain both influential and commercially successful, that is, the possibilities for a more diverse literary market are implicitly opened. Equally, it has been argued that 'By fetishizing so-called indigenous languages, [Ngũgĩ] seems to lose sight of how a single language is layered in unequal structures of social organization, and to endow it instead with undifferentiated mystic power'.[73] Ngũgĩ's choice to write in Gĩkũyũ, this line of criticism suggests, does not entirely solve the issue of address plaguing African literature. Indeed, as an ethnic language, Gĩkũyũ cannot be said to be an idiom which democratically cuts across the Kenyan context and, for the many minority ethnicities of Kenya, may in fact lead to a distancing effect far greater than the use of English, the very issue cited by Achebe as his primary reason for writing in English.[74] Yet, such commentary fails to consider the primacy of Ngũgĩ's first goal, that of restoring a sense of value to African languages. In this sense, writing in Gĩkũyũ may not be ultimately more accessible than writing in English; yet, writing in Gĩkũyũ remains symbolically potent. The fact that Gĩkũyũ can function both as a literary language and as a source language for translation marks a shift in the dynamics of power, globally-speaking.

To a certain extent, the issues of language use, neo-colonization and psychic determination raised by Ngũgĩ lead to a situation in which the African writer is artificially expelled from inclusion within an English-speaking sphere. In other words, by positioning English as always and inevitably foreign for the African writer, Ngũgĩ betrays an assumption that English cannot be made to suit the African writer's needs, that it must always fall under the provenance of Euro-America. Of course, given the proliferation of dialects, pidgins and creoles, a static and essentialist view of English cannot be taken at face value so easily, and, instead, the question of language use turns into a question of address. Ngũgĩ's public statements about language and his professional turn from English may be read less as an indictment of that language than a way to highlight the structural discrepancies in power, value and literary worth which the automatic assumption of English implicitly encodes. For contemporary African literature, English has become still more entrenched as the de facto language of communication through the prevalence of prizes given only to works available in English, a critical field that is increasingly monolingual (a situation not unique to African literary studies, it should be said) and a publishing sector dominated by London and New York. While this situation is unlikely to change any time soon, its very existence points to the necessity to recall the politics of language as an inherent facet of the politics of re(-)presentation in writing Africa in a global context.

The complications of publishing and dissemination of African literature have not been relegated solely to the early years of the Europhone African tradition. Indeed, the tensions and pressures characterizing the publication of African literature remain to the present day and are in many senses exacerbated by the collapse of affording publishing schemes, including the Heinemann African Writers Series (though this series was certainly not free of the implications of anthropological exoticism outlined above, as I will later discuss) and similar low-cost literary and educational imprints.[75] Today, by contrast, the majority of celebrated contemporary African authors find their publishing audiences through British and American presses including Picador, HarperPerennial, Jonathan Cape, Bloomsbury and Granta. These works, published in the United Kingdom and North America, are rarely to be found on the African continent itself, and, where accessible, are priced well beyond the means of the average reading consumer.[76] As this might indicate, African literature, from a strictly commercial standpoint, is less a cultural artefact written for Africa or an African readership, than one intended for Western eyes or at least predominantly marketed with a Western audience in mind. If this is in fact the case, it seems to be equally the case that a collapse into the anthropological exotic is inevitable in these texts, that the demands of publishing practicalities win out over the imperatives of representation. Expanding beyond the practicalities of purchasing and reading contemporary African literature arises a further issue, that of subject matter and narrative style. Several commentators claim that contemporary African authors, largely diasporic in their geographical positioning, know little about the continent of which they write and, instead, fall prey to the exoticizing impulses of a Western publishing industry and readership. As Tanure Ojaide claims, 'Many in this group suffer from a psychic disconnection from the continent. These "children of the postcolony," to use Adesanmi's phrase, educated in the West, imagine Africa because they have not experienced the continent physically and culturally'.[77] In lieu of an authentic African experience, then, contemporary writers are often accused of tailoring their visions of the African continent to heighten their marketability.

Yet, in both cases of critique, this dichotomous view of African literary production fails to grasp the complexity of cultural transmission and circulation. Complaints that contemporary African literature is priced beyond the scope of an African readership forget, for example, that local presses have begun the work of printing these texts at affordable prices and that, as the last chapter of this study will outline, a robust market of locally-produced literature abounds on the continent. More importantly, the accusation that African literature cannot be accessible to a reading public located on the continent forgets the ingenuity of readers and communities in sharing, reproducing and circulating texts. Similarly the issue of truth in representation is not so straightforward and the notion that an aesthetic re-presentation may somehow capture a form of verisimilitude is itself problematic, rooted in totalizing notions of authenticity and essential identity politics. Indeed, as Metscher reminds us, each 'work of art in a socio-historical period opens up a view of the same reality different from every other work of art'.[78] No single view or version of 'reality' can therefore be privileged as essential or somehow more correct without a far deeper inquiry into the meaning and construction of truth-values. Moreover, it is equally possible that, by jettisoning a close adherence to historical verisimilitude in favour of a broader notion of lifeness, in James Woods' terminology,[79] contemporary African literature emerges in a space where the very constructions of self, other, community and memory may be exposed without reverting to dichotomizing essentialisms, while engaging in what Radhakrishnan has referred to as a utopian notion of representation that 'progresses toward a more inclusive and general politicization that does not make a fetish of inside/outside and us/them distinctions'.[80] Aesthetic re-presentation, in this case, transforms into an effort to free the work of art from the demands of verisimilitude and veracity in order to perceive, within it, its critical function. The question of address, as variable, cannot and does not exist within a simple binary relationship of us and them, West and rest. As Gikandi, writing on the first generation of African anti-colonial nationalist authors, notes, the vision of Africa through which we read 'was produced not simply by the opposition between colonial modernity and African traditionalism, but one that had been produced at that liminal scene where the self becomes the other and the lines between the two were blurred or folded into one another'.[81] Based in a network of relationality which is dispersive and multi-valenced, the relationship between the author, the text and the world is one which defies reduction to a single form of directionality. Instead, the question of address is one which hinges on multiple and simultaneous strategies of reading, writing and encoding which gather the dominant and contrapuntal together to create the dynamic space of the literary text both within the text itself and at the site of reception.

# 2
# Race, Class and Performativity

## National Allegory, Racial Becoming and Performativity

The tensions surrounding re(-)presentation in African literature lead
to a series of questions about the status of the individual subject. Can
an autonomous African subject emerge in a global context in which
the structures and categories of colonial rule persist under a perpetual state of unfinished decolonization? Must the African subject
remain forever in thrall to the exclusionary practices of metropolitan
subjectification? Is the individual in African literature ever simply
an individual, or is the single subject forever doomed to an overdetermined socio-political representational function? In the struggle
to recuperate a space for the individual in African writing, race has
played a central part. The African self, that is to say, only materializes
in the transnational space of reading through the exclusionary practices of racialized becoming and, by extension, its status as 'other'.
The tension which arises from these formations of self is highlighted
in Brian Chikwava's *Harare North*, Nuruddin Farah's *Links* and Tsitsi
Dangarembga's *The Book of Not*. In each novel, the status of the
individual subject is foregrounded in distinct narrative forms which
highlight, in different contexts, the centrality of race and racialized
formations in the development of the African self. Addressing the
dissociation of migrancy, the difficulty of return and the struggle
simply to be within a racially-stratified society, each of these novels
highlights the peculiar anxiety which has marked the construction of the individual subject in African literature. As all three texts
demonstrate, for that individual race functions simultaneously as

a category of being, taken to be absolute, and as a site of performativity, subject to the parameters of the context through which it becomes. Race, in other words, is far from a standalone category in any of these texts. Instead, it intersects with specific local histories and concomitant constructions of class and gender to function as a mark of otherness and as a mode both of administering subjects through the workings of power and resistance to the same. In each, the performance of race occupies a central aspect of the performance of self, coexistent with a broader sense in which simply to be African is to be interpellated as raced, in both general and specific terms.

The status of the individual in African writing is of no little consequence to the broader question of representation in African literature. As that 'other' to a metropolitan self, that is, the emergence of the African subject marks a particular site of tension in the transnational production and reception of African literature more broadly. Perhaps unsurprisingly, given the coexistence of material and epistemic violence brought by colonialism, the question of the individual has become something of a refrain in studies of contemporary African writing. Where, in readings of earlier African literature, the individual has been subsumed to his or her society, turned into a cipher for a broader political cause, scholarship on contemporary African literature has focused more strongly on the affective, psychological dimension of the individual, an attempt to recuperate the privilege of subjectivity for populations long denied its protections. In a recent study of Adichie's acclaimed novel, for instance, Hawley notes how 'one characteristic of *Half of a Yellow Sun* that immediately strikes the reader is the strong light that shines on the book's principal players, rather than on the politics and strategies that shaped the war',[1] while Ojaide refers to 'the evolving nature of African literature and the depiction of the contemporary African condition' as occurring in a manner focused on the individual at the expense of the sociopolitical materiality of life on the continent.[2] Taken together, these comments indicate a broader sentiment where contemporary African literature operates predominantly through a distinctly libidinal function, foregrounding affectivity, intimacy and personal trauma over a pull into an overdetermined representative effect.

In 'Third World Literature in the Era of Multinational Capitalism' Jameson makes the claim that, rooted in a not-as-yet fully-realized split between the public and private spheres, the Third World writer remains locked into a representative political position.³ Third World literature, Jameson argues, thereby functions 'necessarily' as national allegory: '[all Third World texts] are to be read as what I will call national allegories, even when, or perhaps I should say, particularly when their forms develop out of predominantly western machineries of representation, such as the novel'.⁴ In this formation,

> even those [texts] which are seemingly private and invested with a properly libidinal dynamic—necessarily project a political dimension in the form of national allegory: *the story of the private individual destiny is always an allegory of the embattled situation of the public third-world culture and society.*⁵

Jameson's reading of Third World literature as national allegory points directly to the precarious position of the individual; read as representative, the individual, as a particular and specified instance of subjectivity, disappears under a larger imperative to speak for the broader sociality. Jameson's contention that all Third World literature must be read as national allegory has unsurprisingly led to considerable criticism, most emphatically in Ahmad's 'Jameson's Rhetoric of Otherness and the "National Allegory"', an essay which has become the de facto rebuttal to Jameson's claims. Arguing that Jameson's typology of literature relies on categories so broad as to be meaningless and, through its focus on the novel form, presupposes its own ends, Ahmad's response highlights the anxieties which such a denial of the individual commands. While his criticism of Jameson remains salient in the context of literary production, Ahmad, in his eagerness to recuperate a sense of individuality which Jameson denies, neglects the extent to which the very question of individuality remains fraught under the pressures of transnational reception. In other words, while Ahmad's criticism of Jameson soundly points to the difficulty of assuming that all Third World texts are *written* to be national allegories, his critique fails to account for the extent to which, as 'other' texts, Third World writing is inevitably *read* precisely for its socio-political dimensions and assumed to hold a representative function which exceeds the portrayal of individual life.

More pertinent for my discussion are arguments that Jameson's theorization presupposes an absolute split between the libidinal economies of the affective and the politicized valences of national allegory in the reading of a text, a viewpoint which seems to underestimate the creative potential of literary writing and the interpretative flexibility which readers may bring to the text. A text, under Jameson's claims, cannot be both personal and political, and the two realms of being must remain discrete; for the Third World text, a collapse into national allegory utterly effaces its libidinal value. As Susan Z. Andrade has astutely pointed out, however, in his insistence on the necessary appearance of national allegory, Jameson 'repeats in formal terms the same gesture made by many theorists of allegory: making the first meaning (or signifier) disappear in favour of the second meaning (or signifier)'.[6] In so doing, he forgets 'that allegories are neither intrinsic nor natural but learned, and that our ability to perceive them has much to do with systems of education and literacy'.[7] Through a recognition of the contingency of such a collapse, however, the absolute split between the personal and the political recedes, replaced instead with a sense in which this gap appears only because of the practices through which the 'other' text is interpreted by its Western readers. Through this realization, in turn, comes the coexistent understanding that another reading remains possible; in contemporary African literature it is this other reading which continually appears, driven by aesthetic innovation as a means of enabling a political formation of identity which escapes any such absolutes. *Harare North, Links* and *The Book of Not* certainly foreground the libidinal and the psychological; at the same time, each novel equally demonstrates the extent to which a decoupling of the individual from context remains partial. Throughout all three texts, then, the emergence of an individual, raced subject remains determined by the subject's position in a broader social and political context defined by what Butler has called the intersecting vectors of power which determine the performance of individual bodies, selves and identities,[8] while simultaneously foregrounding the inherently contingent nature of such performances.

On first glance it appears that the imperative to national allegory insisted upon by Jameson has little in common with Frantz Fanon's libidinal and affective theories of racial coming-into-being. Yet, a closer examination of the stakes through which each functions reveals a certain productive dialogue which emerges where the two theories meet. Fanon argues that, amongst his fellows in the Antilles, the upper-class Martinician grows up feeling 'normal', identifying himself as white through his exposure to the culture of the colonizer and its overwhelming tendency to ascribe to heroic roles the value of whiteness.[9] Upon his encounter with the white man in France, however, the Martinician is in for a terrible shock: he is perceived as black and, as such, an aberration in a white society that projects upon him its own fears and anxieties. Fanon traces the functioning of this racialized splitting of the self in the fifth chapter of *Black Skin, White Masks*, 'l'expérience vécue du noir' ('The Lived Experience of the Black Man', often translated as 'The Fact of Blackness'[10]). Here Fanon writes that, under the white gaze, the black man becomes 'an object among other objects',[11] citing Sartre's formulation of the alienating look which objectifies the subject.[12] Because the black man lives under the domination of the white man, he can no longer exist as a for-himself, in Sartrean terms. Instead, the 'black man must be black' and live within 'two systems of reference', one black and one white.[13] The black man's negation, far from opening a space for freedom, thrusts upon him the weight of an already-decided identity through an alienation that functions 'in intersubjective and social terms',[14] called into being rather than inherent to the human condition, raced or otherwise. Fanon formulates this through a shift from the Lacanian notion of a bodily schema in the alienation imposed on the individual in the mirror stage to 'a historical-racial schema' which becomes the 'epidermal racial schema' of the alienated black man.[15] The black man, rather than operating as an individual, becomes emblematic of his race, his life story imposed upon him by white society:

> The white gaze, the only valid one, is already dissecting me. I am *fixed*. Once their microtomes are sharpened, the Whites objectively cut sections of my reality. I have been betrayed. I sense, I see in this white gaze that it's the arrival not of a new man, but of a new type of man, a new species. A Negro, in fact![16]

Viewed in this context, the black man cannot be seen as a self in the same way as the white man, nor is he able to turn to his fellow black men for legitimization in place of the authenticating white gaze. He is, instead, subject to 'an alienation from both a self-defined subject position and the modes of symbolic production that inform the development and transformation of the position of "other"',[17] which strips away the privilege of alienation and ambivalence from his subject position. Because of the weight of this imposed history, the black man is no longer free simply to be; shaken from his previously-held notions of self and individuality, the black man becomes another lost object whose skin inscribes his very being, resulting in a sense of Sartrean nausea:

> Shame. Shame and self-contempt. Nausea. When they like me, they tell me my color has nothing to do with it. When they hate me, they add that it's not because of my color. Either way, I am the prisoner of the vicious cycle.[18]

Fanon thus continually slides between the notion of blackness as a sort of fixing of the self, mediated by history and imposed by the white gaze, and the notion of the black man as agent and individual. Oscillating between these two poles, the result, for the black man, is a complete loss of identity under the psychic trauma of colonization.

Despite their apparent differences, reading Fanon via Jameson and vice versa creates a space in which to consider the dynamics of re(-)presentation in the development of identity in contemporary African literature. As Margaret Hillenbrand suggests, at the heart of both Jameson's and Fanon's formulations lies the constant need to question the self and its position in the world, marking a 'search for subjectivity [that] signifies both for the individual and the eth-nonational collective',[19] a comment which highlights the specifically performative nature of both positions. Put slightly differently, both Jameson's and Fanon's frameworks function under the dynamics of power, managed by what Butler calls 'the regulatory norms that govern their materialization and the signification of those material effects'.[20] Both the text and the subject re-presented within that text, in other words, attain their materiality through the shaping work of power and its constituting effects, coming into being through the process of becoming 'other', becoming 'African' in a global context in which 'African' indicates that which is excluded in order to define the domain of the human.[21] Fanon's vision of a crippled black subjectivity may thus be viewed as part of a wider communal and political formation implicated into the constitution of power, functioning in turn as part of a strategic national allegorical position. It is precisely that the libidinal and the socio-political may coexist through their constitution by the dynamics of power that captures the condition of the postcolonial nation as 'not a preexisting entity but something persistently reformulated by the experience of the masses in their ongoing struggle'.[22] Through this constant play between the psychological and the political appears the very image of the Third World nation and the subject within. Viewed in this manner, the libidinal economy upon which Fanon dwells may be seen as operating within a larger field of colonial and postcolonial political formation, one which the late thinker outlined in far greater detail in the posthumous *Wretched of the Earth*.[23] This is not, of course, to suggest that each individual life may be simply extended to an allegory for the nation; rather, the individual functions through a public dimension determined through the effects of power and its material resonances. The literary text, in turn, may be read through both this highly-individualistic notion of self along with its wider embedding in the political, thereby resisting a collapse into one or the other as an absolute imperative.

## Narratorial Address and the Disassociation of Being

Throughout *Harare North*, the unnamed first-person narrator demonstrates an instability of self which functions not just as raced, in individualistic terms, but within a set of socio-historical divisions which resonate more broadly. To do so, Chikwava's novel functions through two large-scale effects, which together create a precarious alternative mode of becoming through the narrator's increasingly unhinged performance of self. Through the use of a first-person narrator who consistently erupts into a second-person mode of address, the reader of Chikwava's text is drawn into an involuntary identification with its protagonist through an autotelic narration which interpellates the reader into the narrator's field of becoming. At the same time, the first-person narrator remains fundamentally unreliable through his often-circular idiomatic language, creating an alienating effect in which the reader of the text is excluded from a total identification with the narrative. Together, these two effects create a push–pull movement which drives the reading of the novel and turns its performance upon itself in a manner made all the more contentious by the apparent distance between presumed reader and text. Through its deployment of specified aesthetic effects and narratorial decisions, *Harare North*'s formal structure produces a series of ellipses and contradictions at its heart, rendering the narrative unstable throughout its course and thereby highlighting the contingency of racial becomings.

*Harare North*'s narrator, a former member of the Green Bombers, the youth wing of Robert Mugabe's ZANU-PF party, arrives in London seeking asylum after a run-in with opposition party members in Harare results in a price on his head. Intending to save a sum of $5000 US in order to pay off the man he calls Comrade Mhiripiri and subsequently return to Zimbabwe, the narrator's textual realization highlights the performativity of his role as temporary refugee against the larger background of the troubled post-2002 Zimbabwean community in London. Beacon Mbiba writes that

> In 2002, The United Nations Development Programme established that there were '479,348 Zimbabweans in the diaspora [...] mainly in the United Kingdom, Botswana and South Africa'. The report (2003) admits that this figure is low and that it underestimates the number of Zimbabweans in South Africa. The difficulty is that official statistics only report breadwinners and not dependents and, as noted earlier, there is no system to track return migration.[24]

Initially, Mbiba continues, the Zimbabwean community in Britain was a privileged one:

> Zimbabwean community members are likely to have better academic qualifications than other African communities in the UK. This is largely to do with the general investment they put in education as the route to progress as well as the higher level of literacy achieved by the ZANU-PF government in Zimbabwe in the 1980s. Coupled with this, migration to the UK is an expensive exercise afforded only by those from middle and upper class families who happen to be better educated as well. Thus prior to 2000, Zimbabweans were a favoured (and preferred) group with regards to UK employment. In addition to their higher education and perceived positive work ethics, until November 2002, Zimbabweans did not have visa restrictions that applied to most African nationals coming to the UK.[25]

The year 2002, in other words, marks a shift in the composition and mobility of Zimbabwean migrant populations in the United Kingdom, a moment in which the community transformed from a marked insiderism, through professional merit and upward economic mobility, to a position of exclusion, marked as 'other' in the context of post-9/11 immigration policy manoeuvres and increasing stereotype against the 'corrupt' and 'broken' Zimbabwean nation-state. The first pages of Chikwava's novel hearken to this transformation of the dynamics of power, as the narrator describes this new performance of black migrancy:

> So people is now getting that old consulate treatment: the person behind the counter window give you the severe look and ask you to bring more of this and that and throw back your papers, and before you even gather them together he have call up the next person. That frighten you and make you feel cheap you don't want to go back again.[26]

The narrative shifts from a first- to a second-person perspective, interpellating the reader into the narrator's degraded experience of new British imperialism. An opposition, between 'you', the Zimbabwean immigrant, and the 'old consulate' staff is highlighted through the case worker's 'severe' disregard; yet, this division, with its work of fixing, is unable to remain static, predicated as it is on the use of the unstable and ever-shifting 'you'. Narrative theorist Brian Richardson has referred to the use of a second-person narration as an instance of what he terms unnatural narration. As a pronoun with no stable referent, the use of 'you' as a means of address implicitly resists the readerly desire for a fixing in narrative stability through its autotelic, or direct, nature. As Richardson writes:

> The defining criterion of [...] 'the autotelic' is the direct address to a 'you' that is at times the actual reader of the text and whose story is juxtaposed to and can merge with the characters of the fiction. [...] Its unique and most compelling feature [...] is the ever-shifting referent of the 'you' that is continually addressed. [...] This intensifies one of the most fascinating features of second person narrative: the way the narrative 'you' is alternately opposed to and fused with the reader.[27]

Here 'you' functions as a means of interpellation which disallows the stagnancy of fixed, Manichean allegiances, simultaneously hailing the reader on an individual level and, through the reproduction of this act, fabricating a dislocated reading public. Significantly, given the observation that performativity operates not as a free-for-all, but is rather constrained by the operations of power, the shift to an ambiguous 'you' form of address leads to a shift in the subjective dynamics of reading. By moving the imperative to be from the text to its reader, hailed as 'you', the text performs a dislodging of power, unmooring its performance from its determinants through a form of displacement.

In *Harare North*, these irruptions into the second person foreground the contingency of performativity. Throughout the novel, it is difficult to discern the precise foundations of the 'you', a shifting referent which may serve as an interpellating hailing of the reader, a socio-political commentary on post-2002 immigration or as a reflection of the narrator as a dissociated voice, lost in an encroaching madness. By reporting these sections in the second person, the narrative highlights the central instability of these constructions of being; told to 'you', ascribed to 'you', the performances of self displayed in these extracts can only ever be in progress, linked, as they are, to an unstable and ever-shifting referent caught at the interstices of incongruent fields of power. At the same time, these extracts demonstrate the fixing potential of an externally-determined notion of self, foregrounded in each passage's forceful positioning of 'you' within a socio-political and historical schema beyond the boundaries of any notion of performance:

> But days push you in waves and soon you is washed off on some new and unfamiliar shore. You want things back to being simple like they was so you can focus on few things only but now you have to tight every muscle because if you don't do that then life collect into one big shapeless thing and soon the whole thing slip off your grasp. (*HN*, p. 96)

Becoming that 'you', the reader of *Harare North* is narratorially implicated with the schema of global inequity into which its narrator falls. Simultaneously, the reader is compelled to replicate, in the act of reading, the narrator's performance of an identity based upon dislocation and dissociation, fleetingly becoming other to the narration's self. Momentarily positioned as the debased other, the reader must cede the authoritative and interpretative floor to the narrator, transformed into that object whose exclusion allows the text to emerge. Through this narratorial intermingling, the 'multi-accentual quality' for which Fanon's theorization of racial subjectivity has been praised takes on a distinct and disturbing form,[28] revealing, beyond the performativity of the self, the ultimate performativity of the very categories of nation, self and other. In a parallel move, London, transformed into Harare North, loses its currency as the centre of imperial and post-imperial power, becoming, instead, a stop gap, a measuring station of sorts through which the narrator must pass in his performance of self and into which the reader is continually drawn and dislodged. At the same time, the particulars of that performance themselves remain mutable, turning from an ontological stability in self to the fleeting movements of appearance as being, a subjective space in which the 'big story' (*HN*, p. 53) you tell about life takes on a value and valence far greater than its lived experience. 'Being many people in one person' (*HN*, p. 53), the narrator forcibly draws the reader into a split, multiple and conflicting mode of subjectivity, enlivening what Oliver calls the 'witnessing structure' of being,[29] in which the self is not a single self, but rather a fragmented and dispersed collection of personas united through the fixing qualities of socio-historical and political interpellation into a history already-written. Significantly, this second-person hailing appears in the present tense. If, as Bhabha suggests, the stereotype functions through a form of fixity which 'must be anxiously repeated',[30] the use of present tense in *Harare North* leverages an ambiguous temporality to reflect a larger ambivalence of identity, as simultaneously given and forever becoming, circulating in a manner both ceaseless and futile, exempt from any teleology and stripped of any final sublation. Instead, the powers of reflection and interpretation are taken away, leaving the reader only with action and movement, defying a moment of rest in the a priori.

Yet, the flexibility of performance is not given free reign throughout the novel. Like any performance, that is to say, the performance of self in *Harare North* remains subject to the demands of its external determiners. Indeed, it would be difficult to see in *Harare North* what has been called 'the tendency to celebrate a free-floating "transnational imaginary" born of "postmodern decolonization" [and] "transcultural hybridity"' so often deployed with the postcolonial.[31] Instead, the narrator is presented as forever becoming within the enforced boundaries of a given notion of being, one which inflicts as much as it inflects. This notion of fixing is particularly highlighted in his interactions at Tim's, the fish and chip shop where he finds employment. In this space, the narrator repeatedly describes his lack of ease with Tim, whose watchful eyes keep him under surveillance:

> But now, me I am cleaning them floors, Tim keep asking too many questions when I don't want any question because me I don't know why he want to know so much things about me now and disturb my thinking.
> 'How is Zimbabwe?'
> 'OK.'
> 'How is your family back there?'
> 'OK.'
> 'What's Zimbabwe like?'
> 'OK.'
> 'How is Mugabe?'
> 'OK.'
> 'Are you all right?'
> 'OK.'
> 'Do you know what Zimbabwe means?'
> Zimbabwe mean house of stone, but me I just shrug my shoulders and say I don't know what it mean because he is hassling me for no reason. Now he start telling me what Zimbabwe mean because he look it up on Internet last week. Me I play dunderhead who don't know nothing. 'It means house of stone,' he say. (*HN*, pp. 89–90)

Describing Tim as 'asking too many questions' and wanting to know 'so much things', the narrator is reduced to a transparent site of total understanding, the object of inquiry to be conquered in its classification, compelled to perform its ignorance. A similar effect arises as the narrator is repeatedly confronted by a group of teenagers from a nearby housing estate:

> Now I am cleaning them tables and the floor on the other side of the counter and they drop in, order chips and sit at the table. They

don't eat them chips and just sit there talking and watching me cleaning around. Then, leaving them chips untouched, they run away off cackling and pissing they pants wet.

Tim watch this and don't say nothing because he is breastfeeding the machine. They is laughing at me and he do nothing about it.

Next day they come again and leave the place bawling with laughter. (*HN*, p. 97)

With their mirth, the teenagers represent a language of significations which escape the narrator. Remaining beyond his grasp, these elusive codes transform into a form of mockery, fixing him as an aberration, a stain on society, in a process reminiscent of Fanon's lamentations that he is 'fixed', cut off from 'sections of [his] reality', by the racist white gaze.[32] In contrast to his earlier performance of hapless immigrant and 'friendly African native' (*HN*, p. 4), the narrator is incapable of manipulating this fixing, unable to be seen as human. Not coincidentally, however, the narrator's fixing departs in one significant manner from Fanon's narrative in *Black Skin, White Masks*, in that the teenagers form a multiracial group rather than a homogeneous white gaze. This reconfiguration of the gaze thus shifts its locus from a singularly raced focus into one driven by the performativity of the broader identitarian categories of migrancy. In this move, Chikwava's narrator embodies the notion 'that white and black are relative terms that refer more to social standing than to some natural skin color in itself; there is no skin color in itself'.[33] Instead, race, as played out in Tim's shop, reveals itself to be a manifestation of power, a means of reproducing the social order of things.

No discussion of Chikwava's novel could neglect the importance of the narrator's idiom in his performance (and eventual disintegration) of self. While colloquially referred to as written in Rotten English, a reference to the late Ken Saro-Wiwa's landmark Nigerian-Biafran War novel, *Sozaboy: A Novel in Rotten English*, the narrator of *Harare North* deploys a distinct creole, drawing largely on idiomatic language, repetition and a foregrounding of the present tense.[34] Chikwava has described his use of language as a mix of silapalapa (Zimbabwean pidgin English), Shona and Ndebele translated idiomatically into English and Creole inspired by the writings of Jean Rhys and Claude McKay. As he explains, 'this, in a way, sharpens the otherness of the character—it cannot be possible to understand everything about him'.[35] The narrator's language is simultaneously syncretic and entirely performative in its nature, drawing upon the multiple traditions of Zimbabwe and the African diaspora, as well as the particular cultural context of contemporary London. More importantly, however, the use of language destabilizes any singular attempt at reading or unitary work of readerly identification. The reading public which the novel fabricates is thus forced, through this linguistic play, into a hetero-geneous self-reflection, identified through difference. Put rather bluntly, it is not possible to simply read the novel and construct a single version of the story; instead, the reader of *Harare North* is left in a continual process of comprehension and revision, leading to a perpetual slippage in signification. With this nexus of narratorial modes and themes, *Harare North* refuses any attempts at a singular or straightforward reduction to national allegory, an overdetermined blackness or unitary mode of being. The narrator can neither be seen as a cipher for national allegory, nor can his relationships be taken as a microcosm of a wider Zimbabwean community because the narrative remains forcibly contingent, both reflecting upon the political while engaging the aesthetic to resist an ethical collapse. Through its use of an unreliable first-person narrator whose desta-bilizing performance of multiple selves implicates the reader, the narrative forcibly cleaves re-presentation and representation in its inscrutability.

## Typification, Migration and Conflict

If *Harare North* demonstrates a mode of subject formation in which linguistic innovation and narrative instability foreground the con-tingency of performance, *Links* demonstrates the ways in which this individual coming-into-being is mired within a larger field of collec-tive becoming through the malleability of memory. Like the former, the latter novel, too, serves a sort of representative function which is not one, resisting a collapse into a unitarily-coded prescription of alienation and subjectivity. The novel tells the story of Jeebleh, a Somali resident in New York, who returns to Mogadiscio to reunite with his old friend Bile and help secure the return of Bile's recently-kidnapped niece, Raasta. As one commentator has noted, the novel 'functions as a counter-representation to the mainstream US media's sensationalist, therefore reductive, coverage of the Somali war'.[36]

Through this narrative act of recuperation, the formation of individual subjectivity in the novel is implicitly positioned within a larger landscape of raced identity, one defined both by the inscription of clan-based difference and the assumption of racial difference from a presumed Western reader. Throughout *Links*, Jeebleh struggles to find his place in a Mogadiscio vastly transformed through perpetual clan warfare in the wake of dictator Siad Barre's capitulation. While *Links* does not demonstrate linguistic innovation in the vein of *Harare North*, it nonetheless leverages an aesthetic thrust constitutive to its larger performance of a troubled Somalia, while simultaneously resisting assimilation into representation. The play of communitarian and individual identities enacted in *Links* revolves around the fulcrum of memory, foregrounding the ultimate instability of an insular selfhood. This play comes to the fore in a narrative which, though largely focalized through Jeebleh's increasingly unstable perspective, weaves a communal tapestry through the eruption of alternative narrative voices and forms.

Set in the mid-1990s in the immediate wake of the disastrous American Operation Restore Hope, *Links* evokes a number of references from recent history through its description of two warring clans who, led respectively by StrongmanSouth and StrongmanNorth, seek to consolidate power following the abdication of the Tyrant. While references to the aforementioned figures lends an immediate frame of reference to the novel as a whole, the narrative refuses to explicitly name the real-world figures for whom Tyrant and the Strongmen stand in. For the reader familiar with the Battle of Mogadiscio, these figures will be recognizable as Siad Barre, Mohamed Farrah Aidid and Ali Mahdi Muhammad. Yet, the narrative does not encourage this extratextual act of linking; instead, in its refusal to bestow a proper name upon these players in the conflict, *Links* operates as a typification of African conflict, where the literary serves as a historical abstraction that nonetheless remains particular. Following the early Lukácsian insight that 'art must render reality in a more intensified, condensed and rounded form, one ultimately more meaningful, coherent, sensuous and *recognisable*',[37] it is precisely this act of typification which resists a collapse into a singular narrative of atavistic savagery. Here typification allows the narrative to highlight its subjective, personal and libidinal work as central to its arc, the very work which presents a strong counterdiscursive response to the stereotypical and flattening images portrayed in the media and in films like *Black Hawk Down*. References to the disastrous American intervention/invasion are present throughout the narrative; at the same time, this particular frame of reference is never given total priority over the psychic traumas it foregrounds in Jeebleh and his friends. Along with a series of narrative strategies, including the use of folkloric techniques, the recurrence of dreams as a framing device and the use of intertextual references and epigraphs, this typification of recent Somali history creates a narrative effect in which the desire to excavate a sense of purity in representation is thwarted, replaced instead with a reliance on aesthetic re-presentation.

*Links* is perhaps most challenging in the range of narrative frameworks upon which it calls, both within the diegetic frame of the novel and through its paratextual elements; these references span influences from Dante's *Inferno*, an intertext to the novel as a whole, to the Somali tradition of oral literature, defying a singular point of entry to the novel. Coupled with re-told folkloric extracts and references to the material artefacts of a pan-African tradition,[38] this range of influence creates a multivocal narrative fabric which refuses to choose a single line of filiation. It would be easy to view this play of reference as a form of cultural hybridity, where the interplay of incongruent traditions gives rise to a celebration of the interstitial and inventive, and indeed, this track of criticism has been widely followed in critical readings of Farah's oeuvre. Derek Wright, for instance, has stated that Farah's writing 'is a living testament to the process of cultural hybridization that is a standard feature of the postcolonial world',[39] while Gikandi has characterized it by its blend of 'the culture of the Somali state and the esthetic of African modernism'.[40] Beyond hybridity, however, *Links* performs a form of universalism that is not one, a universalism that is rooted at a semiotic level where the cultures and codes from which the novel draws interact less as a sanctioned cosmopolitan celebration of difference and liminality and more as a testament to the foundational discrepancy of symbolic systems. Through the constant oscillation of registers and occlusions of influence, the novel functions through a form of haunting, narratively embodied in its preoccupation with dreams and the dream world (see, for example, *L*, p. 178; pp. 181–2).[41] In this manner, it presents a vision of the self in the world which relies less on the logic of pluralism and hybridity than in the engagement of what Amanda Anderson, in a discussion of Butler, refers to as 'the enabling disruption of any given universality at the linguistic level', a state in which 'the disruptive vicissitudes of the given norms of universality' are foregrounded to challenge the very structures of subjectification.[42]

As the plurality of referential spaces drawn on in Farah's novel indicates, a sense of dispersal is central to the narrative's presentation of individual becoming, particularly in the figure of Jeebleh himself. For Jeebleh, the instability of his being in Mogadiscio is initially expressed through a sense of migratory unease, a migration of memory based upon a fundamental unhomeliness in being. As Bhabha, in a gloss on Freud, writes, 'to be unhomed is not to be homeless, nor can the "unhomely" be easily accommodated in that familiar division of social life into private and public spaces. The unhomely moment creeps up on you as stealthily as your own shadow'.[43] For Jeebleh, this moment of unhomeliness is mediated through his experience first as a political detainee in Somalia, beneficiary to a moment of reprieve whose understanding eludes him, and later as an exile, made unhomely by his absence. This private experience of dislocation is thus mediated through its public register, becoming both, yet neither, and caught within the discourses of civic life and those of individual survival. Jeebleh's decision to return to Mogadiscio, a city from which he had remained estranged since the moment of his unexplained release from prison, is one couched in inscrutability:

> He reminded himself that he had felt a strange impulse to come, after an alarming brush with death. He had nearly been run over by a Somali, new to New York and driving a taxi illegally. He hoped that by coming to Mogadiscio, the city of death, he might disorient death. Meanwhile, he had looked forward to linking up with Bile and, he hoped, meeting his very dear friend's niece Raasta, who had lately been abducted. (*L*, p. 5)

Mogadiscio, Jeebleh's 'city of death', the city of his childhood and the city of his torment, becomes in this reckoning the only place in which the larger ironies of the constant encroachment of death upon life may be confronted. A city maligned in the international media as lawless and irrevocably broken becomes something else entirely through Jeebleh's intervention. That which is seen as aberrant is normalized through its implications with the mundane coincidences of quotidian existence. This transfiguration is echoed in the manner in which Jeebleh introduces his friends and the situation of Raasta's abduction. Almost an aside, the blasé mention of his friend and his missing niece resists both sensationalism and sentiment; rather than operating as a melodrama, then, Jeebleh's decision to return to the city of his birth after so many years is presented as matter of fact, a pre-given and uninteresting decision based off of a moment of pure contingency. This blasé return itself complicates any overdetermined reading of migrancy in the novel. Farah has spoken extensively on the role of the diaspora, stating that 'they are connected because they know the past, and they want to compare the past, when Somalia was peaceful and beautiful, with the present-day situation, when Somalia is in chaos. But because of their distance, they feel they are objective. They become part of the story when they have been there long enough'.[44] In other words, contra the notion that members of the diaspora contribute to the romanticization of the home nation, Farah's comments indicate a perspective in which it is that very distancing which allows for a normalization through an ascribed objectivity. In similar terms, Jeebleh's departure at the end of the narrative is presented in equally contingent and almost forcibly quotidian terms:

> He had opened a parenthesis with his decision to visit Mogadiscio on a whim, to elude death at the same time that he reclaimed his mother, whom he had neglected into an early grave. Now the parenthesis seemed to be closing, but he felt that it wouldn't have served his purpose for that to happen just yet. After all, he was not prepared to dwell in pronominal confusion, which was where he had been headed. He had to find which pronoun might bring his story to a profitable end. (*L*, p. 329)

Closing the parenthesis, Jeebleh's diasporic return resists stereotype by its very mundanity. The configurations of power which impel a return to the sensational are replaced in this moment by a liberatory banality.

The reference to pronominal confusion in the passage referenced above is not insignificant. Throughout the novel, the concept of a pronominal confusion is leveraged to foreground the instability and ultimately contradictory means through which individual identities are fashioned and re-fashioned against a constantly-shifting field of relation. This recurring narrative meditation on the nature of self-construction, the negotiation of incongruent circulated selves, functions as an explicit commentary on the nature of self-representation, self-in-community and the multiplicity of identities forever caught in a constant war of fixing and shifting. For Jeebleh, the links between pronominal confusion and identitarian conflict are based in the imperative towards clan identity as a fundamental facet of the self in Somali lived experience. Unlike his compatriots, Jeebleh voices his disgust with the idea of the clan as a meaningful category of organization or negotiation, thinking with relief that 'he felt no clan-based loyalty himself—in fact, the whole idea revolted and angered him' (*L*, p. 7). Yet, despite the strength of his conviction against the clan as a basis for identification, throughout the narrative, Jeebleh is entrapped time and again by clan politics, overtly in his aggressive courting by the elders of his clan, who hope to procure money for two battlewagons from him (*L*, p. 128), but also in his very navigation of the city, where staying on the 'right' side becomes a guarantor of safety. It is in this space that Jeebleh is first forced to confront his own implication within the dangerous fundamentalism of clan-based identity politics through his immediate interpellation into the clan's 'we'. This moment of inclusion is, for Jeebleh, more difficult to resolve than his feeling of foreignness in Mogadiscio. As he remarks to himself, to be an outsider is tolerable, given its liberating severing of the fixing ties of the clan's interpellations: 'It had been one thing talking to the Major, who thought of him as an outsider; it was altogether another to be in the company of the manager, with his inclusive "we"! What was he to do?' (*L*, p. 41). In his discomfort, Jeebleh exemplifies what has been described as the need 'not only to recreate national identity and consciousness [...] but also to go beyond and create a social consciousness at the moment of liberation',[45] a means of escaping the endless cycle of domination and oppression through the fabrication of novel modes of belonging, as yet undefined by the trappings of power. Instead, forcibly interpellated into becoming part of the 'we', hailed as part of an undesired in-group in a compulsory act of identification, Jeebleh finds that it is precisely this handling of pronouns which entrenches the self into a false notion of stability in identity which constantly works to truncate the freedom of a shifting self.

For Jeebleh, this condition of becoming/being is exacerbated by the material realities of contemporary Somalia:

> He thought of how it was characteristic of civil wars to produce a multiplicity of pronominal affiliations, of first-person singulars tucked away in the plural, of third-person plurals meant to separate one group from another. The confusion pointed to the weakness of the exclusive claims made by first-person plurals, as understood implicitly in the singled-out singular. (*L*, p. 41)

This double bind, where pronominal confusion edges against the enforced multiplicity of being, characterizes the portrayal of subjective becoming in *Links*. Through Jeebleh's inability to come to terms with his pronominal confusion, his inability to settle upon a modality through which to define himself, the narrative slides across multiple registers and forms of becoming, collapsing the self into the collectivity only to recuperate the self as an end in itself: 'Jeebleh knew [...] that in moments of great anxiety, one may mistake the self for the world' (*L*, p. 6). These two poles of being, being-for-self and being-in-the-world, continually haunt one another without resolution. Yet, this vision of an oscillating self does not lead to an acritical celebration of mutability. Instead, for Jeebleh, the experience of perpetual modulation across becomings is a source of destabilization and dissociation, reminiscent of the degeneration of *Harare North*'s unnamed narrator: 'And now that Jeebleh was alone, the demons were back. His agitation was due, in part, to a lack of clarity in his mind—how to define himself here. His difficulty lay elsewhere, in his ability to choose whom he would associate himself with' (*L*, p. 41). In the end, for Jeebleh, the only solution is to close the parenthesis, drawing a line under his pronominal confusion and departing from Mogadiscio with little forewarning. Musing that 'He and his friends were forever linked through the chains of the stories they shared' (*L*, p. 334), this act of flight is presented not as a betrayal,[46] but rather as the only possible resolution that is not one for the constant movement of rupture brought on by the contradictory imperatives of selfhood.

## Retrospective Alienation and National Disillusionment

Perhaps more than either *Links* or *Harare North*, Tsitsi Dangarembga's *The Book of Not* lends itself to a Fanonian analysis of alienated racial subjectivity and its enforced performance of a raced identity. The second of a planned trilogy (at the time of this writing, the proposed third novel, *The River Running Dry*, remains in preparation) beginning with Dangarembga's acclaimed *Nervous Conditions* (1988), *The Book of Not* tells the continuation of protagonist Tambudzai's story in a Zimbabwe at the threshold of independence. Unlike its relatively optimistic predecessor, *The Book of Not* develops a sense of alienation with no escape; at the novel's end, Tambu, jobless and soon-to-be homeless, flounders in utter estrangement from any sense of being in the world, left adrift by the resonances of colonialist prejudice in a Zimbabwe which has not yet realized the promise of its independence struggles:

> I had forgotten all the promises made to myself and providence while I was young concerning carrying forward with me the good and human, the *unhu* of my life. As it was, I had not considered *unhu* at all, only my own calamities [...]. So this evening I walked emptily to the room I would soon vacate, wondering what future there was for me, a new Zimbabwean.[47]

Tambu's ultimate failure, the narrative implies, comes from her inability to reconcile her subjective becoming with its public dimensions. This very failure, however, is narratively mediated through Tambu's position as a citizen of the new Zimbabwe, creating a self-perpetuating circling effect at the narrative's core. In its contemporary historical mode, *The Book of Not* develops a parallel between Zimbabwe's uneasy emergence into an independence which will not escape from the oppressive dictates of the past and Tambu's own development into a young woman for whom the promise of *Nervous Conditions* cannot be met. As Roseanne Kennedy writes:

> Dangarembga innovatively uses irony, humor, and farce to dramatize the absurdities of racism in a colonial society and the impediments to witnessing it, thereby bringing into visibility what is unspeakable in (post)colonial Zimbabwe. The novel dramatizes the narrator's struggle to break out of a repetition compulsion, manifested in her obsessive desire for recognition, which continually leaves her deflated and depressed. Dangarembga's use of fiction to articulate the Rhodesian legacy of colonialism and racism is particularly significant given the taboo on speaking about race in Zimbabwe today.[48]

As Kennedy's comments suggest, Tambu's story extends beyond the purely affective to a modality more in line with Jameson's national allegory, a distortion of the process of *Bildung*. At the same time, and in direct contrast to the dominant reading of *Nervous Conditions*, the more pessimistic sequel cannot be so easily reduced. While it is certainly the case, as Kennedy posits, that 'Tambu's experiences of loss and denial are therefore not merely personal; they are symptomatic of larger national struggles',[49] this parallel reading of nation and protagonist fails to capture the complexity of identification and alienation as presented in the novel. From a narratorial perspective, this work of undoing is emphasized through the novel's telescoping of time. Midway through the narrative, Tambu remarks that 'What happened after that took a long time, although it seemed as if it took no time at all; as if I stayed always in the same place, trudging, exhausted, and stayed exactly where I was, treading space and time like water' (*BN*, p. 97). Indeed, throughout the novel there appears a series of ellipses, where years are compressed into mere sentences, and moments of dwelling where passing episodes expand. In lieu of Benedict Anderson's notion of the novel as 'moving calendrically through homogeneous, empty time' comes a distorting effect which, through its refusal of a teleological march through history, subverts a reversion to national allegory and disrupts the development of *Bildung*.[50] The two roles through which Tambu's development unravels, her individual psychological transformation and her allegorical position as stand-in for newly-independent Zimbabwe, maintain their singularity, negotiating without collapsing.

Following this reading, in *The Book of Not* is an apparent undoing of Tambu's inter-subjective becoming in *Nervous Conditions*, a story which the narrator describes as 'not after all about death, but about my escape and Lucia's; about my mother's and Maiguru's entrapment; and about Nyasha's rebellion',[51] 'the story of four women whom I loved, and our men, this story [of] how it all began'.[52] In contrast to this collective, feminine experience of becoming, the Tambu of *The Book of Not* is portrayed as isolated to the extent of solipsism, ending her narrative development in a devastating solitude. In place of a rootedness in the earlier text through which Tambu 'stands poised to become part of the national elite',[53] the follow-up novel displays a fragmentary sense of alienation which no connectivity can challenge, mired in a set of material conditions which it cannot overcome. If its predecessor in the planned trilogy takes its narrative inspiration from the famous translation of Sartre's remark, in his preface to Fanon's *The Wretched of the Earth*, that 'the status of the "native" is a nervous condition',[54] then *The Book of Not*, too, can be read as a play on its title, one in which the process of subjectification is continually mediated through its very negation at the cusp of arrival, a product of expulsion. In so doing, *The Book of Not* undermines the reconciliatory mode on which *Nervous Conditions* concludes, turning its promise of development and progression through education into another hollow negation of its own effects in this 'novel of "unbecoming"'.[55]

Where *Nervous Conditions* begins with a deliberate destruction of empathy through the narrator's confession that she was pleased to see her brother die, *The Book of Not* begins in a mode which highlights its inward turn, refusing the reader easy access into the narrative or its narrator's fictional mind: 'Up, up, up, the leg spun. A piece of person, up there in the sky. Earth and acrid vapours coated my tongue. Silence surged out to die away at the ragged shriek of a cricket in the bushes at the edge of the village clearing' (*BN*, p. 3). These lines serve to obfuscate any easy act of interpretation, setting a scene that remains shrouded in darkness and haunted by lacunae. At one level, the image of the severed leg, flying through the sky, gestures towards a sense of debilitating alienation, engaging the way in which 'the very metaphor of *amputation* [...] suggests unconscious knowledge [...] of the colonial process as causing loss or confusion of identity'.[56] Importantly, however, this passage reveals a more generalized moment of destabilization at the site of reading. The origin of the leg, its fate and its relevance to Tambu remain unspoken, opening the narrative onto a scene of fragmentation which tacitly parallels the degeneration of Tambu's sense of self throughout the novel. As the passage develops, it comes to light that this opening is a moment of violence doubled in its intimacy. The leg, it reveals, belongs to Netsai, Tambu's younger sister who has joined the 'elder siblings', a colloquial term for Mugabe's freedom fighting militia, trained in guerrilla warfare in the hills of Mozambique. Having stepped on an errant landmine, it is Netsai whose leg 'arcs through the sky', crystallizing into a leitmotif that will appear throughout the narrative as a symbol of Tambu's psychic degeneration. At the same time, the narrative reveals, this moment of violence is itself embedded within a larger field of violence and power as the scene simultaneously introduces Sacred Heart, the convent school at which Tambu studies as one of five black students, the apex of her achievement at the end of *Nervous Conditions*. The dismembered violence of the mutilated limb is metonymically displaced onto the site of colonialist development, crippling its allegedly benevolent mission. Tambu's journey throughout *The Book of Not* is similarly stunted, turning the *Bildungsroman* form upon itself as a teleology that leads to nowhere, circling itself like the arc of Netsai's leg. This deformation of the *Bildungs* form is of no little significance to the narrative. As Morton observes, 'the aesthetic form of the *Bildungsroman* is marked by the imperialist determinants of European aesthetics, and by the civilising mission of English literature',[57] a case in which the aesthetic form of the text serves a distinct, if occluded, political purpose. In *The Book of Not*, however, the disfiguration of the *Bildungsroman* aesthetic, through Tambu's psychic fragmentation, serves to foreground the destructive force of colonial education.

As this opening moment of displacement indicates, Sacred Heart holds a central place in Tambu's emerging sense of alienation. In the family village, Tambu's status as educated in the school, a space normally reserved only for the white population, results in a cleaving between her self-image and that of her community, in which she begins to see herself as 'grown too old and too fine' (*BN*, p. 8) to return. Having rejected the confines of her family life in favour of the possibilities of formal education at the end of *Nervous Conditions*, Tambu, in *The Book of Not*, fails to develop the promised self-image of success and liberation. Instead, Tambu finds her selfhood displaced from the confines of an idealized, pre-colonial traditional family unit to the racial hierarchy of Sacred Heart, echoing the earlier act of metonymic displacement:

> You were awarded a copper plate, laced at the edges and patterned with dots on the rim. Your name was in it, your very own name, Tambudzai Sigauke. Like a miracle, that name that you hardly ever read anywhere else appeared in the centre of the plate, as though it was something special. [...] If I learnt what was required, my name would be placed together thus, with the institution that offered the most prestigious education to young women in the

country, and so I would drop into my pocket, from where it could not be taken away, the key to my future. (*BN*, p. 27)

Receiving one of these copper plates becomes Tambu's primary goal throughout much of her time at Sacred Heart, an aim intended to combat against the alienation which threatens her. By seeing her name engraved onto one of these plates, Tambu supposes, her inclusion into the Sacred Heart community would be guaranteed, a confirmation of a self authorized by the norms of the (white) school and exempt from alienation. Yet, a passage midway through the novel suggests that this desired performance is not to be:

> You came to a school where you frequently had to pinch yourself to see if you really existed. Then, after that was confirmed, you quite often wished you didn't. So you ducked away to avoid meeting a group of people. That's when you found out how you were going to manage after all, when you'd almost given up hope, to bring people to admire and respect you. (*BN*, p. 114)

In place of a fully-realized self, Tambu is called upon to play the native, the excluded and degraded other. The narrative evokes this expulsion through the repeated image of the severed, alien limb, appearing first when, having grabbed her teacher's hand, Tambu regards her black skin against the white skin of the older woman, recoiling at 'soiling' her teacher in this way and 'horrified to see [her] hand disobedient and motionless' (*BN*, p. 32). During a room inspection, as Tambu finds herself unable to recognize the sound of her own voice or feel her hands gripping her bed sheets, this alienation returns: 'I was just as worried about another encounter with myself. What if I did something else I didn't know I could do, like pull the sheets! What would it be, and wouldn't it be awful?' (*BN*, p. 57). Later, having failed at her attempts at a good degree, due largely to racist structures which deny her equal classroom access with her white colleagues, and resigned to a life of menial work, Tambu again sees herself as that unacknowledged amputation: 'Stumbling on stones on my way to catch a *combi* to work, holding my hand to my face against the putrid evaporate from rotten pipes, I was soon petrified by intense surges of aggression' (*BN*, p. 199). In each case, Tambu experiences herself as other. Yet, unlike that enabling otherness that might bring her into being through its productive alienation, Tambu's otherness, crippled by its doubling, can only be experienced as an expulsion which refuses acknowledgement. Where the 'possibility of subjecthood lies in the [...] willingness and ability to accept that point of explosion, which blasts apart the black [...] body as it is known within colonial culture',[58] for Tambu, any moment of reconstruction remains impossible. In contrast to her cohort, notably Ntombi, whose love for languages and desire to 'enable communication later between Africans who could not understand each other' (*BN*, p. 152) demonstrates a means of putting the body back together, reaching a productive alienation through the generation of a new self in a larger communal framework, Tambu, afraid even to speak Shona for fear of 'getting another [black] mark' (*BN*, p. 126), is literally left without a language of expression, a means of rebuttal. In stark contrast to claims that 'freedom from the past is possible if one breaks with its heritage. [...] To repair oneself, burdened with an identity that has been constructed [...] is to *dis-identify* with it',[59] Tambu is left with no space from which to dis-identify, no space from which to articulate an alternative means of being in the world and no space from which to embrace destabilization for its forward thrust, so fully materialized by the norms which give rise to her performance is she.

This displacement of the self onto the norms and regulations of the school thus develops into a form of alienation that takes its shape in the epistemic and material breaks of a self-fragmentation. Tambu is debilitatingly alienated, in Oliver's terms, through her double displacement, both from the family sphere, with its attendant notion of past in tradition and community, destroyed through the violence of settler colonialism, and from her idealized self at Sacred Heart, forever out of grasp by virtue of the racist ideology which the school and nation purport. As Oliver suggests, 'Fanon points toward a debilitating alienation inherent in colonialism that not only adds another layer to the idea that alienation is inherent in the human condition but also works against primary alienation'.[60] In other words, by forcing the subject into an alienation based on race, the debilitating alienation of colonialism prevents the subject from engaging in that more general alienation through which the self is actualized. Instead, the raced subject is made party, by colonial power, 'to a double command: be like me, don't be like me; be mimetically identical, be totally other. The colonial other is situated somewhere between difference and similitude, at the vanishing point of subjectivity'.[61] In turning from the destroyed and impossible traditional sphere to the supposed meritocracy of the school environment, Tambu turns from a notion of development through the empowerment of knowledge to a utilitarian notion of achievement in which any potential for self-knowledge is stripped and left abject through this command to perform the impossible:

> Besides, I suffered secretly a sense of inferiority that came from having been at the primitive scene. Being a student at the Young Ladies' College of the Sacred Heart, I possessed images from the school's films and library: cavemen dragging their women where they wanted them by the hair or bludgeoning their prey. And in the final analysis there was everyone, sitting mesmerised and agreeing about the appropriateness of this behaviour. (*BN*, p. 28)

Universalized into an inclusion with the 'cavemen' and their 'primitive scene', Tambu, despite her zeal to wholly adopt the normative values of the convent, remains unable to reconcile her necessary expulsion from its norms. Recurring perpetually, the inassimilable negation upon which her selfhood balances is highlighted, butting up against and preventing an acknowledgement of that other, productive negation of human subjectivity. Yet, this inability to dismantle the self indicates a different form of resistance at the level of narrative, one which refuses to collapse the aesthetic with the political. Embittered and utterly bereft, Tambu, as narrator, offers no entry for identification. Instead, Tambu's affective degeneration can only be read as a single narrative strand, unreliably told, against a plethora of alternative options. If, in *Nervous Conditions*, Tambu's progressive development can be marked as a national allegory against the degeneration of Nyasha,[62] here, marked against the success of Ntombi, Tambu's stagnancy refuses this same generalization through allegory, remaining, as it were, singularly affected.

*Harare North, Links* and *The Book of Not* all demonstrate, to differing degrees, the ways in which the demand to perform a contextually-derived racial identity lays the foundation of an African self, forever compelled to exclusion and objectification, in contemporary

Anglophone African writing. While none of the three novels presents an entirely liberating or optimistic vision of the possibilities of self-hood or the status of the individual, each nonetheless demonstrates the mechanisms through which an objectification of the African self and concomitant extrapolation from individual formations to a totalizing representation function may be deferred. Each text, through its aesthetic function, serves to destabilize the governing norms through which the self is materialized as always more than a self, while remaining rooted in a specific history of becoming. At the same time, each text demonstrates the very ambiguity of the individual in contemporary African writing, always compelled to perform a form of a selfhood that may never speak solely for itself.

# 3
# Gender and Representing the Unrepresentable

## Race, Gender and Articulated Identities

Women's identities in African literature form a particularly difficult facet of representation due, in large part, to the problem of articulating an intersectional identity in language.[1] As Kimberlé Crenshaw has aptly stated, 'Because of their intersectional identity as both women and of color within discourses shaped to respond to one or the other, women of color are marginalized within both'.[2] African women, in other words, are identified as both other by virtue of gender and other by virtue of ethnic identity, two facets which can be neither separated nor treated as equivalent but instead function through a complex relational process. Based in this context, this chapter focuses particularly on the contested space where gender meets ethnic or racial identity,[3] that space in which, as Spivak has famously claimed, the subaltern cannot speak. Yet, despite the constant threat of appropriation and assimilation, it should be recalled, as Benita Parry reminds us, that 'discourses of representation should not be confused with material realities'.[4] Rather than viewing feminine subjectivities in African writing as inherently irretrievable, that is to say, an attentive reading remains attuned to the ways in which these identities speak differently, persistently emerging in alternate codes which go beyond the discursive. This chapter furthers this discussion by considering the articulation and intersection of race and gender in three contemporary global African texts by women writers: Chimamanda Ngozi Adichie's *Half of a Yellow Sun*, Yvonne Vera's *The Stone Virgins* and Aminatta Forna's *Ancestor Stones*. Along with their shared critical success, each of these three texts shares a preoccupation with the particular amplification of intersectional identities in the context of war. Adichie's *Half of a Yellow Sun* serves as a memorialization of the Nigerian-Biafran War of 1967–70, while Vera's *The Stone Virgins* confronts the genocidal violence that overtook Zimbabwe's Matabeleland in the aftermath of the Second Chimurenga, a period known as the Gukurahundi. In Forna's *Ancestor Stones* the narrative, spanning nearly eighty years, is shadowed by the persistent violence of Sierra Leone's postcolonial development, particularly in and around the Civil War of 1992–2001. In each case, discourses of gender and race intersect, and this intersection is complicated by its location in conflict. As all three texts demonstrate, attempts to subvert the trope of feminization in conflict, particularly women's roles as sexual guardians and victims, repeatedly emerge in contemporary African writing. At the same time, alternative models of gendered identity remain limited in their effectiveness, subject to the tension between subversion and domestication in the construction of contrapuntal discourses of gender.

The representation of gender in African literature has been fraught since the inception of global African writing in the Anglophone sphere with Chinua Achebe's *Things Fall Apart*. As critics of that text have supposed, Achebe's portrayal of the feminine in Umuofia raises a series of questions surrounding representation, violence and agency.[5] The occlusion of the feminine from the world of the literary text seen in that early novel would be reproduced across early Anglophone African literature, a body of work largely written by men in which, as Florence Stratton has demonstrated, 'woman' is continually figured 'as an index of the changing state of the nation'.[6] In other words, the representation of woman as a metonymic figuration of the nation in early African writing was both commonplace and damaging to women's broader social and political interests. In particular, the Mother Africa trope, as I will discuss below, was reconfigured as one which 'operates against the interests of women, excluding them, implicitly if not explicitly, from authorship and citizenship' through a construction of woman as both emblem of the nation and keeper of its cultural purity.[7] Women, thus stereotyped, become 'at once the custodians of national identity and culture and the wards of the nation-state, central to the preservation of the state and relegated to the margins of the body politic'.[8] In its contemporary formations, this role may be described as one in which women 'serve as a barometer of progress',[9] relegated to a form of objectification and instrumentalization. Pertinently, Stratton's comments that 'contact brought about by intrusions into Africa by patriarchal cultures from both the East in the form of Islam and the West from the time of the slave trade up to the neocolonial present [...] resulted in a deterioration in the condition of women and, some suggest, in the suppression of once-powerful feminine values' highlight the extent to which the literary re-presentation of the feminine continually functions against larger shifts in the representative possibilities available for women,[10] intertwining the textual re-presentation of feminine subjectivities with broader issues of socio-political representation. Indeed, across the continent, ethnographic and anthropological research suggests that a central facet of colonialism's epistemic violence was its imposition of stringent constructions of gender, virtue and femininity, which helped to flatten and dislodge the more varied and complex cultural formations which had once existed. For the Igbo in what is now the southeast of Nigeria, for instance, prior to colonial conquest existed a system of social intercourse in which gender was both flexible and mutable across an individual lifetime.[11] Through the subject positions of 'male daughter' and 'female husband', women, in pre-colonial times, could occupy masculine social roles and positions of authority. In addition, as members of the *umuada*, or association of daughters of the clan responsible for jurisdiction in the domestic sphere and social policing, women, prior to marriage, held a central role in the maintenance and ordering of society. Likewise, in pre-colonial Sierra Leone, numerous matrilineal societies persisted, along with a similarly mutable system in which an individual's gender may be shifted or renounced over the course of a lifetime, an action portrayed in Asana's story in *Ancestor Stones*. Even in what is now Zimbabwe, though often described as having long operated through patriarchal systems of control, the pre-historic San demonstrate the pervasiveness of alternative models of social arrangement and alternative structures of power beyond the masculine/feminine binary.[12] Yet with colonialism these heterogeneous systems of gender were displaced, replaced with a rigid and binary system codified in law and custom and amplified through the erasure of the subsistence economy, where women played a central role, by a cash-based system of colonial trade.[13]

This is not to suggest that a single paradigm of gender flourished across Africa; social formations across the continent, from any perspective, remained and continue to remain highly variable. Equally, these comments are not intended to suggest that prior to colonialism, women in African societies did not face subjugation due to gender. Rather, these comments highlight how, prior to colonial rule, the subject positions available to women remained broader in their scope and more widely varied across geographies, a point which sociologists including Ifi Amadiume and Oyèrónke Oyĕwùmí have returned to in their studies of gender, colonialism and African identity formations.[14] As Forna has written in the context of Sierra Leone, with colonialism came an obligation to erase the heterogeneity of the past through a large-scale cultural forgetting, an act of symbolic violence with far wider ramifications:

> We were obliged to forget who we were in the same way: to adopt different customs and different ways of thinking and different systems of governing. It has been to the detriment of the country hugely and I think it was a major cause of the war. To destroy a country's systems and not replace them with something that the country knows and has lived with and has come organically from the centre of that country, leaves the field wide open for the sorts of events that took place.[15]

As a result of this imperative to forget, one which echoes more broadly across Africa, writ large, not only was historical memory truncated across the continent, but the very forms and functions of subjectification which once existed were erased, giving at least some credence to Fanon's assertion that colonialism marked a total epistemic break with the past.[16] Part of the project of reclamation, then, particularly in the realm of gender, has been to testify to, witness and give voice to the now-silenced articulations of identification and subjectification of what once was.

A further challenge in the representation of women in the African context appears through the ubiquity of the Mother Africa trope in writing, a sense in which the land and landscape become identified with the female form and a holistic notion of femininity, what Gillian Rose, writing more broadly, has identified as a 'conflation of Woman with place'.[17] In the landscape of African literature as published in the West, the use of the Mother Africa trope has been identified by Stratton as a commonplace tropology of men's writing. On its surface figured as an emancipatory celebration of the feminine, the Mother Africa trope 'belies the real "position of women in Africa," camouflaging their subordination by the patriarchal sociopolitical systems of African states from which they need to be liberated'.[18] Indeed, the feminization of Africa served both as an alibi for colonial conquest and on-going (neo)colonial intervention and as a means of perpetuating hegemonic structures dominated by a largely male and middle-class strata of post-independence rulers. This identification of Africa, as a landscape, with the feminine is explicitly hearkened to in the opening pages of *Ancestor Stones*: 'I see her sometimes, usually when I least expect it: a reminder of her. In the bow of a lip: an outline a blind man could trace with his fingertips. The curve of the continent in the sweep of a skull, in the soft moulding of a profile'.[19] Mother Africa is figured as a spectral presence in Abie's Scottish life, a remainder which draws her back to the land of her birth and early childhood in a manner reminiscent of Vera's Thenjiwe and her identification with the Matabele landscape. Based in a context in which, through colonization, the control of land implied a control of power, the identification of the land with the feminine may potentially be read as an emancipatory move, reclaiming a sense of agency in the formation of identity. At the same time, this identification of the landscape as feminine leads back to the tension surrounding the Mother Africa trope; the notion of 'woman' is both domesticated, and instrumentalized, while obscuring the workings of this nexus of identification through the deployment of an essentialized and nostalgic notion of feminine virtue and purity.

Along with a preoccupation with gender, Forna's, Vera's and Adichie's novels specifically position themselves in a conflict or post-conflict context. This is of particular relevance to the representation of gender because of the ways in which war, violence and militarization have contributed to the naturalization of binary paradigms for gender. Where conflict, writ large, 'relies on gendered constructions and images of the state, state militaries, and their role in the international system',[20] it simultaneously creates a system in which 'women are— as the traditionally appointed guardians of racial [or ethnic] purity, patriarchal order, and cultural authenticity—the foremost victims of and collaborators (willing or coercively) in the new wars'.[21] Through the normalization of the trope of the warrior man and victim woman, situations of conflict simultaneously amplify and normalize codified gender hierarchies in ways which both limit the possibilities available to women and render them deeply vulnerable. Writing on the 2003 United States invasion of Iraq, Hayat Imam has pinpointed 'the hidden subtext of war' as that situation in which 'men are punished, tortured, and made powerless and then women, in turn, are targets of that transferred anger and violence',[22] highlighting the means through which women's bodies are further instrumentalized in the quest to recuperate the male subject in conflict. While written in a different context, Imam's comments nonetheless point to an applicable sense in which the feminine body is instrumentalized in war, stripped of agency and transformed into an object upon which male anxieties are written. This process of feminization thus 'invokes a deeply internalized and naturalized binary—the essentialized concept of sex difference—which is then available to naturalize diverse forms of structural oppression',[23] effectively ordering the political sphere while depoliticizing its effects.

In the context of conflict, rape becomes a particularly potent sign of women's vulnerability, as the examples of *Half of a Yellow Sun*, *Ancestor Stones* and *The Stone Virgins* foreground in various ways. Where, as Natalja Zabeida writes in reference to the Bosnian War, 'women are allocated the "honor" and responsibility for keeping the nation and, hence, the right to self-rule alive',[24] their bodies become the canvas upon which struggles over the meaning of that nation are enacted. This situation has been described by one critic as that in which 'the defiling of women's bodies becomes both symbolic and material/physical, and the culture itself, through the bodies of women, becomes defaced and deracinated'.[25] Zabeida continues:

> Women's bodies thus become a message board for accusations, denials, and symbolic killing. Through rape, the enemy sends a message to the adversary that the claim to purity and integrity is no longer valid. Rape also points to the inability of the protecting male to save his woman and his territory from harm. In the communication between men, this serves as proof of his impotence and his failure as a man and as a soldier. Therefore, in the rape of women, men are seen and see themselves as 'actual' targets of this sexual violence.[26]

While Zabeida's comments remain applicable to the African context, the three novels under discussion in this chapter demonstrate the extent to which the use of rape in war is not simply a tool of ethno-nationalism. Indeed, in Nigeria during the Nigerian-Biafran War, Sierra Leone during the Civil War and Zimbabwe during the Gukurahundi, rape was used by all sides and forces not just against the 'other' woman, but rather, against all women. During the Nigerian-Biafran War this position became exacerbated through women's active participation in the conflict; as Axel Harneil-Sievers, Jones O. Ahazuem and Sydney Emezue write, 'Women also contributed considerably to the effort to win the war, while their sex exposed them to peculiar risks and temptations during and immediately after the war'.[27] Women thus held positions which, while vital to the on-going conflict, betrayed their relatively subordinate positions in society. Women were active in the Civil Defence League (illustrated most famously in Achebe's short story 'Girls at War'),[28] participated in the land army and co-operative societies, organizations intended to cultivate and distribute food for the armed forces,[29] and comprised the majority of traders in *afia attack*, or the cross-border supply trade.[30] Equally, however, women were used for their sexual labour both in providing 'female sexual services' to army members and as 'conscripted' wives and girlfriends.[31] During Sierra Leone's decade-long civil war, in a similar vein, women occupied positions as fighters and providers of material support, facing exclusion from the normative social sphere and heightened sexual vulnerability as a result.[32] For women not involved directly in combat, too, rape and sexual exploitation were all-too commonplace, cutting across all classes, ages, ethnicities and loyalties in over 250,000 reported cases of rape and sexual slavery.[33] During Zimbabwe's Gukurahundi, too, continuing this pattern, women were made particularly vulnerable, subject to sexual torture, rape and mutilation as an especially commonplace means of enforcing terror.[34]

In broader terms, the use of sexual violence as a tool of war may be seen as a response to the feminization of the African continent under colonial rule. This feminization, part of the process of turning the colonies into the other of Europe, saw a narrative pattern emerge in which the colonial other was cast as essentially weak, irrational and feminine in opposition to the strong masculine rationality of the metropolitan power. Stratton has written that colonial writers used 'their feminization of Africa and Africans [to contribute] to the justification of the colonial presence in Africa'.[35] Indicating the continuities between imaginative writing and socio-political patterns of representation, Geraldine Moane describes the ways in which 'a common pattern of regarding the colonized country and the colonized people as "feminine" occurs. Discourses of femininity involving weakness and emotionality were invoked to reinforce the inferiority of the colonized country and people'.[36] In so doing, colonialism 'linked the sexual division of labour to the global division of labour, and enabled the further elaboration of ideologies of white and male superiority'.[37] Crucially, this work of feminization functioned in tandem with what V. Spike Peterson calls 'the development of European nationalism and normalization of bourgeois respectability [which] produced an idealized model of femininity: pure, dutiful, and maternal',[38] effectively intertwining the subordination of colonial conquest with the reification of gender binaries more broadly. In the era of anti-colonial political activism, nationalist movements in the colonized world thus sought to rectify their projection onto the global stage through what Ashis Nandy has termed 'hypermasculinization'.[39] While it would be reductive to suggest that the West and colonialism are therefore responsible for sexual violence and feminization in the formerly colonized world, the experience of colonization nonetheless may be seen as having put in motion a discursive system in which masculinity and masculinization became marked as laudable and the feminine and feminization as aberrant in a particularly charged manner. Set against this backdrop, the depiction of sexual violence against women in African narrative draws upon a range of local, national and global contexts, implicating discrepant, but not incongruous, systems of domination.

## The Limits of Resistance

As my discussion so far has indicated, violability and sexual vulnerability are central themes in *Half of a Yellow Sun*, *Ancestor Stones* and *The Stone Virgins*. In each novel, the particular vulnerability of women is explored in challenging ways; more precisely, each text both reinforces the fragile position of intersectional identities while engaging in the critical recuperation of these very subjectivities. In *Half of a Yellow Sun*, the precarious position of the feminine is represented through the narrative trajectories of a woman who initially seems to defy these norms, Kainene. The novel, set in the period immediately preceding, during and after the Nigerian-Biafran War, centres on the intellectual Odenigbo household. Running in three strands, the novel is focalized by Olanna, Odenigbo's lover and eventual-wife, Richard, an Englishman new to Nigeria who falls in love with Olanna's twin sister, Kainene, and Ugwu, a rural houseboy who, under Olanna and Odenigbo's tutelage, rises to become the custodian of Biafra's memory. Kainene, at first appearance, seems to transcend the subjugation of the feminine, particularly through her relationship with her lover, one in which Kainene is repeatedly characterized as dominant, aloof and detached in contrast to Richard's needy passion. Yet, upon closer examination this narrative inversion of the gendered binary of power is rendered incomplete. In the novel, Richard's initial desire for Kainene is subsumed into a metonymic connection to his desire for the Igbo-Ukwu roped pot, figured in the narrative as his sole reason for being in Nigeria.[40] Richard places her in parallel to the pots as another object which moors his attempts at subject-formation in Nigeria. By identifying Kainene with the roped pots, Richard constructs both as what Spivak has termed 'signifiers' of otherness,[41] which, rather than functioning as independent entities, operate as markers of a larger abstract notion, in this case that of Africa as a totalizing concept. Despite critical claims that Richard 'undergoes the full processes of wooing and genuinely feeling the anxieties and jealousies of falling in love before he happily gets engaged to a cynical Nigerian girl, Kainene',[42] it is important to note that throughout the narrative Richard's longing for Kainene remains distinctly linked to his anxiety at belonging in Africa. Contrary to the claims above, Richard is never able to enter into an engagement with Kainene, mired, instead, in the paralysis of his bad faith with regards to their connection; Kainene is thus figured less as a person and more as a possession signifying authenticity and belonging. Kainene's objectified state becomes most plain following her disappearance on *afia attack*. After she fails to return for a day, Richard and Olanna go searching for her. Asking soldiers and civilians along the way to the disputed border if they had seen her, 'Richard showed them Kainene's picture. Sometimes, in his rush, he pulled out the picture of the roped pot instead. Nobody had seen her' (*HYS*, p. 407). In her absence, Richard conflates Kainene with the roped pot, metonymically confirming her objectification. While Richard, facing the loss of his existence with Kainene, slips into a form of abjection wherein his conflated subject and object relations result in the 'darkness' which takes him over (*HYS*, p. 430),[43] it is in fact Kainene who, within the context of the novel, becomes the irretrievably suppressed; like Biafra itself, Kainene embodies the jettisoned object whose exclusion is necessary for the narrative's progression. It is Richard who remains and is given the opportunity to develop his existence in Nigeria after Biafra, described as returning to Nsukka to join the new Institute for African Studies (*HYS*, p. 429), while Kainene disappears never to be seen again. With this conclusion to their respective narrative arcs, Kainene no longer may occupy the dominant position, instead becoming the very sacrifice which permits Richard's elevation to a position of agency and total subjectification.

In broader narrative terms, Kainene is figured as an aberration from normative standards of womanhood as a male daughter of sorts. Throughout the narrative, her aloof mannerisms are set against her twin Olanna's socially-endorsed femininity. Kainene is repeatedly described, in contrast to her sister's voluptuousness, as boyish in her looks, alluding to a type of dehumanizing sterility.[44] This has been reflected in critical commentary that marks her as 'play[ing] the role of son',[45] having an 'androgynous look',[46] her 'eyes more clearly focused' than the romantic Olanna.[47] Framed by her disavowal of normative gender stereotypes and the demands of her sex, Kainene is punished for her transgressions within a narrative which appears to abandon the male daughter of the pre-colonial tradition for the imposed femininity of colonialism. Kainene's disappearance falls into further ambiguity because of its occasion on *afia attack* which, while a name for cross-border supply trade, was also an alibi for sexual trafficking, rape and abduction.[48] Situating Kainene's disappearance in this particular context, Adichie thereby inverts her androgyny into a forced feminine sexuality through an assertion of sexualization through physical violation. Through this ending, Kainene's characterization loses its force, serving instead as a warning to the woman who attempts to step outside of her biologically-determined subject position.

This notion of vulnerable, sexualized femininity resounds through Adichie's text. This becomes particularly striking at the end of the text, as Ugwu, having been conscripted into the Biafran Army, participates in the gang rape of a woman known only as 'the bar girl':

> Ugwu pulled his trousers down, surprised at the swiftness of his erection. She was dry and tense when he entered her. He did not look at her face, or at the man pinning her down, or at anything at all as he moved quickly and felt his own climax, the rush of fluids to the tips of himself: a self-loathing release. He zipped up his trousers while some soldiers clapped. Finally he looked at the girl. She stared back at him with a calm hate. (*HYS*, p. 365)

Hawley has written that, when Ugwu is conscripted into the army, 'what he is actually called upon to do there is only mildly hinted at';[49] yet, the scene of the bar girl's rape suggests otherwise. Though Adichie refrains from excessive physical detail, the bar girl and her return gaze, through its visceral hatred, foreground the atrocities of war and Ugwu's implication in them. The calm, hateful gaze shatters Ugwu's carefully-constructed and nurtured self, fixing him as the monster he becomes. Yet, despite his 'self-loathing', Ugwu is unable to stop himself from raping the girl, and it is this very self-hatred which is released upon his victim, echoing the notion that it is the feminine body onto which masculine rage is inscribed.

Throughout Ugwu's tenure as a conscript in war, Adichie utilizes a prominent intertextual motif through Ugwu's repeated readings of, and attempts to find solace in, Frederick Douglass's *Narrative of the Life of Frederick Douglass, An American Slave: Written by Himself* (*HYS*, p. 360). In the narrative, the discovery and subsequent readings of this book become particularly significant for Ugwu, figured as the means through which he discovers the power of giving himself voice through language and rhetoric and inspiring his eventual rise to become the chronicler of Biafra. As written elsewhere, the inclusion of Douglass's *Narrative* provides Adichie's narrative with a textual connection to the discourses of slavery and emancipation;[50] this intertextual reference, however, may also be read as of particular interest in the context of Adichie's portrayal of the bar girl's rape and Ugwu's role as rapist. Prior to raping the girl, having entered her bar, Ugwu notices his colleagues rolling a joint: 'Ugwu thought he made out something familiar on an unrolled portion of paper, the word *narrative*, but it could not be' (*HYS*, p. 364). Flying into an uncharacteristic rage at this discovery, Ugwu is described as out of control, where, rather than operating as an agent, he feels that 'life was living him' (*HYS*, p. 364). Positioning the discovery of the violated *Narrative* immediately before the rape of the bar girl, the narrative inextricably intertwines the two situations. The book, as a source of knowledge and Ugwu's outlet for his discovery of agency through writing, is violated, physically manifesting Ugwu's internal fragmentation and confusion, then bodily inscribed on the feminine object. It can be no coincidence that the *Narrative* itself contains scenes of horrifying, racist male domination in the brutal torture and rape of Douglass's Aunt Hester. Maurice O. Wallace, writing on this scene, describes the terrified Douglass's reaction to witnessing this brutality as 'reveal[ing] his own sexual vulnerability by a scopophobic worry betraying the spectragraphic surrogacy of the black woman's body for Douglass's frightful fantasies of male rape'.[51] The female figure and her violation are thus subsumed into a discourse of male bodily sanctity. In *Half of a Yellow Sun*, Ugwu and his metonymic violation through the disfiguring of the book may be similarly seen as displaced and bodily inscribed onto the bar girl who, as the feminine excess, becomes the site on which anxiety may be deposited without material retribution in the form of physical counter-violence. The bar girl's perceived moment of agency in her hateful stare is denied through this metonymic displacement, reverting her to an object of the superordinate male gaze, an act in which, as Brenda Cooper notes, Adichie's novel is 'sucked into the tropes of the dominant discourse, both with regard to representations of Africa and also in relation to portrayals of gender violence'.[52]

In *Half of a Yellow Sun*, sexual violence appears in a number of forms. In addition to Ugwu's participation in the gang rape of the bar girl are Anulika, Ugwu's sister who is brutally raped and assaulted during the war; Amala, a young servant girl coerced into carrying Odenigbo's child; Arize, Olanna and Kainene's cousin, who, the narrative implies, is raped and tortured before her murder in the pogroms preceding the war, and Eberechi, a neighbour who survives the war by becoming an officer's conscripted 'girlfriend'. Despite the prevalence of gendered violence in the novel, however, rape and violability remain largely episodic. In Yvonne Vera's *The Stone Virgins*, however, sexual violence comprises the central event around which the narrative turns. The novel provides a graphic account of the state-sanctioned violence of the Gukurahundi through the fates of two sisters, Thenjiwe and Nonceba. Throughout, the text operates in a narrative register distinct from both Adichie's and Forna's novels, relying on a highly-aestheticized lyricism. Like *Half of a Yellow Sun*, a novel Adichie has explained she wrote as a means of reclaiming a lost history for the generations which have come after Biafra,[53] Vera's novel, too, uncovers a lost and officially unspoken episode of post-colonial trauma. While the bulk of the novel addresses Nonceba and Thenjiwe's attack by dissident Sibaso and subsequent aftermath, the text as a whole spans from 1950 to 1986, encapsulating Zimbabwe's struggle for liberation and emergence as postcolonial nation-state. The novel has been lauded for its work of 're-membering', a task in which it 'recover[s] for women the power of language denied them by patriarchy's silencing power',[54] as well as how it 'ensures that its readers know the cost of political silence' through their engagement with the text's heroines.[55] As a text, *The Stone Virgins* demands an ethical engagement, defamiliarizing the grotesque and aestheticiz-ing the quotidian, towards the end of destabilizing the stringent categories of being which the violence of colonialism required. In this manner, *The Stone Virgins* forms a central part of what Paul Zeleza identifies as Vera's larger project to 'engage and reconstruct Zimbabwean history' by 'engaging unflinchingly with potentially shocking substance of content, such as rape, abortion, incest, suicide and mutilation'.[56]

From early 1983 to the end of 1986, the Gukurahundi names a period in which an estimated 20,000 individuals were killed in Matabeleland in atrocities carried out by the North Korean-trained Fifth Brigade of the Zimbabwe National Army. Named by ZANU leader and Prime Minister Robert Mugabe for 'the rain that washes away the chaff before the summer rains',[57] the Gukurahundi was justified as necessary action against rebelling dissidents from the Zimbabwe People's Revolutionary Army (ZIPRA), affiliated with Joseph Nkomo's rival ZAPU party. Despite the scale of the atroci-ties committed during the Gukurahundi, the period remains largely forgotten in official historical discourse both within and beyond Zimbabwe. Indeed, as the events unfolded, they remained largely ignored by the international community. Recent evidence suggests that a central motivation for the violence was the need to maintain a sense of economic stability for white farmers and foreign investors and that, for Western governments, 'being the time of the Cold War, the imperative was to get the Zimbabwean government on their side'.[58] Despite the government's claims to be acting on behalf of the general population against dissident factions, the majority of victims of the Gukurahundi were not dissidents or soldiers, but rather, ordinary civilians. Jocelyn Alexander writes that

> The Fifth Brigade introduced a qualitatively new and more horrific kind of war. For those civilians who bore its brunt, all preceding armies paled in comparison. Civilians stressed the explicitly tribal nature of the brigade's attacks, the forced use of Shona, the invoking of a mythical past of Ndebele raids against the Shona to justify the brigade's brutality.[59]

Certainly, much of the brutality was ethnically motivated, split, as it was, along ZANU/ZAPU lines, reflected in Mahlathini's murder and the razing of the Thandabantu Store in *The Stone Virgins*. Current research, however, suggests that government claims of dissident violence were largely exaggerated, with potentially as few as 400 dissidents operating in the areas around Gulati and Matabeleland.[60] Equally, it is important to recall that many incidences of violence were not enacted across ethnic lines, as Sibaso's attack of Thenjiwe and Nonceba illustrates, and that recourse to ethnic absolutisms and stratification does not and cannot constitute an ethical response to the terror of the times. Set in this context, *The Stone Virgins* functions as an unmasking of this largely-ignored and often-misrepresented period in Zimbabwe's postcolonial history. In particular, Vera, in her re-presentation of the violence brought by the Gukurahundi, portrays a scene which refuses absolutes, both by way of gender and by way of ethnicity. Instead, Vera's portrayal of the carnage that ensued remains nuanced and complex, unravelling the binaries of identification whose fossilization abetted the unfurling of violence.

The central episode of the novel depicts Thenjiwe's murder and decapitation and Nonceba's rape and mutilation at the hands of Sibaso, a ZIPRA dissident who has returned to the bush, hiding in caves in a half-life of sorts. This fact of geography is itself of particular significance for the novel's depiction of sexualized violence; as Ranka Primorac has noted, 'the stony landscape of Gulati stands for violence and death',[61] linking Sibaso, in his wanderings across the land, to the spectral scene of negation in life. At the same time, however, his haunting of the caves of Gulati points to a desire to exceed the strictures of racialized norms in independent Zimbabwe. These hills and caves, originally inhabited by the prehistoric San, were later used as a refuge by both Shona and Ndebele female spirit mediums, linking Sibaso's drifting amongst them to 'a physical and metaphysical transgression across histories and the ethnic divide'.[62] As a dissident, one of those persecuted by Mugabe's army for his ethnic identity, Sibaso's attack on the sisters foregrounds what Dorothy Driver and Meg Samuelson call 'the use to which women are put as compensation for male loss and male terror',[63] a re-presentation of the feminization of conflict. Later in its narrative, the novel reveals that Sibaso was once an ardent supporter of the Independence cause, fighting with the army; yet, expelled and subjugated for racial and ethnic reasons, he turns to sexual violence and terror as a means of ratifying his now-disintegrated sense of selfhood, attempting, through his attack on Thenjiwe and Nonceba, to return to a state of becoming now denied to him. In those attacks, Sibaso's attempts to become are explicitly displaced onto the bodies of the sisters, marked by his total ownership of the surviving Nonceba: 'She does not look at him. Her face is turned from him. She is silent, without worth, with nothing precious but time. She is nothing to him. An aftermath to desire'.[64] As 'nothing' to Sibaso, Nonceba's rape and mutilation represents the instrumentalization of feminine subjectivity to the project of solidifying a masculine subject position of agency and authority in the context of the post-conflict postcolonial. Despite her attempts to undercut Sibaso's presence by avoiding his stare, Nonceba is forced to look at him, with his fingers on her tongue signifying his total control (*SV*, p. 70). Crucially, Sibaso metonymically links Nonceba and the stone virgins, sacrificial virgins who would be buried with the kings of the land, memorialized in San paintings in the caves of Gulati that he roams. In so doing, he frames both Nonceba and the virgins in a discourse of instrumentalization, where the sacrifice of the feminine form serves to underwrite the authority of the masculine. Through this form of displacement, Nonceba, like the stone virgins, is inscribed onto the land, symbolically entrapped in the romanticized discourse of Mother Africa in, following Sofia Kostelac, 'a mythologized, circumscribed femininity, which forecloses the possibility of female autonomy'.[65]

Caught in the midst of a violent struggle for masculine becoming, Thenjiwe and Nonceba serve as mere objects, highlighted in Nonceba's need to submit to Sibaso:

> His name is Sibaso, a flint to start a flame. Him. Sibaso. I follow him closely. My life depends on it. I follow the shape of his body. I follow his arms. He has killed Thenjiwe. He is in the midst of that death. (*SV*, p. 81)

The narrative does not present this ultimate act of subjugation and ownership in simplistic terms, however. Nonceba and Thenjiwe are lost when faced with Sibaso's violent attack, forced into a space in which their bodies no longer belong to them; yet, the narrative problematizes the efficacy of this domination. This comes to the fore in the lyrical register of this passage, one which, in its aestheticizing of extreme violence and terror, renders it unknowable and inassimilable to the a priori. Both in the quotidian sense in which Sibaso's murder, rape and violation are depicted and in the intimate idiom of the attacks, that is to say, the narrative forces its reader to witness the act of violence, the sort of event which has become the already-known signifier of African savagery and postcolonial inadequacies, as a moment of sheer alterity, utterly foreign and impenetrable to closure. This destabilization is heightened through the slippages in narrative voice which the passage foregrounds. Switching seamlessly between Sibasio's focalized narration, a third-person narrative account and Nonceba's first-person experiences, *The Stone Virgins*, in its narrative form, unmoors the locus of control through its multiperson form. Sibaso may 'own' Nonceba, rendering 'Kezi, her place of birth [...] no longer her own' (*SV*, p. 90), literally silencing her through the removal of her lips and physically invading her body through the violent rape, but his subjectivity is never given narrative authority. Instead, it is continually displaced, as traces of Nonceba's mental resistance come to the fore, creating a narrative structure which, as Kostelac suggests, both 'interrupts the negation of her subjectivity by the brutal violation that Sibaso conducts' and 'focuses on the distortion of subjective space wrought by the atrocities Nonceba is forced to endure'.[66] The two perspectives, moreover, are radically inassimilable, forcing a continued negotiation of the terms of narrative representation and discourse. In so doing, the narrative site of readerly entry is continually shifted, rendering the scene deeply ambiguous and deferring the moment of closure in favour of a perpetual sense of movement. Through these workings, a sense of reconstitution is available, in which, as Nonceba, gazing upon her dead sister's decapitated form reflects, 'The body is no longer his. The body is hers' (*SV*, p. 76). The literal body of the narrative, in this moment, escapes from Sibaso's singular grasp. Through this interweaving of voices, Vera's novel resists the binary oppositions of violator and victim, undercutting their Manichean logic with a complex and rhizomatic notion of interdependency. The ethical imperative to recognize that which is radically other, to see the faceless, is foregrounded by this continual work of narrative displacement and re-entry. Despite its narrative complexity, however, the aftermath of Sibaso's attack cannot be said to be entirely liberating in its presentation of Nonceba's continued existence. Here survival can only be partial; symbolic in its force it does little to restore the physical, material damage that Sibaso inflicts. Physically marked, Nonceba, throughout her recovery, is left exposed and made more visibly subject to the outside gaze, forever having 'to deal with other people, looking, watching, turning their bodies toward her, wondering about her' (*SV*, p. 95). The imposition of this gaze thus undercuts the more triumphant moments of Nonceba's resistance against Sibaso. With this physical marking, and the vulnerability which it implies, the novel extends the impact of Sibaso's attack to a normalized condition of perpetual haunting that serves as the culmination of feminine ambiguity throughout the novel.

The remainder of Vera's novel occupies itself largely with Nonceba's tormented recovery, subject to a doubled haunting by the recurrent intrusion of Sibaso in her thoughts, narratively re-presented through the intertwining of their narrative voices and perspectives, and the repeated appearance of Thenjiwe to her in her recovery. When Nonceba finally begins to recuperate, the catalyst for this healing appears in Cephas, Thenjiwe's former lover, who returns to Kezi in order to take Nonceba to Bulawayo where she may remain safe under his protection. It is here that Nonceba undergoes the reconstruction and recovery which enable her to find her voice again and, with it, a possibility for a future existence. The novel has been lauded for its presentation of recuperation as an act that can only exist with men and women approaching one another as equal participants in healing.[67] Certainly, the ending of Vera's final novel creates a sense that another way is possible, that hope can be restored and that bodies and subjectivities may be recuperated through precisely this act of co-creation. At the same time, the agency for this recuperative action remains with Cephas, the masculine protagonist. In a detail which is far from insignificant, *The Stone Virgins* describes Cephas's occupation as historian, a position replete with potency in its implications with what Terrance Ranger has called Zimbabwe's 'patriotic history'.[68] In this vocation, Cephas is endowed with a potent form of power in the keeping, shaping and selecting of the past which will inform history and tradition, turning memory into fact. While his desire to build this historical moment from kwoBulawayo is significant in its reconstitution of a people's history written out of small narratives against the grain of orthodox, patriotic history which serves to silence, this positioning contains an alternative reading where, through the bestowal of historical and communal guardianship to Cephas, the narrative ultimately undermines its ambivalent destabilization of the dominant tropes of feminization. As in *Half of a Yellow Sun*, in which it is Ugwu who becomes the chronicler of Biafra, it is ultimately the male, the masculine, who is enshrined with the task of preserving the nation and the collective, empowered through the feminine sacrifice which enables him. At the same time, Cephas's relationship to Nonceba remains ambiguous, signified in the two characters' differing experiences of memory and trauma in the aftermath of the Gukurahundi. For Cephas, this relationship is encountered in his desire to remove Nonceba from her traumas and, through her recovery, find his own sense of self recuperated, a reinstrumentalization of the feminine which he thinks of as his yearning '[t]o remove her from her memories, as though that indeed could be done as easily as tossing a coin. His version of escape; her version of surrender' (*SV*, p. 161). Yet, for Nonceba, this same act of forgetting, of severing the traumatic past in the name of a hopeful future, is described as 'surrender', marking a refusal of this return to form. Where Cephas casts himself as saviour, shielding, the narrative tells us, Nonceba from 'invisible scars (*SV*, p. 172), Nonceba, in her daily ability to carry her physical scars, occupies an alternative mode of persistent becoming in the face of atrocity.

While *The Stone Virgins'* portrayal of the masculine historian/ chronicler is tempered by Cephas's relationship with Nonceba, in

*Half of a Yellow Sun*, it stands in stark relief. Towards the end of the novel, after escaping conscription with minor injuries, Ugwu returns to his home with Odenigbo and Olanna; the war wanes and Ugwu slowly begins to return to his role as burgeoning intellectual and eventual chronicler of Biafra. Yet, the bar girl's hateful gaze remains, entangled with his own heroic role as writer of the Biafran story:

> Later, Ugwu murmured the title [of his book] to himself: *The World Was Silent When We Died*. It haunted him, filled him with shame. It made him think about that girl in the bar, her pinched face and the hate in her eyes as she lay back on the dirty floor. (*HYS*, p. 396)

For Ugwu, the book he would write becomes synonymous with his own shame at his role in the war, despite, as Marx has identified, his attempts to use the book as 'a way of repressing his memories of soldiering'.[69] The memory of the girl's hateful gaze returns him to the fragmentation of that moment and denies him any sense of satisfaction in his writing or his work, turning the rape into something more than 'a vehicle of social and historical criticism' or narrative tool, as has been suggested elsewhere.[70] Ugwu, from this point in the narrative onwards, is described as split, fearful of himself and fearful that the secret of his monstrous acts could come out and destroy his existence. Paradoxically, the act of rape and his violation of the bar girl create the very conditions which give rise to Ugwu's role as voice of Biafra, indicating the extent to which Asha Varadharajan's claim that the feminine is that which is 'excluded as it were from its self-fashioning, reappear[ing] in the self-deprecatory postmodern ego as the difference within' may be applicable.[71] It has been claimed that Adichie is 'unwilling to abandon Ugwu', her protagonist, and instead 'reasserts his goodness, as Ugwu saves a child during a bombing raid and suffers immense guilt'.[72] Under this line of criticism, Ugwu's writing, too, serves as an act of atonement through which he absolves himself of the rape.[73] In this sense, then, *Half of a Yellow Sun* appears to complete what is gestured towards in *The Stone Virgins*, drawing an ultimate conclusion in which the restoration of history, memory and the encounter with trauma is only given (masculine) voice through the sacrifice of the feminine.

In contrast to both Vera's and Adichie's novel, in Forna's *Ancestor Stones* it is Abie, the daughter of the land, who is tasked with recovering and recording the collective history of Sierra Leone told by her aunts. In another departure from the previous two texts, Forna's does not deal with explicit physical violence in quite the same way, relying on a more subtly-embodied notion of the intersection between an articulated African femininity and violence. Violence, in *Ancestor Stones*, appears in myriad forms, both material and symbolic. Nouri Gana and Heike Härting write that 'if narrative configures and disfigures the body in symbolic, physical, and gender-specific terms, then narrative violence designates the inseparability of symbolic and physical processes of subject formation'.[74] In *Ancestor Stones*, this is certainly the case; throughout the novel, these two registers of violence remain intertwined, where the symbolic weight of metaphorical domination underscores the physical manifestation of violation and trauma. In Asana's story, beginning the embedded aunts' tale, this intertwining of the symbolic and the material appears first in the story of her name. Explaining that Asana was not what she was originally called, the elder aunt recounts how her name, and with it her birthright, were taken from her by her mother as a means of appeasing her ailing twin brother: 'That was when she took my name away from me and gave it to him. If only he would come back, she promised, he would be the firstborn' (*AS*, p. 17). While much of my discussion thus far has focused on the forms of violence and oppression brought upon women by men, here, it is Asana's mother who perpetuates Asana's loss of identity, promising her name and the title of first born to her ailing son if only he would remain on this earth. In so doing, the novel demonstrates the perpetuation of feminine subjugation across all levels of the sociality as a normalized and naturalized subordinate subject-position. Women, inculcated into this realm, are tasked with both the literal and metaphoric reproduction of the social order, a sentiment echoed in Asana's musings, on the women who would become her co-wives, that she 'learned about women—how we are made into the women we become, how we shape ourselves, how we shape each other' (*AS*, p. 107). Asana's sense of violation through the removal of one name and bestowal of another resonates across the narrative in the other women's stories. Hawa describes how her mother, a slave, was given her name by her owner, the aunts' father. Hawa herself is renamed Josephine Baker by Mr Blue, a mining officer for whom she works. Serah describes her disastrous marriage in which she, reacting against African tradition, changes her name to her husband's, mistaking for cosmopolitan sophistication a form of domination. These episodes together highlight the potency of naming as a means of consolidating control and removing a larger sense of subjective agency, a symbolic stripping which provides the rationale for material abuse. This shift to the material is developed later in the novel when, having 'thrown [herself] away to become some man's third wife' (*AS*, p. 107), losing any sense of a proper name, Asana finds herself at the mercy of a petty man whose physical abuse of her pregnant body and mind echo and amplify that first violation. Rather than simply strip her of name, however, Asana's first husband removes her from her very being through his abuse. Becoming 'a woman who existed only as what she saw reflected in the eyes of others' (*AS*, p. 125), Asana is unable to escape the fixing qualities of an external communal gaze that sees her as nothing, until the time when her alcoholic co-wife engineers her escape (*AS*, pp. 128–9).

The all-pervasiveness of violence against women is further reflected in the stories of Abie's other aunts, ranging across the aforementioned naming of Hawa's mother, much beloved by her husband, but a slave nonetheless, Serah's mother's inability to testify on her own behalf when accused of an affair because 'she knew in her heart that she had wished it' (*AS*, p. 103), Serah's abuse and abandonment by a husband determined to show her 'what a wife is for' (*AS*, p. 227) and Mariama's experiences in a racially-charged Britain where she is warned that black women were not to 'go behaving the way girls here do' (*AS*, p. 204). These episodes reinforce the means through which women's agency becomes subject to administration through a set of institutional norms which privilege the masculine, regulate women's sexuality and relegate women to supporting roles in the quest for postcolonial subjectification. Yet, throughout the novel, disparate sites of resistance appear. As previously mentioned, Asana is able to escape her abusive marriage through the cunning of her co-wife. Later, she escapes the entrapment of still another marriage by leaving the society of women entirely, becoming a *mambore*, a member of the society of men and thus reclaiming the flexibility of gendered subject positions by 'relinquishing the birth right of womanhood in exchange for the liberty of a man' (*AS*, p. 248). For Serah, escape from her unhappy marriage comes through her mother's legacy. Despite the older woman's disappearance in the wake of her inability to defend herself from accusations of infidelity, her very absence provides the material means for Serah's escape through her portion of the bride price. Later, this inheritance bears its fruit as Serah, now empowered, leads a collective 'woman's song' against government soldiers bent on disrupting free and fair voting in the 1996 elections (*AS*, pp. 272–3), persevering against military force through a collective act of resistance which enlivens what has been called 'the remarkable role played by civil society and the electoral commission in ensuring that the elections were not hijacked or postponed by a government reluctant to give up power'.[75] In the very recollection of their stories, moreover, the aunts form a collective which exceeds the trappings of the larger sociality, coming together to re-create an unvoiced and complex history which speaks not in one voice but four, demonstrating the ways in which the private and the intimate may be re-articulated as a means of empowerment in the public sphere.[76] Indeed, the very form of the novel, presented to its reader as the collective oral history of the subaltern, signals such a form of feminine authorization. Throughout, these are women's stories, told by, about and to women, in which masculine authority remains peripheral.

## Alternative Codes and Hidden Voices

As this discussion of *Ancestor Stones* implies, beyond the complexities of representation which arise with the intersection of violence and sexuality in the construction of feminine subjectivities in these three novels, another mode of femininity exists, one which further complicates the representation of articulated identities and provides a possible contrapuntal reading of gender. This contrapuntal feminine ideology may be loosely defined as a reclamation of the sacred maternal. In contrast to the fixity of the Mother Africa trope, the deployment of the sacred maternal renders femininity malleable, mutable and coexistent in multiple realms, registers and planes of being. This form of maternal power appears in *Half of a Yellow Sun* through Mama, Odenigbo's mother. On his initial meeting with Mama, Ugwu immediately notices her resemblance to her son: 'Master's mother had the same stocky build, dark skin, and vibrant energy as her son; it was as if she would never need help with carrying her water pot or lowering a stack of firewood from her head' (*HYS*, p. 94). Mama is described as a female equivalent to Odenigbo, who, in Ugwu's world, occupies the position of symbolic and literal authority. Unlike the other women in Ugwu's life, Mama, in her vitality and strength, gives the impression of autonomy. Ugwu is quickly irritated by her, as she assumes control of the kitchen, sending him out while she prepares 'proper soup', and asking him, 'What does a boy know about real cooking?' (*HYS*, p. 94). Through her ascendancy to the control of all food preparations, Mama stakes her ownership and sole ruling of subsistence within the household while embodying the role of *Omu*, or female monarch.[77] To Ugwu's ears, Mama's bearing and voice give an air of triumph (*HYS*, p. 95), as though in her control of the kitchen and, by extension, the running of the household, Mama has won a battle for dominance. Mama, too, controls the destiny of other women, here through her authority over Amala who, unsure of herself, is described as wandering 'around the kitchen, as if eager to do something to please Master's mother but uncertain what to do' (*HYS*, p. 96). As Mama's bought and paid for servant, Amala functions, at least initially, as a wife of sorts, underwriting Mama's authority within the domestic sphere, and, by later bearing the child that will continue Mama's lineage, invoking an image of pre-colonial woman–woman marriage, despite its later subversion through Amala's rejection of her maternal role.[78]

It soon becomes apparent that Mama's perceived triumph comes from her victory over Olanna, a woman she refers to as a witch who did not nurse from her own mother (*HYS*, p. 97). Faced with Mama's anger, Olanna immediately leaves the house, cast out by the dominant maternal force which rejects her, a move which repeats the tradition of discord between lineage daughters and wives.[79] Yet, Mama's victory is only partial; dismissed by Odenigbo, in explanation to Olanna, as a small woman who knows little outside of her own village (*HYS*, p. 99), Mama is quickly positioned on the losing side of what Mabura has called a 'clash between *dibia* medicine and the modern postcolonial world'.[80] Following this supposed Manichean division, the narrative marginalizes Mama, representing her as a superstitious and jealous woman left behind as the nation progresses into modernity, eventually killed through her own inability to cope with the changes of a society at war and her insistence on staying on her land even as the federal troops advance towards it (*HYS*, p. 196; p. 298). Yet, this effort at marginalization remains incomplete through Mama's narrative inscrutability. During her second visit to the Odenigbo home, unexpected and coinciding with Olanna's absence on a trip to London, Ugwu begins to see in Mama what he had feared on her first visit, suspecting her of engaging in a potent magic to kill Olanna. Entering the kitchen one day, Ugwu witnesses Mama rubbing ointment into Amala's back: 'Perhaps Mama was rubbing a potion on Amala. But it made no sense because if Mama had indeed gone to the *dibia*, the medicine would be for Olanna and not Amala' (*HYS*, p. 214). Despite his suspicion that Mama is working magic to dispose of Olanna, Ugwu cannot decipher her actions. Already dismissed as mere superstition and anachronistic tradition by Odenigbo, Mama's means of control over the feminine within the household escapes Ugwu. Instead, throughout Mama's visit, Ugwu remains watchful, though unsure of what he is looking for (*HYS*, p. 215). Perceiving her behaviour as a desire to kill Olanna, Ugwu misreads her intentions, leaving himself unable to either warn his guardians or prevent what transpires. Mama's plan, to coerce Odenigbo into impregnating Amala, is thus never known by any of the other characters. Instead, Mama's influence hangs over the household like a shadow, casting its anxiety on the home through her control of the discourses of reproduction and procreation.[81] Later, when Amala becomes pregnant, Odenigbo is quick to blame his mother for her influence, claiming that, without her hand in it, nothing would have happened (*HYS*, pp. 240–1). For all of the members of the Odenigbo household, Mama remains beyond comprehension, her motives opaque and only explicable through recourse to the stereotype of the ignorant villager. Even upon Amala's child's birth and eventual adoption by Olanna and Odenigbo, Mama remains a mystery, explained away through the more comprehensible discourses of tradition and ignorance.

In *Ancestor Stones*, the notion of the sacred maternal permeates the text from early in its pages. The story itself, framed as the restitution of a maternal legacy through the sharing of Abie's aunts' stories, functions in large part as an elegy to the sacred discourses of the maternal and its vestiges in postcolonial sociality, one in which 'it is women's work, this guarding of stories' (*AS*, p. 12). Within the aunts' stories, a sense of collective and communal femininity is continually enacted, made more potent, for each character, with her entry into motherhood. As Asana's story describes, the very event of childbirth emerges as a collective feminine experience, superseding the masculinist framework of village life. Describing the collective 'clicking' (*AS*, p. 16) of the village women as her mother birthed her and her twin, Asana's early recollections thus display an indication of the alternative codes of the sacred maternal. Heard, understood and reproduced by each of the mothers in the community, the collective sound of clicking appears in a register which only the initiated may decode. In this pre-verbal semiotic space, the quotidian norms of masculine domination and feminine subjugation are temporarily superseded. Indeed, the very separation of women in the village, enacted through the relegation of each wife to her hut and her conjugal role, is surpassed through the aural coming together of the mothers of the community to welcome another woman into their fold. The role of the maternal is echoed towards the conclusion of Asana's story, as she recalls her escape from the RUF forces which overrun her village. Like Serah's earlier escape from her unhappy marriage, Asana's escape from certain death is enabled by a maternal legacy, as she hides within the safety of her mother's beloved treasure box (*AS*, pp. 292–5). Where Stratton describes the trope of enclosure in African writing as one in which 'female characters are enclosed in the restricted spheres of behavior of the stereotypes of a male tradition, their human potential buried in shallow definitions of their sex',[82] enclosure, in *Ancestor Stones*, is transformed by its resonance with a maternal inheritance. The trope of enclosure, in other words, is re-articulated, transformed into a strategic means of empowerment. Rather than serving as a means of psychic splitting and destruction, Asana's recourse to enclosure instead functions as a means of salvation, marking a space enshrined by the sacred maternal and thus protected from the masculinist discourses of war and its attendant violence.

As with *Half of a Yellow Sun* and *Ancestor Stones*, *The Stone Virgins*, too, presents a glimpse of an alternative coding of gender and an alternative discourse of gendered identity through the figure of Sihle. As Nonceba and Thenjiwe's paternal aunt, it is Sihle who discovers Nonceba's mutilated form following Sibaso's attack, and it is Sihle who takes Nonceba for emergency medical treatment, willing her to survive and caring for her in the immediate aftermath. It is not insignificant, then, that Sihle, this figure of healing and survival, is figured in terms radically departing from patriarchal femininity. As the novel explains,

> Everyone calls her Sihle, even though all the mothers in Kezi are called by the names of their children, especially if these children are sons. [...] There is silence and speech, fall and rise, whenever Sihle is about. There is a steady rhythm. The silence marks the times when Sihle talks and gives us our histories, like treasures. [...] Sihle is not married to Ndabenhle Dlodlo, the man with whom she has had her four sons. However, everyone in the village calls him by the name of his first son [...] sekaZenzo. (*SV*, pp. 112–13)

Thus characterized, Sihle emerges in an alternative feminine subject position, empowered and driven by personal choice. Defying convention and remaining independent from her potential roles as wife and mother, Sihle embodies a form of feminine agency whose potency stems from its very ability to conjure histories and places. In the larger context of the novel, this is of no little significance; as Carolyn Martin Shaw explains, the paternal aunt 'in Shona and Ndebele cultures of Zimbabwe sits with her brothers in making decisions for the extended family and [...] conventionally instructs girls in a young woman's proper behavior and in what to do and expect as a wife'.[83] The father's sister, in other words, forms part of the patriarchal system of authority which inculcates and interpellates young women into their subordinate subject positions, echoing the sort of reproduction of norms earlier seen in Asana's renaming, enabling the reproduction of the gendered division of labour. Sihle, however, is different; by renouncing her children's name and a pre-ordained conjugal script, Sihle recuperates a space for autonomous action, one which, through her nurturing of her wounded niece, she attempts to transmit across generations. At the same time, Sihle's feminine authority remains ambivalent, undercut by her social marginalization through her rejection of marriage. Sihle, by denying the authorization of her position, both exceeds patriarchal authority and is subordinated to it through her exclusion from the larger sociality, leaving her openly 'blamed for anything the women in the Gumede family fail to do or do improperly' (*SV*, p. 113) as the price of her independence.

Of course, in *The Stone Virgins*, Sihle is not the only symbol of feminine agency; instead, the figure of Nehanda, a spirit medium associated with the First Chimurenga, remains the most overt reference to another way of reading gender. Nehanda, oral tradition and popular mythology recount, was the daughter of Mutota, defiant after being forced into an incestuous act intended to give supernatural power to her father's Mutapa state. After her death, Nehanda's spirit would possess a number of mediums, most notably Charwe, who, at the end of the nineteenth century, led resistance against the British South Africa Company and its settlers. Captured in 1897, the Nehanda medium remained defiant until her execution in 1898, famously proclaiming that her bones would rise again.[84] As 'the most memorable hero of the first Chimurenga',[85] Nehanda has become a potent nationalist figure in contemporary Zimbabwe, with streets, hospitals and numerous other institutions named for her, and the spirit has been said to have possessed numerous other mediums in the intervening years. With this historical continuity, 'the memory of the 1896–97 medium continued to be linked to the theme of resistance', particularly in the Second Chimurenga, starting in 1972.[86] While this is of little surprise, given her potency as a symbol against colonial rule and a defiant self-determination, the contemporary usages of her name are perhaps less triumphant than this may indicate, characterized by her assimilation into the patriotic narrative of masculine resistance authored by Mugabe and his governmental allies. In these scripts, Nehanda is domesticated, 'divested of independence, militancy and "masculine" powers to support the story of nationalism as a movement driven and conceptualised by men'.[87] So shifted, Nehanda transforms from a figure of resistance to what has been called 'an archetypical figure of protection, woman as passive mother whose value revolved only on her capacity to give birth to the nation's sons or to symbolise the nation's birth',[88] an ironic return to the Mother Africa trope.

In *The Stone Virgins*, Nehanda's appearance appears both to lend credence to charges of domestication while also serving as a warning against the dogmatic adherence to totalizing mythological formations. Nehanda is not called upon by the mutilated and traumatized Nonceba, as may be expected; instead, she is the figure of strength upon whom Sibaso relies as he wanders the hills and caves of Matabeleland: 'Nehanda, the female one. She protects me with her bones. I embrace death, a flame' (*SV*, p. 117). Significantly, Nehanda's famous vow that her bones will rise is transformed into Sibaso's claim for a lasting identity through death and destruction. In this move, Nehanda's transformation from a figure of feminine agency to a marker of masculine violence and aggression is complete, rendering her subordinate to the ends of masculine authority and thus subject to exclusion. In place of an intersectional and articulated identity, Nehanda is taken purely as a marker of racial or ethnic difference, her gendered power neutralized. At the same time, the novel suggests, this use of Nehanda is strategic, standing as a warning against the force of naturalization. By associating Nehanda with Sibaso, that is to say, the novel foregrounds the deformation of a mythologized femininity, rendering its continuities with violence, both symbolic and material, apparent. The obfuscating power of Mother Africa, as a form of naturalized feminization, is laid bare in a warning against the danger of these appropriations.

Despite the ambiguities of representing gender in the post-conflict African context, it is nonetheless important to highlight the positive work that these narratives do in the representation of an African femininity on a global scale. Certainly, none of the three novels under analysis here presents an entirely straightforward or celebratory narrative of female resistance. At the same time, all three give voice to an all-too-often unvoiced subjectivity. In all three novels, that is to say, women characters remain central, voicing their stories, emotions and perspectives in a manner that is both nuanced and, crucially, human. Moving away from the naturalized image of the African woman as victim in need of saving, each novel retains a sense of agency for its women characters by the very fact of portraying them in action and foregrounding their perspectives. While their ultimate role remains ambiguous, this work of giving voice to the voiceless and showing the face of the anonymous serves a critical political purpose in the context of transnational literary circulation. Writing on the novels of Emecheta and Nwapa, who figured rape as central to their narratives of women's lives during the Nigerian-Biafran War from the subjective centre of these victimized women, Stratton points out that, 'rape is one of the hidden facts of the Nigerian conflict. Recording the conflict from the point of view of women [...] breaks through this conspiracy of silence'.[89] In the context of the conflict, rape served as a means through which control was naturalized, quite literally inscribed upon the feminized body of the nation as a means of silencing dissent. By portraying, at times in graphic language, the embodiment of this silencing and using the tool of imaginative narrative to voice what is voiceless, then, these three novels contribute to the de-naturalization of the African woman as victim paradigm. While this work is not yet finished, these novels signal a means through which to enact and continue this line of resistance.

# 4
# Mythopoetics and Cultural Re-Creation

This chapter moves from questions of subjectivity and the individual to a broader consideration of address and narrative strategy in contemporary Anglophone African writing. Throughout this chapter, I refer predominantly to two primary texts, Chris Abani's *GraceLand* and Ngũgĩ wa Thiong'o's *Wizard of the Crow*, to interrogate the means through which contemporary African writers negotiate the multiple audiences for whom they write through the re-inscription of mythopoetic motifs. The latter text, in particular, as a work produced in Gĩkũyũ, translated into English and more widely read in this second form, makes for a particularly potent example of textual innovation, narrative form and rhetorical address. Indeed, it is the particular fact of the novel's creation, as a work produced within a local tradition with a view towards its global audience, that most explicitly highlights the issues of re-inscription and multiplicity which this chapter explores. This polyvocality, in turn, forms a central facet of the work of contemporary African writing in negotiating the supposed binaries of modernity and tradition, West and rest, which have marked the emergence of African writing on the global stage.

The notion of authenticity has been widely discussed in scholarship on African literature, evidenced in debates surrounding the Négritude movement and the often-vitriolic disagreement on the 'decolonization of African literature' between the troika of Chinweizu, Onwuchekwa Jemie and Ihechukwu Madubuike and Wole Soyinka.[1] In these conflicts, the status of African literature as 'in a situation of change, of "upheaval"' comes particularly to the fore.[2] Rooted in this sense of perpetual transition, African aesthetic movements have been characterized by critics as torn between two opposing desires: that of an entry into Euro-American notions of modernity imposed with colonialism and that of a retrieval of a suppressed and idealized past lost by the same. While the intricacies of these debates are largely beyond the scope of this chapter, they nonetheless indicate the long-standing conversation surrounding tradition, authenticity, form and function in African literature and its particular importance to the creation and maintenance of a global image of Africa. With this backdrop in mind, this chapter addresses the use of mythopoetic motifs in *GraceLand* and *Wizard of the Crow*, viewing the reconfiguration of traditional discourses in each text both as a means of collective identification and as a form of resistance against the normative circulation of an idea of Africa in a Euro-American world literary market. Operating as a form of strategic address, the creation of newly-formed mythologies allows these novels to escape the universalizing tendencies of a totalizing discourse which seeks to erase difference in favour of a Manichean view of African identity. This cultural re-appropriation functions as a means of historical and material contextualization in both texts; through their very transformation of traditional tropes they moreover demonstrate a re-appropriation which remains variable and multiply-articulated. Both novels thus interrogate the means through which discourses old and new are blended and reformulated to create a cultural context which exceeds a singular notion of authenticity and tradition, ultimately questioning the veracity, as well as the utility, of these very terms. At the same time, both demonstrate the limitations of such shifts in address and narrative form through their mixed receptions, an indication of the relative powers of the market and of the text.

## Authenticity, Tradition and Modernity

Tradition is important to any minority group embedded within a global culture of white supremacy; it restores dignity and pride in origins to a displaced and disenfranchised population, a crucial function which has been highlighted by even the most radical thinkers. Pal Ahluwalia, writing on the Négritude movement, has explained how even ultimately essentializing formations become, through their championing of a restorative African spirit, 'essential to the process which sought to break down the tyranny of the web of representations which had been forged over centuries'.[3] More precisely, as Lewis Nkosi explains, 'Negritude, after all, was nothing if not an exploration of the collective dreams of black men who had only just awakened from the nightmare of colonialism', rooted in a particular historical and intellectual moment.[4] In the context of this study, these visions may be said to operate as a corrective against the deformed vision of the African continent circulated through global cultural flows. Yet, those who engage in this restorative use of tradition need forever remain self-conscious of the encroachment of totalizing and defensive positions, particularly in order to guard against a coeval collapse into exoticism, a risk outlined in work ranging from Huggan's theorization of the anthropological exotic in African literature to Brouillette's more general discussion of postcolonial publishing. In his essay 'On National Culture', Fanon draws out this argument further, transposing the existential argument of *Black Skin, White Masks* to the communal scene of revolutionary and post-revolutionary societies. In the first stage of national culture, roughly analogous to what Abdul JanMohamed has termed the 'hegemonic phase' of (neo)colonialism,[5] the native elite fall prey to the values of the colonizer, 'using techniques and a language borrowed from the occupier'.[6] Boehmer has called this process approximation, where the native elite runs 'the risk paradoxically of mirroring the authoritative poses of the colonizer'.[7] Fanon explains that colonialism, using 'a kind of perverted logic, [...] turns its attention to the past of the colonized people and distorts it, disfigures it, and destroys it'.[8] This degradation thus creates a need, on independence, to recuperate the discarded past through traditional discourse; in this second stage, the colonial elite attempt to grasp what Stephanie Newell has described as the 'outworn "mummified fragments"' of an idealized past as national culture.[9] Neither the first nor second stage of national culture effectively engages with the newly-independent nation as whole because of their reliance on the outmoded poles of a binary opposition between modernization and traditionalism. Indeed, for Fanon, national culture may only take its truly authentic form in its third and final stage, one which Kobena Mercer describes as 'an intellectual reflection on the transformational practices, made possible by new democratic antagonisms, that were bringing new forms of collective subjectivity into being'.[10] This third stage thus strikes an entirely novel balance between the modern and the traditional, the situated and the universal, in what has been termed a 'relationship [...] of mutual constitution'.[11] In this movement through the three stages of national culture, Fanon presents an argument that is much more in line with his earlier theorization of black subject-formation in *Black Skin, White Masks* than is often acknowledged. As Parry puts it, Fanon already 'struggles with and ultimately refuses an identification with a past, and projects himself towards "a restructuring of the world"'[12] in parallel to his struggle to restructure national culture. Much like the individual, who strives to escape the binaries of a racialized identity-formation, large-scale cultural formations, too, struggle to surpass oppositional frames of identification towards more liberatory futures.

Where traditional systems of knowledge have been replaced by the imposition of external values and epistemological categories, a singular return to an idealized pre-colonial nativism paradoxically supports the colonialist notion that 'African human experience [...] can only be understood through a *negative interpretation*'.[13] Africa and African societies have been forced to re-imagine themselves through categories based in a Western episteme, resulting in what Boehmer has described as the need, for postcolonial writers, to recreate 'from the position of their historical, racial, or metaphysical difference a cultural identity which had been damaged by the colonial experience' in order to forge 'roots, origins, founding myths and ancestors, national fore-mothers and -fathers'.[14] In different terms, Gikandi has expressed a similar sentiment through his claim that, for African literature, 'the simultaneous existence of a modern and a traditional world could only be negotiated through works of imagination'.[15] To further respond to the debilitating effects of epistemic violence, Soyinka advises that 'on the continent must come a reinstatement of the values authentic to that society, modified only by the demands of the contemporary world'.[16] Thus, Soyinka expresses a not uncommonly-held belief that, in order to dismantle the discourses of colonial domination, any return to the pre-colonial African past must remain coupled with a view of the contemporary world, echoing Fanon's warnings against an unequivocal turn to tradition.[17] A movement towards an idealized African past must be accompanied by vigilance against the colonialist perception that 'societies in which mythicoreligious ideas and social traditions play a significant role in intellectual culture must not [...] be rational or capable of "philosophy"'.[18] This balance may therefore be attained through a contextualization in both the materiality of the contemporary era and specificity of the historical moment.

The importance of navigating between the dual poles of traditionalism and Eurocentrism and the danger inherent to this difficult task thus cannot be overstated with reference to contemporary cultural production emanating out of Africa and the African diaspora. Any imagining of the African continent and its nations which relies entirely on traditionalism runs the risk of stagnation and nostalgia, remaining, as Jean Marie Makang has stated, 'incapable of helping present Africans in their striving for control over their own destiny'.[19] Indeed, as Wright notes, none of these moves towards the past '[has] proved be the "open sesame" to the closed door of postcolonial dictatorship and the blocked path to genuine independence'.[20] Similarly, a view of Africa which relies wholly on Eurocentric conceptions of development and progress would fall prey to a neocolonialist stripping of culture and a removal of historicity from the continent. As Wendy Griswold states, no view of Africa can take the continent as static because 'Traditional African communities [...] changed irrevocably under colonialism'.[21] Any vision of the continent which denies these changes only serves to continue the suppression of liberationist discourses striving towards true independence.

In his discussion of the double consciousness which characterizes the black Atlantic, Paul Gilroy states that it

> emerges from the unhappy symbiosis between three modes of thinking, being, and seeing. The first is racially particularistic, the second nationalistic in that it derives from the nation state in which the ex-slaves but not-yet-citizens find themselves, rather than from their aspiration towards a nation state of their own. The third is diasporic or hemispheric, sometimes global and occasionally universalist.[22]

In the context of contemporary African literature, this triple splitting can be reconceived as that which is culturally particularist, marking the return to traditionalist tropes seen in Abani's and Ngũgĩ's novels, nationalistic, in that it derives from a specific national experience marked by the effects of 'arrested decolonization', to use Biodun Jeyifo's phrase,[23] and, finally, transnational and inherently blended.

As a conceptual whole, this sort of split or double consciousness serves to modulate its own object, preventing what Gilroy calls a 'cultural insiderism' that privileges ethnicity as 'an incontestable priority over all other dimensions of their social and historical experience, cultures, and identities'[24] while maintaining the interaction between 'roots' and 'routes' so crucial to black identities. Like Fanon's third stage of culture, neither wholly traditional nor wholly Western-derived, the narrative spaces opened up through these forms of multiply-articulated blending instead represent an emerging and ever-shifting culture of liminality in which the inassimilable is given voice.

## Re-framing the *Ogbanje*

In the traditional Igbo mythicoreligious conception of the world, existence is divided between three planes: the spirit world, inhabited before birth, the material world of human beings and the spirit world of the ancestors.[25] These three planes are not seen as discrete, but instead function together to create the world in total in a dualist notion of the seen and unseen worlds.[26] Spirits may interact with human individuals and vice versa, as the binary conception of mind and body is replaced with an open system of thought. In this system, the *ogbanje* refers to the spirit-child caught between oppositional pacts in the spirit world and human world.[27] Once born, these *ogbanje* children wish to quickly return to their spirit-companions and so desire to terminate their human lives. However, this directly violates the Igbo directive that every individual must live out a full life in accordance with their *chi*, or destiny-giving personal deity, and, as a result, the *ogbanje* child enters into a cycle of birth, death and rebirth. The *ogbanje* is forced to exist in a liminal space that is neither entirely human nor entirely spirit but instead reflects the ambiguity of its divided existence.[28] In its traditional inception in Igbo society, the *ogbanje* story is used to explain the actions of individuals who are seen as outside the norms of expected social behaviour.[29] It is said that, because these individuals have divided loyalties in the spirit and human worlds, so their conduct must betray conflict,[30] reflecting the paradoxical duality that they embody.[31] More recently, the *ogbanje* myth has been used as an analogy for the Nigerian postcolony, conceptualizing the nation as the spirit-child forced to continually reinvent itself.[32] While this application of the *ogbanje* myth minimizes the complexities of Nigerian national politics and presents a homogenous view of the society which, given its construction of ethnic divisions, is suspect, it nonetheless indicates the importance and wide application of the mythological figure in contemporary discourse. In other terms, the myth has been described as embodying 'a Nigeria-centric signification' for postcolonial trauma,[33] serving as an allegorical figure of sorts, one through which to conceptualize the specific history of disillusionment which followed Nigeria's emergence as a nation-state.

Approaching *GraceLand*, the *ogbanje* myth provides one layer of meaning within the narrative and presents one possible master plot through which to read it. The novel, which tells the story of Elvis Oke, a sixteen-year-old aspiring dancer navigating life in the slums of 1980s Lagos following his mother's death from cancer and father's electoral losses in the short-lived Second Republic, is told in five narrative strands, one encompassing Elvis's childhood in Igboland, prior to, during and in the immediate aftermath of the Nigerian-Biafran War, sections recounting his contemporary experiences in Lagos, religious mythology taken from Igbo tradition, statements on Igbo cultural practice from Western ethnographic anthropology and a collection of recipes, information on herbal cures and extracts from Elvis's deceased mother's journal.[34] Immediately, then, the novel structures itself through multiple frames of reference, positioning divergent modes of knowledge in tandem with one another, an indication of the text's larger work of conceptual re-inscription. Throughout the narrative, Elvis is represented through a series of dislocations and displacements, mimicking the birth–death–rebirth cycle of the *ogbanje*. Over the course of these cycles, Elvis transforms from an idealistic child, safely ensconced in the rural world overseen by his mother and grandmother, to a hardened, solitary teenager involved in the criminal underworld of Lagos. Throughout, his idealized image of his childhood is demolished, while his dreams of fame and fortune as a dancer are reborn in the decidedly more realist dream of survival. Physically, Elvis disappears from his home and reappears, fundamentally changed, at several different climactic occasions in the narrative. Nowhere, however, is the enactment of the *ogbanje* myth in *GraceLand* more evident than at the narrative's conclusion, marking its final *ogbanje* cycle. Having progressed through several cycles of dislocation and return, Elvis is portrayed as less and less able to cope with the realities of his life on the streets of Lagos. With his home in the slums destroyed by the government and having survived both a price on his head and days of torture, Elvis, the narrative makes evident, will not persevere through indefinite homelessness. In a last-minute miracle, Elvis is given a visa to America, somehow procured by his friend Redemption for a fantasized emigration. Elvis is initially reluctant to take this gift, wondering about its ability to effect change in his life: 'Even though it had become painfully clear to him that there was no way he could survive in Lagos, there was no guarantee he would survive in America'.[35] Eventually convinced to take the passport and visa, Elvis, at the narrative's end, waits in the airport for his flight to be called. Immediately, the staging of this conclusion reflects the ambivalence of the *ogbanje*. As a liminal space, the airport waiting lounge functions as a setting without a nation, neither technically in the country of departure nor in the land of destination; in the conditions of transnational migrancy and contemporary exile, it is a place that is simultaneously no place at all, a non-place *par excellence*.[36] By positioning its conclusion in this setting, the narrative structurally highlights its undecidability, marking the text as one which, finishing without a setting, may display a conclusion without closure.[37] While in traditional Igbo society the mutilated corpse of the *ogbanje* child would be left outside the village in the Evil Forest, also called the Bad Bush, to ensure it will not return,[38] Elvis, under the conditions of global neoliberalism and the ravages of structural adjustment, is left in the no-place of the airport, narratively abandoned so as never to return.

In this moment, Elvis is unable to articulate his emotions:

> He wasn't sure how to feel. On the one hand, he had the opportunity to get away from his life. On the other, he felt like he was abandoning everything that meant anything to him. Oye, Efua, his father, the King, Redemption, Okon, Blessing, even Comfort. (*GL*, p. 318)

Igbo mythology mandates a social view of the world where individuals exist not in a vacuum but through their society and as part of a social whole.[39] As part of a communal fabric, the individual exists beyond his or her own skin through the existence and perpetuation of the family clan, emphasized through the belief in reincarnation within a family line. Elvis is explicitly shown as breaking this communal pact, foregrounding its contingency. He is aware that, by leaving Lagos, he will cut himself out of the traditional tapestry-like existence of the community, effectively enacting his own death therein, but continues nonetheless in what Rita Nnodim calls his final loss of belief.[40] Elvis, through this departure, embodies the desire of the *ogbanje* 'to be allowed *just to be*, to occupy their own place in the universe's grand scheme of things, to live and perform fully and consistently that *atypical self*, no matter how aberrant or grievous others experience them to be'.[41] In choosing escape, Elvis marks his desire to exist outside of dominant, pre-written and static master narratives of tradition and society, as well as the impossibility for those narratives to persist under the conditions of late capitalist global imperialism. For Elvis, this is a final departure which escapes rationalization:

> He knew that what he thought he was leaving behind wasn't much, and after all, his aunt Felicia was in America. No, what he was leaving had nothing to do with quantity; nor, in spite of Redemption's protestations, did it have to do with quality. This was something else, something essential. (*GL*, pp. 318–19)

Neither qualitative nor quantitative evaluations can provide a justification for his departure. It is simply, as the narrative says, something essential in his being which does not allow him to stay. For the *ogbanje*, societal norms serve as a constraint; where others abide by norms which dictate that life progress through set stages in line with a community of values, the *ogbanje* operates as a singularity, choosing to reject the demands of socially-driven destinies. Despite his awareness of the comparatively difficult material conditions of Nigerian society, for Elvis, his desire to leave is unarticulated and beyond the possibilities of description within any symbolic framework, rendered, as it is, undecidable; critically, then, the flight to America is removed from any developmentalist counter-narrative. Instead, Elvis must face the fundamental qualities of his character and follow his need to depart from his home indefinitely.

The novel ends as Elvis, by the assumed name on his visa, is called to his boarding gate:

'Redemption,' the airline clerk called.
Elvis, still unfamiliar with his new name, did not respond.
'Redemption!' the clerk called louder.
Elvis stepped forward and spoke.
'Yes, this is Redemption.' (*GL*, p. 321)

The narrative closes with this excerpt, and, by denying the reader any scene of Elvis in transit or in America, its ability to reorient Elvis's existence in this new setting is left ambiguous. His textual existence is suspended; as an entity, Elvis is left in a middle ground. Elvis is gone; instead, he is reborn in Redemption, an acknowledgement of the power, through the act of naming, of re-inscription. With this ending, the narrative demonstrates the impossibility of giving closure to Elvis's uncontainable existence, where, as an *ogbanje*, he is finally represented as neither here nor there, condemned to ambivalence. With its inconclusive ending, *GraceLand* motions towards the inability of mythology, as a governing framework, to delineate conclusive order to its world and situates itself within a popular tradition which reflects the interests and anxieties of its society.

Yet, *GraceLand* fails to function as a straightforward retelling of the *ogbanje* myth. Elvis, as *ogbanje*, does not die in the physical sense; instead he attempts to disappear to a new land. Nor is Elvis reborn; instead, his character shifts through a series of manifestations and is ultimately left ambiguous. Elvis-as-*ogbanje* is not, by any means, directly analogous with the traditional myth in the manner of previous literary plays on the *ogbanje-abiku* tradition, notably in Achebe's *Things Fall Apart* and Okri's *The Famished Road*. Rather, the *ogbanje* in *GraceLand* mirrors the historicity of its postcolonial setting, reflecting Emmanuel Chukwudi Eze's remark that 'modern African writings operate on several other historical levels. On one level, the traditions one presumably writes about [...] is experienced by the writer as alive [...] But on another level, the writer also knows that the tradition in question has been damaged and transformed in an irreversible manner'.[42] In shifting the elements of the traditional myth, *GraceLand*, as a narrative, reflects the changed and dynamic society it re-presents and from which it springs. As a modern *ogbanje*, Elvis's narrative progress operates within the conditions of postcoloniality as well as traditional mythology, functioning beyond the sphere of an easy nativism in order to engage with the complexities of identity-formation and communal belonging in contemporary Nigerian society.

Crucially, *GraceLand* transforms the site of the *ogbanje*'s split allegiances through spatial substitution. Rather than develop as a struggle between loyalties in the human world and the spirit world, *GraceLand* stages the conflict of the *ogbanje* as one between a desire for an indigenous homeland and a desire for the chance at prosperity promised in the mythical West, represented in the narrative by America. Throughout the novel, *GraceLand* is peppered with references to this other form of mythology, that of developmentalism and the myth of postcolonial progress through immigration to the global north. Elvis, like his companions, indulges in occasional fantasies of success and fame in America, and references to American popular culture, particularly through Hollywood cinema, are on a par with references to African media within the narrative. For some critics, in fact, *GraceLand* is most powerfully read as a statement of postcolonial development through migrancy and the transnational circulation of Western commodity culture, where, as Adélékè Adéèkó claims, 'America rescues the narrative and its protagonist when Elvis runs out of escape outlets from the confining destinies that beset him in Lagos'.[43] America is thus where he 'finds moral salvation from the ambiguity of life in Nigeria',[44] highlighting what Hunt calls the 'particularly nefarious blend of poverty, disenfranchisement and violence' that is all Nigeria may offer to its citizens.[45] Read in this way, the narrative's promise may only be fulfilled through the invocation of the West and its epistemic and economic values, subsumed under the mythological discourse of salvation through emigration and the irredeemable stagnation of the postcolonial nation-state. The novel's conclusion, seen as such, shifts from a staging of indigenous mythology to a staging of exile and asylum, leading to a tendency to read the narrative entirely through the lens of Western-driven developmental progress.

Because the narrative also functions through its transformed indigenous mythology, however, it fails to allow such an acritical view of America and the adoption of a totalizing discourse of neocolonialist progress. This is particularly evidenced by Elvis's own ambiguity towards America. Early in the narrative, Elvis begins to ruminate on his feelings towards the country: 'He mused over his mixed feelings. His fascination with movies and Elvis Presley aside, he wasn't really sure he liked America. Now that the people he cared about were going there, he felt more ambivalent than ever' (*GL*, pp. 55–6). For Elvis, America is not simply the place of dreams, idealized, as Albert Memmi discusses with reference to the youth of North Africa, as a utopia of maximum possibility.[46] While Memmi presents a straightforward picture of yearning and certainty that in the Western metropole, happiness and prosperity will be found, Abani's Elvis presents a much more complicated picture. America is not a guarantor of success; it is simply another, different place. For Elvis, America may be seen as the cause of Nigeria's economic and postcolonial ills and as complicit in neo-imperialist global domination (*GL*, p. 280). It is a place which is taking his loved ones from him (*GL*, pp. 165–8), reducing his already fractured family unit to none. America, for Elvis, while a pleasant dream, would in reality change nothing.

Perhaps most evocatively, the narrative complicates the question of America through a reference to James Baldwin's *Going to Meet the Man*, a reference both powerful and complex enough to warrant its full quotation:

> As he read, Elvis began to see a lot of parallels between himself and the description of a dying black man slowly being engulfed by flame. The man's hands using the chains that bound him as leverage to pull himself up and out of the torture. He flinched at the part where the unnamed white man in the story cut off the lynched black man's genitalia. He closed the book and imagined what kind of scar it would leave. It would be a thing alive that reached up to the sky in supplication, descending to root itself in the lowest chakra, our basest nature. Until the dead man became the sky, the tree, the earth and the full immeasurable sorrow of it all. He knew that scar, that pain, that shame, that degradation that no metaphor could contain, inscribing it on his body. And yet beyond that, he was that scar, carved by hate and smallness and fear onto the world's face. He and everyone like him, until the earth was aflame with scarred black men dying in trees of fire. (*GL*, pp. 319–20)

At the moment of the narrative's conclusion, America's spell over Elvis is completely broken. No longer seeing America as a place of salvation or the land of grace to which the novel's title alludes, Elvis, instead, sees himself in America, one with the victims of racist oppression throughout history, collateral damage under imperialist and capitalist calls for expansion at all costs. America can no longer be seen as the natural developmental conclusion to a progressive life; it becomes instead another ambivalent space rife with pain, corruption and the struggles which mark Elvis's existence as part of the underclassed and underrepresented. By holding America at a critical distance, the narrative complicates any attempts to read its conclusion as a wholesale validation of migrancy and progress through the assimilation of American value systems, highlighting the artifice of what Mudimbe has called 'the strong tension between a modernity that often is an illusion of development, and a tradition that sometimes reflects a poor image of a mythical past'.[47] Instead, Elvis's ultimate departure must be read, at least in part, as the outcome of his trajectory as *ogbanje*, leaving the status of his final journey both uncertain and ambivalent. America is not salvation; Elvis is not guaranteed happiness, and, in fact, his actual chances are low. The American myth must contend with the discourse of the *ogbanje*, triangulated over the black Atlantic and transforming America into another liminal space.

In his reading of *GraceLand*, Obi Nwakanma refers to Elvis's flight to America as marking a tendency, in contemporary Nigerian literature, 'to question, as a result of disillusionment, the value of nation and national belonging'.[48] Yet the narrative complicates the issue beyond national belonging as a binary marker. Communal belonging is both questioned and affirmed; traditions are respected while simultaneously displaced. No statement wholeheartedly supporting any totalizing discourse may be maintained; instead, the narrative demands a consistently dynamic negotiation and re-imagination of meaning throughout its course. In this way, *GraceLand* becomes an emergent space for narrating the postcolony, free from the nostalgia of nativism implied in the return to indigenous mythology and its attendant yearning for lost origins, as well as from the contemporary view of the West as saviour and economic and social development as the mythological slayer of ills. In its structure, the narrative answers back to the inherent contradiction of postcolonial narrative which, as Boehmer has noted,

> cannot bring what it promises: a completely united and unifying history, an absolute unity with the national body. To conceptualize that fusion demands self-division. In effect, to transfigure body into narrative, to escape from being only a figure in another's text, is to effect a break in the self.[49]

In *GraceLand*, this method of self-division appears through the transformation of the traditional through the intrusion of the contemporary. Critically then, the use of the *ogbanje* myth as a latent master narrative, in tandem with contemporary mythologies and subject to conceptual blends, serves to situate the text in its cultural and historical context, while drawing upon global continuities in the asymmetrical distribution of power and capital. Simultaneously, the use of the *ogbanje* motif places *GraceLand* well within the larger tradition of Nigerian literature and, to a lesser extent, the wider scope of the black Atlantic.[50] Yet, in contrast to Cooper's claims that such re-formulations of the past in the service of a re-imagined present function predominantly as magical realism,[51] *GraceLand* remains within a predominantly realist narrative frame, where the metaphorical nature of the *ogbanje* allows for a broader interpretation of the term which may escape the closure which threatens static tropes. Throughout the novel, the contemporary reworking of the *ogbanje* myth becomes a shadow upon the text itself, maintaining the liminal and inassimilable, while demanding a constant renegotiation of meaning through the dynamism of the narrative form. The use of mythology elicits this uneasy unity in fragmentation through the organization of the narrative as inherently split within itself, expressing the capacity of narrative to make impossible meanings accessible. *GraceLand* critiques and presents a new imagining of Nigeria as unchained from the oppressive dictates of mythology and the domination of culture heroes. At the same time, the nation-state is also imagined as no longer at ease with neoliberal mythologies of development; instead the narrative functions as a re-imagining of Nigeria which surpasses any binary or static notion of tradition and modernity, forcing instead a continual shift in register that opens all meanings.

## Language, Orality and Myth

Any reader of Ngũgĩ wa Thiong'o would be unsurprised by the statement that, like Abani's, Ngũgĩ's work is riven with multiple codes, discourses, narratives and frames of reference. In a certain sense, the very existence of Ngũgĩ's work embodies a form of conceptual blending and narrative hybridity through its creation. Describing his early career as a writer in the English language, Ngũgĩ explains how '[he] heard [his characters'] voices in Gĩkũyũ but wrote them down in English sounds', a process he glosses as 'a mental translation' where 'for every novel that [he] wrote in English, there was an original text'.[52] While on the surface a largely pragmatic description of the mechanics of writing in a secondary language, Ngũgĩ's comments on his early creative practice point further to the inherent blending that characterizes his writing, a product of the need to relegate narrative to a single language always haunted by another. As a writer who self-consciously creates with a view towards multiple audiences, local and global,[53] moreover, Ngũgĩ cannot be said to have escaped this sense of the spectral even in his Gĩkũyũ-language works. Instead, in these later texts, too, a similar and constant encroachment of otherness, both through English, the language, and English, an aesthetic code bound up in the novel form, creates a sense of alterity in the very symbolic structures of narration. Impelled by this perpetual motion towards that which is not, Ngũgĩ's works mark a space where self-described 'innovations in language' render the translatability of the text forever in the process of becoming, but never quite complete.[54]

Criticism of Ngũgĩ's works has largely focused upon the ways in which his Gĩkũyũ-language texts, as part of what has been called 'his quest for an authentic African cultural regeneration, natural pride, and dignity',[55] have sought to inscribe the rhetorical and cultural tokens of orality into the written word. Ngũgĩ's first novel written in Gĩkũyũ, 1980's *Caitaani mũtharaba-Inĩ* (*Devil on the Cross*), written during his imprisonment in Kamiti Maximum Security Prison, has been described as 'a modern oral narrative' that 'is situational, presentist, and contingent' and displays an easy 'oral eclecticism' in its very structure and form.[56] In a similar vein, 1986's *Matigari* has been regarded as a novel which leverages oral form, myth and the socio-political import of rumour in order to 'reopen and recontextualize the history that the state has sought to repress in the name of truth',[57] a textual act which only 'acquires political agency in the process of being read'.[58] The novel itself became part of oral legend, when, upon hearing reports of the eponymous truth-seeker traversing the Kenyan countryside, the oppressive Moi regime ordered the capture and arrest of its protagonist; undaunted by the discovery that the dissident in question was a fictional invention, the regime coordinated the mass-scale seizure and destruction of the novel, transforming the text, as a material object, into the object of myth and legend and ironically guaranteeing its popular success. It is of course no coincidence that these novels, written in Gĩkũyũ for a class of workers and peasants typically excluded from the global market of readers and consumers, noted as the first instance in which 'a work of high fiction saw as its principal readership a group other than the complacent postcolonial bourgeoisie',[59] would function in this way. Throughout Ngũgĩ's career, what has been called his 'attempt to synthesize aesthetic forms and cultural formations in a continuous state of flux' has emerged as a central concern, spanning both the question of aesthetic form,[60] through a redefinition of the literary, and a deeply-rooted political engagement, drawing on the particular potency of the cultural in the work of mass mobilization and liberation. Here, what Andrade has called the novel form's 'complex relation to Africa and cultural nationalism' is of particular importance. As Andrade explains,

> unlike poetry and drama, [the novel] is the genre commonly believed to have originated outside the continent and therefore to have become African only as part of the colonial enterprise. Second, although the novelistic tradition in indigenous languages such as Kiswahili, Wolof, Yoruba, and Xhosa has mushroomed in the twentieth century, the African literature that is most significant to the world is written in European languages.[61]

The very choice of the novel form, then, positions Ngũgĩ's work in a space of transformation, recreation and reclamation. In his quest to transform the Euro-American cultural form of the novel to serve the specifically-situated political needs of Kenya, writ small, and a Third World still emerging from arrested decolonization, writ large, it is only natural that Ngũgĩ should attempt to surpass the universalizing aesthetic imperatives of literary value.

Given this background and career to date, it should be of little surprise that Ngũgĩ's most recent novel, *Mũrogi wa Kagogo* (*Wizard of the Crow*, published in its original Gĩkũyũ in three volumes from 2004 to 2006 and in English in 2006), displays a similar preoccupation with the transformation of orality, myth, legend and folklore in order to serve a materially-grounded political end. The novel has been described as a 'conspicuously oral narrative' that is inherently performative in its nature,[62] 'a composite tale, a global epic [...] but with an African foundation and an African voice',[63] 'the culmination of a long process by the novelist to simulate the art of the oral storyteller in writing, and thus to overcome the ostensible gap between orality and writing'[64] and a 'picaresque Rabelaisian novel'.[65] In translating orality into the novel form, moreover, Ngũgĩ's work sharply refutes what Abiola Irele has criticized as the 'inherent evolutionism' of orthodox conceptions of orality which inevitably view oral cultures as atavistic, degraded and developmentally lagging.[66] Because of this focus, *Wizard of the Crow*'s performative nature, as a literary work which seeks to re-define the literary as a function, has been described as staging the dynamics of power 'in order to dramatize power's precariousness and expose it to censure and disavowal'.[67] In so doing, the novel imbues itself with the traces and rhetorical effects of a transformed and transcribed grounding in folklore; at the same time, like *GraceLand*, this recourse to the allegedly atavistic is not single-minded in its force. Rather, the recourse to authentic and traditional narrative structures and communicative modes, through its transformational interpretative imperative, constructs a commentary on the very impossibility of the single authentic story, narrative or voice in the context of an Africa still battered by the material effects of an arrested decolonization.

With its opening lines that 'There were many theories about the strange illness of the second Ruler of the Free Republic of Aburĩria, but the most frequent on people's lips were five',[68] *Wizard of the Crow* begins with an explicit rumination on its multiplicity of narratives, grounded in a distinctly oral register. This use of rumour, as Robert L. Colson suggests, opens a narrative frame in which the hierarchical ordering of discourses is subverted, problematizing the notion of authorization on a broader scale.[69] In the novel, storytelling appears in several forms, none more significant than the narrative's foregrounding of its meta-function. Throughout, the narrative voice is consciously positioned as one voice among others, shifting between tenses, moods and perspectives, enabling a form in which a single sanctioned narrative is unable to emerge as a privileged site; instead, the very form of the narrative is one in which multiple codes coexist, not so much as equivalent as in a state of constant flux, in which authority is given and rescinded and frameworks of truth emerge and recede:

> Let me say as the narrator that I cannot confirm the truth or falsity of the existence of the chamber [where the Ruler is rumoured to keep daemons]; it may turn into a mere rumor or tale from the mouth of Askari Arigaigai Gathere. (*WC*, p. 11)

> It is difficult, even today, to make sense of what happened afterward. Even A.G., despite his gift of words, was taciturn, but people claimed this was because he, Tajirika, Njoya, and Kahiga had been sworn to secrecy under the penalty of their tongues being cut out for blabbering. (*WC*, p. 550)

Amongst the primary narrative voices present are those of a self-conscious narrator, whose shifts between first-person singular, first-person plural and third person foreground the inherent untenability of omniscience as a narrative model. In addition, the novel presents the voices of Askari Arigaigai Gathere, known as A.G., a police constable-turned storyteller; Kamītī and Nyawīra, who, together, share the role of Wizard of the Crow; the Ruler; Tajirika and his wife Vinjinia; devout Christian couple Maritha and Mariko; the garbage collectors who first find Kamītī's body passed out on a trash heap and the Soldiers of Christ. These voices appear in parts and in whole throughout the narrative, often with little warning or indication that a shift in perspective or voice is forthcoming. Through this form of multiperson narrative, *Wizard of the Crow* joins a body of work written in what Richardson has termed extreme narration,[70] leveraging the particularly literary qualities of the novel form to destabilize naturalized ideological values of truth and authenticity. In *Wizard of the Crow* this form of unnatural narration is a direct by-product of the novel's inscription of orality, a mode of communication which is arguably the single *most* natural form, within the aesthetics of the novel. In following this unnatural–natural form of narration, *Wizard of the Crow* escapes the barriers of empty and homogenous time,[71] shifting from a singular work of remembrance to a multifaceted and contingent reminiscence. Remembrance, in Walter Benjamin's terms, 'is dedicated to one hero, one odyssey, one battle', essentially codifying the historical memory which will pass from generation to generation through the individualistic, isolated form of the novel. Reminiscence, the short-lived and multiply-articulated domain of the storyteller, by contrast manifests in 'many diffuse occurrences'.[72] In *Wizard of the Crow*, this shift from remembrance to reminiscence is felt particularly through its telescoping of time and shifts in temporality, written in a narrative form in which months and years pass in mere sentences, while moments draw on for scores of pages. Through these shifts in register, time and address, the multiperson communicative effect of the novel allows for a foregrounded reckoning with the inherent unreliability of narrative, the very contingency of all stories and claims to truth which, by virtue of their subjective grounding, remain partial.

Rife with references to pan-Africanism, Hindu scripture, Chinese philosophy, Biblical traditions, Freudian psychoanalysis and more, *Wizard of the Crow* is inherently hybrid in its frame of reference. This sense of the global and the multiple has been described as Ngũgĩ's position 'between the universalizing rhetoric of multiculturalism, cosmopolitanism, and postcolonial nostalgia, on one hand, and the two competing sites of enunciation, the American academy and an increasingly present and relocated Kenya on the other'.[73] In different terms, the novel can be read as 'rooted in an imaginary African country, but [...] situated in many parts of the world',[74] pointing again to the multiplicity of influence that permeates the text. Yet, this opening towards the global is not a case of bland universalism, commoditized hybridity or cosmopolitan artifice. The opening performed by the novel is one of a rooted cosmopolitanism,[75] where a materially-grounded critique blended with a specified cultural location informs and enables a broader appraisal of the discourses of power, authority and authenticity. Like *GraceLand*, *Wizard of the Crow* engages in an act of conceptual blending, operating simultaneously on multiple levels to allow the emergence of a form which is more than the sum of its parts. In *Wizard of the Crow*, this comes to the fore in the interaction between what can loosely be termed its twinned dictator and pastoral narratives. The former, as the dominant master narrative of the novel, engages with what has become a well-rehearsed and a priori tale of African neocolonial mismanagement, corruption and inadequacy, chronicling the Ruler's manic struggle to maintain power at all cost and the indifferent corruption of his ministers in the face of rampant poverty and misery for the masses.[76] In this sense, *Wizard of the Crow* re-stages Fanon's warning against the pitfalls of national consciousness, joining a long line of works focused on the disillusionment that followed independence, including Achebe's *A Man of the People* (1966), Soyinka's *Season of Anomy* (1973), and, most significantly, Armah's *The Beautyful Ones Are Not Yet Born* (1968).[77] This is made particularly evident in the novel's description of the Ruler's rise to power, from an activist teacher committed to the anti-colonial cause to a humble servant of the newly-independent republic to a megalomaniacal despot 'baffled by anyone not moti-vated by greed' and utterly beholden to the neocolonial interests of Western powers and the Global Bank (*WC*, pp. 231–5). In this nar-rative, the Ruler is described as an adept and adroit player in world politics, successfully leveraging the West's fear of communism to his own favour with a wilfully-blind global community, 'rendering the Ruler the African leader most respected by the West and landing him numerous state visits with kings, queens, and presidents receiving him in their palaces at lavish dinner parties' (*WC*, p. 234). The Ruler's success at courting Western favour continues with the climactic birth of Baby D, the Ruler's disfigured manipulation of democratic ideologies, a shift in rhetorical manoeuvring resulting in the Ruler being hailed 'for his bold and courageous steps, [with] some edito-rial writers going so far as to call him a democratic visionary whose balance of pragmatism and ideology had caught his foes with their pants down' (*WC*, p. 703), and ending with the Ruler's 'Self-Imposed Disappearance' (*WC*, p. 753) and Tajirika's rise as the new African darling of global capitalism.

At the same time, *Wizard of the Crow* calls upon another master plot, hearkening to an alternative form of knowledge and under-standing connected to the mythic qualities of the land and the healing properties of traditional knowledge from a primordial past corrupted by colonial modernity. Critics have read land as a meta-phor in Ngũgĩ's works which 'serves a metonymic function, figuring the glorious past of the community, now in ruins, and a past whose restoration is only possible through land restitution',[78] a perspective which this second master narrative appears to confirm in its depiction of the land and its rural populations. In the Gĩkũyũ context from which Ngũgĩ writes, the importance of land and its loss, as a symbol of colonial occupation and settler domination, cannot be overemphasized, grounding this second master narrative in the long and contested historical context of Kenyan freedom and independence. Early in its pages, the novel describes how, driven by her experiences following a devastating automobile accident, Nyawĩra turns away from her upbringing as part of the pampered and alienated elite in favour of a life amongst the masses. In this description, the modernized middle and upper classes are described as corrupt, set adrift from their fellow citizen and remote from the immediacy of authentic experience. By contrast, the rural peasant class exist in tune with nature, enabled with a near-spiritual connection with the world around them:

> What surprised her then and later when she recalled her near fatality was the number of cars that simply passed her by; no one had stopped to see if anyone was hurt or needed help. The people who hurried to her rescue were the barefooted, mostly. One unloaded his donkey cart to rush her to the nearest medical center many miles away, the donkey announcing their arrival at the emergency room by braying loudly and shitting. (*WC*, p. 79)

In this juxtaposition between an uncaring bourgeoisie and compassionate peasantry, depicted as pure of heart despite material decrepitude, the narrative, through Nyawĩra's memories, presents an idealized and pastoral vision of the downtrodden masses, gesturing towards a tradition of romanticization seen from Fanon's early writings on the revolutionary potential of the lumpenproletariat to the present day. Later, it is in this idyllic rural space, naturalized outside of history, that Kamĩtĩ and Nyawĩra first come together, a union of innocence and wonder described as occurring in a landscape where love manifests itself 'in the tree branches where the nests of weaverbirds hung; in the murmurings of the Eldares River as it flowed eastward before turning into a roaring waterfall; in the sun's rays, which pierced through the waterfall, splitting into the seven colors of the rainbow' (*WC*, p. 205). The land, and by extension its people, becomes a site of purification, a timeless space where the ravages of global imperialism cannot penetrate. Yet, the narrative complicates this romanticized and atavistic view; despite their initial bliss, the land cannot indefinitely defer the 'chill' between Nyawīra and Kamītī (*WC*, p. 206). Instead, this chill, a product of their different views on material, political engagement under dictatorship, stems from Nyawīra's inability to surrender her political principles to the land; rather than viewing the prairie as an escape, that is to say, Nyawīra continues to view the land as valuable only inasmuch as it may aid and abet liberation through radical politics, the ultimate conclusion of her experience following her accident years before. Where Kamītī sees the abundance of nature, Nyawīra sees a need for human action, remembering that 'it is also good to build a granary for when nature has the flu' (*WC*, p. 204). As one half of the Wizard of the Crow, Nyawīra, particularly in her hesitance to view the land as an alternative to history, is significant, placing the novel's pastoral-traditionalist narrative under erasure and creating, instead, a coeval commitment to the political. The mythic force of the land cannot be privileged, as the land is lauded for its pragmatic use as a refuge from the surveillance of power, one which, for the Movement of the Voice of the People, becomes 'a school to which they often came to hear what it had to tell them' (*WC*, p. 758), where the principles of survival and cooperation flourish, taught as they practise their 'right to political struggle' (*WC*, p. 75).

Given its complexity of focus and form, it is of little wonder that *Wizard of the Crow*'s reception has been mixed. Mainstream reviews in North America and Europe, while largely positive, have displayed a gently patronizing quality, exemplified in comments that highlight its genesis in a 'traditional' orality and 'fantastic' folklore as an excuse for its 'broad strokes of caricature'.[79] Such commentary, alluding to the text's re-configuration of the universalized Euro-American aesthetics of the novel, indicates a sense of benevolent bemusement with its structural and linguistic blending and narrative innovation. More positive reviews focus on the novel's instrumental nature, insisting that, faced with its deficiencies, 'it is worth remembering that Ngũgĩ's works are often read aloud in public spaces',[80] and that any inconsistencies might be explained by this steadfast adherence to strategic forms of address. Despite critical complaints about the novel's more magical interludes, however, more problematic appear to be the moments in which it becomes most realist in focus, turning to what are called 'didactic set pieces on AIDS and domestic violence'.[81] Critical commentary on the novel, too, points towards these episodes as instances of literary failure, exemplifying Ngũgĩ's overt political intentions, told through narrative forms which, in Jameson's terms, appear 'conventional or naïve'.[82] Throughout commentary on the novel, there appears to be a sense in which the Western reader is placed on the defensive, exemplified in complaints that Ngũgĩ finds, in the realm of Western modernity, nothing of value, seeing instead a Manichean binary where nothing remains to be salvaged.[83] Certainly, Ngũgĩ is singularly invective in his criticism of neoliberal globalization. Yet, this passionate critique is not one which can be read as absolute or totalizing precisely because of its blended narrative form. *Wizard of the Crow*, that is to say, displays a more complex engagement with its multiple inheritances than its harsher critics might suppose, demonstrated particularly in the centrality of education and the university-model in the development and dissemination of a political consciousness. Considered in this light, the Movement may be seen as inspired more by the Europe of 1968 than a primordial past, its inheritance as much a product of Enlightenment virtues as it is a struggle against the corruption of the same, and its folkloric register continually mediated by a materialist engagement with postcolonial African history and vice versa.

Perhaps more surprising has been the novel's reception in its original Gĩkũyũ. Serialized into three volumes containing its six books (*Mũrogi wa Kagogo: Mbuku ya Mbere na ya Keri*, *Mũrogi wa Kagogo: Mbuku ya Gatatũ* and *Mũrogi wa Kagogo: Mbuku ya Kana, Gatano na Gatandatũ*), *Mũrogi wa Kagogo* was published between 2004 and 2006, with the arrival of the English-language text delayed as long as was reasonably possible to better facilitate the original text's circulation. Like its predecessor texts, it was the author's intention that the novel would be read out loud and discussed in groups, part of his own myth-making surrounding his larger cultural production as an internationally-celebrated author. Writing on the experience of teaching *Wizard of the Crow*, William Slaymaker describes how a Gĩkũyũ-speaking student, approaching the original,

> was sure his male (not female!) relatives had bought or would buy the serialization of the Gĩkũyũ version and discuss it with real interest over some beers. In short, everything critics and Ngũgĩ

himself would say about the oral importance of his narratives would be played out in the brew of the male imaginations of family members of his father's generation.[84]

For these readers, the novel's orality and reliance on folklore would be instantly recognizable. While the novel does not draw on a specific set of folktales or Gĩkũyũ myth, its framework would be easily identifiable as such, particularly with allegorically-named characters such as Silver Sikiokuu (Large Silver Ear), Machokali (Dangerous Eyes), and Tajirika (Seek or Get Wealthy).[85] The very storytelling frame would be further recognizable through the figure of the Wizard of the Crow who, while not a literal character from Gĩkũyũ legend, would be easily interpreted as a representative figure, a case of Ngũgĩ 'winking to some of his readers—the insiders—as he unties the cords of power and unspells the poison apple of politics'.[86] Despite this cultural grounding, however, the novel's reception by its Gĩkũyũ-language readers remains markedly less positive than that of its Euro-American readers.

This mixed reception is due in part, no doubt, to the changed circumstances of context in which the novel has been published. As Mike Kuria suggests, without the censorship of a dictatorial regime, *Mũrogi wa Kagogo* claims less inherent subversive appeal than its predecessors,[87] resulting in its reduced clandestine circulation as a cultural marker of political resistance. Following from this observation has been the criticism of the novel's relative success in achieving Ngũgĩ's goal of reaching a reading public of peasants and workers. The novel has been criticized for placing 'certain demands on [Ngũgĩ's] Gĩkũyũ readers to be familiar with his key languages— Kiswahili and English—in addition to Gĩkũyũ',[88] through a reliance on a form of Gĩkũyũ which only a highly-educated and English-literate reader would be able to navigate.[89] This, in turn, ends by 'not only alienating [those readers] but also requiring that they are literate in the very language whose shackles [Ngũgĩ] seeks to free them from'.[90] The novel has further been castigated for its tendency to Kikuyunize English words, rather than Sheng or Swahili, 'suggest[ing] that [Ngũgĩ] is entering the Kikuyu world from an English linguistic world's perspective or as a person largely linguistically alienated from the people he wishes to reach'.[91] One commentator, writing in the *Kenya Times*, highlights the chasm between Ngũgĩ and his purported reading public, complaining that '[t]he man himself works and lives in a Western country and even if he started from 1970s chucking out some random publications in vernacular literature, he has eventually been translating those very publications to "Western languages"'.[92] In tandem with complaints about the type of language used, critics have pointed to the dense intertextuality of the novel, one which calls upon Enlightenment philosophy, Marxist thought and Shakespearian allusions, claiming that, through the sheer volume of allusion, the novel appears remote from the cognitive and cultural spheres of its intended audience of Gĩkũyũ workers and peasants,[93] and indicating a concomitant and incompatible form of insidership in the text. Despite the polemicism of these comments, it remains important to at least reflect on the question of address in *Wizard of the Crow*. By all accounts, it seems that the novel is not and cannot be said to be written for Ngũgĩ's romanticized population of workers and peasants; if nothing else, the fact that the novel was written with translation into English in mind indicates that the issue of reception and address is not as simple as Ngũgĩ may claim. Equally, however, suggestions that the novel remains intellectually inaccessible to a wide readership are troubling in their implications and assumptions. Rather, it appears evident that *Wizard of the Crow* is a novel written for multiple purposes, to multiple audiences, with multiple frames of reference and levels of encoding. For the Gĩkũyũ reader able to translate its allusions to orality, play on Gĩkũyũ vocabulary and allegorical namings, the novel contains a different story than for the reader ignorant in these traditions but perhaps more competent at decoding its references to classical European philosophy and its tradition of letters. In each case, the novel presents a rich and complex narrative structure with a multiplicity of meaning, where the meaning of the text is co-created through the act of reading and interpretation beyond the limits of a single narrative.

## The Pitfalls of Magical Realism

As the discussion above has implied, a critically confounding facet of *Wizard of the Crow* has been its adherence, or lack thereof, to the conventions of realism and its play with the universalized aesthetics of the novel form. The novel has been called, amongst other things, an example of 'grotesque realism',[94] 'satirical magic realist',[95] 'fantastical, surreal and scatological',[96] 'marvelous-realist satirization'[97] and part of 'the new realism'.[98] These attempts at categorization imply that, by failing to conform to the conventions and expectations of realism, the novel must therefore conform to the amorphous category of postcolonial magical realism. While it is undoubtedly the case that the novel contains elements which exceed the boundaries of orthodox realist conventions, this compulsion to categorize the novel as part of a category as ill-defined as magical realism remains problematic for two primary reasons. On a general level, the recourse to magical realism, in the context of postcolonial writing, has become so commonplace as to have lost all sense of meaning or specificity in intention.[99] This is to say that, through the overwhelming critical desire to mark 'other' texts as 'magical', the very category has lost any sense of intentionality or import, hindered by what Eva Aldea describes as its 'careless' ascription.[100] More precisely, the recourse to magical realism contains within it a sense of estrangement from the material which reifies its artificial cleaving from the aesthetic. Cooper, for instance, has described magical realism as 'seeing with a third eye', a result of the 'syncretizing of cultures as creolized communities are created'.[101] Seen in this light, magical realism is a consequence of 'the fact that these countries [in the Third World] encountered Western capitalism, technology and education haphazardly',[102] leading to a need to re-imagine the pre-capitalist, pre-colonial world, what Stephen Slemon has referred to as magical realism's import as a form of counter-colonial writing marked by an inherent hybridity.[103] Writing on *Wizard of the Crow* in particular, Spencer has argued that 'the fantastic or magical aspects of a magical realist novel are less pure fantasy than metaphors that beseech decipherment or interpretation and therefore rejuvenate or re-perform conventional ways of understanding and describing the problem of dictatorship'.[104] While none of these readings of magical realism states outright that this literature functions apolitically, and indeed some commentators even claim an explicitly political intention in the deployment of magical realism, they nonetheless share a reliance on a strict oppositional model of literary aesthetic choice, splitting pre- and post-, West and rest, and implicitly bracketing the aesthetic from the material, the 'traditional' from the 'modern'. The turn away from conventional modes of realism is coupled with a seeming compartmentalization in which the folkloric, the pre-colonial and the traditional are seen as separate from, and thereby supplemental to, any engagement with modernity. In his postulation of 'animist realism' as a conceptual frame through which to read cultural production from the African continent, Harry Garuba addresses the artificiality of this hierarchal perspective, highlighting the extent to which magical realism remains overly-narrow as a concept and unable to grasp the 'multiplicity of representational practices' developed in African literature.[105] Through this constriction of purpose, material engagement is reduced to satire and disillusionment, closing off the possibility for action grounded in material conditions. Even where a political value is given space to emerge, as in readings of *Wizard of the Crow*, a critical dependency on magical realism as an epistemic frame of reference leads to concurrent charges of 'prolixity, stiffness and didacticism',[106] which fail to consider the full complexity of representational strategies in the text.

The tendency to view *Wizard of the Crow* as magical realist likely stems from its use of oral folklore as a mediating narrative structure. Ngũgĩ himself has stated that he 'accept[s] the term because of its contradictory nature, realism and magic. [...] But then you realize this has been part of the storytelling tradition of the world over, Africa included'.[107] Certainly, several of the episodes deemed 'magical' by criticism can be read otherwise, ranging from the augmentation of the ministers Machokali and Sikiokuu to Tajirika, who, as a means of combatting his persistent 'whiteache', visits Genetica Incorporated to have his black limbs replaced by white (*WC*, pp. 741–2). Even Kamĩtĩ's habit of leaving his body and flying across the globe could be potentially read as part of a larger series of spiritual and meditative phenomena, a gesture to the tradition of yogic practice from the India of his university days. Less explicable, however, is what is arguably the narrative's central motif, that of the Ruler's swollen, floating body, and its eventual reduction to a snake-like figure with the birth of Baby D(emocracy):

> The Ruler was quite candid with the doctor. He explained that when he read the news from the Global Bank, he had become so angry that his body started to expand even more. He had called his special adviser to have somebody to talk to in the hope that this would ease the anger within. While waiting for Tajirika, he had read some more newspapers, only to feel his anger mount

until it almost choked him, and that was when he felt himself lifted uncontrollably. He could not tell exactly when it started, but it was definitely when he was already in the air that his tummy began to ache. At first the pain was manageable, but now it had become unbearable. (*WC*, p. 652)

Certainly, this passage displays many of the hallmarks of the surreal and the magical. The Ruler, his body grotesquely expanded and released to flight, functions metaphorically as an index of corruption and vanity. Yet, this other-worldly expansion is itself a literalization of a very real phenomenon, embodying the Ruler's anger at his impotence under neo-imperial control and his powerlessness in the face of the Global Bank. Realized in a context of structural adjustment and financial politicking, the very magic of this moment is turned mundane, surpassing the fantastic to become another sort of socio-political commentary grounded in the materialism of twenty-first century structures of global inequity and the new colonialism of an Africa ravaged by structural adjustment and neo-imperialism. To dismiss this narrative episode as exemplary of a universalized notion of magical realism, then, neglects both the novel's political engagement and its position within a specific and localized oral and folkloric tradition. In both *Wizard of the Crow* and *GraceLand*, magical elements remain distinctly rooted within a set of cultural, historical and political contexts whose reading requires attention to specificity. Rather than viewing these elements as exotic or other, these elements constitute a central framework through which to conceive of the work in which each text engages. Much like the typification seen in Farah's *Links* and the aestheticism of *The Stone Virgins*, these moments of the fantastic signal an attempt to prevent a simplistic collapse into an a priori discourse of African otherness through their very difference. By remaining inassimilable to a single narrative framework, that is to say, these specifically-rooted moments create a means of forcing a perpetual work of interpretation beyond closure.

Like *Wizard of the Crow*, *GraceLand* too features episodes and structural narratives drawn from beyond the Western novelistic aesthetic. In *GraceLand*'s case, critical commentary reflects the risk inherent in simply dismissing these episodes as part of a generic magical realism. These comments are exemplified in claims that the narrative uses a non-realist mode to avoid direct engagement with the political realities of 1980s Lagos and that the text runs rife with 'mysterious events that cannot be fully explained or rationalized'.[108] In the novel, the most mysterious of these moments emerges as, in an episode central to its second book, Maroko, the slum in which Elvis and his father live, is scheduled for destruction as part of Operation Clean the Nation, one of many programmes driven by structural adjustment intended to rid the city of its vestiges of poverty. The slum's planned destruction, it transpires, is part of a plan to create space for upper-class housing projects to bring money to the military government while displacing the estimated 300,000 residents, a novelistic re-imagination of a now-infamous episode in Nigeria's recent history.[109] Previously depicted as a broken man deep in the throes of alcoholism, Elvis's father Sunday emerges to take a leading role in organizing protests of the slum's destruction, seemingly recalling his civic past and, in the context of mythologies of personal redemption, embarking on a hero quest. As Maroko is knocked to the ground, Sunday remains, the last man standing in the battle against the authorities (*GL*, pp. 285–7). In this episode a number of mythological elements coincide. Beatrice, Sunday's beloved wife, appears as a spirit along with a leopard, totem of his ancestors, congruous with the Igbo mythicoreligious belief that the spirit and human worlds interact and coexist as parts of a totality. As a spirit-entity, Beatrice entreats Sunday to remember his son, re-situating him into the social and communal fabric of Igbo life so crucial to traditionalist conceptions of society. At the same time, Sunday sees the leopard, a spirit-animal which could not possibly exist within the urban geography of Maroko. Yet, as a man far from religious or spiritual, Sunday dismisses these figures as 'too much' when juxtaposed with the more pressing concern of the approaching bulldozers. Always described as practical and sceptical of his late wife's religious beliefs, Sunday immediately reverts to a rationalist explanation for these spirits:

> If he ignored [Beatrice], she would disappear. She was, after all, a drunken hallucination. He laughed. Madam Caro must have laced his palm wine with some narcotic. Whatever it was, it was good, and he was glad he was a regular. (*GL*, p. 286)

At this point in the narrative, the interaction of the human and spirit planes reflects the ambiguity of its situation. It is very possible that Sunday, an end-stage alcoholic, simply hallucinates his dead wife and the leopard. Yet, this explanation becomes equally impossible, given his lack of attention to them and lack of a foundational spiritual belief structure. As Sunday himself muses, 'If Beatrice and the leopard were only hallucinations, why had they remained even when he wasn't paying any attention?' (*GL*, p. 286).

The ambiguity of the spiritual elements at Maroko reaches its apex at the moment of Sunday's death:

> [The bulldozers] were almost upon him and the vibrations were coming from everywhere. Grabbing a cutlass Comfort had dropped earlier, Sunday sprang with a roar at the 'dozer. The policeman let off a shout and a shot, and Sunday fell in a slump before the 'dozer, its metal threads cracking his chest like a timber box as it went straight into the wall of his home. Sunday roared, leapt out of his body and charged at the back of the policeman, his paw delivering a fatal blow to the back of the policeman's head. With a rasping cough, Sunday disappeared into the night. (*GL*, p. 297)

As he dies, Sunday merges with the leopard, a powerful spirit-animal talismanic within Igbo mythology.[110] Roaring against the bulldozers and police, Sunday-as-leopard, here, beckons explicitly to the tradition of Igbo folktale. Coinciding with these indigenous elements are elements of the contemporary mythology of urban development in the Third World, marked by the policeman, soldiers and bulldozers bent on progress at all human cost. As mythological elements, all three figures mark the initiation of progress and development defined in singular terms, while functioning similarly as bringers of destruction. Sunday's death is thus developed in a fully-hybridized register, incorporating the contemporary elements of the policeman and his gun and the bulldozer alongside the leopard, Sunday's spirit totem, in his final act of freedom. Framed in this context, his death becomes an event inassimilable to any master narrative. Part spiritual, part developmentalist, Sunday's death scene escapes charges of magical realism or mystification through its materialized setting, as a product of structural adjustment. Instead, Sunday, in his final moments, operates at the very boundary of the symbolic and the real where clashing epistemologies coexist under a dual sense of time and space. As Nnodim remarks, Sunday's 'dying body is united with the material fabric of the city as he dies an absurd, heroic and almost mythical death',[111] a scene which forces the incongruous to coexist within a single narrative moment. 'Limping off' through this conceptually hybridized scene, Sunday, his life and his death become marked as uncontainable by the text, asserting the porosity of the boundaries of the narratable and the permissible.

The very real coexistence of the mythic and the material in this scene is confirmed later in the narrative, as Elvis finds his father's body:

> What puzzled him, though, was the policeman. What has killed him? He approached the body. The entire back of the head was missing and there were claw marks all over the body. It looked like he had been mauled by some large predator. That was really strange, because there were no animals of that size anywhere near Lagos or Maroko. It certainly wasn't the work of a ghetto rat. (*GL*, pp. 304–5)

Here the narrative forcibly narrates myth within the consciously realist register of the text, assimilating the one within the space of the other, and vice versa, to animate the abstract in the moment of Sunday's death.[112] Elvis does indeed find his father's body crushed by bulldozers. Yet, the slashes of his claws remain, marking the point where the human and the spirit intersect and rendering the mythic ordinary. Sunday's death, through its morphology and combination of these disparate elements, functions to maintain the coexistence of both planes of being, while situating them within the context of contemporary material specificity within a single narrative form. Through this concerted hybridization of forms, Abani's narrative surpasses its cultural difference, inscribing its polyglossic epistemic register and refusing the marginalized notion of cultural binaries in its narrative space.

While the re-inscription of mythopoetics in *GraceLand* and *Wizard of the Crow* cannot be distilled to a single cause or seen as producing a single narrative effect, one particularly felt consequence is its rhetorical function. Mythology, pre-colonial tradition and folkloric motifs in these novels serve as markers of collective identification, suggesting that the novel written for the audience for whom these tropes and narratives are readable is different to that read by the audience who fails to recognize these elements. This, in turn, results in a constituted narrative voice which is either directly heard or implicitly overheard depending on its context. The effects of this double-coding may be borne out by the tendency, in popular review, to reduce these narratives to forms familiar to a Western readership, such as Bill Ott's infamous review of *GraceLand*, in which he comments that the novel is 'a fine example of the universality of teen experience across cultures' whose 'cross-cultural humor is irresistible'.[113] Equally, with its transformed mythologies, *GraceLand* has been accused of a certain touristic exoticism where the novel fails to reflect 'the reality of the society portrayed'.[114] In both cases, the novel is read as universal, alternatively praised for its disinterested detachment or vilified for its lack of authenticity. Yet, the very construction of these notions of universality, truth-value and authenticity remains obscured. Gikandi has written that

> nowhere is this overtly political dimension of language as marked as in the use of myths. I am not simply referring to traditional myths which have become de-historicized over time and hence appear to be independent of ordinary experience, but also to contemporary myths which are promoted by the daily media.[115]

Both *Wizard of the Crow* and *GraceLand*, in their melding of traditional and contemporary mythology, use the politicization of mythology and its tendency to distort to create narratives that explicitly question the categories marked by the postcolonial and its reification of mythology, enacting the questioning of myth that Isidore Okpewho describes as critical to any hope for a liberationist future.[116] In so doing, both novels create narrative spaces where transgressive identities may be maintained and the oppositional pull of binary choices may be avoided. As Stuart Hall has written, 'Cultural identities come from somewhere, have histories. But, like everything which is historical, they undergo constant transformation. Far from being eternally fixed in some essentialized past, they are subject to the continuous "play" of history, culture and power'.[117] The fusion of traditional mythological motifs with the mythologies of postcoloniality becomes a way of expressing this play while navigating what Òlakunle George has referred to as the difficult task of all African writers, 'the need to speak of and for a collective identity and destiny, from within an enunciatory space that is exterior to that identity'.[118] These texts thus fill in the gap between two discontinuous modes of thinking, often seen as the primary point of conflict between Western and African epistemological systems,[119] through the emergence of blended spaces and conceptual narratives which are neither entirely one myth nor the other, nor the sum of their parts.

Each narrative's use of mythology shifts from what could be seen as an attempt to recuperate the traditional notions of the past or idealize a society forever altered by colonialism to a commentary on the fragmentation of individuals and communities in the postcolonial era and a questioning of the drive to development through the wholesale embrace of neoliberal values. Ahluwalia has remarked that scholarship on and representations of Africa must demonstrate 'a better understanding of the manner in which African identity constantly is constituted and reconstituted, thus forcing Africanists to rethink the manner in which Africa has been conceptualised through the dominant category of the nation-state'.[120] In *GraceLand* and *Wizard of the Crow*, this understanding of an ever-shifting conceptualizing of self and community is enacted through the appropriation and restaging of indigenous mythology which, through its ethnic and historical connotations, defies the delineations of national boundaries and discrete categories. Each narrative represents the need for an epistemology which operates as a palimpsest containing the traces of multiple views. James Snead claims that, despite

> their hesitancy about coming to terms with the specificity of African literature, few western readers seem unwilling to talk about its 'universality'. The new critical valorisation of 'universal appeal' [...] is frequently applied to African works [...] even though the word 'universality' seems often to function as a code word meaning 'comprehensibility for the European reader'.[121]

Through their re-imagining of Africa through the dual lenses of traditional and contemporary mythologies, both novels disallow the easy universals of the metropole and force a reckoning with the historicity of the nation, while the recourse to a timeless pre-colonial idyll is subverted by the imperatives of a situated postcolonial modernity. Any universal within the narrative must come to terms with the specificity of its mythopoetic positioning as well as its localized context. Both *GraceLand* and *Wizard of the Crow* thus subvert the demand for a single national culture or authorized continental vision, instead presenting the collectivity as multifaceted. As re-imaginings of Africa on a global scale, they present a dynamic, fragmented collection of communities where the simplicity of essentialized categories and distinct narrative roles becomes subverted through conceptual blending and the complications therein. Through the emergence of blended spaces and inassimilable viewpoints, these narratives transform to gesture beyond what they articulate, subverting both the uncritical embrace of Western ideologies and the idealistic nativism of traditionalism, while re-imagining a vision of the African postcolony where the respective chains of mythologies old and new may be transformed into a discourse of liberation.

# 5
# Global African Literature: Strategies of Address and Cultural Constraints

## Material Cultures and Rhetorical Address

From its earliest days as a viable global market category, the emergence of African literature in English has been an exercise in asymmetrical relations of cultural capital, realized through shifts in transnational economic exchange and global fields of power. As an institution, the development of African literature can be traced back to 1957, when a young Nigerian broadcaster named Chinua Achebe, on the advice of friends, showed a manuscript for a novel chronicling the saga of three families in pre-colonial Nigeria to an instructor at his BBC training course in London. The manuscript, overhauled, revised and rescued from consignment to the dustbin of an unscrupulous typewriting service, would eventually make its way to Alan Hill who, working for William Heinemann, would publish it first in hardback in 1958 and later in paperback as the inaugural offering of the Heinemann African Writers Series in 1962.[1] The publication of that novel, *Things Fall Apart*, has come to mark the founding of modern African literature, the first foray of a new body of work which has since been hailed for its revitalization of English-language literature and its centrality in the consecration of world literatures on a global scale. Outstripping all publisher expectations, *Things Fall Apart* has since become the most widely-read literary work from the continent, selling over ten million copies, translated into nearly fifty languages and enabling Achebe's legacy as the father of African literature.[2] The story of *Things Fall Apart*'s publication has become a founding myth of sorts in the canon of modern African writing, repeated ad nauseam in stories of its genesis. Of course, Achebe was far from the first writer in English from the African continent; English-language writing in Africa has existed since at least the eighteenth century, beginning with slave narratives such as Olaudah Equiano's *The Interesting Narrative of the Life of Olaudah Equiano, Or Gustavus Vassa, The African, Written by Himself,* and imaginative literature on the continent can be traced nearly as far back through contributions commissioned by missionary presses, literary bureaux and popular imprints.[3] Nor was Achebe the first African literary writer to be feted by the international publishing market; six years before the publication of *Things Fall Apart,* Amos Tutuola's *The Palm-Wine Drinkard* had been published by Faber and Faber and hailed as a fine example of 'authentic' and 'primitive' writing, naïve art at its best.[4] It is indeed true, as Robert Fraser suggests, that 'practically all the grand foundational myths espoused by agencies, literary historians and other interested parties [...] are misplaced' and that, instead, the origins of African literature stem from a far more complex and lengthy process than the Achebe story suggests.[5] Equally, as Newell has demonstrated, it would be inaccurate to suggest that, prior to the publication of *Things Fall Apart,* writing from the continent was no more than 'an expectant, Achebe-shaped pause'.[6] Yet, the shape of African literature as we know it today would be unthinkable without Achebe and his involvement with the African Writers Series; dwelling upon this foundational myth, moreover, highlights the tensions which have marked the emergence of African literature as an institution, since these incipient moments.

As Patrick Williams has so rightfully stated, the publication of *Things Fall Apart* 'marks an epoch of its own' in the formation of African literature both on the continent and abroad.[7] The subsequent dissemination and reception of *Things Fall Apart* has served as a template of sorts, engendering from the outset the tensions and contradictions which have been persistently reproduced in the circulation of African literature around the world to the present day. Described in its initial publishers' reports as 'a very exciting discovery' chronicling 'the break-up of tribal life in one part of Nigeria',[8] the novel was lauded for its simplicity and feted for its ethnographic inquiries, finding its way into discussions of literary value, anthropology and colonial discourse. 'Writing back' to the vision of Africa as a land of savagery and darkness, the distorted reflection of the continent depicted in the work of writers like Joseph Conrad and Joyce Cary,

Achebe's novel became a cornerstone in the project of recuperating a positive notion of African culture and heritage, what the author has described as part of an effort to 'teach [his] readers that their past— with all its imperfections—was not one long night of savagery from which the first Europeans acting on God's behalf delivered them'.[9] Through what has been called a 'deliberate revisionist strategy',[10] which leveraged the imaginative and aesthetic possibilities of the novel form, *Things Fall Apart* would portray, instead, an Africa of dignity and tradition, populated by rounded individuals and rich cultural collectivities. Proving definitively that the privileges of literary voice and aesthetic re-presentation in imaginative writing were no longer the sole property of the colonial masters, Achebe's novel marked the first occasion in which the continent's cry back to its masters might be heard, consecrating anti-colonial sentiment and humanizing, for the first time on a global scale, a distinctly African story of colonialism.

While the novel's positive impact on African writing and in the recuperation of a global image of Africa cannot be overstated, there remains something rather problematic in the way in which, over time, the novel has travelled. In its transnational circulation, that is to say, the novel has been continually marked by a reception rooted in what Henry Louis Gates Jr has termed the 'anthropological fallacy' in black writing,[11] a critical corollary of sorts to Huggan's notion of the anthropological exotic. Arguing that criticism of African and African diaspora writing has emphasized an overdetermined ethnographic dimension to the text, Gates suggests that 'this curious valorization of the social and polemic functions of black literature' has led to a certain repression of the text as a literary work.[12] In other words, by approaching African and African diaspora literature as containing a set of anthropological and ethnographic truths about the society from which it arrives, criticism, Gates contends, has relied upon an overdetermined reading of black social formations and an underdetermined sense of the aesthetic, what Kadiatu Kanneh calls the 'long-standing habit of shunting African literature into a space outside art and literary figuration and into sociological data'.[13] In the case of *Things Fall Apart*, as can be extended to African writing in English more broadly, this appears in the notion that the text teaches us, its Western readers, something about Africa, providing an authentic point of entry into the continent's storied past. Indeed, as Gates points out, until recently, Achebe was more likely to appear on the syllabus of a course in anthropology than English literature, a situation in which, as Low notes, 'the authenticity of the cultural information [has been] presented at the expense of aesthetic complexity'.[14] In the case of *Things Fall Apart*, this sleight of interpretation occurs in spite of the novel's destabilization of totalizing narratives and singular readings of tradition.[15] Based in a critical matrix which valorizes an externally-enforced notion of authenticity, the reception of contemporary African literature shows a similar tension in the desire for imaginative works to teach the global reader something about the continent, to express a certain reality which, while remote and exotic, may remain nonetheless accessible to the Western reader. Literature, in this context, is caught in the contradictory imperatives of a crisis of representation which demands that it be both particular, in its authentic Africanness, and universal, in its accessibility to its Western readers.

To a large degree, the development of this tension has been driven less by strictly literary needs and desires than by external economic forces. As Caroline Davis has illustrated in her study of Oxford's Three Crowns Series, in the context of African literature the two supposedly-discrete realms of symbolic and economic value have long been mutually-implicated, creating a 'paradoxical situation' in which cultural capital is mediated by commercial measures.[16] The African Writers Series, for instance, began with the interrelated goals of developing a body of literature for an emerging middle class, written by, for and from the continent itself, while also providing an international platform and reading public for African writers. Yet, the Series would over time find its ability to sell and market texts on the continent eroded by monetary crises, the spectre of structural adjustment and the attendant 'book famine' of the 1980s and 1990s.[17] For the African Writers Series, this resulted in a reduction of sales on the continent from 80 per cent of net sales at the beginning of the 1980s to only 20 per cent by the decade's end.[18] Today, a situation persists in which African writers must largely look to the West for their audiences, driven perhaps less by a lack of interest in literature on the African continent than has been supposed, and more by the economic imperatives of publishing. Indeed, claims regarding the lack of a reading public on the continent, including Griswold's observation that few, if any, individuals in Nigeria read for pleasure and Achebe's complaint that African readers show a predisposition towards what may be thought of as instrumental, rather than literary, reading,[19] should be tempered by an understanding that, in Africa, local publishing was severely eroded under structural adjustment and general governmental mismanagement throughout the 1980s.[20] Thus, the erosion of public services and subsidies led to a situation in which literary texts, imported by multinational publishers, were priced beyond the means of the average citizen.[21] In valuing literary reading above the so-called instrumental, moreover, a certain generic hierarchy emerges, discounting popular literature, short-form works and other forms of writing crafted for discrete, localized markets.[22] Equally, literary engagement has been far from static on the continent, and a number of factors continues to shape the relative accessibility of texts: continental literary festivals, prizes and workshops; the institution of local presses and publications such as Kenya's *Kwani?* and South Africa's *Chimurenga*; the possibilities brought up by the growing popularity of internet-based publishing and the insistence, from some celebrity writers like Chimamanda Ngozi Adichie and  Ngũgĩ wa Thiong'o, that their works be published both locally and affordably.[23]

In its contemporary guise, African writing in English is no longer subject to the direct patronage of colonial institutions or publishers' series. This is not, however, to suggest that contemporary African writing in English is entirely free from external influence; rather, the institutions with a hand in the formation of African literature today come from more diffuse locations which have become particularly relevant in light of new media. It is certainly true that early African writers, notably figures like Achebe, Ngũgĩ and Soyinka, were significant public figures and spokespeople in their own right. Still, with the spread of internet technologies in an increasingly frenetic global field of transmission and consumption, the situation for the contemporary purveyor of African literature has become exacerbated, its global resonances amplified by the neoliberal impulse to telescope context into slogan. Increasingly, in this scene, sound bites shared on Facebook, one liners easily retweeted and production-laden, feel-good moments of reflection which draw comfortable conclusions in eighteen minutes or less have taken prevalence in the shaping of a collective vision of Africa and the delimitations of the African writer's position. In this era of Internet-based communication and social media, contemporary African writers are simultaneously public figures, called upon to comment on African politics, culture and current affairs, and taken as sagacious experts in representing African for a European and American audience.

Given this context, it is of little surprise that prize culture has become increasingly important in the dissemination and marketing of African literature. In his study of contemporary literary prizes, James English writes that the awarding of literary prizes

> remains a strange practice inasmuch as we continue to be discomfited by what seems an equation of the artist with the boxer or discus-thrower, by a conception of art as a contest or competition from which there must emerge a definite winner, and by the seeming incommensurability of gold-plated medals or crystal statuettes, mounted certificates or outsized checks, with the rare achievements of artistic genius that these objects are supposed to honor and reflect.[24]

Prizes, English supposes, are deeply ambivalent through their inherent contradiction between disinterested creativity and commerce. Yet, in the case of African literature, a body of work which, through its implication into an a priori notion of Africa as that 'other' space, is anything but disinterested, the tensions English describes are both heightened and displaced. Based in a context where 'art's relationships to money, to politics, to the social and the temporal' are already foregrounded,[25] that is to say, the role of prizes and other esteem-based institutions has been particularly fraught. The 'rare achievements of artistic genius', in this context, are already displaced by a global will-to-knowledge and imperative to represent. The Caine Prize for African Writing is perhaps most notable and exemplary in this regard. As an award which offers a significant monetary prize, international exposure and participation in a range of workshops and colloquia, the prize has played an undoubtedly positive role in the fostering of African literature both on the continent and around the world. At the same time, the prize has proven to be an ideal target for critics intent on exposing the neocolonial ramifications of literary prize culture, accused of 'market[ing] certain authors as authentic representatives of something called "Africa", providing authentic access to the "African experience"', while 'participat[ing] in promoting African literature as an exotic commodity and thus contribut[ing] to its "othering" while appropriating it into the Anglo-American cultural capital'.[26] More damningly, the prize restricts itself to works published in English or available in English translation, a pragmatic decision with far-reaching and often-troubling implications for the shaping of African writing on a world stage. Set in a context of increasing stratification, both of the global production of knowledge and of economic power, the prize has been described as simultaneously necessary for the growing transnational profile of African literature and debilitating in its inadvertent fostering of a certain 'aesthetic of suffering', to use Helon Habila's phrase, in global African writing.[27] The debates surrounding the Caine Prize point to the way in which even those most scrupulous institutions and organizations remain subject to a form of international branding, an inadvertent assimilation into a system of inequity in representation where the creation of 'Africa', as a literary vision, is always subject to mediation from the outside. It is certainly not my intention to suggest that institutions such as the African Writers Series, Commonwealth Prize, Caine Prize and now-defunct Noma Prize have nefarious intentions towards the promotion, circulation and diversification of African literature around the globe. Yet, neither are these institutions innocent in their participation in the power structures which shape the asymmetrical system of representation that guides the creation of Africa, as concept, an image and an idea.

The observation that publishing patterns may be ultimately directed by motives beyond the literary is hardly surprising. Indeed, it is difficult to imagine any enterprise, no matter how well-intentioned, which would not be constrained at least to some degree by external factors. In the case of African literature, however, the economic imperative to write Africa through a certain vision is complicated by a concomitant issue of aesthetic production. In her study *World Republic of Letters*, Pascale Casanova makes the claim that literary study in Europe and America has suffered from a distrust of context and an attendant over-valorization of the universal. While much of Casanova's argument focuses on the development and institutionalization of major and minor literatures in Europe, she makes the crucial point that international literary space, as she terms it, functions through an uneven distribution of literary value.[28] As she argues,

The classics are the privilege of the oldest literary nations, which, in elevating their foundational texts to the status of timeless works of art, have defined their literary capital as non-national and ahistorical—a definition that corresponds exactly to the definition that they have given of literature itself.[29]

Put slightly differently, these remarks point to the notion that the very concept of aesthetic universality is itself a sort of mystification. The forms and conventions which we, as readers rooted in Europe and North America, take to be universal, are in fact both particular and realized only through the consolidation of literary value and creative capital in certain parts of the world. For writers from outside of these spheres of literary power, the only path available to literary success is to 'therefore yield to the norms decreed to be universal by the persons who have a monopoly on universality'.[30] As Pierre Bourdieu reminds us, moreover, our evaluations of style are themselves the products of an uneven field of production, where the wielding of cultural capital intersects with the workings of economic power and the construction of social difference:

> A work of art has meaning and interest only for someone who possesses the cultural competence, that is, the code, into which it is encoded. The conscious or unconscious implementation of explicit or implicit schemes of perception and appreciation which constitutes pictorial or musical culture is the hidden condition for recognizing the styles characteristic of a period, school or an author, and, more generally, for the familiarity with the internal logic of works that aesthetic enjoyment presupposes. A beholder who lacks the specific code feels lost in a chaos of sounds and rhythms, colours and lines, without rhyme or reason.[31]

For literary aesthetics, too, such a precarious construction of value persists. Despite claims of artistic autonomy, that is to say, the writer of African literature is caught within a situation in which, through the demands of publishing and the desire for a wide readership, certain aesthetic forms are tacitly endorsed as more valuable, and therefore more apt for consumption, than others. As readers, we evaluate literary works through this framework, in which the work must respond, if only unconsciously, to the codes and patterns which have come to be naturalized as universal, an operation of power and prestige which guides the vision of Africa as the exotic and the already-known.

Recalling 'the dependence of the aesthetic disposition on the past and present material conditions of existence which are the precondition of both its constitution and its application and also to the accumulation of a cultural capital',[32] the construction and consumption of literary aesthetics shifts from a question of disinterested artistic success, or lack thereof, to a question of power and translatability. Deploying the insight that, through their ascription of literary value and prestige, certain national and localized traditions acquire the illusion of universality, alongside the market-oriented imperatives of global publishing, a situation emerges in which the African writer must function in an asymmetrically-weighted transnational sphere of creation and dissemination where the very token 'African' remains perpetually counterbalanced by a universal transparency in form, both exotic and homogenous, strange, but anticipated.[33] Indeed, as has been the case with *Wizard of the Crow*, it is precisely when an author attempts to break away from the supposed universals of literary function that the form of African writing becomes most contentious, open to charges of didacticism, mysticism or obfuscation.

Through the continuing legacies of colonialism, patronage and external economic control, the will to authenticity in African writing and a coexistent imperative towards the universal, African literary writing in English remains to a large degree overdetermined both by the spectre of Africa as the already-known and by the well-rehearsed saga of the African writer operating through the cultural, literary and economic institutions of the West.[34] At the same time, however, African writing remains almost systematically underread. As Brennan reminds us,

> If we look to the future as well as the past, we are met with incompatible visions of community that still suggest binaries of an intractable sort: not three worlds, as might be expected in a discussion of colonialism, but two. In these, one knows the other and the other sees in the one only a closed book. To put the matter another way, Puerto Ricans and Liberians field a larger knowledge of the United States than North Americans do of Puerto Rico and Liberia; the socialist knows the workings of capital with excessive (often even useless) detail, whereas the organic intellectual of capital typically approaches socialism with an uncontested ignorance.[35]

In this situation of asymmetrical knowledge, those with power retain the privilege of ignorance, while those without are destined to learn the rules of the game from without. Those of us who make our profession through the teaching of non-European literatures are all too familiar with the difficulty for students, upon approaching the 'other' text, to separate the literary from the ethnographic and the tendency of students to take single works of literary art as socio-political representative truths of heterogeneous geographies and complex historical moments. As Slaymaker, discussing his experience of teaching *Wizard of the Crow* notes,

> The average undergraduate junior or senior I encounter in a world literature survey class will have little knowledge of African political cultures other than what they might learn from extremely violent films about Africa, or from following various Hollywood and other popular culture celebrities who have adopted African children, established African schools, contributed to AIDS relief, and reveled in their global goodness on various talk shows.[36]

In this context of both presumed mastery and sanctioned, if complex, ignorance, a double bind for the writers of African literature arises, in which the writer is compelled to teach the Western reader something about Africa, displaying the continent in all its strange wonder, while remaining within the boundaries of the a priori. Knowledge, in this context, must never come at the expense of the predetermined, and only that which is already anticipated may come forth as the new.

## Reading 'Africa' on a Global Stage

At the intersection of the economic imperatives of global publishing, the universalizing politics of representation and the struggle over aesthetic form in African writing lies the question of address, what has been called the 'double public' of the African writer.[37] In studies of African literature, the related issues of audience and rhetoric have become commonplace sites of inquiry. For whom does the African author write? Who reads? Are these two imagined groups contiguous? For the writer of contemporary African literature, these questions are particularly heightened through the material circuits of transnational production and reception. Brouillette has described this as a situation in which

> writers' anxiety tends to stem from the dissemination of their texts to reading communities accessing privileged metropolitan markets that are often (though not exclusively) Anglo-American in location and orientation. Writers are compelled to resist, justify, or celebrate precisely this aspect of the postcolonial field's arrangement, in accordance with their own circumstances.[38]

Brouillette's remarks are certainly applicable to African writing published and read in Europe and North America; at the same time, her comments minimize the inherent flexibility of literary writing, as an aesthetic form with an extra-literary representative function. With its powers of naturalizing and normalizing, that is to say, imaginative literature in particular displays a rhetorical function which exploits the perceived gap between author and readership.[39] In his influential work on literary audiences, Peter Rabinowitz identifies four distinct audiences implicit within any text: the actual audience, authorial audience, narrative audience and ideal narrative audience, the former two of which are of the most interest to African writing as discussed here. The actual audience is constituted 'of the flesh-and-blood people who read the book' over whom authors have little control and in whom booksellers have the most interest,[40] while the authorial audience is that audience for whom the author of a book 'designs his work rhetorically'.[41] Rabinowitz suggests that, through authorial reading, actual readers attempt to uncover the author's intentions and meaning, thereby engaging in what he calls the 'politics of interpretation',[42] continuing that 'since the structure of a work is designed with the authorial audience in mind, actual readers must come to share its characteristics as they read if they are to experience the text as the author wished'.[43] Of course, Rabinowitz acknowledges, reading is not always successful in this sense, and, more importantly, misreadings and misfires between the reader, the text and the author are the result of cultural assumptions and predispositions, rather than ignorance or malice, per se. As James Phelan has noted, narratives are acts of purposeful communication,[44] where the 'doubling effect' of textual and readerly dynamics transforms the very act of reading into one complicated by interpretive, ethical and aesthetic judgements.[45] In the context of African literature, this doubling effect is foregrounded because of the geographic and cultural distance assumed between writers, implied readers and actual readers, an effect of the critical notion that African writing today is more widely produced and read in Europe and North America. This presumed distance becomes one which requires what has been characterized as 'a sustained effort of contextualization of the discursive event' and 'a serious adjustment of [the reader's] modes of interpretation', in order that the text may achieve its communicative effect.[46]

The question of multiple audiences and multiple forms of address raises a particular issue in the context of African literature, writ small, and postcolonial literatures, writ large, due in no small part to the aforementioned asymmetry in global knowledge production and ownership. For Gikandi, this problem is one of the missing referent, in which these 'other' texts are read 'without a proper understanding of [their] context or [their] implied and real readers, [their] conditions of production and reception'.[47] In other words, the reading of African literature, Gikandi argues, has displayed a pattern in which specificity and positionality have been minimized in the name of universal discursive forms, resulting in a loss of the text's own position within a local context.[48] While this observation may seem at first curious, given Gates' complaints against the anthropological fallacy in readings of African writing, these two positions are not entirely incompatible. In fact, it is through the very elision of specified historical knowledge and social context that the anthropological fallacy emerges, relying on an overdetermined notion of African authenticity, rather than discrepant and localized forms of contextualized understanding. While not without their own merits, these efforts to read African writing outside of its specificity serve equally to suppress the text as, quite simply, a text. Driven by marketing practices which brand literary production from the continent as 'postcolonial' or 'world literature', African literature, at least that which has found a market in Europe and North America, comes to its reader largely already-read, its interpretation premeditated. In the face of these issues, a number of competing strategies have come to the fore, ranging from Christopher Miller's assertion that particular reading practices need to be developed for African literature based not in 'self-reflexivity and Eurocentrism' but in anthropological inquiry, to Gates' rebuttal that such an act would only serve to further ghettoize African and African diaspora literary production.[49] Comforting though the notion of a 'correct' or specified mode of reading African writing may be, in implying or in supposing that the Western reader flattens the text by reading it incorrectly, it is nearly impossible to avoid a simultaneous suggestion that there exists a single, authorized meaning to the text which can be retrievable through a distinct set of reading practices. This sort of idea is, as Brouillette has pointed out, embedded within the premise of even such nuanced and considered options as Huggan's anthropo-logical exotic, where the idea that a text may be read as exoticized or anthropologized itself indicates that there is another, more genuine reading available, a logic that simply reproduces the divisions it seeks to dismantle.[50] Rather than focusing on a correct or authorized method for reading African literature, then, it seems that turning to the question of multiple audiences presents an alternative paradigm, one which both attends to the specificity of the text, as arising from a certain set of historical, social and cultural formations, while allow-ing for a notion of meaning as dynamic, created both behind it, that is to say, and before it simultaneously. In looking at contemporary writing, the coexistence of multiple levels of address, intended to speak to multiple audiences which may sometimes, but not always, overlap, is both commonplace and frequently strategic in its force. As with *Wizard of the Crow* and *GraceLand*, where the reader versed in Gĩkũyũ folklore and Kenyan history, for the former, or Nigerian Igbo religious belief and postcolonial Nigerian state politics, for the latter, receives one version of the text, while the reader not literate in these contexts receives another, so, too, across the body of work comprising global African literature such multiple stories emerge from the relative ease with which referents, contexts and historical specificities are recognized and read. The text appears not through a single authorized reading, an authentic understanding or an expert perspective, but rather, as a unique event which arises at the interface of actual and possible readings, readers and contexts, enlivening the single text with multiple and coexisting constructions of meaning.

Strategies of address come to the fore in globally-published African literature in a variety of ways which straddle questions of form and content. In works like *Ancestor Stones* and *Wizard of the Crow*, complex forms of narrative play mark one means of exceeding any simplistic or binary-based reader–text relationship, offering, instead, multifaceted modes of communicative exchange which revel in their destabilizing effects. Embedded texts, self-conscious narrators and shifts in voice function together to highlight the contingency of narrative as a communicative act and to render a single reading of the text impossible. Plurality, in both texts, is foregrounded, displacing the singular authority of the monolithic, universal narrator with a formal structure that pushes beyond. In *Harare North*, linguistic innovation creates a similar effect, continually evading mastery and averting fossilization in a voice which foregrounds partial becomings over totalizing beings. Both *Links* and *The Stone Virgins*, meanwhile, illustrate the effects of an elided historical context against a referent which, though unspoken, maintains its spectral hold over the text, allowing the possibility of alternative modes of reading based upon specific historical, social and cultural forms of knowing. Across these works, the unreliability of narrative as a communicative form is not only posited, but centralized as a textual force, as illustrated in *The Book of Not*'s cynical narratorial voice. Speaking to the past from some unspecified future, with all of the shortcomings and revisionism of hindsight on display, Tambu's retrospective narration continually betrays its work as narrative, destabilizing its own attempts at naturalization. The directive to authenticity, in this context, lays bare its contingency and its always-only retrospective ordering. Across this body of work, language, the very act of communication through oral and written forms, becomes a means of foregrounding these rhetorical impulses, providing a sort of meta-commentary both on the power of knowledge and on questions of authority and authorization in the creation and dissemination of any story.

In *GraceLand* and *Half of a Yellow Sun*, this appears through the narrative trope of the book within the book, a paratextual play on the deployment of writing as a form of legitimizing authority. In Adichie's novel, this emerges through the textual insertion of eight extracts, initially titled only 'The Book', which is later revealed to be 'The World Was Silent When We Died', the history of Biafra written by Ugwu, the subaltern houseboy-turned chronicler of the nation.[51] Of the eight extracts of The Book, six are placed immediately following chapters focalized by Richard (*HYS*, p. 82; p. 115; p. 155; p. 237; p. 258; p. 375). Of the remaining two, the fourth extract comes at the end of a chapter focalized by Ugwu and the eighth and final extract, definitively delineating authorship, comes at the novel's conclusion, following a chapter focalized by Olanna (*HYS*, pp. 204–5; p. 433). Throughout, these extracts re-imagine moments from the narrative, recounting their process of re-telling through descriptions which highlight the act of writing in a multiplicity of registers, including historical analysis, personal narrative and poetry. The tendency for the extracts from The Book to occur at the end of Richard's chapters, in tandem with Richard's own musings on his desire to write a book about Nigeria-Biafra, creates a narrative effect which, throughout the novel, leads the reader to believe that they are from Richard's work in progress. It is only in the novel's antepenultimate chapter, focalized by Ugwu, that the novel reveals The Book's true authorship. In the context of the narrative as a whole, the revelation that The Book is authored by Ugwu, rather than Richard, serves as a rhetorical gesture that engages the questions of authorship and the larger right to speak for any people, invoking an authorial audience incongruous with *Half of a Yellow Sun*'s presumed actual audience.

While Adichie makes an explicit statement about cultural ownership and the right to narrate history, Abani creates a subtler narrative statement on collective identifications and authenticity. *GraceLand* similarly functions through the embedding of a book-within-the-book, here figured through twenty-seven extracts, written in an italic font and set on separate pages between each of the novel's chapters. Taken from Elvis's mother's journal, the Bible, the call to prayer of Islam and an Onitsha market chapbook entitled *Mabel, the Sweet Honey that Poured Away*, these extracts are diverse and vary widely in their content and tone. At the same time, each insert relates directly to the main narrative, appearing either as part of a specific narrative episode or as part of the larger narrative frame of Elvis's attempts to reconcile himself with his repressed past and bleak present, while remaining external to it. The inserts thus embody the twin notions of the Derridean supplement, that which extends an original as an extraneous addition while completing it as an integral element, and the frame, that which both encloses from the exterior while also giving rise to the main narrative, in an incongruous relation of dependence and erasure.[52] As the texts within the text show, the narrative's cultural contact zone is far broader than any singular notion of African or Nigerian experience, escaping the Manichean division of the West versus rest. Abani has stated that his intention, in presenting these extracts, was to force a different engagement with the text;[53] by representing traditional, Christian, Islamic and popular beliefs, the inserts in *GraceLand* reflect the diversity and often oppositional interactions of Nigerian society at a wider level, marking the liminality and porosity of collective identifications. Thus, the use of these inserts becomes a means of escaping the binary-based entrapment of cultural thinking which functions in absolutes, viewing itself either as traditional or modern, authentic or false.

The peculiar difficulties apparent in the act of 'reading' African literature on a global stage are not, however, entirely avoided through these sorts of rhetorical gestures, aesthetic manoeuvres and strategic encodings of address, as the example of *Things Fall Apart* has illustrated. Indeed, there remains a sense in which the power of the text to resist assimilation and appropriation remains beyond its boundaries. The text, that is to say, is never just the text and the strategies encoded within are never subject to a strictly literary interpretation. Instead, functioning within a broader public sphere, the literary text remains subject to mediation by its conditions of production and reception, one in which it is entrapped between the twinned but oppositional imperatives to represent an authentically African experience and voice that is nevertheless mediated and determined by a universalized set of Euro-American valuations and constraints. The issues which arise with this double bind are not isolated incidents, as a recent change to the wording of the Caine Prize's eligibility criteria reflects. In February 2012, a section stating that eligible texts should capture an 'African sensibility' was removed. Both that from the prize's founding until 2012 this call to the deliberately vague notion of 'an African sensibility' was considered a salient criterion and its subsequent removal are cause for reflection. Huggan has criticized prize culture for its complicity with commodity fetishism based around an aesthetic of exoticism.[54] On the surface, it appears that a similar criticism may be applied to the notion of an 'African sensibility', as developed by the Caine Prize committee. Certainly, it is impossible to define a concrete set of guidelines which might delineate the parameters of an 'African sensibility' without reverting to stereotype or satire. It is precisely this notion which critics like Ikheloa and Dobrota Pucherová critique in their contention that the Caine Prize encourages a 'stereotypical' view of the continent in which writers themselves are complicit.[55] Yet, there is a degree to which this line of commentary misses the point: it is precisely because there is no way to define or engender an 'African sensibility' that the term has such potency. Like the continent itself, the idea of 'an African sensibility' both alludes to a sense of closure while simultaneously defying any single statement of being or unified interpretation. It is this quality of the impossible, the multiple and the ever-shifting which the ambiguous wording captures, existing under erasure to open up the possibility of becoming otherwise. Yet, this more positive reading of the term evidently was not sustainable in the context of an asymmetrically-loaded publishing industry where such a sentiment was recognized as both 'impossible to define' and 'also potentially predetermin[ing] content'.[56] Beyond being simply a case of bureaucratic minutia, the struggle over the wording of the Caine Prize guidelines points to a more general tension surrounding African literature read globally: African writing has to be, in some way, identifiable as African, be it through its authorial subject, content, form or function. At the same time, it is impossible to identify a text as simply African because such a singular ascription does not exist.

Rather than rely on notions of 'correct' or 'incorrect' reading, then, it is perhaps more useful to remember that the African literary text is a global artefact of sorts, existing in the world and circulating across an uneven field of cultural and social capital, creating different readings and valuations through its different uses and contexts. As cultural artefacts actually-existing in the world, African literary texts, with all of their discursive and textual innovations, are nonetheless subject to closure, erasure and commoditization. Through their circulation in an uneven field of literary value and cultural capital, these works, their dissemination and their reception, aptly illustrate the notion of uneven cultural sharings in different, and often incompatible, regimes of value.[57] As exchangeable objects circulating across cultural borders, that is to say, these texts demonstrate the ways in which the travelling of cultural objects, at the interface of commodified exchange value and universalized literary value, marks out a site of uneven valuation, translation, and transformation in the construction of meaning, created through the constraints of circulation in the public sphere and the 'specificity of material domains'.[58] Critically, this meaning and its attendant notion of value are constructed precisely through the systems of social exchange through which these texts travel the world, arriving in Europe and North America for consumption and exchange. Through what Daniel

Miller terms 'externalization and sublation', 'Africa', travelled to Europe and North America, gets its very meaning.[59] It is because of this uneasy movement and transformation, perhaps, that critical and popular readings of these novels have shown a decided hesitancy to reckon with their multifocality, demonstrated in the repeated return to invocations both of Africa, as a defining notion in these works, and 'universality', as a yardstick for success, throughout maintaining a sense of the anxiety that comes with any effort to represent or to write Africa. Of course, writers and readers are not passive dupes in this regard, and numerous possibilities for resistance, both in writing and reading, persist. At the same time, the conditions which place these possibilities under constant threat remain salient in their materiality.

## Local Engagements and Transnational Constraints

Francis B. Nyamnjoh's *The Disillusioned African*, G. A. Agambila's *Journey* and Valerie Tagwira's *The Uncertainty of Hope* are not likely to be familiar to global readers of African literature; certainly, none of these three texts nor their authors can be said to have reached the critical or commercial success of Adichie, Abani, Forna, Farah, Dangarembga, Vera, Chikwava or Ngũgĩ. All three have been published by local African presses (*The Disillusioned African* by Bamenda's Langaa Research and Publishing Common Initiative Group, *Journey* by Accra's Sub-Saharan Publishers and *The Uncertainty of Hope* by Harare's Weaver Press), and though all three are currently marketed internationally through the African Books Collective none have received the same level of international attention as the aforementioned authors. It is tempting, based on this information, to suggest that these locally-published authors form a category strictly opposed to their globally-published counterparts. This is not, however, entirely evident. Like many of the more celebrated authors of African literature, Agambila, Nyamnjoh and Tagwira have all spent significant periods of their lives in Europe and North America for both study and work. Agambila holds degrees from Brandeis University and a PhD from New York University, while Nyamnjoh earned a PhD from the University of Leicester and currently lives outside of his native Cameroon as a professor of social anthropology at the University of Cape Town. Tagwira, who took her medical degree in Harare, nevertheless spent a period of years working in London, joining the Royal College of Obstetricians and Gynaecologists, and she has also been included in the 2010 Caine Prize anthology for her short fiction, exposing at least some of her work to a broader global audience. Equally, globally-recognized authors like Adichie and Wainaina maintain residences on the African continent, while others remain active in the nurturing of local literary voices through participation in continental literary festivals and workshops. By all accounts, then, these two bodies of work cannot be distinguished by invoking authorial identity or a simple local/global dichotomy; instead, a more complex set of factors surrounding textual production, literary form and transnational consumption appears at the heart of what separates these two groups of writers.

Neither Nyamnjoh, Agambila nor Tagwira work full time as professional authors. This is not, of course, to say that none of the three writes in a polished or developed style, but rather to simply point out that all three maintain careers outside of the literary world. Agambila is a prominent Ghanaian politician, having served as a Deputy Minister of State in the Ministries of Finance and Economic Planning, Harbours and Railways, and Environment and Science and unsuccessfully running for Minister of Parliament for Bolgatanga Central in 2012, Tagwira is a practising OB-GYN and lecturer at the University of Zimbabwe's Medical School, and Nyamnjoh is best known as an anthropologist. These facts of occupation are of no little significance given Brouillette's observation 'that literary production is influenced by the development of authorship as a profession and by the process through which writers consume images of themselves and reinterpret those images in order to negotiate and circulate different ones'.[60] Through the relative (in)feasibility of professional authorship, there appears a fundamental distinction between these two loosely-categorized bodies of writing, in which a different, if not entirely incongruous, set of anxieties, motivations and constraints comes into play in the way each author re(-)presents Africa. These locally-published texts, in other words, may be distinguished from their globally-recognized counterparts not through invocations of locality versus globality or authenticity versus modernity, necessarily, but through their patterns of production, address and reception. As non-professional writers, published largely outside of the global literary market and its attendant demands, Tagwira, Agambila and

Nyamnjoh may become subject to a certain freedom from what has been alternately termed the postcolonial aura, the aesthetics of post-modernism or the geopolitical aesthetic of postcolonial writing,[61] a shift in both reference and address which resonates through their respective literary works.

Significant in this regard are critical observations that contemporary African literature, by which is always meant African writing published in North America and Europe, is distinct from earlier African writing through its hesitancy to directly engage with the political, as such, in favour of the personal. *Half of a Yellow Sun*, for instance, has been praised as 'a defense of the personal against the dehumanizing effects of war',[62] a novel that dwells 'on the book's principal players, rather than on the politics and strategies that shaped the war'.[63] In similar terms, both Adichie's and Forna's work have been cited as particularly preoccupied with interpersonal intimacy,[64] while, as Annie Gagiano points out, much of the criticism on *The Stone Virgins* has centred on 'debates about [its] historical and/or political adequacy or inadequacy'.[65] More broadly speaking, Ojaide has complained that contemporary African writing, written by the 'children of the post-colony', in Adesanmi's phrase,[66] because of its diasporic location, is largely estranged from the realities of life on the continent,[67] a sentiment echoed in comments which highlight the diasporic and diffuse characteristics of this body of work. In each case, contemporary African writing is seen as strikingly libidinal in its force, escaping the vestiges of the political in favour of the personal in a seeming inversion of Jameson's classification of national allegory. Yet, despite these claims and in stark contrast, *The Disillusioned African*, *Journey* and *The Uncertainty of Hope* display a preoccupation with the political as a central fulcrum around which each novel pivots. Here, this 'other' African literature grapples repeatedly and overtly with the legacies and continuities of colonial violence on the African continent in three distinct geographical locations, foregrounding the political as a central force in the everyday lives of its characters, inescapable and all-permeating of even the most private of spaces.

*The Disillusioned African* takes the form of four long letters written in the late 1980s and early 1990s from Charles, a thirty-something philosophy student from Douala, the 'economic capital' of Cameroon,[68] who has travelled to the United Kingdom for a period of study, to his friend Moungo, as well as a short epilogue authored by the latter.

Through its epistolary form, the novel functions primarily as a screed against the economic and political stagnation of contemporary Cameroon, in particular, and the African continent, in general, breaking into extended reflections which castigate not only the continued neocolonial influence of the former colonizers, but also the postcolonial hijacking of the African nation-state by an alienated bourgeois class of elite compradors. Drawing on the controversy which marked Cameroon's 1992 presidential elections, the novel rails against the complacency of a population content to accede to the dictates of an alienated leadership. For Charles, the development of colonialism and all its legacies are intimately entwined with larger structures of capitalist rule and inequality. As he informs Moungo, 'the first time Europeans convinced themselves that Africans were fools, inferiors, and monkeys [...] was when Capitalism was beginning to take shape, and slaves sold like tea and coffee would be here in the heart of winter' (*DA*, p. 4). Through their control of capitalist systems of exchange, Charles continues, 'The Europeans succeeded in "infusing into Africans strange ideas of themselves as superior beings"' (*DA*, p. 5), engendering a centuries-long global situation in which Africa would be 'milked' (*DA*, p. 17) for its resources by a Europe authorized with the legitimacy to import systems of valuation which would function to subordinate Africans 'from all sorts of angles—religious, cultural, political, economic, etc' (*DA*, p. 80). Pointing to the hypocrisy at the heart of colonial intervention, which purports to save but can only do so by destroying, *The Disillusioned African* portrays an African continent still reeling from global systems of inequality and misrule.

This sentiment is echoed in *Journey*, a novel which tells the story of Amoah, former prefect and recent graduate from a European-led secondary school in Ghana. Hailing from the northern village of Tinga, a place which 'has never appeared on any map',[69] Amoah is sent by his grandfather to the school in the hopes that he might return home and use his education to help his village fight against a corrupt government that is gradually stealing all of their land. Instead, Amoah falls prey to the ideological dictates of the school environment, content in his place in its rigid hierarchy. The narrative is split into three parts, following Amoah in his final days at school, a brief visit to his grandfather's home in Tinga and, finally, to Accra, where he goes to find work in the hopes of raising money for his ailing grandfather's medical care. Throughout, the first-person narrative adopts an inadvertently ironic tone, subtly satirizing Amoah's steadfast belief in the system and his ability to rise through its ranks. From its early pages, where Amoah absorbs his Headmaster's lessons about African inadequacies, reflecting that 'Punctuality is important. The Headmaster has said this a million times. He says we Africans have no sense of time, that is why we've been tardy in our development. It is true' (*J*, p. 27), to the novel's end when the seduction of schoolgirl Mmah provides Amoah with momentary respite from his hopeless existence, the novel narrativizes the lasting legacies of colonialism in the inadequacies of everyday life in Ghana, a nation of strangers with polarized loyalties. As Mr Doe, the master of Amoah's significantly-named Rhodes house, informs him in his final days at school:

> We sit here and shout about our independence. Independence from who? Independence for who? We cannot talk of independence while our peoples' minds remain enslaved. Real freedom lives in the mind. The struggle against neo-colonialism must be waged in our peoples' minds. The problem is that our nation is led by a pack of ignorant stooges. (*J*, p. 97)

Drawing a direct link between the perpetuation of neocolonial hierarchies of power and the institutional structures put in place under colonialism, Mr Doe laments the continued subjugation of the nation and its people, viewing independence as little more than a sham. Despite his belief that Mr Doe was 'a strange man' (*J*, p. 99) with his distrust of the elite, Amoah, as the narrative progresses, cannot help but observe the debilitating effects of colonial systems of value on the population at large, despite his determination not to. Dwelling upon the dilapidated buses which move the majority of the population in their daily travels, the inadequacy of public services priced beyond the average citizen's means and the stunted mind-set of villagers 'still talking about pounds, shillings, and pence' in an independent Ghana (*J*, p. 115), *Journey*'s narrative functions through a pattern of oppositions and stunted progressions which foregrounds the contingency of postcoloniality's developmentalist mythologies. As in *The Disillusioned African*, in *Journey*, the African nation-state is figured less as a space of freedom than one of arrested decolonization, where true independence remains remote.

Despite this focus on the continuities linking colonial and postcolonial systems of inequity, neither *Journey* nor *The Disillusioned African* depicts colonialism as the singular cause of Ghana's or Cameroon's postcolonial malaise, complicating each narrative's political thrust. Indeed, as *The Disillusioned African*'s Charles remarks, that viewpoint would be a 'myopia [...] too dangerous to harbour' (*DA*, p. 169). Rather, colonialism is presented as part of a longer process of alienation and stratification whose perpetuation is implicated in the very social fabric of each nation, written into its founding under neo-imperial interests. Much of *Journey*'s narrative dwells upon the gaping chasm between the upper and lower classes in contemporary Ghana, a hierarchal reproduction of inequity from which Amoah cannot escape. Describing the ways in which government policies both consolidate the subordination of rural populations stripped of their land rights (*J*, pp. 30–1), and perpetuate their material diminishment through the nationalization of industry and attendant requirements to sell crops and services to the government at below-market rates (*J*, p. 219), *Journey*'s narrative depicts Ghana as a place in which the average citizen finds little outlet for upward mobility or economic stability. Through 'the knowledge that failure will sentence [him] to life with hard labour and endless drudgery', Amoah is driven to educational success, seeing it as his one opportunity to 'have all those things [he has] seen others have' and find a route to happiness through material prosperity (*J*, p. 72). As he wonders, 'What is the use of education if it doesn't free your hands from calluses and grime?' (*J*, p. 93). Yet, this meritocratic view of society can never be fully realized, as Amoah is instead driven, time and again, to manual labour as his only option for survival. Though educated and relatively privileged as such, Amoah remains constrained by his subject position as a child of the village, consigned to the very life of 'endless drudgery' which he hopes to forestall and at the mercy of public facilities which, in an era of structural adjustment, remain inaccessible to the everyday citizen (*J*, pp. 96–7).

Joining his uncle and family in Accra, Amoah's life is dictated by the conditions of the Sabon Zongo, a place in which homes are built on top of one another and sewage runs freely in the small spaces between not, as he supposes, to 'promote intimacy' (*J*, p. 223), but to enclose. Separated from the rest of the city by a sewage-infested river called the Black Nile, the Sabon Zongo represents the postcolonial slum, a space in which urbanization, decoupled from industrialization, leads to the rapid reproduction both of poverty and of the Manichean binaries of colonialism, now transformed into a binary between the bourgeois elite and the everyday citizen.[70] In this stratified city, Amoah's one hope for change comes through employment with the National Beef Corporation, overseeing quality control in the production of corned beef. Here, too, however, the promise of economic emancipation remains remote, as a full month's salary gives Amoah barely enough to afford his grandfather's transportation to Accra, let alone his medical fees. Summarily laid off with nothing but 'a casual labourer's wage' when cattle supplies run short (*J*, p. 274), Amoah is brought face to face with his disposability as an exchangeable commodity, an unskilled worker, and the futility of a life spent working for naught, emphasized when his grandfather dies before he is able to bring him to the city. In so doing, the novel serves as a morality tale of sorts, a caution against those who, like Amoah in its first sections, revel uncritically in the status quo, taking the everyday at face value.

*The Disillusioned African*'s Charles, in his letters to Moungo, takes a harsher stance against 'arrested decolonization' on the African continent, stating that 'Africa's greatest enemy is its leaders' (*DA*, p. 44) and repeatedly castigating the 'black pawns' who have frittered away the freedom brought by peasant sacrifices (*DA*, p. 29). Highlighting the alienation, excess and inferiority of a leadership educated in Europe and North America, who continue to fly to London for supper on a whim at the expense of the everyday citizen (*DA*, pp. 46–7), Charles laments the hypocrisy of those 'Europhiles [who] have always made the world believe that what they do is representative of Africa. Quite tragic, for they are precisely the sort of people who ought not to be contacted, if one is interested in the truth about Africa' (*DA*, p. 60). For Charles, the continuities between colonialism and contemporary governmental corruption are made clear through the actions of 'the self-elected watchdogs of the National Cake' (*DA*, p. 40), whose self-interest guides governmental policy at the expense of the peasantry. In a distinctly Fanonian sentiment, Charles expresses his admiration for those underrepresented rural subjects, who he sees as the only true force of revolutionary potential on the continent, lamenting their 'pathetic' position as they 'toil[] under the sun, moon and stars, like Jimmy Cliff's slave-parents did, in order to sustain the urban centres with their bunches of consumerist civil servants and professional idlers of [Moungo's] calibre' (*DA*, p. 31), 'exploited by two forces' (*DA*, pp. 33–4). Indeed, it is out of a desire to take action with these people that Charles, by the novel's end, leaves the United Kingdom for Zaire. In a mode which is as reminiscent of Ngũgĩ as it is Fanon, Charles decries the 'blanchification' of the continent and the self-imposed alienation of the African middle classes, lamenting his own entrapment within a colonial mentality which led him to 'come all the way to Europe to study what [he] should study in Africa' (*DA*, p. 158). As he explains it, 'being educated in Europe is like paying money to be trained into a mercenary or a crusader for European cultures and values in Africa' (*DA*, p. 158). The only solution, the novel concludes, is to turn away from these institutions of false consciousness towards the peasantry, working to combat the continent's problems through the liberation and education of its masses. Yet, this solution, too, remains partial, mediated through Charles's often-pontificating and unsympathetic voice and his fate as one literally cut in pieces by his dogmatic romanticism, losing limbs in two separate attacks while he attempts to 'educate' the rural populations.

The concerns developed in *The Disillusioned African* and *Journey* are echoed in *The Uncertainty of Hope*, as protagonist Onai struggles to eke out a subsistence living for herself and her three children in Mbare, one of the largest slums of Harare. Like *The Disillusioned African* and *Journey*, *The Uncertainty of Hope* addresses the general misgovernment of contemporary African nation-states and the corruption amongst those that are intended to help the needy, depicting an array of characters from a broad range of social and economic positions to highlight the disparities, discrepancies and possibilities of contemporary Zimbabwe. Throughout the novel, Onai reckons with her unfaithful, alcoholic husband Gari, whose physical abuse sends her to the hospital early in its pages. As she attempts to better her life in a declining economic situation in which everyday commodities remain inaccessible to those unable to pay in US dollars, Onai is repeatedly brought face to face with the disinterest and corruption of a disillusioned bureaucracy. Tagwira's novel is particularly insightful in its depiction of the relatively unknown 2005 Operation Murambasvina (literally, 'Drive Out Trash'). As Mike Davis describes it, 'In the aftermath of the corruption-tainted 2005 Zimbabwe elections, President Robert Mugabe turned his wrath against the street markets and shantytowns of Harare and Bulawayo, where the poor had voted in large numbers for the opposition Movement for Democratic Change'.[71] In its first stage, the Operation destroyed thirty-four local markets across Harare, leading to the arrest of 17,000 stallholders and informal drivers, and displaced over 700,000 slum dwellers in what the UN would term 'a catastrophic injustice' that would hit women, children, the disabled and the elderly with particular force.[72] At first met with disbelief, Operation Murambasvina marks a watershed moment in *The Uncertainty of Hope*: 'For the majority, the market had been their sole source of livelihood. It had been bad enough before, but this new calamity would remove their only means of supporting their families'.[73] Describing the carnage as 'Rocks, fruits, vegetables and other objects flew in the air as angry people hit back at the police, who were assaulting them and launching tear-gas canisters into the air' (*UH*, p. 133), the novel depicts the transformation of 'thriving market area' into 'piles of rubble' (*UH*, p. 164). For many of the novel's characters, this assault marks a breaking point, forcing some deeper into the informal economy and others into exile and homelessness. For Onai, her fellow stallholders and slum dwellers, the ramifications of Operation Murambasvina are amplified through an official rhetoric intent on development at any human cost. Forced to send her children to trade small foodstuffs at the local bus depot, Onai finds herself plunged deeper and deeper into poverty in a Zimbabwe where 'a poor woman will always be a poor woman' (*UH*, p. 18), with little left to hope for.

Beyond its fictionalized portrayal of Zimbabwe's recent history, the novel spends much of its length engaged in an extended discourse on the problem of HIV and AIDS in contemporary Africa and the particular dangers which women face. Unlike *Wizard of the Crow*, where Ngũgĩ's discourse on AIDS prevention appears in an isolated narrative episode, here, AIDS, the fear of AIDS, and women's vulnerability to AIDS function as central narrative themes. Indeed, for many of the novel's women, AIDS seems a matter less of prevention than resignation, where the fear of hunger remains more imminent than fear of the disease (*UH*, p. 82). Onai, after learning that her philandering and abusive husband Gari has taken up with Gloria, a notorious local prostitute, worries that she, too, would now be infected with the virus. With few drugs available, those donated by international agencies filched by the unscrupulous for sale at inflated prices on the street (*UH*, p. 61), HIV and AIDS '[hang] over [Onai] like a hangman's noose' (*UH*, p. 126). In a rare display of personal assertiveness that she terms 'Her biggest failure as a wife' (*UH*, p. 69), Onai goes so far as to refuse intercourse with Gari without a condom. Like the novel's other women, Onai is drawn into a situation in which, treated as an exchangeable commodity by a patriarchal system of power, few options remain available for self-protection. The one promise of hope lies in the novel's extended plea for the contemporary Zimbabwean woman to use the female condom, described in the text as 'a blessing' that allows some semblance of freedom (*UH*, p. 70), sounding a call for an alternative form of feminine agency which, while working within systems of patriarchal inequity, nonetheless finds a space for action.

In contrast to *Ancestor Stones*, *The Stone Virgins* and *Half of a Yellow Sun*, *The Uncertainty of Hope* develops a more pessimistic reading of patriarchal norms and women's oppression in contemporary Zimbabwe. Onai remains steadfastly faithful to her marriage, despite Gari's continued violence and infidelities. Even her rebellion against unprotected sex is tempered by Gari's role of head of the household:

> However, her stance had cost her a great deal. The escalating beatings were ample testimony of Gari's reaction to her defiance. According to him, condoms were what a man used when he thought of sleeping with a prostitute, not with his own wife for whom he had paid a grand total of ten cows and an expensive coat for her father, as *marooro*. (*UH*, pp. 69–70)

As she later muses, 'It was a man's prerogative to run his household as he wished, with no allegiance to any rules, especially those dictated by a woman. Her husband was no exception. He was, after all, a man, no less so than the next' (*UH*, p. 121). Faced with her friends' pleas to leave Gari, Onai reflects upon the precarity of a woman's situation in a contemporary Zimbabwe still under the thrall of traditionalist modes of social organization:

> How could she possibly face a world that despised divorcees; looked down on single mothers? Marital status was everything. It did not really matter how educated or otherwise skilled a woman

was. A woman's worth was relative to one man, her husband: westernised values about women surviving outside marriage help no authenticity *mumusha*. (*UH*, p. 46)

Onai's attitude towards her relationship proves a point of frustration for her friends, who cannot understand why she continues to persist in a family where, even after Gari's death, 'as a woman, a widow, she had no rights to take any independent initiative' (*UH*, p. 248). Yet, even the more vocally-liberated characters display a similar pragmatism towards the subject positions and options available to women in contemporary Zimbabwe. Katy, Onai's closest confidante, goes so far as to purchase condoms for her husband to carry on his cross-border trips to South Africa, viewing infidelity as an inevitability. Even 'enlightened' university student Faith dispiritedly acknowledges the need, for her less-fortunate classmates, to find wealthy men to support their educations. Yet, rather than appear as passive victims, the women of *The Uncertainty of Hope* are rounded characters who survive through their sheer tenacity in the face of seemingly insurmountable odds, gesturing beyond the monolithic ideologies portrayed in the novel towards discrepant futures and alternative possibilities. Throughout the novel, these women are depicted both as aware of the precarity of their social positions and as singularly flexible in their methods of coping, illustrating an adherence to what novelist Chike Unigwe has called 'negofeminism', a mode of engagement 'which stays within the boundaries of social and cultural norms, but which also manipulates that space'.[74] As pragmatic agents, the women of *The Uncertainty of Hope* appear aware of the need for alternative modes of protest and deliberate engagement to confront a corrupt and uncaring system without fear of retribution. These women thus recognize the very rootedness of the political, remaining situated within a localized context in their calls for change, rather than reverting to a universalized plea for human rights that erases specificity. Hope for the future may appear bleak in this situation, and yet it remains through the work of Kushinga Women's Project, where Faith, an aspiring lawyer, and Emily, a medical doctor, fight to empower voiceless women like Onai and struggle for structural change. Across the generations, feminist engagement deepens and, while progress remains gradual, the narrative nonetheless gestures towards a horizon of possibility.

Throughout all three novels, ideals of development and postcolonial progress are continually brought to question through narrative forms which place seemingly intractable institutional powers side by side with the multifarious tactics of everyday life. Where, in *Journey* and *The Disillusioned African*, these issues arise through the function of education in the perpetuation of an alienated elite and the inability of the average citizen to find a piece of the so-called national cake, in *The Uncertainty of Hope* the rhetoric of developmentalism is questioned through the material ravages of Operation Murambasvina upon the local population. In the latter novel, debates between Faith and her fiancé, wealthy farm-owner Tom, highlight the discrepant attitudes to human rights and development in a national context where 'varying degrees of protection existed for particular groups in society' (*UH*, p. 170). Placing Tom's assertions that the clearing of market places and slums would provide space and resources for the building of better homes and more beneficial public services alongside Onai's futile quest to find housing and employment, the novel foregrounds the human toll of international financial rhetoric and the collateral damages that a single-minded quest for development, defined in unitary terms and pursued at all costs, leaves in its wake. All three novels, then, highlight the inadequacy of universalized human rights discourses, and the feasibility of alternative strategies for Africa, based at the level of local engagements and populist movements which function not through the benevolence of multinationals and NGOs, but from the bottom up. At the same time, none of these three novels is myopic in its focus on the African continent, seeking, instead, to expose the global continuities through which development, structural adjustment, and the notion of a postcolonial progress function in imaginative forms which foreground the human.

Given these comments, the observation that *Journey*, *The Uncertainty of Hope* and *The Disillusioned African* function within distinctly national frames of reference may come as little surprise. Indeed, even the very language of each text belies this focus: *Journey* reproduces much of its dialogue in Ghanaian pidgin, while *The Uncertainty of Hope* and *The Disillusioned African* gesture to Zimbabwe's and Cameroon's multilingual histories, blending Shona, Ndebele and English in the former and French and English in the latter. Still, the observation that these are novels embedded within specific national contexts is of no little significance given the growing tendency to think beyond the nation in commentary on African literature. In his introduction to *The Granta Book of the African Short Story*, Habila writes that contemporary African literature can be characterized by its 'post-national' character, an attribute in which the global, the diasporic, the cosmopolitan and the multiply-rooted are privileged over the local, tacitly deemed static. Explaining that his 'use of the term "post-nationalist" is aspirational', Habila argues that contemporary African writing has

> the best potential to liberate itself from the often predictable, almost obligatory obsession of the African writer with the nation and national politics, an obsession that at times has been beneficial to African writing, but more often has been restrictive and confining to the African writer's ambition.[75]

While not, by any means, an observation without reason, these locally-published works display a distinct preoccupation with the nation that challenges Habila's claims. With these novels, then, two interrelated observations arise. First, it appears that, through the very centrality of the nation to their narrative frames, these novels aptly represent the problem of the referent as outlined by Gikandi, necessitating a direct engagement with the specificity of historical and social context in the act of consumption. These portrayals of the nation are far from static or predictable, depicting the national space as multifocal, complex and particular in its formation. *The Disillusioned African* functions through the development of resistance in the aftermath of the 1992 elections, sounding a call for political engagement in the face of structural adversity. *Journey*, meanwhile, operates fully within the context of contemporary Ghana, attempting to recover from the erosion of public life brought on by structural adjustment. In *The Uncertainty of Hope*, the ravages of Mugabe's regime against its most vulnerable citizens form a crucial component of character motivation and development. In each case, the extra-literary referent provides critical grounding for the discursive functions of the text. Emerging from this observation is a second, more potent effect, suggesting that reports of the death of the nation in African literature have been greatly exaggerated. Throughout Tagwira's, Agambila's and Nyamnjoh's novels, the nation persists, both as a salient power and as a form of personal identification for its subjects. For those everyday citizens not endowed with the privilege of migrancy or peripatetic celebration, the nation remains a central point both of identification and of materiality. Where, paradoxically, the emphasis on the post-national and the cosmopolitan has inadvertently defined a vision of Africa and African writing dictated by the allegedly disinterested norms of the universal, these other voices risk suppression. Yet, positioned outside of the celebratory rhetoric of migrancy, these works display a sense of locality as dynamic and productive.[76] Rather than cry for liberation from the nation, it is the imagined national space which enlivens each text, obscuring attempts to assimilate each into a bland universalism. Where, as Newell writes, authors in the era of independence were compelled to 'imagine new national communities for themselves',[77] Tagwira, Nyamnjoh and Agambila, it seems, reflect a desire to imagine newly-awoken, politically-committed, and locally-rooted national communities.

Each of these novels presents a picture of Africa that is simultaneously part of the a priori notion of Africa as the already-known, and yet startlingly different. In each novel, Africa appears as a broken space, corrupt and poorly managed. Yet, none of these three novels allows for an acritical view of this breakdown in governance and civic life. Rather, this continental collapse is contextualized as part of intersecting local, global and postcolonial histories, depicting an Africa rarely given voice in the global imaginary, where disillusionment and stagnancy coexist with individual ingenuity and personalized modes of agency. This is not an Africa of exoticism or primordial wisdom, nor is it an Africa of tribal mysticism or folkloric knowledge. Rather, this is an urban and working-class Africa, where cultural tradition permeates without obfuscating, populated by characters with distinct visions of the world and perspectives which may not be entirely comprehensible to the Western reader, but which remain nonetheless coherent. The Africa that emerges from these texts is released from its absorption into the universal, embedded within its local histories and discrepant modernities. The anxieties of the a priori, through this depiction of an Africa that is not one, are made irrelevant, as the call to personal action and responsibility triumphs over apprehension. In so doing, these novels reveal themselves to be positioned not towards the international vision of the Western reader, but rather towards the local, middle-class reader. If, as critics ranging from Derek Attridge to Robert Spencer have suggested, the power of literature for the Western reader, particularly postcolonial writing, is to engender an openness to the other, a certain cosmopolitan sentiment,[78] these texts display a rhetorical function intended to effect an alterity which demands political engagement for the locally-situated African reader. The opening to the other seen as characteristic of all imaginative writing, here, transforms into a plea for action at the collective level. As *The Disillusioned African*'s Charles writes, few forces 'can beat the resolve of a people who believe they've had enough of a tyrant' (*DA*, p. 234). With this shift in external perspective, these texts appear to be driven less directly by the anxieties of re(-)presentation and more by the socio-political function of the novel as a means of engagement and consummation of a national collective feeling which comes with a sense of responsibility towards one's fellow citizens.

As the examples discussed from each text might indicate, from a formalist perspective, all three of these texts display some of the 'conventional and naïve' aesthetics which, following Jameson, the First World reader may decry, in a departure from the universalized, postmodern, postcolonial aesthetic of contemporary global fiction. Here, however, it is crucial to recall that these matters of taste function simultaneously as operations of power, rather than objective facts of literary value. Functioning through local systems of publishing and alternative modes of marketing, these texts retain a certain scope in which to develop another voice and another perspective, rooted in a set of preoccupations, codes and contexts which remain marginal to the global literary construction of Africa, perhaps, but central to another, overlapping field of production and reception. In a certain sense, then, these texts, unlike their global counterparts, remain outside of the postcolonial, as a literary category, beyond the aesthetic formations and economic imperatives which, together, map across its field of production and reception. Yet, neither do these three novels display what Appiah refers to as the neotraditional in their aesthetic form,[79] a situation in which a fabricated traditionalism is called upon for an approving Western gaze in a sanctioned nativism. Instead, these novels show a particular preoccupation with a form of modernity rooted in the material realities of contemporary Africa, rather than a normative global order. This literary vision of discrepant modernity takes its roots in a form of urban realism which portrays Africa not through the idiom of the exotic but through the language of the everyday, looking not to the Western reader but to a locally-situated audience, seeking not international prestige but bounded affectivity. As contemporary tales intended for a middle-class audience, these narratives display a third and incompatible set of aesthetic principles centred on political engagement and the heightening of social consciousness in the context of the contemporary African middle classes. Certainly, none of the three novels discussed here display a sense of being untouched by colonialism; indeed, each heavily features colonialism and its uneasy legacy as central to its depiction of contemporary African societies. If anything, these texts display what seems to be a far more striking continuity with early African writing, notably the politically- and nationally-engaged work of the 1970s and 1980s, the literature of disillusionment, as Lazarus calls it,[80] in that these texts, too, foreground their referents as a means of direct political engagement and effect.[81] Yet, unlike these predecessor texts, none of the three texts discussed here can be said to be characterized entirely by a sense of hopelessness or despair. Despite a shared sentiment of betrayal by the lost promises of an independence which, in its contemporary guise, appears more remote than ever, each of these three texts nonetheless ends with an invocation of hope, where the possibilities of becoming-otherwise persist at the level of individual agency and responsibility. For *The Uncertainty of Hope*'s Onai, this appears at the novel's conclusion as, through a series of coincidences and twists of fate, she finally realizes her dream of opening a dress-making shop, providing a better life for her children, while in *The Disillusioned African*, the possibility of a different future appears through Charles's struggle for direct political engagement on the African continent. Even in *Journey*, where the narrator appears to lose all faith by the end of the novel, a spark of possibility appears through Amoah's sexual congress with upper-class Mmah, suggesting that forms of cross-demographic alliance and allegiance may remain possible.

   In a certain sense, each of these three texts is more straightforwardly African than any of the globally-published texts discussed in this study. All three are explicitly concerned with issues and debates located on the African continent itself and tied to specific, local contexts, all three have been published in Africa by African presses and all three are written by authors who remain resident in and engaged professionally on the African continent. At the same time, by virtue of their publication and relative spheres of influence in distribution, consumption and dissemination, each of these three texts is far less likely to appear under the banner of African literature as a global market category. Instead, that descriptor remains under the auspices of global belonging. As has always been the case, Africa remains very much a colonial invention, something that becomes elsewhere, without ever really being. What this might tell us about African literature, as a category, is that the application of the label is less about the work and its relation to the continent and more about our image of the world, as the global readers of the text, and what we see as constituting that world. As a market category, African literature, a form of world literature, may well be, as some critics have charged, complicit in the exoticization and commoditization of the once-colonized world. Rather than bringing disparate populations closer together, it may contribute to a sense of global estrangement through its inherent and inevitable assimilation into the discourse of the already-known. At the same time, however, African literature is much more than this, containing within it many more potent possibilities for understanding, reading and engaging otherwise.

# Conclusion: Writing Africa's Futures?

From 5 to 7 July 2013, the Royal African Society held its second annual Africa Writes festival at the British Library in central London. A celebration of African literature, the three-day event featured writers, critics and thinkers working across a range of forms, geographies and media related to the continent, to both celebrate the vibrancy of African writing across the world today and discuss the future of African writing, as a global literary category. Throughout the festival, conversations returned time and again to a series of interrelated questions: What is the future of African writing? Is there pressure, for the African writer, to accede to the demands of stereotype in depicting the continent? Does the label 'African writer' have any meaning when applied de facto? Faced with these questions, the festival returned to a series of refrains which have dominated discussions of African literature: African literature is mobile; African literature is post-national; African literature is read mostly in Europe and North America. Despite the vibrancy of the festival and the deep investment in African literature which it displayed, the persistence of these conversations indicates a disheartening anxiety at the heart of contemporary African literature on a global scale, one linked to trends in criticism, scholarship and popular discussion. No single event could realistically answer these questions in any definitive way, and, indeed, it would be equally impossible, here, to draw a set of easy conclusions about the landscape of African literature and its future trajectories. Instead, the exchanges which dominated Africa Writes demonstrate the persistence of a certain unease which has characterized African literature since its institutionalization. Developed under systems of external patronage and written in languages arguably alien to the continent, African literature has never been an easy classification with which to come to grips, always remaining to some extent determined from the exterior. Nor has African literature, despite appearances, ever been a homogenous or unified field. Indeed, as Caroline Davis reminds us, it was publishers who 'served to group disparate African writers under a single umbrella category, and to promote a concept of African literature as a homogenous entity',[1] not a uniformity inherent to the body of work itself. From its earliest appearances in slave narratives and missionary writing, the Africa in African literature has always been about much more than simply the continent. Facing outwards, it has always been part and parcel of the circulation of the a priori and marked by the condensation of global anxieties and local imperatives.

At the heart of these concerns lies the question of where African literature is produced and where it is read, a question which has driven this study. While early writers like Achebe and Ngũgĩ sought international audiences as part of the project of authorizing African literature as an institution (and, by extension, African civilizations as human), in its contemporary forms the perceived disparity between author and audience has led to a more deeply-felt disquiet about the commoditization of African literature and the global trafficking of otherness. Akin Adesokan characterizes what he calls 'new African writing' by its transnational market, commenting that contemporary African literature may be 'appreciated as manifestations of reproducible difference based on race and culture, and [is] underwritten by actually existing global inequalities'.[2] Problematic for Adesokan, then, are the ways in which contemporary African writing celebrated in North America and Europe encapsulates a certain postcolonial aesthetic, one aimed 'at courting a readership invested in the representation of contemporary Africa as a sight of perennial political and humanitarian emergencies',[3] and linked in increasingly complex ways to the continual reproduction of material injustices. Equally, Adesokan's comments highlight a specific cultural mechanism through which to be African in the global literary field requires a form of displacement, a sense in which the author and the text take on their valuation through their passage across transnational circuits of material exchange. Those African authors who remain cloaked in relative obscurity in the West, by extension, are not perceived as contributing quite as fully to African literature, mired, instead, in the provincial and the particular in their literary efforts. As Habila has written, the majority of African authors celebrated in the world literary market are products of the diaspora, living and working in the West,[4] a characterization widely echoed in scholarship through remarks on the dislocation and distance which marks contemporary writing as distinct from earlier works of African literature. This line of commentary thus takes as given the premise that African literature is a largely diasporic form, and that this sense of diasporic post-nationality remains both constitutive of this body of work and, to varying degrees, central to any project of evaluation or interpretation which may confront it. While there is certainly something to be said for this line of criticism, particularly given the force of the world literary market in the promotion and dissemination of certain types of texts, rather than others, Adesokan's comments simultaneously reveal a tendency reproduced more broadly in scholarship which de-emphasizes the inherent multiplicity of literary expression from and around the continent. Early writers, as has been well documented,[5] wrote both for an international audience and a local readership, balancing aesthetic codes and literary practices of address. Likewise, in contemporary writing, as my readings have shown, multiple levels of rhetoric coexist, leading to simultaneous and overlapping modes of literary communication. Within the text itself, a certain space for a resistant aesthetics remains open, pushing back against the political closure which Adesokan describes by leveraging the imaginative possibilities of fiction, complicating any single reading of African literature as a global body of work.

The opening up of 'Africa' to its heterogeneous, disparate and multiple forms, faces and guises is a crucial task for unlocking the static and atavistic image of Africa, and, in this sense, a focus on the mobile and the post-national can be seen in broadly positive terms. The recuperative possibilities of such a perspective can be seen in such recent works as Adichie's *Americanah* (2013), which travels from Nigeria to America and England and back again to tell the story of two star-crossed lovers; Forna's *The Hired Man* (2013), a novel which escapes Africa entirely, exploring post-war Croatia to engage with themes of conflict, betrayal and forgiveness with resonances on the continent; Taiye Selasi's *Ghana Must Go* (2013), a novel that travels across West Africa, the East Coast of America and London to chart the disintegration and reconstitution of the Nigerian-Ghanaian-American Sai family, and Teju Cole's *Open City* (2011), which tells the story of half-German, half-Yoruban Julius, a psychiatric resident living in New York City. Yet, the easy celebration of the mobile and the multiple may equally lead to a set of uneasy conclusions about what it means to be African and what a preoccupation with Africa should or should not entail. In one sense, this preoccupation with the peripatetic has contributed to a paradoxical fossilization in African writing, where a predictable aesthetic has repeated itself at the expense of other visions and other voices.[6] To be legitimately African, in this context, is to embody a sort of cosmopolitan sentiment, one which might enable the text and the author to enter a supposedly universal set of codes and conversations. With this movement into universality, however, ambiguity appears as conflict recedes into the shadows. In place of a reckoning with the very real inequalities and systems of domination which have determined Africa's place in the world today, this celebrated, post-national Africa remains curiously neutral. Through the promotion of this diasporic, post-national vision of the continent, there appears a concomitant sense in which, to be African and celebrated as such, the text and its author must embody a certain transparency, a translatability of sorts. Once again, it seems, the a priori returns and with it the imperative both to simultaneously teach while conforming to the already-known, to fascinate without threatening. Simultaneously, this preoccupation with the mobile misses the totality of literary work emanating from the continent and, more precisely, the complex strategies of address and partial rootedness embedded even in the most cosmopolitan of texts. In *GraceLand*, this appears through the reconceptualized *ogbanje* narrative, while in *Half of a Yellow Sun*, repeated invocations of Mami Wata and the sacred feminine call upon a framework of knowledge which cannot be entirely translated. More broadly, in narrative terms, the return to Gĩkũyũ folklore and a particular preoccupation with the land informs *Wizard of the Crow*, while *Links* develops an aestheticism based upon Somali oral poetics. In each case, the specificity of aesthetic work in the text coexists with its more cosmopolitan concerns, opening the specific to the universal in a dialectical relationship more nuanced than any single label might indicate. Conversely, a sense of cosmopolitanism, as *Journey*, *The Disillusioned African* and *The Uncertainty of Hope* show, is not necessarily under the sole ownership of these globally-circulated texts, nor is it entirely evident that a sense of locality, in literary terms, is synonymous with atavism. Rather, the local may itself be enlivened by multiple forms of being that coexist across the horizontal sprawl of any single location, what Primorac has identified as 'local cosmopolitanism', a sense of 'cultural and political pluralism, tolerance, and willingness to accommodate strangeness and difference' which may nonetheless remain rooted in a single geographic location.[7] The focus on the diasporic and the post-national, moreover, seems to cast a shadow over the very real, pressing and material concerns of the local, concerns which, through the top-down workings of the state, permeate daily life and, through the many discrepant, bottom-up forms of engagement which persist on the continent, provide material for the dense richness of everyday life.

Due in no small part to its characterization as a transnational phenomenon, African literary writing has remained mired in a series of debates about what it should mean to write Africa and what Africa should be, on a global stage. In his review of Caine Prize winner NoViolet Bulawayo's debut novel, *We Need New Names*, Habila identifies a certain sense of 'performing Africa' in the literary text, a sense in which to write Africa is 'to inundate one's writing with images and symbols and allusions that evoke, to borrow a phrase from Aristotle, pity and fear, but not in a real tragic sense, more in a CNN, western-media-coverage-of-Africa, poverty-porn sense'.[8] African literature, he complains, has become too deeply mired in the imperatives to represent a certain type of space and place for the satisfaction of the Western consumer, leading to an exploitative, repetitive and largely predictable aesthetic of suffering throughout. The Caine Prize, in particular, has been castigated for encouraging this aesthetic of suffering, creating a transnational vision of Africa as precisely the land of refugee camps and slums that authors like Adichie rail against. Prize culture, under these accusations, has led to the fossilization of certain conventions in the writing and representation of Africa, conventions which have fed back into the a priori vision of the continent as a land of despair and misery. Equally, Eleni Coundouriotis claims, the very aesthetic of trauma which permeates African writing seeks to flatten context in order to placate a foreign readership uninterested in nuance, a result of neocolonial domination.[9] Yet, as the examples of *GraceLand*, *The Stone Virgins* and *Links* show, to reflect or represent suffering on the African continent is not necessarily to enter into a single-minded discourse or a one-dimensional portrait of the continent. Instead, as the works of global African literature repeatedly demonstrate, Africa, whatever its vision, remains heterogeneous, re-presented in multifaceted, multi-layered aesthetic forms which demand a realignment of the political. In writing Africa and reading Africa, aesthetic sensibilities and a flexibility of expression result in a literary perspective which demands innovation, mutability and creativity at the site of reading, too, in order to grapple with the complexity of a re-presentation that persistently eludes representation. Rather than serve as unproblematic descriptions of African literary writing, then, these debates foreground the continued precarity of Africa's place in an asymmetrically-loaded world system despite all claims of cosmopolitan reconciliation. Based in a context of global inequality and transnational exploitation, that is to say, African literary writing remains subject to external mediation, seemingly unable simply to be, without the authenticating gaze of the Western reader-consumer and inevitably transfigured from an aesthetic artefact into a material commodity through which a certain political script is rehearsed and repeated.

Yet, as the locally-published novels discussed in this study demonstrate, the anxiety surrounding these debates is not all-permeating. Examining Tagiwira's and Agambila's novels, for instance, one could equally argue that, based within a material context still largely determined by the ravages of multinational capitalism and neocolonial conquest, to write contemporary Africa is precisely to re-present a form of degradation. Critically, as these novels show us, this aesthetic need not turn on a sentimentalist notion of pity or on an exploitative sense of humanitarian guilt. Rather, the depictions of suffering in these works act as a call to responsibility, an ethical interpellation that gestures past the Western reader in hailing a local audience. These performances of African suffering remain highly particular in their context, evoking a texturally-dense sense of the referent. Simultaneously, these works develop specified strategies for combatting structural disillusionment within its particular manifestations, an act which, far from victimizing its subjects, depicts in them a form of localized agency. These works thus display a sense of urgency in which Africa is no longer available simply for the satisfaction of a touristic gaze; rather, this Africa is one which speaks to itself, preoccupied not with the aesthetic imperatives of universalism, but with the immediacy of the present moment and the concomitant need for political engagement and action across all levels of society. Rather than dwell upon the vision of Africa pointing outwards, this is an Africa which has turned inwards, more concerned with the immediacy of action and local engagements than with the anxieties of the a priori. Equally, there exists a range of non-canonical forms of contemporary African writing which betray the diversity through which Africa may come to appear in all its discrepancy, forms such as thrillers and crime novels, romances, science fiction, graphic literature, and popular writing. As critics have noted, these popular and 'low' forms of literary production are able, through their mass circulation and dissemination, to 'express complex insights and propositions relating to national communities' in specific, rooted contexts,[10] enabling a large-scale dialogue amongst populations denied official channels of recognition.[11] All of these forms retain a central place in the landscape of African writing and the landscape of African reading today, despite their critical neglect. As Fraser reminds us, 'boundaries between such divisions are drawn along historically over-determined lines. They are, for example, largely meaningless in the worlds of orality or manuscript lying behind so much reading practice in Asia and Africa'.[12] Rather than take a vertical approach to literary valuation, then, one which valorizes those works of 'high' fiction published by multinational presses, African literary production today remains dynamic and multifocal, operating along contrasting axes of verticality and horizontality in its realization.

Regardless of the form it takes, it is apparent that Africa, as a concept, an image and an idea, remains a powerful force within the global imaginary. The anxieties that have shaped and continue to shape African writing are driven as much by the creativity of writers from the continent as they are by the persistence of a global gaze. Driven by the unfinished process of decolonization and still under the international yoke of financial conquest and multinational control, the continent remains a potent site of global anxiety around which notions of ownership and agency, development and modernity, independence and control circulate. Based within a global literary market which continues to label it by virtue of this affiliation, contemporary African literature remains subject to the vestiges of this anxiety, always extending beyond itself to a more global reckoning with the unspoken legacies of conquest. It may well be the case that, under the condition of transnational production and reception, the imperative to perform Africa is inescapable, if not as part of the creation of the text than as a characteristic of its consumption. Yet, this compulsion to perform Africa, as the texts read in this study demonstrate, need not exist as a burden. Rather, to write Africa and to read it may open up space for tremendous creativity, ingenuity and imagination. To perform Africa is not necessarily to fall back into a script of poverty, misery and exoticism; instead, performing Africa can take on multiple forms which contradict even as they coexist and which remain rooted even as they travel. Performing Africa need not be a singular act, but rather one which, both globally-mediated and locally-modulated, encompasses multiple spaces, audiences, frames of reference and histories.

Whatever the future of African writing, without a radical shift in global markets the accompanying questions surrounding representation are unlikely to disappear in the foreseeable future. Indeed, in an era of increasingly frenetic neoliberal expansion, it seems more likely that the divisions and tensions outlined here will only multiply. At the same time, this globally-authorized form of African literature is not the sole arbiter of value in the trafficking of Africa's image and, indeed, myriad other forms of African literatures continue to exist. It would be reductive to suggest that either one or the other body of writing forms the 'true' African literature or is more deserving of critical merit, however. Instead, when thinking of African literature, it is important to recall the ways in which actors like locally-published authors, institutions like the African Books Collective and forms like popular writing coexist with their international, institutionalized counterparts. Neither body of writing defines African literature or African writing, much like any single description would fail to capture the enormity and complexity of the continent itself. Without a view towards this plurality, one which, rather than seek to position these works in a hierarchy, views them as part of a horizontal sprawl, the anxiety that surrounds Africa as a literary space created and circulated across the globe will not, it seems, be destined to dissipate anytime soon.

# Notes

## Introduction: Writing Africa in a Global Marketplace

1. Binyavanga Wainaina, 'How to Write About Africa', *Granta*, 92 (2005), 92.
2. Harish Trivedi, 'Ngũgĩ wa Thiong'o in Conversation', *Wasafiri*, 18.40 (2003), 5–10 (p. 8).
3. Timothy Brennan, *At Home in the World: Cosmopolitanism Now* (Cambridge: Harvard University Press, 1997), p. 36.
4. Sarah Brouillette, *Postcolonial Writers in a Global Literary Marketplace* (Basingstoke: Palgrave Macmillan, 2007), p. 5.
5. Neil Lazarus, *The Postcolonial Unconscious* (Cambridge: Cambridge University Press, 2011), p. 117.
6. See, for instance, Brenda Cooper, *Magical Realism in West African Fiction: Seeing with a Third Eye* (Abingdon: Routledge, 1998), Chinweizu, Onwuchekwa Jemie and Ihechukwu Madubuike, *Toward the Decolonization of African Literature* (Enugu: Fourth Dimension, 1980), Ato Quayson, *Strategic Transformations in Nigerian Writing* (Oxford: James Currey, 1997), amongst numerous others.
7. Examples of this strand of criticism include Chidi Amuta, *The Theory of African Literature: Implications for Practical Criticism* (London: Zed, 1988), George M. Gugelberger (ed.), *Marxism and African Literature* (London: James Currey, 1985), Neil Lazarus, *Resistance in Postcolonial African Fiction* (New Haven: Yale University Press, 1990), Emmanuel Ngara, *Ideology and Form in African Poetry: Implications for Communication* (London: James Currey, 1990).
8. Caroline Davis, *Creating Postcolonial Literature: African Writers and British Publishers* (Basingstoke: Palgrave Macmillan, 2013), p. 4. Other examples of this line of inquiry include Gail Low, *Publishing the Postcolonial: Anglophone West African and Caribbean Writing in the UK 1948–1968* (New York: Routledge, 2011), Graham Huggan, *The Postcolonial Exotic: Marketing the Margins* (London: Routledge, 2001), Robert Fraser, *Book History Through Postcolonial Eyes* (London: Routledge, 2008).
9. Simon Gikandi, *Reading the African Novel* (London: James Currey, 1987), p. ix.
10. Benedict M. Ibitokun, 'The Dynamic of Spatiality in African Fiction', *Modern Fiction Studies*, 37.3 (1991), 409–26 (p. 424).
11. Chidi Amuta, 'The Nigerian Civil War and the Evolution of Nigerian Literature', *Canadian Journal of African Studies*, 17.1 (1983), 85–99 (p. 94).
12. Chinweizu, Onwuchekwa Jemie and Ihechukwu Madubuike, 'Towards the Decolonization of African Literature', *Transition*, 48 (1975), 29–57 (p. 57).

13. Guari Viswanathan, 'Introduction', in *Power, Politics and Culture: Interviews with Edward W. Said*, ed. by Guari Viswanathan (London: Bloomsbury, 2001), p. xii.
14. Edward W. Said, *Orientalism* (London: Penguin, 2003 [1978]).
15. Said, *Orientalism*, pp. 282–3.
16. Kojin Karatani, 'Use of Aesthetics: After Orientalism', trans. by Sabu Kohso, *boundary 2*, 25.2 (1998), 145–60 (pp. 146–7).
17. Judith Butler, *Precarious Life: The Powers of Mourning and Violence* (London: Verso, 2003), p. 91.
18. Gayatri Chakravorty Spivak, *A Critique of Postcolonial Reason: Towards a History of the Vanishing Present* (Cambridge: Harvard University Press, 1999), p. 127.
19. Lee Brown, 'Introduction', in *African Philosophy: New and Traditional Perspectives*, ed. by Lee Brown (New York: Oxford University Press, 2004), pp. 3–20; Emmanuel Chukwudi Eze, 'Introduction', in *Postcolonial African Philosophy: A Critical Reader*, ed. by Emmanuel Chukwudi Eze (Oxford: Blackwell, 1997), pp. 1–21; D. A. Masolo, 'The Concept of the Person in Luo Modes of Thought', in *African Philosophy: New and Traditional Perspectives*, ed. by Lee Brown (New York: Oxford University Press, 2004), pp. 84–106; I. A. Menkiti, 'Physical and Metaphysical Understanding', in *African Philosophy: New and Traditional Perspectives*, ed. by Lee Brown (New York: Oxford University Press, 2004), pp. 107–35.
20. V. Y. Mudimbe, *The Invention of Africa: Gnosis, Philosophy, and the Order of Knowledge* (Bloomington: Indiana University Press, 1988), p. 12.
21. V. Y. Mudimbe, *The Idea of Africa* (Bloomington: Indiana University Press, 1994), p. xi.
22. Mudimbe, *Invention*, p. 186.
23. Mudimbe, *Invention*, p. 1.
24. Mudimbe, *Invention*, p. 4.
25. Mudimbe, *Invention*, p. 12.
26. Ezekiel Mphahlele, *The African Image*, second edition (London: Faber and Faber, 1974), p. 36.
27. Alex de Waal, 'Getting Somalia Right This Time', *New York Times* (21 February 2012) <http://www.nytimes.com/2012/02/22/opinion/getting-somalia-right-this-time.html?pagewanted=all> [accessed 19 July 2013]; Petina Gappah, 'Where Citizenship Went to Die', *New York Times* (22 March 2013) <http://www.nytimes.com/2013/03/23/opinion/where-citizenship-went-to-die-in-zimbabwe.html?pagewanted=all> [accessed 19 July 2013]; Jeffrey Gettleman, 'Kenya, Known for Its Stability, Topples Into Post-Election Chaos', *New York Times* (3 January 2008) <http://www.nytimes.com/2008/01/03/world/africa/03kenya.html?pagewanted=all> [accessed 19 July 2013]; Adam Nossiter, 'Election Fuels Deadly Clashes in Nigeria', *New York Times* (24 April 2011) <http://www.nytimes.com/2011/04/25/world/africa/25nigeria.html> [accessed 19 July 2013]; David Smith, 'Scores Hacked to Death in Nigerian Sectarian Clash', *Guardian* (7 March 2010) <http://www.guardian.co.uk/world/2010/

mar/07/scores-hacked-death-nigerian-sectarian> [accessed 19 July 2013]';
Michael Binyon, 'Sierra Leone: A Tale of Post-colonial Disaster: How
Prosperity Declined into Bloody Revolution', *Times* (31 May 1997), p. 2.

28. Yvonne Abraham, 'Orchard Gardens Graduate Excels with Determination,
Support', *The Boston Globe* (30 June 2013) <http://www.bostonglobe.com/
metro/2013/06/29/abraham/KjovFRAZjw3Yz351ADcIkL/story.html>
[accessed 11 July 2013].

29. Gayatri Chakravorty Spivak, 'Resident Alien', in *Relocating Postcolonialism*,
ed. by David Theo Goldberg and Ato Quayson (Oxford: Blackwell, 2002),
pp. 47–65 (p. 61); Gayatri Chakravorty Spivak, *Other Asias* (Malden:
Blackwell, 2008), p. 15.

30. Simon Gikandi, 'Cultural Translation and the African Self: A (Post)colo-
nial Case Study', *Interventions: International Journal of Postcolonial Studies*,
3.3 (2001), 355–75.

31. Gayatri Chakravorty Spivak, *Outside in the Teaching Machine* (New York:
Routledge, 1993), p. 44.

32. Bill Ashcroft, *On Post-Colonial Futures: Transformations of Colonial Culture*
(London: Continuum, 2001); Bill Ashcroft, *Caliban's Voice: The Transformation
of English in Post-Colonial Literatures* (London: Routledge, 2009).

33. Stephen Morton, *States of Emergency: Colonialism, Literature and Law*
(Liverpool: Liverpool University Press, 2013), p. 121.

34. Edward W. Said, *Culture and Imperialism* (London: Vintage, 1993), p. xiii.

35. Mark Currie, *Postmodern Narrative Theory* (Basingstoke: Palgrave
Macmillan, 1998), p. 2.

36. Kwame Anthony Appiah, *The Ethics of Identity* (Princeton: Princeton
University Press, 2005), p. 29.

37. Chinua Achebe, *The Education of a British-Protected Child* (London:
Penguin, 2009), p. 62.

38. Timothy Brennan, 'The National Longing for Form', in *Nation and
Narration*, ed. by Homi K. Bhabha (London: Routledge, 1990), pp. 44–70
(p. 47).

39. Chris Tiffin and Alan Lawson, 'Introduction', in *De-Scribing Empire: Postcolonialism and Textuality*, ed. by Chris Tiffin and Alan Lawson (London:
Routledge, 1994), pp. 1–11 (p. 2).

40. Tsenay Serequeberhan, 'The Critique of Eurocentrism and the Practice of
African Philosophy', in *Postcolonial African Philosophy: A Critical Reader*,
ed. by Emmanuel Chukwudi Eze (Oxford: Blackwell, 1997), pp. 141–61
(p. 144).

41. Edward W. Said, 'Beginnings', in *Power, Politics and Culture: Interviews with
Edward W. Said*, ed. by Guari Viswanathan (London: Bloomsbury, 2001),
pp. 3–38 (p. 25).

42. bell hooks, *Yearning: Race, Gender, and Cultural Politics* (Boston: South End
Press, 1991); Kelly Oliver, *Colonization of Psychic Space: A Psychoanalytic
Social Theory of Oppression* (Minneapolis: University of Minnesota
Press, 2004); Paul Gilroy, *Postcolonial Melancholia* (New York: Columbia
University Press, 2005).

43. Mudimbe, *Invention*, p. 1.
44. Neil Lazarus, 'The Politics of Postcolonial Modernism', in *Postcolonial Studies and Beyond*, ed. by Ania Loomba, Suvir Kaul, Matti Bunzl, Antoinette Burton and Jed Etsy (Durham: Duke University Press, 2005), pp. 423–38 (p. 427).
45. John C. Hawley, 'The Colonizing Impulse of Postcolonial Theory', *Modern Fiction Studies*, 56.2 (Winter 2010), 769–87 (pp. 778–9).
46. Eli Park Sorensen, *Postcolonial Studies and the Literary: Theory, Interpretation and the Novel* (Basingstoke: Palgrave Macmillan, 2010), pp. x–xi.
47. Mudimbe, *Idea*, p. 177.
48. Elleke Boehmer, *Colonial and Postcolonial Literature: Migrant Metaphors* (Oxford: Oxford University Press, 2005), p. 251.
49. Robert Spencer, *Cosmopolitan Criticism and Postcolonial Literature* (Basingstoke: Palgrave Macmillan, 2011); Spivak, *Teaching Machine*, p. 197.
50. Forest Pyle, '"By a Certain Subreption": Gayatri Spivak and the "Level" of the Aesthetic', *Interventions: International Journal of Postcolonial Studies*, 4.2 (2002), 186–90 (p. 190).

# 1    Ethics, Conflict and Re(-)presentation

1. This 'ethical imperative', as I have been calling it, is one which has been expanded upon at length in criticism of South African literature, particularly in the work of critics including David Attwell, Derek Attridge and Stephen Clingman. As the introduction to this study indicated, this ethical focus is no doubt in due, at least in part, to the immediacy of representation under apartheid and long-standing debates in South Africa around the role of aesthetic representation under a regime of terror (see, for instance, Lewis Nkosi, *Home and Exile* (London: Longman, 1965) and J. M. Coetzee, 'Into the Dark Chamber', in *Doubling the Point*, ed. by David Attwell (Cambridge: Harvard University Press, 1992), pp. 361–8). While certain theoretical insights from these critics will be deployed over the course of this study, literary writing from South Africa remains outside of its remit, given both the positioning of global African literatures as both sub-Saharan and produced by non-white (usually black) authors (a position which I do not necessarily endorse, but which remains the dominant global narrative of African authenticity, writ large) and South Africa's singular historical trajectory.
2. Paul Gilroy, *The Black Atlantic: Modernity and Double Consciousness* (Cambridge: Harvard University Press, 1993), pp. 38–9.
3. Thomas Metscher, 'Literature and Art as Ideological Form', trans. by Kiernan Ryan, *New Literary History*, 11.1 (1979), 21–39 (p. 24).
4. Tobin Siebers, 'Ethics ad Nauseam', *American Literary History*, 6.4 (Winter 1994), 756–78 (p. 776).
5. Terry Eagleton, 'The Ideology of the Aesthetic', *Poetics Today*, 9.2 (1988), 327–38 (p. 330).
6. See Chapter 3, 'History', in Spivak, *Critique*.

7. Spivak, *Critique*, p. 259.
8. Lazarus, *Postcolonial Unconscious*, p. 114.
9. Lazarus, *Postcolonial Unconscious*, p. 146.
10. Peter Hitchcock, *The Long Space: Transnationalism and Postcolonial Form* (Stanford: Stanford University Press, 2010), p. 19.
11. Spivak, *Critique*, p. 259.
12. Dina Al-Kassim, 'The Face of Foreclosure', *Interventions: International Journal of Postcolonial Studies*, 4.2 (2002), 168–75 (p. 170).
13. Peter Hitchcock, 'They Must Be Represented? Problems in Theories of Working-Class Representation', *PMLA*, 115.1 (2000), 20–32 (p. 29).
14. Lazarus, *Postcolonial Unconscious*, p. 125.
15. Thomas Keenan, 'The Push and Pull of Rights and Responsibilities', *Interventions: International Journal of Postcolonial Studies*, 4.2 (2002), 191–7 (p. 193).
16. R. Radhakrishnan, 'Culture as Common Ground: Ethnicity and Beyond', *MELUS*, 14.2 (Summer 1987), 5–19 (pp. 9–10).
17. Gayatri Chakravorty Spivak, 'Responsibility', *boundary 2*, 21.3 (Autumn 1994), 19–64 (p. 58).
18. Fredric Jameson, 'Third World Literature in the Era of Multinational Capitalism', *Social Text*, 15 (1986), 65–88 (p. 69).
19. An expanded version of this essay appears as 'Jameson's Rhetoric of Otherness and the "National Allegory"', in Aijaz Ahmad, *In Theory: Class, Nation and Identity* (London: Verso, 1993), pp. 95–122.
20. See Lazarus, *Postcolonial Unconscious*, p. 97.
21. Julie McGonegal, 'Postcolonial Metacritique', *Interventions: International Journal of Postcolonial Studies*, 7.2 (2005), 251–65 (p. 251).
22. McGonegal, 'Metacritique', p. 257.
23. Imre Szeman, 'Who's Afraid of National Allegory? Jameson, Literary Criticism, Globalization', *The South Atlantic Quarterly*, 100.3 (2001), 803–27 (pp. 806–7).
24. Arjun Appadurai, 'Introduction: Commodities and the Politics of Value', in *The Social Life of Things*, ed. by Arjun Appadurai (Cambridge: Cambridge University Press, 1986), pp. 3–63 (p. 15; p. 17).
25. Charles Kimber, 'Interview: Chimamanda Ngozi Adichie', *Socialist Review* (October 2006) <http://www.socialistreview.org.uk/article.php?articlenumber=9845> [accessed 20 March 2011].
26. Stephen Moss, 'Madonna's Not Our Saviour', *Guardian* (8 June 2007) <http://www.guardian.co.uk/books/2007/jun/08/orangeprizeforfiction2007.orangeprizeforfiction> [accessed 20 March 2011].
27. John Marx, 'Failed-State Fiction', *Contemporary Literature*, 49.4 (2008), 597–633 (p. 620).
28. Carlye Archibeque, 'An Interview with Chris Abani', *Poetix* <http://poetix.net/abani.htm> [accessed 20 March 2011].
29. See Ikhide R. Ikheloa, 'The Trials of Chris Abani', *Ikhide: Email from America* (25 November 2011) <http://xokigbo.wordpress.com/2011/11/25/the-trials-of-chris-abani and-the-power-of-empty-words/> [accessed 1 December 2011] for a full account of these charges.

30. Lazarus, *Postcolonial Unconscious*, p. 141.
31. Edward W. Said, *Representations of the Intellectual* (New York: Vintage, 1994), p. 11.
32. Mark Sanders, 'Representation: Reading-Otherwise', *Interventions: International Journal of Postcolonial Studies*, 4.2 (2002), 198–204.
33. Edward W. Said, *The World, the Text, and the Critic* (Cambridge: Harvard University Press, 1983), p. 2.
34. Park Sorensen, pp. 8–11; Said, *WTC*, p. 3.
35. Hitchcock, *Long Space*, p. 16.
36. Judith Butler, *Giving an Account of Oneself* (New York: Fordham University Press, 2005), p. 7.
37. Robert Spencer, 'Cosmopolitan Criticism', in *Rerouting the Postcolonial: New Directions for the New Millennium*, ed. by Janet Wilson, Cristina Şandru and Sarah Lawson Welsh (London: Routledge, 2010), pp. 36–47 (p. 41).
38. Said, *WTC*, p. 32.
39. Said, *WTC*, p. 39.
40. Mudimbe, *Invention*, p. 185.
41. See Chapter 1, 'African Literature and the Anthropological Exotic', in Huggan, *Postcolonial Exotic*.
42. José F. Colmeiro, 'Exorcising Exoticism: Carmen and the Construction of Oriental Spain', *Comparative Literature*, 54.2 (2002), 127–55 (p. 128).
43. Robert J. C. Young, *White Mythologies: Writing History and the West*, second edition (London: Routledge, 2004), p. 184.
44. Colmeiro, pp. 128–9.
45. Frederick N. Bohrer, 'Inventing Assyria: Exoticism and Reception in Nineteenth-Century England and France', *The Art Bulletin*, 80.2 (1998), 336–56 (pp. 347–9).
46. Tzvetan Todorov, *On Human Diversity: Nationalism, Racism and Exoticism in French Thought* (Cambridge: Harvard University Press, 1993), p. 264.
47. Huggan, *Postcolonial Exotic*, p. 13.
48. Lyn Innes, 'Reading Africa', *Interventions: International Journal of Postcolonial Studies*, 3.3 (2001), 317–21 (p. 317).
49. David Scott, *Refashioning Futures: Criticism after Postcoloniality* (Princeton: Princeton University Press, 1999), p. 124.
50. Scott, p. 124.
51. Huggan, *Postcolonial Exotic*, p. 34.
52. Huggan, *Postcolonial Exotic*, p. 37.
53. Wole Soyinka, 'The Writer in an African State', *Transition*, 31 (1967), 10–13 (p. 12).
54. Soyinka, 'African State', p. 12.
55. Soyinka, 'African State', p. 11.
56. For an exhaustive discussion of the ways in which Achebe manipulates both the question of address and the use of tradition, see Rhonda Cobham, 'Problems of Gender and History in the Teaching of *Things Fall Apart*', in *Chinua Achebe's Things Fall Apart: A Casebook*, ed. by Isidore Okpewho (New York: Oxford University Press, 2003), pp. 165–80.

57. Homi K. Bhabha, *The Location of Culture* (London: Routledge, 1994), pp. 77–8.
58. Huggan, *Postcolonial Exotic*, p. 40.
59. Low, p. xiv.
60. Low, p. 17.
61. Thomas Brückner, 'Across the Borders: Orality Old and New in the African Novel', in *Fusion of Cultures?*, ed. by Peter O. Stummer and Christopher Balme (Amsterdam: Rodopi, 1996), pp. 153–60 (p. 154); Wendy Griswold, *Bearing Witness: Readers, Writers and the Novel in Nigeria* (Princeton: Princeton University Press, 2000), p. 36.
62. Quayson, *Strategic Transformations*, p. 44.
63. Griswold, *Bearing Witness*, pp. 33–4.
64. Abiola Irele, *The African Experience in Literature and Ideology* (Bloomington: University of Indiana Press, 1990), p. 174.
65. Low, p. 2.
66. Obiajunwa Wali, 'The Dead End of African Literature?', *Transition*, 10 (1963), 13–16 (p. 14).
67. Trivedi, p. 8.
68. Trivedi, p. 7.
69. Ngũgĩ wa Thiong'o, *Decolonising the Mind: The Politics of Language in African Literature* (London: James Currey, 1986), p. 12.
70. Ngũgĩ, *Decolonising*, p. 26.
71. Trivedi, p. 6.
72. Angela Lamas Rodrigues, 'Beyond Nativism: An Interview with Ngũgĩ wa Thiong'o', *Research in African Literatures*, 35.3 (2004), 161–7 (p. 163).
73. Apollo Obonyo Amoko, *Postcolonialism in the Wake of the Nairobi Revolution: Ngũgĩ wa Thiong'o and the Idea of African Literature* (Basingstoke: Palgrave Macmillan, 2010), p. 107.
74. Chinua Achebe, 'English and the African Writer', *Transition*, 18 (1965), 27–30 (p. 28).
75. See, for example, chapters devoted to the series in Huggan, *Postcolonial Exotic* and Low.
76. Griswold, *Bearing Witness*, pp. 88–119; Ogaga Okunyade, 'Weaving Memories of Childhood: The New Nigerian Novel and the Genre of the *Bildungsroman*', *ARIEL: A Review of International English Literature*, 41.3–4 (2011), 137–66 (pp. 137–8).
77. Tanure Ojaide, 'Migration, Globalization, and Recent African Literature', *World Literature Today*, 82.2 (2008), 43–6 (p. 44).
78. Metscher, p. 37.
79. James Wood, 'Truth, Convention, Realism', in *How Fiction Works* (London: Vintage, 2009), pp. 168–87.
80. Radhakrishnan, p. 18.
81. Gikandi, 'African Self', p. 357.

## 2  Race, Class and Performativity

1. John C. Hawley, 'Biafra as Heritage and Symbol: Adichie, Mbachu, and Iweala', *Research in African Literatures*, 39.2 (2008), 15–26 (p. 20).

2. Ojaide, 'Migration', p. 46.
3. I retain use of the term 'Third World', following Jameson as well as scholars including Robert J. C. Young and Ella Shohat, to describe the interventionary and political valences of the formerly-colonized world. See Young, p. 43; Ella Shohat, 'Notes on the "Post-Colonial"', *Social Text*, 31/32 (1992), 99–113 (p. 111).
4. Jameson, p. 69.
5. Jameson, p. 69, emphasis original.
6. Susan Z. Andrade, *The Nation Writ Small: African Fictions and Feminisms, 1958–1988* (Durham: Duke University Press, 2011), p. 26.
7. Andrade, *Writ Small*, p. 23.
8. Judith Butler, *Bodies that Matter: On the Discursive Limits of "Sex"* (London: Routledge, 1993), pp. xxv–xxvi.
9. Frantz Fanon, *Black Skin, White Masks*, trans. by Richard Philcox (New York: Grove Press, 2008 [1952]), pp. 124–6.
10. While 'the fact of blackness' is certainly a mistranslation of Fanon's original French text, and therefore cannot be attributed to him, given the critical breadth and depth of work that this phrase has spawned, it remains relevant to discussions of Fanon and his legacy in postcolonial studies.
11. Fanon, *Black Skin*, p. 89.
12. Jean-Paul Sartre, *Being and Nothingness: A Phenomenological Essay on Ontology*, trans. by Hazel E. Barnes (New York: Washington Square Press, 1992 [1943]).
13. Fanon, *Black Skin*, p. 90.
14. Nigel Gibson, 'Losing Sight of the Real: Recasting Merleau-Ponty in Fanon's Critique of Mannoni', in *Race and Racism in Continental Philosophy*, ed. by Robert Bernasconi and Sybol Cook (Bloomington: Indiana University Press, 2003), pp. 129–50 (p. 130).
15. Fanon, *Black Skin*, p. 91. For Lacan's 'bodily schema' of alienation, see 'The Mirror Stage as Formative of the I Function, as Revealed in Psychoanalytic Experience' in Jacques Lacan, *Ecrits: A Selection*, trans. by Bruce Fink (New York: W.W. Norton, 2002 [1966]).
16. Fanon, *Black Skin*, p. 95.
17. Maurice Stevens, 'Public (Re)Memory, Vindicating Narratives, and Troubling Beginnings: Toward a Critical Postcolonial Psychoanalytic Theory', in *Fanon: A Critical Reader*, ed. by Lewis R. Gordon, T. Denean Sharpley-Whiting and Renée T. White (Oxford: Blackwell, 1996), pp. 203–19 (p. 207).
18. Fanon, *Black Skin*, p. 96.
19. Margaret Hillenbrand, 'The National Allegory Revisited: Writing Private and Public in Contemporary Taiwan', *positions: east asia cultures critiques*, 14.3 (2006), 633–62 (p. 634).
20. Butler, *Bodies*, p. xii.
21. Butler elaborates on this process in the context of sex and sexuality, arguing that 'the body is not an independent materiality that is invested

by power relations external to it, but it is that for which materialization and investiture are coextensive' (Butler, *Bodies*, p. 9). While the processes through which race and the token 'African' are constructed and performed remain distinct, if at times coextensive, with those of sex, Butler's general notion of 'performativity not as the act by which a subject brings into being what she/he names, but rather, as that reiterative power of discourse to produce the phenomena that it regulates and constrains' (Butler, *Bodies*, p. xxi) remains central to the production of African identities.

22. Pheng Cheah, *Spectral Nationality: Passages of Freedom from Kant to Postcolonial Literatures of Liberation* (New York: Columbia University Press, 2003), p. 218.

23. Robyn Dane has explained this as a condition in which the earlier work 'tells how colonization looks from inside the skull; the latter tells how it should theoretically look, albeit not completely, after the world ceases to be insane' (Robyn Dane, 'When Mirror Turns Lamp: Frantz Fanon as Cultural Visionary', *Africa Today*, 41.2 (1994), 70–91 (p. 76)). In other terms, this has been referred to as Fanon's 'insistence on the possibility of a dialectical transcendence which, in the end, amounts to nothing less than a "right to citizenship" in a world of "reciprocal recognitions"' (Michael Azar, 'In the Name of Algeria: Frantz Fanon and the Algerian Revolution', in *Frantz Fanon: Critical Perspectives*, ed. by Anthony C. Alessandrini (London: Routledge, 1999), pp. 21–33 (p. 31)).

24. Beacon Mbiba, 'Zimbabwe's Global Citizens in "Harare North": Some Preliminary Observations', in *Skinning the Skunk—Facing Zimbabwean Futures: Discussion Papers 30*, ed. by Mai Palmberg and Ranka Primorac (Uppsala: Nordska Afrikainstitutet, 2005), pp. 26–38 (p. 29).

25. Mbiba, p. 30.

26. Brian Chikwava, *Harare North* (London: Vintage, 2009), p. 6; henceforth cited in-text as *HN*.

27. Brian Richardson, *Unnatural Voices: Extreme Narration in Modern and Contemporary Fiction* (Columbus: Ohio State University Press, 2006), pp. 30–2.

28. Kobena Mercer, 'Busy in the Ruins of a Wretched Phantasia', in *Frantz Fanon: Critical Perspectives*, ed. by Anthony C. Alessandrini (London: Routledge, 1999), pp. 195–218 (p. 197).

29. Oliver, p. 72.

30. Bhabha, *Location*, p. 66.

31. Graham Huggan, 'Postcolonial, Globalization, and the Rise of (Trans) cultural Studies', in *Towards a Transcultural Future: Literature and Society in a 'Post'-Colonial World*, ed. by Geoffrey V. Davis, Peter H. Marsden, Bénédicte Ledent and Marc Delrez (Amsterdam: Rodopi, 2004), pp. 27–36 (p. 31).

32. Fanon, *Black Skin*, p. 95.

33. Oliver, p. 67.

34. Chikwava has stated that he considers the narrator's language to be a 'creole', rather than a 'pidgin', because 'pidgin English, or broken English,

is a stunted language that is used mainly used by traders or labourers who don't use it as soon as they get to their homes, [while] Creole is a full language that has developed to express a broader range of experience at all levels of social intercourse and is not the poor cousin to English in the same way that pidgin or broken English is'. See Marianne Dutrion, 'A propos d'*Harare North*. Une conversation avec Brian Chikwava', *Malfini: Publication exploratoire des escapes francophones* <http://malfini. ens-lyon.fr/document.php?id=170> [accessed 10 January 2013].

35. Dutrion.
36. Ines Mzali, 'Wars of Representation: Metonymy and Nuruddin Farah's *Links*', *College Literature*, 37.3 (2010), 84–105 (p. 85).
37. Park Sorensen, p. 67, emphasis original.
38. Nuruddin Farah, *Links* (London: Duckworth, 2005), pp. 55–6; pp. 61–2; p. 165; henceforth cited in-text as *L*.
39. Derek Wright, 'Nations as Fictions: Postmodernism in the Novels of Nuruddin Farah', *Critique: Studies in Contemporary Fiction*, 38.3 (1997), 193–204 (p. 195).
40. Simon Gikandi, 'Nuruddin Farah and Postcolonial Textuality', *World Literature Today*, 72.4 (1998), 753–8 (p. 754).
41. This preoccupation with haunting and the spectral is precisely what Pheng Cheah sees as characteristic of postcolonial anti-imperialist nationalism and literary production, particularly in its enlivening of the cultural work of the political.
42. Amanda Anderson, 'Cosmopolitanism, Universalism, and the Divided Legacies of Modernity', in *Cosmopolitics: Thinking and Feeling Beyond the Nation*, ed. by Pheng Cheah and Bruce Robbins (Minneapolis: University of Minnesota Press, 1998), pp. 265–89 (p. 282).
43. Bhabha, *Location*, p. 9.
44. Minna Niemi, 'Witnessing Contemporary Somalia from Abroad: An Interview with Nuruddin Farah', *Callaloo*, 35.2 (2012), 330–40 (p. 336).
45. Pal Ahluwalia, *Politics and Post-Colonial Theory: African Inflections* (London: Routledge, 2000), p. 48.
46. Despite this optimistic spin, it should be noted that the second volume of Farah's trilogy, *Knots*, presents Jeebleh's visit and departure in a less than optimistic light, as Seamus refers to the visit as having 'set off a tremor that became an earthquake' (Nuruddin Farah, *Knots* (London: Penguin, 2007), p. 326).
47. Tsitsi Dangarembga, *The Book of Not* (Banbury: Ayebia Clarke Publishing, 2006); henceforth cited in-text as *BN*.
48. Roseanne Kennedy, 'Mortgaged Futures: Trauma, Subjectivity, and the Legacies of Colonialism in Tsitsi Dangarembga's *The Book of Not*', *Studies in the Novel*, 40.1/2 (2008), 86–107 (p. 86).
49. Kennedy, 'Mortgaged Futures', p. 89.
50. Benedict Anderson, *Imagined Communities: Reflections on the Origin and Spread of Nationalism*, revised edition (London: Verso, 1991), p. 24.
51. Tsitsi Dangarembga, *Nervous Conditions* (New York: Seal Press, 1988), p. 1.

52. Dangarembga, *Nervous Conditions*, p. 208.
53. Andrade, *Writ Small*, p. 119.
54. The phrase 'nervous condition' is Constance Farrington's 1963 translation of Sartre's assertion that 'l'indigénat est une névrose introduite et maintenue par le colon chez les colonisés avec leur consentement'. The term 'névrose' has been more recently translated 'neurosis', by Richard Philcox.
55. Kennedy, p. 89.
56. E. Ann Kaplan, 'Fanon, Trauma and Cinema', in *Frantz Fanon: Critical Perspectives*, ed. by Anthony C. Alessandrini (London: Routledge, 1999), pp. 146–57 (p. 150).
57. Morton, p. 135.
58. Anjali Prabhu, 'Narration in Frantz Fanon's *Peau noire masques blancs*: Some Reconsiderations', *Research in African Literatures*, 37.4 (2006), 189–210 (p. 194).
59. Françoise Vergès, '"I am not the slave of slavery": The Politics of Reparation in (French) Postslavery Communities', in *Frantz Fanon: Critical Perspectives*, ed. by Anthony C. Alessandrini (London: Routledge, 1999), pp. 258–75 (p. 267).
60. Oliver, p. 3.
61. Diana Fuss, 'Interior Colonies: Frantz Fanon and the Politics of Identification', *Diacritics*, 24.2/3 (1994), 20–42 (p. 23).
62. Andrade, *Writ Small*, pp. 155–61.

## 3   Gender and Representing the Unrepresentable

1. See Jonathan Rutherford, 'A Place Called Home: Identity and the Cultural Politics of Difference', in *Identity: Community, Culture, Difference*, ed. by Jonathan Rutherford (London: Lawrence & Wishart, 1990), pp. 9–27 on articulation and Kimberlé Crenshaw, 'Mapping the Margins: Intersectionality, Identity Politics and Violence Against Women of Color', in *Identities: Race, Class, Gender, and Nationality*, ed. by Linda Martín Alcoff and Eduardo Mendieta (Malden: Blackwell, 2003), pp. 175–200 for a discussion of intersectionality, gender and race.
2. Crenshaw, p. 176.
3. Despite the widespread distinction between 'race' and 'ethnicity' in scholarship across disciplines, in this chapter I use the two terms interchangeably to demarcate the host of constructed, contingent and performative practices which delineate the boundaries of cultural 'otherness' in the postcolonial African context.
4. Benita Parry, *Postcolonial Studies: A Materialist Critique* (London: Routledge, 2004), p. 19.
5. See Cobham for a full analysis of gender in *Things Fall Apart*.
6. Florence Stratton, '"Periodic Embodiments": A Ubiquitous Trope in African Men's Writing', *Research in African Literatures*, 21.1 (1990), 111–26 (p. 112).

7. Stratton, 'Periodic', p. 112; see also Florence Stratton, *Contemporary African Literature and the Politics of Gender* (London: Routledge, 2004), p. 40; Geraldine Moane, *Gender and Colonialism* (Basingstoke: Macmillan, 1999), p. 50.

8. T. Denean Sharpley-Whiting, *Frantz Fanon: Conflicts and Feminisms* (Lanham, MD: Rowman & Littlefield, 1998), p. 58.

9. John Marx, 'The Feminization of Globalization', *Cultural Critique*, 63 (2006), 1–32 (p. 23).

10. Florence Stratton, 'The Shallow Grave: Archetypes of Female Experience in African Fiction', *Research in African Literatures*, 19.2 (1988), 143–69 (p. 144).

11. See Ifi Amadiume, *Male Daughters, Female Husbands: Gender and Sex in an African Society* (London: Zed Books, 1987); Ifi Amadiume, *Re-Inventing Africa: Matriarchy, Religion and Culture* (London: Zed Books, 1997); Nkiri Iwechia Nzegwu, *Family Matters: Feminist Concepts in African Philosophy of Culture* (Albany: State University of New York Press, 2006); Egodi Uchendu, *Women and Conflict in the Nigerian Civil War* (Trenton: Africa World Press, 2007).

12. See Lily G. N. Mabura, 'Black Women Walking Zimbabwe: Refuge and Prospect in the Landscapes of Yvonne Vera's *The Stone Virgins* and Tsitsi Dangarembga's *Nervous Conditions* and Its Sequel, *The Book of Not*', *Research in African Literatures*, 41.3 (2010), 88–111 (p. 99).

13. Amadiume, *Male Daughters*, p. 141.

14. See, for example, Oyěwùmí's chapter 'Colonizing Bodies and Minds: Gender and Colonialism' in Oyèrónke Oyěwùmí, *The Invention of Women: Making an African Sense of Western Gender Discourses* (Minneapolis: University of Minnesota Press, 1997), pp. 121–56.

15. 'Aminatta Forna in Conversation and Valeriu Nicolae in Conversation: Memory and Forgetting', *Index on Censorship*, 35.2 (2006), 74–81 (p. 79).

16. See Fanon, 'The Trials and Tribulations of National Consciousness', in *The Wretched of the Earth*, trans. by Richard Philcox (New York: Grove Press, 2004 [1961]), pp. 97–144.

17. Gillian Rose, *Feminism and Geography: The Limits of Geographical Knowledge* (Minneapolis: University of Minnesota Press, 1993), p. 56.

18. Stratton, 'Periodic', p. 121.

19. Aminatta Forna, *Ancestor Stones* (London: Bloomsbury, 2006), np; henceforth cited in-text as *AS*.

20. Laura Sjoberg and Sandra Via, 'Introduction', in *Gender, War, and Militarism: Feminist Perspectives*, ed. by Laura Sjoberg and Sandra Via (Santa Barbara: ABC-CLIO, 2010), pp. 1–14 (p. 3).

21. Nouri Gana and Heike Härting, 'Introduction: Narrative Violence: Africa and the Middle East', *Comparative Studies of South Asia, Africa and the Middle East*, 28.1 (2008), 1–10 (p. 7).

22. Hayat Imam, 'Aftermath of U.S. Invasions: The Anguish of Women in Afghanistan and Iraq', in *Women, War, and Violence: Personal Perspectives and Global Activism*, ed. by Robin M. Chandler, Lihua Wang and Linda K. Fuller (New York: Palgrave Macmillan, 2010), pp. 117–34 (p. 126).

23. V. Spike Peterson, 'Gendered Identities, Ideologies, and Practices in the Context of War and Militarism', in *Gender, War, and Militarism: Feminist Perspectives*, ed. by Laura Sjoberg and Sandra Via (Santa Barbara: ABC-CLIO, 2010), pp. 17–29 (p. 19).

24. Natalja Zabeida, 'Not Making Excuses: Functions of Rape as a Tool in Ethno-Nationalist Wars', in *Women, War, and Violence: Personal Perspectives and Global Activism*, ed. by Robin M. Chandler, Lihua Wang and Linda K. Fuller (New York: Palgrave Macmillan, 2010), pp. 17–30 (pp. 21–2).

25. Sondra Hale, 'Rape as a Marker and Eraser of Difference: Darfur and the Nuba Mountains (Sudan)', in *Gender, War, and Militarism: Feminist Perspectives*, ed. by Laura Sjoberg and Sandra Via (Santa Barbara: ABC-CLIO, 2010), pp. 105–13.

26. Zabeida, p. 23.

27. Axel Harneil-Sievers, Jones O. Ahazuem and Sydney Emezue, *A Social History of the Nigerian Civil War: Perspectives from Below* (Ogete, Enugu: Jemezie Associates, 1997), p. 132.

28. Harneil-Sievers, Ahazuem and Emezue, p. 133.

29. Harneil-Sievers, Ahazuem and Emezue, pp. 129–30.

30. Harneil-Sievers, Ahazuem and Emezue, p. 144.

31. Harneil-Sievers, Ahazuem and Emezue, p. 48; p. 148.

32. Susan Shepler, 'Post-war Trajectories for Girls Associated with the Fighting Forces in Sierra Leone', in *Gender, War, and Militarism: Feminist Perspectives*, ed. by Laura Sjoberg and Sandra Via (Santa Barbara: ABC-CLIO, 2010), pp. 91–102.

33. Elisabeth Jean Wood, 'Sexual Violence during War: Toward an Understanding of Variation', in *Gender, War, and Militarism: Feminist Perspectives*, ed. by Laura Sjoberg and Sandra Via (Santa Barbara: ABC-CLIO, 2010), pp. 124–37 (p. 128); Megan Gerecke, 'Explaining Sexual Violence in Conflict Situations', in *Gender, War, and Militarism: Feminist Perspectives*, ed. by Laura Sjoberg and Sandra Via (Santa Barbara: ABC-CLIO, 2010), pp. 138–54 (p. 139); Ibrahim Abdullah, 'Bush Path to Destruction: The Origin and Character of the Revolutionary United Front (RUF/SL)', in *Between Democracy and Terror: The Sierra Leone Civil War*, ed. by Ibrahim Abdullah (Dakar: Council for the Development of Social Science Research in Africa, 2004), pp. 41–65 (p. 61).

34. Sandra Chait, '*The Stone Virgins* by Yvonne Vera', *Africa Today*, 50.4 (2004), 132–5 (p. 133); Sabelo J. Ndlovu-Gatsheni, *Do 'Zimbabweans' Exist? Trajectories of Nationalism, National Identity Formation and Crisis in a Postcolonial State* (Bern: Peter Lang, 2009), p. 182; Martin Meredith, *Mugabe: Power, Plunder and the Struggle for Zimbabwe* (New York: Public Affairs, 2002), p. 66; The Catholic Commission for Justice and Peace in Zimbabwe, *Gukurahundi in Zimbabwe: A Report on the Disturbances in Matabeleland and the Midlands, 1980–1988* (New York: Columbia University Press, 2008); Michael Bratton and Eldred Masunungure, 'Zimbabwe's Long Agony', *Journal of Democracy*, 19.4 (2008), 41–55 (p. 50).

35. Stratton, *Contemporary African Literature*, p. 37.

36. Moane, p. 33.
37. Moane, p. 34.
38. Peterson, p. 22.
39. Ashis Nandy, *The Intimate Enemy: Loss and Recovery of Self Under Colonialism* (New Delhi: Oxford University Press, 1983), pp. 7–11.
40. Chimamanda Ngozi Adichie, *Half of a Yellow Sun* (London: Harper Perennial, 2006), p. 53; henceforth cited in-text as *HYS*.
41. Spivak, *Critique*, p. 131.
42. Chima Anyadike, 'The Global North in Achebe's *Arrow of God* and Adichie's *Half of a Yellow Sun*', *The Global South*, 2.2 (2008), 139–49 (p. 143).
43. Julia Kristeva, *Powers of Horror: An Essay on Abjection*, trans. by Leon S. Roudiez (New York: Columbia University Press, 1982 [1980]).
44. The necessity for a woman to enter into motherhood in order to become fully human has been explored in depth in earlier Anglophone African writing, especially the works of Flora Nwapa and Buchi Emecheta.
45. Mabura, 'Walking Zimbabwe', p. 207.
46. Elleke Boehmer, 'Achebe and his Influence in some Contemporary African Writing', *Interventions: International Journal of Postcolonial Studies*, 11.2 (2009), 141–53 (p. 148).
47. Hawley, 'Biafra', p. 21.
48. Stephanie Newell, *West African Literatures: Ways of Reading* (Oxford: Oxford University Press, 2006), p. 157; Harneil-Sievers, Ahazuem and Emezue, p. 146; Marion Pape, 'Nigerian War Literature by Women: From Civil War to Gender War', in *Body, Sexuality, and Gender: Versions and Subversions in African Literatures 1*, ed. by Flora Veit-Wild and Dirk Naguschewski (Amsterdam: Rodopi, 2005), pp. 231–41 (p. 238).
49. Hawley, 'Biafra', p. 20.
50. Brenda Cooper, *A New Generation of African Writers: Migration, Material Culture & Language* (Woodbridge: James Currey, 2008), p. 147.
51. Maurice O. Wallace, *Constructing the Black Masculine: Identity and Ideality in African American Men's Literature and Culture 1775–1995* (Durham: Duke University Press, 2002), p. 86.
52. Cooper, *New Generation*, p. 134.
53. Chimamanda Ngozi Adichie, 'African "Authenticity" and the Biafran Experience', *Transition*, 99 (2008), 42–53 (pp. 49–50; p. 53).
54. Duncan Brown, 'National Belonging and Cultural Difference: South Africa and the Global Imaginary', *Journal of Southern African Studies*, 27.4 (2001), 757–69 (p. 758); Carolyn Martin Shaw, 'Turning Her Back on the Moon: Virginity, Sexuality, and Mothering in the Works of Yvonne Vera', *Africa Today*, 51.2 (2004), 35–51 (p. 37).
55. Stephen Chan, 'The Memory of Violence: Trauma in the Writings of Alexander Kanengoni and Yvonne Vera and the Idea of Unreconciled Citizenship in Zimbabwe', *Third World Quarterly*, 26.2 (2005), 369–82 (p. 374).
56. Paul Zeleza, 'Colonial Fictions: Memory and History in Yvonne Vera's Imagination', *Research in African Literatures*, 38.2 (2007), 9–21 (p. 11); Ranka

Primorac, *The Place of Tears: The Novel and Politics in Modern Zimbabwe* (London: Tauris Academic Studies, 2006), p. 145.

57. Ian Phimster, '"Zimbabwe is Mine": Mugabe, Murder, and Matabeleland', *Safundi: The Journal of South African and American Studies*, 10.4 (2009), 471–8 (p. 471).

58. Maurice T. Vambe, 'Zimbabwe Genocide: Voices and Perceptions from Ordinary People in Matabeleland and the Midlands Provinces, 30 years on', *African Identities*, 10.3 (2012), 281–300 (p. 282); Brian Chikwava, 'Free Speech in Zimbabwe: The Story of the Blue-Stomached Lizard', *World Literature Today*, 80.5 (2006), 18–21 (p. 20).

59. Jocelyn Alexander, 'Dissident Perspectives on Zimbabwe's Post-Independence War', *Africa: Journal of the International African Institute*, 68.2 (1998), 151–82 (p. 159).

60. Vambe, p. 282.

61. Primorac, *Place of Tears*, p. 163.

62. Mabura, 'Walking Zimbabwe', p. 97.

63. Dorothy Driver and Meg Samuelson, 'History's Intimate Invasions: Yvonne Vera's *The Stone Virgins*', *English Studies in Africa*, 50.2 (2007), 101–20 (p. 110).

64. Yvonne Vera, *The Stone Virgins* (New York: Farrar, Staus and Giroux, 2002), p. 69; henceforth cited in-text as *SV*.

65. Sofia Kostelac, '"The body is his, pulse and motion": Violence and Desire in Yvonne Vera's *The Stone Virgins*', *Research in African Literatures*, 41.3 (2010), 75–87 (p. 82).

66. Sofia Kostelac, '"The Voices of Drowned Men Cannot Be Heard": Writing Subalternity in Yvonne Vera's *Butterfly Burning* and *The Stone Virgins*', *English Studies in Africa*, 50.2 (2007), 121–32 (p. 128).

67. Arlene A. Elder, *Narrative Shape-shifting: Myth, Humour and History in the Fiction of Ben Okri, B. Kojo Laing and Yvonne Vera* (Surrey: James Currey, 2009), p. 127.

68. Terrance Ranger, 'Nationalist Historiography, Patriotic History and the History of the Nation: The Struggle Over the Past in Zimbabwe', *Journal of Southern African Studies*, 30.2 (2004), 215–34 (pp. 218–19).

69. John Marx, 'Fiction and State Crisis', *Novel: A Forum on Fiction*, 42.3 (2009), 524–30 (p. 527).

70. Shona N. Jackson, 'The Economy of Babel or "Can I Buy a Vowel?"', *Callaloo*, 32.2 (Spring 2009), 581–90 (p. 581).

71. Asha Varadharajan, *Exotic Parodies: Subjectivity in Adorno, Said, and Spivak* (Minneapolis: University of Minnesota Press, 1995), p. 21.

72. Nathan Oates, 'Political Stories: The Individual in Contemporary Fiction', *The Missouri Review*, 30.3 (2007), 156–71 (p. 165).

73. Cooper, *New Generation*, p. 133.

74. Gana and Härting, p. 4.

75. Jimmy D. Kandeh, 'In Search of Legitimacy: The 1996 Elections', in *Between Democracy and Terror: The Sierra Leone Civil War*, ed. by Ibrahim Abdullah (Dakar: Council for the Development of Social Science Research

in Africa, 2004), pp. 123–43 (p. 143); for more detail on the centrality of women to the success of the elections, see Filomina Chioma Steady, *Women and Collective Action in Africa* (New York: Palgrave, 2006), pp. 50–3.

76. Rose, p. 126.
77. Nzegwu, p. 11.
78. Nzegwu, p. 15.
79. Nwando Achebe, *Farmers, Traders, Warriors, and Kings: Female Power and Authority in Northern Igboland 1900–1960* (Portsmouth: Heinemann, 2005), p. 37.
80. Lily Mabura, 'Breaking Gods: An African Postcolonial Gothic Reading of Chimamanda Ngozi Adichie's *Purple Hibiscus* and *Half of a Yellow Sun*', *Research in African Literatures*, 39.1 (2008), 203–22 (p. 210).
81. The link between the sacred maternal and fertility in Igbo tradition has been well documented, perhaps mostly thoroughly by Sabine Jell-Bahlsen, *The Water Goddess in Igbo Cosmology: Ogbuide of Oguta Lake* (Trenton: Africa World Press, 2008), pp. 72–3.
82. Stratton, 'Shallow Grave', p. 147.
83. Martin Shaw, p. 47.
84. See Diana Auret, 'The Mhondoro Spirits of Supratribal Significance in the Culture of the Shona', *African Studies*, 41.2 (1982), 173–87; D. N. Beach, 'An Innocent Woman, Unjustly Accused? Charwe, Medium of the Nehanda Mhondoro Spirit, and the 1896–97 Central Shona Rising in Zimbabwe', *History in Africa*, 25 (1988), 27–54.
85. Emmanuel Chiwome, 'The Role of Oral Traditions in the War of National Liberation in Zimbabwe: Preliminary Observations', *Journal of Folklore Research*, 27.2 (1990), 241–7 (p. 243).
86. Beach, pp. 27–8.
87. Desiree Lewis, 'Biography, Nationalism and Yvonne Vera's *Nehanda*', *Social Dynamic: A Journal of African Studies*, 30.1 (2004), 28–50 (p. 33).
88. Lewis, p. 33.
89. Stratton, *Contemporary African Literature*, p. 123; see also Ann Marie Adams, 'It's a Woman's War: Engendering Conflict in Buchi Emecheta's *Destination Biafra*', *Callaloo*, 24.1 (Winter 2001), 287–300 (p. 295).

## 4   Mythopoetics and Cultural Re-Creation

1. See, for example, Aimé Césaire, *Discour sur le colonialism, Suivi de Discour sur la Négritude* (Paris: Présence Africaine, 2000 [1955]); Aimé Césaire, *Cahier d'un retour au pays natal* (Paris: Présence Africaine, 1956); Léopold Sédar Senghor, *Anthologie de la nouvelle poésie nègre et malgache de langue française* (Paris: Presses universitaires de France, 1948); Chinweizu, Onwuchekwa Jemie and Ihechukwu Madubuike, *Decolonization*; Soyinka, 'African State'.
2. Brückner, p. 153.
3. Ahluwalia, p. 21.
4. Lewis Nkosi, *Tasks and Masks: Themes and Style of African Literature* (Harlow: Longman, 1981), p. 14; p. 27.

5. Abdul R. JanMohamed, 'The Economy of Manichean Allegory: The Function of Racial Difference in Colonialist Literature', *Critical Inquiry*, 12.1 (1985), 59–87 (p. 62).
6. Fanon, *Wretched*, p. 160.
7. Boehmer, *Migrant Metaphors*, p. 100.
8. Fanon, *Wretched*, p. 149.
9. Newell, *West African*, p. 90.
10. Kobena Mercer, 'Welcome to the Jungle: Identity and Diversity in Postmodern Politics', in *Identity: Community, Culture, Difference*, ed. by Jonathan Rutherford (London: Lawrence & Wishart, 1990), pp. 43–71 (p. 60).
11. Rahul Rao, *Third World Protest: Between Home and the World* (Oxford: Oxford University Press, 2010), p. 137.
12. Benita Parry, 'Fanon and the Trauma of Modernity', in *After Fanon* (New Formations, 47) (London: Lawrence & Wishart, 2002), pp. 24–9 (p. 25).
13. Achille Mbembe, *On the Postcolony* (Berkeley: University of California Press, 2001), p. 1, emphasis original.
14. Boehmer, *Migrant Metaphors*, p. 177.
15. Simon Gikandi, 'African Literature and the Colonial Factor', in *Cambridge History of African and Caribbean Literature*, vol. 1, ed. by F. Abiola Irele and Simon Gikandi (Cambridge: Cambridge University Press, 2004), pp. 379–97 (p. 382).
16. Wole Soyinka, *Myth, Literature and the African World* (Cambridge: Cambridge University Press, 1976), p. x.
17. Fanon, *Wretched*, p. 159.
18. Peter Amato, 'African Philosophy and Modernity', in *Postcolonial African Philosophy: A Critical Reader*, ed. by Emmanuel Chukwudi Eze (Oxford: Blackwell, 1997), pp. 71–99 (p. 76).
19. Jean Marie Makang, 'Of the Good Use of Tradition: Keeping the Critical Perspective in African Philosophy', in *Postcolonial African Philosophy: A Critical Reader*, ed. by Emmanuel Chukwudi Eze (Oxford: Blackwell, 1997), pp. 324–38 (p. 327).
20. Derek Wright, 'African Literature and Post-independence Disillusionment', in *Cambridge History of African and Caribbean Literature*, vol. 1, ed. by F. Abiola Irele and Simon Gikandi (Cambridge: Cambridge University Press, 2004), pp. 797–808 (p. 808).
21. Wendy Griswold, 'The Writing on the Mud Wall: Nigerian Novels and the Imaginary Village', *American Sociological Review*, 57.6 (1992), 709–24 (p. 710).
22. Gilroy, *Black Atlantic*, p. 127.
23. Biodun Jeyifo, 'The Nation of Things: Arrested Decolonization and Critical Theory', *Research in African Literatures*, 21.1 (1990), 33–48.
24. Gilroy, *Black Atlantic*, p. 3.
25. Chigekwu Ogbuene, *The Concept of Man in Igbo Myths* (Frankfurt am Main: Peter Lang, 1999), p. 5.
26. G. G. Darah, 'Introduction', in *Radical Essays on Nigerian Literature*, ed. by G. G. Darah (Lagos: Malthouse Press, 2008), pp. xv–xlvii (p. xx); Ichie

P. A. Ezikeojiaku, 'Towards Understanding Ndi Igbo and their Cosmology', in *Radical Essays on Nigerian Literature*, ed. by G. G. Darah (Lagos: Malthouse Press, 2008), pp. 35–48 (p. 38).

27. *Ogbanje* is a term taken from Igbo tradition, while the more widely-known corollary, *abiku*, comes from the Yoruba mythopoetic and religious traditions.

28. Menkiti, p. 108.

29. Chinwe Achebe, *The World of the Ogbanje* (Enugu: Fourth Dimension, 1986), pp. 30–1.

30. Chinwe Achebe, p. 60.

31. Christopher Okonkwo, 'A Critical Divination: Reading *Sula* as Ogbanje-Abiku', *African American Review*, 38.4 (2004), pp. 651–68 (pp. 653–4).

32. Ato Quayson, 'Looking Awry: Tropes of Disability in Postcolonial Writing', in *Relocating Postcolonialism*, ed. by David Goldberg and Ato Quayson (Oxford: Blackwell, 2002), pp. 217–30 (p. 227); Chikwenye Okonjo Ogunyemi, 'An Abiku-Ogbanje Atlas: A Pre-Text for Rereading Soyinka's *Ake* and Morrison's *Beloved*', *African American Review*, 36.4 (2002), 663–8 (p. 667).

33. Hamish Dalley, 'Trauma Theory and Nigerian Civil War Literature: Speaking "Something that was Never in Words" in Chris Abani's *Song for Night*', *Journal of Postcolonial Writing*, 49.4 (2013), 445–57 (p. 452).

34. Stefan Sereda's analysis of *GraceLand* provides an illuminating discussion of the interweaving of these many discourses as a means of fashioning a polyglossic resistance at the text's structural level. Stefan Sereda, 'Riffing on Resistance: Music in Chris Abani's *Graceland*', *ARIEL: A Review of International English*, 39.4 (2008), 31–47 (pp. 35–8).

35. Chris Abani, *GraceLand* (New York: Picador, 2004), p. 318; henceforth cited in-text as *GL*.

36. Marc Augé, *Non-Places: Introduction to an Anthropology of Supermodernity*, trans. by John Howe (London: Verso, 1995 [1992]), p. 3.

37. For the distinction between completion and closure, see James Phelan, *Reading People, Reading Plots* (Chicago: The University of Chicago Press, 1989), pp. 17–18.

38. Boehmer, 'Achebe', pp. 144–5.

39. Ogbuene, p. 135.

40. Rita Nnodim, 'City, Identity and Dystopia: Writing Lagos in Contemporary Nigerian Novels', *Journal of Postcolonial Writing*, 44.4 (2008), 321–32 (p. 325).

41. Okonkwo, p. 657, emphasis original.

42. Emmanuel Chukwudi Eze, 'Language and Time in Postcolonial Experience', *Research in African Literatures*, 39.1 (2008), 24–47 (p. 26).

43. Adélékè Adéèkó, 'Power Shift: America in the New Nigerian Imagination', *The Global South*, 2.2 (2008), 10–30 (p. 16).

44. Obi Nwakanma, 'Metonymic Eruptions: Igbo Novelists, the Narrative of the Nation, and New Developments in the Contemporary Nigerian Novel', *Research in African Literatures*, 39.2 (2008), 1–14 (p. 13).

45. Katherine Hunt, 'Book Review: Abani, Chris. *Graceland*', *Journal of Asian and African Studies*, 43 (2008), 241–3 (p. 243).
46. Albert Memmi, *Decolonization and the Decolonized* (Minneapolis: University of Minneapolis Press, 2006), p. 70.
47. Mudimbe, *Invention*, p. 5.
48. Nwakanma, p. 13.
49. Elleke Boehmer, 'Transfiguring: Colonial Body into Postcolonial Narrative', *NOVEL: A Forum on Fiction*, 26.3 (Spring 1993), 268–77 (p. 274).
50. Toni Morrison's *Beloved*, in particular, has frequently been read in the *ogbanje-abiku* tradition.
51. Cooper, *Magical Realism*, p. 1; p. 44.
52. Ngũgĩ wa Thiong'o, 'Recovering the Original', *World Literature Today*, 78.3/4 (2004), 13–15 (p. 14).
53. Michael Andindilile, 'Beyond Nativism: Translingualism and Ngũgĩ's Engagement with Anglophonism', *Perspectives: Studies in Translatology* (2013), 1–19 (p. 15); Raoul J. Granqvist, 'Reflections: Ngũgĩ wa Thiong'o in/and 2006', *Research in African Literatures*, 42.4 (2011), 124–31 (p. 129); James Ogude, *Ngũgĩ's Novels and African History: Narrating the Nation* (London: Pluto Press, 1999), p. 88.
54. Trivedi, p. 8.
55. Nick Mdika Tembo, 'Subversion and the Carnivalesque: Images of Resistance in Ngũgĩ wa Thiong'o's *Wizard of the Crow*', in *Spheres Public and Private: Western Genres in African Literature*, ed. by Gordon Collier (Amsterdam: Rodopi, 2011), pp. 337–61 (p. 343).
56. Obonyo Amoko, pp. 105–6.
57. Simon Gikandi, *Ngũgĩ wa Thiong'o* (Cambridge: Cambridge University Press, 2000), pp. 232–3.
58. Gikandi, *Ngũgĩ*, p. 291.
59. Obonyo Amoko, p. 103.
60. Gikandi, *Ngũgĩ*, p. 2.
61. Andrade, *Writ Small*, p. 2.
62. Robert Spencer, 'Ngũgĩ wa Thiong'o and the African Dictator Novel', *Journal of Commonwealth Literature*, 47.2 (2012), 145–58 (p. 152).
63. Granqvist, p. 126.
64. Simon Gikandi, 'The Postcolonial Wizard', *Transition*, 98 (2008), 156–69 (p. 156).
65. William Slaymaker, 'Digesting Crow: Reading and Teaching Ngũgĩ's *Wizard of the Crow*', *Research in African Literatures*, 42.4 (2011), 8–19 (p. 8).
66. F. Abiola Irele, *The African Imagination: Literature in Africa and the Black Diaspora* (New York: Oxford University Press, 2001), p. 25.
67. Spencer, 'African Dictator Novel', p. 147.
68. Ngũgĩ wa Thiong'o, *Wizard of the Crow* (New York: Anchor, 2006), p. 3; henceforth cited in-text as *WC*.
69. Robert L. Colson, 'Arresting Time, Resisting Arrest: Narrative Time and the African Dictator in Ngũgĩ wa Thiong'o's *Wizard of the Crow*', *Research in African Literatures*, 42.1 (2011), 133–53.

70. See Chapter Four, 'I, etcetera: Multiperson Narration and the Range of Contemporary Narrators', in Richardson, *Unnatural Voices*.
71. The term, taken from Walter Benjamin, has also been used by Benedict Anderson to describe the link between the novel and the nation: 'The idea of a sociological organism moving calendrically through homogeneous, empty time is a precise analogue of the idea of the nation, which also is conceived as a solid community moving steadily down (or up) history'. Benedict Anderson, p. 24.
72. Walter Benjamin, *Illuminations*, trans. by Harry Zohn (New York: Schocken Books, 1968), pp. 98–100.
73. Granqvist, p. 128.
74. Angela Lamas Rodrigues, 'Beyond Nativism: An Interview with Ngũgĩ wa Thiong'o', *Research in African Literatures*, 35.3 (2004), 161–7 (p. 167).
75. On the notion of a cosmopolitanism in which the universal is rooted in the local, see Sheldon Pollock, Homi K. Bhabha, Carol A. Breckenridge and Dipesh Chakrabarty, 'Cosmopolitanisms', in *Cosmopolitanisms*, ed. by Sheldon Pollock, Homi K. Bhabha, Carol A. Breckenridge and Dipesh Chakrabarty (Durham: Duke University Press, 2002), pp. 1–14; Walter Mignolo, 'The Many Faces of Cosmo-polis: Border Thinking and Critical Cosmopolitanism', in *Cosmopolitanisms*, ed. by Sheldon Pollock, Homi K. Bhabha, Carol A. Breckenridge and Dipesh Chakrabarty (Durham: Duke University Press, 2002), pp. 157–88; Bruce Robbins, 'Introduction Part I: Actually Existing Cosmopolitanism', in *Cosmopolitics: Thinking and Feeling Beyond the Nation*, ed. by Pheng Cheah and Bruce Robbins (Minneapolis: University of Minnesota Press, 1998), pp. 1–19; Bruce Robbins, 'Comparative Cosmopolitanisms', in *Cosmopolitics: Thinking and Feeling Beyond the Nation*, ed. by Pheng Cheah and Bruce Robbins (Minneapolis: University of Minnesota Press, 1998), pp. 246–64; Kwame Anthony Appiah, *Cosmopolitanism: Ethics in a World of Strangers* (London: Penguin, 2006).
76. See Spencer, 'African Dictator Novel' for a full reading of *Wizard of the Crow* as part of a global tradition of dictator novels.
77. *Wizard of the Crow* develops a number of parallels and intertextual references to Armah's novel, notable through Kamĩtĩ's obsession with smell and its use of the abject as a metaphor for neocolonial corruption.
78. Ogude, p. 47; Gikandi, *Ngũgĩ*, p. 18.
79. John Updike, 'Extended Performance: Saving the Republic of Aburira', *New Yorker* (31 July 2006) <http://www.newyorker.com/archive/2006/07/31/060731crbo_books> [accessed 19 June 2013].
80. Aminatta Forna, 'Speaking in Tongues', *Washington Post* (10 September 2006) <http://www.washingtonpost.com/wp-dyn/content/article/2006/09/07/AR2006090701167.html> [accessed 19 June 2013].
81. Forna, 'Speaking in Tongues'.
82. Jameson, 'Third World Literature', p. 66.
83. See Ogude, p. 47; Gikandi, *Ngũgĩ*, pp. 15–17, on earlier works by Ngũgĩ.
84. Slaymaker, p. 14.

85. Translations taken from Mike Kuria, 'Speaking in Tongues: Ngũgĩ's Gift to Workers and Peasants through *Mũrogi wa Kagogo*', *Journal of Literary Studies*, 27.3 (2011), 56–73 (p. 61).
86. Gikandi, 'Postcolonial Wizard', p. 165.
87. Kuria, p. 62.
88. Andindilile, p. 15.
89. Kuria, p. 62.
90. Kuria, p. 61.
91. Kuria, p. 64.
92. Mwangi Muriruri, cited in Granqvist, pp. 128–9.
93. See Kuria, p. 65; Andindilile, p. 16.
94. Mdika Tembo, p. 357.
95. Joseph McLaren, 'From the National to the Global: Satirical Magical Realism in Ngũgĩ's *Wizard of the Crow*', *The Global South*, 2.2 (2008), 150–8.
96. Forna, 'Speaking in Tongues'.
97. Colson, p. 137.
98. Updike.
99. See, for example, Bhabha's claim that magical realism is the language of the emergent postcolonial world in Homi K. Bhabha, 'Introduction: Narrating the Nation', in *Nation and Narration*, ed. by Homi K. Bhabha (London: Routledge, 1990), pp. 1–7 (p. 7).
100. Eva Aldea, *Magical Realism and Deleuze: The Indiscernibility of Difference in Postcolonial Literature* (London: Continuum, 2011), p. 1.
101. Cooper, *Magical Realism*, p. 15.
102. Cooper, *Magical Realism*, p. 15.
103. Stephen Slemon, 'Magical Realism as Post-Colonial Discourse', in *Magical Realism: Theory and History*, ed. by Lois Parkinson Zamora and Wendy B. Faris (Durham: Duke University Press, 1995), pp. 407–26 (pp. 420–2).
104. Spencer, 'African Dictator Novel', p. 153.
105. Harry Garuba, 'Explorations in Animist Materialism: Notes on Reading/ Writing African Literature, Culture, and Society', *Public Culture*, 15.2 (2003), 261–85 (p. 272).
106. Granqvist, p. 126.
107. Nnedi Okorafor, 'Organic Fantasy', *African Identities*, 7.2 (2009), 275–86 (p. 283).
108. Susan Z. Andrade, 'Adichie's Genealogies: National and Feminine Novels', *Research in African Literatures*, 42.2 (2011), 91–101 (p. 95); Gwendolyn Etter-Lewis, 'Dark Bodies/White Masks: African Masculinities in *Graceland, The Joys of Motherhood* and *Things Fall Apart*', in *Masculinities in African Literary and Cultural Texts*, ed. by Helen Mugambi and Tuzyline Jita Allen (Banbury: Ayebia Clarke, 2010), pp. 160–77 (p. 172).
109. The destruction of Maroko in 1990 has been called 'One of the most notorious and heartbreaking' of the 'repeated forced exoduses' brought

on by structural adjustment (see Mike Davis, *Planet of Slums* (London: Verso, 2006), p. 101). In *GraceLand*, the episode is a reference not to this final destruction of the slum, but to an earlier episode of clearance in 1983 (see Sarah Harrison, '"Suspended City": Personal, Urban, and National Development in Chris Abani's *GraceLand*', *Research in African Literatures*, 43.2 (2012), 95–114 (p. 97)).

110. Ezikeojiaku, p. 44.
111. Nnodim, p. 323.
112. Garuba, p. 274.
113. Bill Ott, 'review of *GraceLand*', *Booklist* (13 November 2003), 570.
114. Ojaide, 'Canonisation', p. 16.
115. Simon Gikandi, *Reading the African Novel* (London: James Currey, 1987), p. 150.
116. Isidore Okpewho, 'Home, Exile, and the Space In Between', *Research in African Literatures*, 37.2 (Summer 2006), 68–83 (p. 69).
117. Stuart Hall, 'Cultural Identity and Diaspora', in *Identity: Community, Culture, Difference*, ed. by Jonathan Rutherford (London: Lawrence & Wishart, 1990), pp. 222–37 (p. 225).
118. Òlakunle George, 'The "Native" Missionary, the African Novel, and In-between', *NOVEL: A Forum on Fiction*, 36.1 (Autumn 2002), 5–25 (p. 18).
119. Menkiti, p. 107.
120. Ahluwalia, p. 131.
121. James Snead, 'European Pedigrees/African Contagions: Nationality, Narrative, and Communality in Tutuola, Achebe, and Reed', in *Nation and Narration*, ed. by Homi K. Bhabha (London: Routledge, 1990), pp. 231–49 (p. 237).

## 5   Global African Literature: Strategies of Address and Cultural Constraints

1. Jerome Brooks, 'Chinua Achebe: The Art of Fiction no. 139', *The Paris Review*, 139 (1994) <http://www.theparisreview.org/interviews/1720/the-art-of-fiction-no-139-chinua-achebe> [accessed 16 July 2013]; Chinua Achebe, *There Was A Country: A Personal History of Biafra* (London: Allen Lane, 2012), pp. 34–8.
2. James Currey, *Africa Writes Back: The African Writers Series and the Launch of African Literature* (Oxford: James Currey, 2008), p. 28.
3. See, for example, Fraser, pp. 88–99; Gareth Griffiths, *African Literatures in English: East and West* (Harlow: Pearson Education, 2000); Patrick Williams, 'West African Writing', in *Writing and Africa*, ed. by Mpalive-Hangson Msiska and Paul Hyland (Harlow: Addison Wesley Longman, 1997), pp. 31–45 (pp. 31–3).
4. Low, p. 2.
5. Fraser, p. 88.
6. Newell, *West African*, p. 98.

7. Williams, p. 33.
8. Currey, p. 30.
9. Chinua Achebe, *Hopes and Impediments* (New York: Anchor Books, 1988), p. 45.
10. Williams, p. 34.
11. Henry Louis Gates, Jr, 'Criticism in the Jungle', in *Black Literature and Literary Theory*, ed. by Henry Louis Gates, Jr (New York: Methuen, 1984), pp. 1–25 (p. 5).
12. Gates, p. 5.
13. Kadiatu Kanneh, 'What is African Literature? Ethnography and Criticism', in *Writing and Africa*, ed. by Mpalive-Hangson Msiska and Paul Hyland (Harlow: Addison Wesley Longman, 1997), pp. 69–86 (p. 73).
14. Gates, p. 5; Low, p. 90.
15. Newell, *West African*, pp. 85–100.
16. Caroline Davis, p. 2. Throughout her extensive study, Davis demonstrates the limits of Bourdieu's contention that, in the realm of art, symbolic and economic value remain discrete. Instead, as she illustrates through an extensive study of Oxford University Press and the Three Crowns Series, in the realm of postcolonial writing, the economic and the symbolic enter into a symbiotic relationship driven by oppositional aims and desires.
17. Currey, p. xxiv.
18. Fraser, p. 182.
19. Griswold, *Bearing Witness*, p. 11; Chinua Achebe, *Morning Yet on Creation Day: Essays* (Garden City: Anchor Books, 1975), p. 39.
20. Walter Bgoya and Mary Jay, 'Publishing in Africa from Independence to the Present Day', *Research in African Literatures*, 44.2 (2013), 17–34 (pp. 19–20).
21. Williams, pp. 43–4.
22. Fraser, p. 166; p. 175; Caroline Davis, p. 35; Newell, *West African*, pp. 6–7.
23. Ngũgĩ's Gikuyu-language texts are published by East African Educational Publishers (Kenya) and Adichie's by Kaficho Limited (Nigeria). Similarly, authors like Doreen Baingana and Zoe Whitcomb are represented by local publishers in Kenya and South Africa, respectively.
24. James English, *The Economy of Prestige: Prizes, Awards and the Circulation of Cultural Value* (Harvard: Harvard University Press, 2005), p. 2.
25. English, p. 3.
26. Dobrota Pucherová, '"A Continent Learns to Tell its Story at Last": Notes on the Caine Prize', *Journal of Postcolonial Writing*, 48.1 (2012), 13–25 (p. 14; p. 22).
27. Helon Habila, '*We Need New Names* by NoViolet Bulawayo—review', *Guardian* (20 June 2013) <http://www.guardian.co.uk/books/2013/jun/20/need-new-names-bulawayo-review> [accessed 16 July 2013]. Ikhide R. Ikheloa, for instance, exhorts African writers and critics to 'Keep the Caine Prize, lose the contrived stories. Africa has suffered enough as it is', in an essay which argues that, through the prize's popularity and high profile, aspiring African writers have been driven to conform

to a certain expected aesthetic in their portrayal of Africa. Equally, the idea that prize culture and prestige-based institutions have fostered an artificially unified aesthetic in African writing is nothing new. Gareth Griffiths, for instance, argues that, because of the prevalence of the African Writers Series and celebrity authors like Achebe, early African writing, too, displayed a more unified aesthetic than the continent's diversity might suggest. Ikhide R. Ikheloa, 'The 2011 Caine Prize: How Not to Write About Africa', *Ikhide: Email from America* (11 March 2012) <http://xokigbo.wordpress.com/2012/03/11/the-2011-caine-prize-how-not-to-write-about-africa/> [accessed 16 July 2013]; Griffiths, pp. 84–5.

28. Pascale Casanova, *The World Republic of Letters*, trans. by M. B. Debevoise (Cambridge: Harvard University Press, 2004 [1999]), pp. 11–12.
29. Casanova, p. 15.
30. Casanova, p. 156.
31. Pierre Bourdieu, *Distinction: A Social Critique of the Judgement of Taste*, trans. by Richard Nice (London: Routledge, 1984 [1979]), p. 2.
32. Bourdieu, p. 53.
33. Huggan, *Postcolonial Exotic*, pp. 35–7; Brennan, *At Home in the World*, pp. 36–41.
34. Huggan, *Postcolonial Exotic*, p. vii.
35. Brennan, *At Home in the World*, p. 3.
36. Slaymaker, p. 8.
37. Neil ten Kortenaar, *Postcolonial Literature and the Impact of Literacy: Reading and Writing in African and Caribbean Fiction* (Cambridge: Cambridge University Press, 2011), p. 189.
38. Brouillette, pp. 3–4.
39. H. Porter Abbott, *The Cambridge Introduction to Narrative* (Cambridge: Cambridge University Press, 2002), p. 36; Wayne Booth, *A Rhetoric of Irony* (Chicago: The University of Chicago Press, 1974).
40. Peter J. Rabinowitz, 'Truth in Fiction: A Reexamination of Audiences', *Critical Inquiry*, 4.1 (Autumn 1977), 121–41 (p. 126).
41. Rabinowitz, 'Truth', p. 126.
42. Peter J. Rabinowitz, *Before Reading: Narrative Conventions and the Politics of Interpretation* (Columbus: Ohio State University Press, 1987), p. 8.
43. Rabinowitz, *Before Reading*, p. 25.
44. James Phelan, *Narrative as Rhetoric: Technique, Audiences, Ethics, Ideology* (Columbus: Ohio State University Press, 1996), p. 8.
45. James Phelan, 'Rhetorical Aesthetics and Other Issues in the Study of Literary Narratives', in *Narrative—State of the Art*, ed. by Michael G. W. Manberg (Philadelphia: John Benjamins, 2007), pp. 103–12 (p. 107).
46. Lahcen E. Ezzaher, *Writing and Cultural Influence: Studies in Rhetorical History, Orientalist Discourse, and Post-Colonial Criticism* (New York: Peter Lang, 2003), p. 19.
47. Simon Gikandi, 'Reading the Referent: Postcolonialism and the Writing of Modernity', in *Reading the 'New' Literatures in a Post-Colonial Era*, ed. by Susheila Nastra (Cambridge: D. S. Brewer, 2000), pp. 87–104 (p. 90).

48. Gikandi, 'Referent', p. 91.
49. Christopher Miller, 'Theories of Africans: The Question of Literary Anthropology', *Critical Inquiry*, 13.1 (1986), 120–39 (p. 121); Gates, 'Criticism in the Jungle', p. 5.
50. Brouillette, p. 19.
51. Andrade, 'Adichie's Genealogies', p. 92.
52. Jacques Derrida, *Of Grammatology*, trans. by Gayatri Chakravorty Spivak (Baltimore: The Johns Hopkins University Press, 1976), pp. 144–5; Brian Richardson, 'Introduction: Narrative Frames and Embeddings', in *Narrative Dynamics: Essays on Time, Plot, Closure, and Frames*, ed. by Brian Richardson (Columbus: Ohio State University Press, 2002), pp. 329–32 (p. 330); John Frow, 'The Literary Frame', in *Narrative Dynamics: Essays on Time, Plot, Closure, and Frames*, ed. by Brian Richardson (Columbus: Ohio State University Press, 2002), pp. 333–8 (p. 335).
53. Amanda Aycock, 'An Interview with Chris Abani', *Safundi*, 10.1 (2009), 1–10 (p. 8).
54. See '"Prizing Otherness": A Short History of the Booker', in Huggan, *Postcolonial Exotic*, pp. 105–23.
55. Ikheloa, 'Caine Prize'; Pucherová, p. 20.
56. Lizzy Attree, 'The Caine Prize and Contemporary African Writing', *Research in African Literatures*, 44.2 (2013), 35–47 (p. 41).
57. Appadurai, pp. 3–63.
58. Daniel Miller, 'Why Some Things Matter', in *Material Cultures: Why Some Things Matter*, ed. by Daniel Miller (London: UCL Press, 1997), pp. 3–21 (p. 17; p. 6).
59. Daniel Miller, *Material Culture and Mass Consumption* (Oxford: Blackwell, 1987), p. 62.
60. Brouillette, p. 2.
61. Arlif Dirlik, *The Postcolonial Aura: Third World Criticism in the Age of Global Capitalism* (Boulder: Westview Press, 1997); Aijaz Ahmad, 'The Politics of Literary Postcoloniality', *Race & Class*, 36.3 (1995), 1–20; Brennan, *At Home in the World*, p. 36.
62. Oates, p. 164.
63. Hawley, 'Biafra', p. 20.
64. Zoë Norridge, 'Sex as Synecdoche: Intimate Languages of Violence in Chimamanda Ngozi Adichie's *Half of a Yellow Sun* and Aminatta Forna's *The Memory of Love*', *Research in African Literatures*, 43.2 (2012), 18–39.
65. Annie Gagiano, 'Reading *The Stone Virgins* as Vera's Study of the Katabolism of War', *Research in African Literatures*, 38.2 (2007), 64–76 (p. 72).
66. Pius Adesanmi, 'Of Postcolonial Entanglement and Durée: Reflections on the Francophone African Novel', *Comparative Literature*, 56.2 (2004), 227–42 (p. 236).
67. Ojaide, 'Migration', p. 44; Tanure Ojaide, 'Examining Canonisation in Modern African Literature', *Asiatic*, 3.1 (2009), 1–20 (p. 16).
68. Francis B. Nyamnjoh, *The Disillusioned African*, revised edition (Bamenda: Langaa Research and Publishing Common Initiative Group, 2007 [1995]), p. 11; henceforth cited in-text as *DA*.

69. G. A. Agambila, *Journey* (Accra: Sub-Saharan Publishers, 2006), p. 112; henceforth cited in-text as *J*.
70. Mike Davis, pp. 14–19.
71. Mike Davis, p. 113.
72. Mike Davis, p. 114.
73. Valerie Tagwira, *The Uncertainty of Hope* (Harare: Weaver Press, 2006), p. 131; henceforth cited in-text as *UH*.
74. Daria Tunca, Vicki Mortimer and Emmanuelle Del Calzo, 'An Interview with Chika Unigwe', *Wasafiri*, 75 (2013), 54–9 (p. 56).
75. Helon Habila, 'Introduction', in *The Granta Book of the African Short Story*, ed. by Helon Habila (London: Granta, 2011), pp. vii–xv (p. viii).
76. Simon Gikandi, 'Between Roots and Routes: Cosmopolitanism and the Claims of Locality', in *Rerouting the Postcolonial: New Directions for the New Millennium*, ed. by Janet Wilson, Cristina Şandru and Sarah Lawson Welsh (London: Routledge, 2010), pp. 22–35.
77. Newell, *West African*, p. 21.
78. Derek Attridge, *The Singularity of Literature* (London: Routledge, 2004), p. 24; Robert Spencer, *Cosmopolitan Criticism*, p. 16.
79. Kwame Anthony Appiah, 'Is the Post- in Postmodernism the Post- in Postcolonial?', *Critical Inquiry*, 17.2 (1991), 336–57 (p. 341).
80. Lazarus, *Resistance*.
81. Gikandi, 'Referent', p. 97.

## Conclusion: Writing Africa's Futures?

1. Caroline Davis, p. 109.
2. Akin Adesokan, 'New African Writing and the Question of Audience', *Research in African Literatures*, 43.3 (2012), 1–20 (p. 3).
3. Adesokan, p. 11.
4. Habila, 'Introduction', p. viii.
5. See, for instance, Achebe's 'The Novelist as Teacher' in *Hopes and Impediments* and Ngũgĩ's comments on his transition to Gikuyu writing in *Decolonising the Mind*.
6. Adesokan, p. 1.
7. Ranka Primorac, 'Legends of Modern Zambia', *Research in African Literatures*, 43.4 (2012), 50–70 (p. 52).
8. Habila, '*We Need New Names* review'.
9. Eleni Coundouriotis, 'The Child Soldier Narrative and the Problem of Arrested Historicization', *Journal of Human Rights*, 9.2 (2010), 191–206 (p. 195).
10. Ranka Primorac, *Whodunnit in Southern Africa* (London: Africa Research Institute, 2011), p. 2.
11. Graham Furniss and Abdalla Uba Adamu, '"Go by Appearances at Your Peril": The Raina Kama Writers' Association in Kano, Nigeria, Carving out a Place for the "Popular" in the Hausa Literary Landscape', *Research in African Literatures*, 43.4 (2012), 88–111 (p. 110); see also Stephanie Newell, *Ghanaian Popular Fiction: 'Thrilling Discoveries in Conjugal Life' and Other Tales* (London: James Currey, 2000).
12. Fraser, p. 166.

# Bibliography

Abani, Chris, *GraceLand* (New York: Picador, 2004).

Abbott, H. Porter, *The Cambridge Introduction to Narrative* (Cambridge: Cambridge University Press, 2002).

Abdullah, Ibrahim, 'Bush Path to Destruction: The Origin and Character of the Revolutionary United Front (RUF/SL)', in *Between Democracy and Terror: The Sierra Leone Civil War*, ed. by Ibrahim Abdullah (Dakar: Council for the Development of Social Science Research in Africa, 2004), pp. 41–65.

Abraham, Yvonne, 'Orchard Gardens Graduate Excels with Determination, Support', *The Boston Globe* (30 June 2013) <http://www.bostonglobe.com/metro/2013/06/29/abraham/KjovFRAZjw3Yz351ADcIkL/story.html> [accessed 11 July 2013].

Achebe, Chinua, *The Education of a British-Protected Child* (London: Penguin, 2009).

——, 'English and the African Writer', *Transition*, 18 (1965), 27–30.

——, *Hopes and Impediments* (New York: Anchor Books, 1988).

——, *Morning Yet on Creation Day: Essays* (Garden City: Anchor Books, 1975).

——, *There Was A Country: A Personal History of Biafra* (London: Allen Lane, 2012).

Achebe, Chinwe, *The World of the Ogbanje* (Enugu: Fourth Dimension, 1986).

Achebe, Nwando, *Farmers, Traders, Warriors, and Kings: Female Power and Authority in Northern Igboland 1900–1960* (Portsmouth: Heinemann, 2005).

Adams, Ann Marie, 'It's a Woman's War: Engendering Conflict in Buchi Emecheta's *Destination Biafra*', *Callaloo*, 24.1 (Winter 2001), 287–300.

Adéèkó, Adélékè, 'Power Shift: America in the New Nigerian Imagination', *The Global South*, 2.2 (2008), 10–30.

Adesanmi, Pius, 'Of Postcolonial Entanglement and Durée: Reflections on the Francophone African Novel', *Comparative Literature*, 56.2 (2004), 227–42.

Adesokan, Akin, 'New African Writing and the Question of Audience', *Research in African Literatures*, 43.3 (2012), 1–20.

Adichie, Chimamanda Ngozi, 'African "Authenticity" and the Biafran Experience', *Transition*, 99 (2008), 42–53.

——, *Half of a Yellow Sun* (London: Harper Perennial, 2006).

Agambila, G. A., *Journey* (Accra: Sub-Saharan Publishers, 2006).

Ahluwalia, Pal, *Politics and Post-Colonial Theory: African Inflections* (London: Routledge, 2000).

Ahmad, Aijaz, *In Theory: Class, Nation and Identity* (London: Verso, 1993).

——, 'The Politics of Literary Postcoloniality', *Race & Class*, 36.3 (1995), 1–20.

Al-Kassim, Dina, 'The Face of Foreclosure', *Interventions: International Journal of Postcolonial Studies*, 4.2 (2002), 168–75.

Aldea, Eva, *Magical Realism and Deleuze: The Indiscernibility of Difference in Postcolonial Literature* (London: Continuum, 2011).

Alexander, Jocelyn, 'Dissident Perspectives on Zimbabwe's Post-Independence War', *Africa: Journal of the International African Institute*, 68.2 (1998), 151–82.

Amadiume, Ifi, *Male Daughters, Female Husbands: Gender and Sex in an African Society* (London: Zed Books, 1987).

———, *Re-Inventing Africa: Matriarchy, Religion and Culture* (London: Zed Books, 1997).

Amato, Peter, 'African Philosophy and Modernity', in *Postcolonial African Philosophy: A Critical Reader*, ed. by Emmanuel Chukwudi Eze (Oxford: Blackwell, 1997), pp. 71–99.

'Aminatta Forna in Conversation and Valeriu Nicolae in Conversation: Memory and Forgetting', *Index on Censorship*, 35.2 (2006), 74–81.

Amuta, Chidi, 'The Nigerian Civil War and the Evolution of Nigerian Literature', *Canadian Journal of African Studies*, 17.1 (1983), 85–99.

———, *The Theory of African Literature: Implications for Practical Criticism* (London: Zed, 1988).

Anderson, Amanda, 'Cosmopolitanism, Universalism, and the Divided Legacies of Modernity', in *Cosmopolitics: Thinking and Feeling Beyond the Nation*, ed. by Pheng Cheah and Bruce Robbins (Minneapolis: University of Minnesota Press, 1998), pp. 265–89.

Anderson, Benedict, *Imagined Communities: Reflections on the Origin and Spread of Nationalism*, revised edition (London: Verso, 1991).

Andindilile, Michael, 'Beyond Nativism: Translingualism and Ngũgĩ's Engagement with Anglophonism', *Perspectives: Studies in Translatology* (2013), 1–19.

Andrade, Susan Z., 'Adichie's Genealogies: National and Feminine Novels', *Research in African Literatures*, 42.2 (2011), 91–101.

———, *The Nation Writ Small: African Fictions and Feminisms, 1958–1988* (Durham: Duke University Press, 2011).

Anyadike, Chima, 'The Global North in Achebe's *Arrow of God* and Adichie's *Half of a Yellow Sun*', *The Global South*, 2.2 (2008), 139–49.

Appadurai, Arjun, 'Introduction: Commodities and the Politics of Value', in *The Social Life of Things*, ed. by Arjun Appadurai (Cambridge: Cambridge University Press, 1986), pp. 3–63.

Appiah, Kwame Anthony, *Cosmopolitanism: Ethics in a World of Strangers* (London: Penguin, 2006).

———, *The Ethics of Identity* (Princeton: Princeton University Press, 2005).

———, 'Is the Post- in Postmodernism the Post- in Postcolonial?', *Critical Inquiry*, 17.2 (1991), 336–57.

Archibeque, Carlye, 'An Interview with Chris Abani', *Poetix* <http://poetix. net/abani.htm> [accessed 20 March 2011].

Ashcroft, Bill, *Caliban's Voice: The Transformation of English in Post-Colonial Literatures* (London: Routledge, 2009).

———, *On Post-Colonial Futures: Transformations of Colonial Culture* (London: Continuum, 2001).

Attree, Lizzy, 'The Caine Prize and Contemporary African Writing', *Research in African Literatures*, 44.2 (2013), 35–47.

Attridge, Derek, *The Singularity of Literature* (London: Routledge, 2004).

Augé, Marc, *Non-Places: Introduction to an Anthropology of Supermodernity*, trans. by John Howe (London: Verso, 1995 [1992]).

Auret, Diana, 'The Mhondoro Spirits of Supratribal Significance in the Culture of the Shona', *African Studies*, 41.2 (1982), 173–87.

Aycock, Amanda, 'An Interview with Chris Abani', *Safundi*, 10.1 (2009), 1–10.

Azar, Michael, 'In the Name of Algeria: Frantz Fanon and the Algerian Revolution', in *Frantz Fanon: Critical Perspectives*, ed. by Anthony C. Alessandrini (London: Routledge, 1999), pp. 21–33.

Beach, D. N., 'An Innocent Woman, Unjustly Accused? Charwe, Medium of the Nehanda Mhondoro Spirit, and the 1896–97 Central Shona Rising in Zimbabwe', *History in Africa*, 25 (1988), 27–54.

Benjamin, Walter, *Illuminations*, trans. by Harry Zohn (New York: Schocken Books, 1968).

Bgoya, Walter and Mary Jay, 'Publishing in Africa from Independence to the Present Day', *Research in African Literatures*, 44.2 (2013), 17–34.

Bhabha, Homi K., 'Introduction: Narrating the Nation', in *Nation and Narration*, ed. by Homi K. Bhabha (London: Routledge, 1990), pp. 1–7.

———, *The Location of Culture* (London: Routledge, 1994).

Binyon, Michael, 'Sierra Leone: A Tale of Post-colonial Disaster: How Prosperity Declined into Bloody Revolution', *Times* (31 May 1997), p. 2.

Boehmer, Elleke, 'Achebe and his Influence in some Contemporary African Writing', *Interventions: International Journal of Postcolonial Studies*, 11.2 (2009), 141–53.

———, *Colonial and Postcolonial Literature: Migrant Metaphors* (Oxford: Oxford University Press, 2005).

———, 'Transfiguring: Colonial Body into Postcolonial Narrative', *NOVEL: A Forum on Fiction*, 26.3 (Spring 1993), 268–77.

Bohrer, Frederick N., 'Inventing Assyria: Exoticism and Reception in Nineteenth-Century England and France', *The Art Bulletin*, 80.2 (1998), 336–56.

Booth, Wayne, *A Rhetoric of Irony* (Chicago: The University of Chicago Press, 1974).

Bourdieu, Pierre, *Distinction: A Social Critique of the Judgement of Taste*, trans. by Richard Nice (London: Routledge, 1984 [1979]).

Bratton, Michael and Eldred Masunungure, 'Zimbabwe's Long Agony', *Journal of Democracy*, 19.4 (2008), 41–55.

Brennan, Timothy, *At Home in the World: Cosmopolitanism Now* (Cambridge: Harvard University Press, 1997).

———, 'The National Longing for Form', in *Nation and Narration*, ed. by Homi K. Bhabha (London: Routledge, 1990), pp. 44–70.

Brooks, Jerome, 'Chinua Achebe: The Art of Fiction no. 139', *The Paris Review*, 139 (1994) <http://www.theparisreview.org/interviews/1720/the-art-of-fiction-no-139-chinua-achebe> [accessed 16 July 2013].

Brouillette, Sarah, *Postcolonial Writers in a Global Literary Marketplace* (Basingstoke: Palgrave Macmillan, 2007).

Brown, Duncan, 'National Belonging and Cultural Difference: South Africa and the Global Imaginary', *Journal of Southern African Studies*, 27.4 (2001), 757–69.

Brown, Lee, 'Introduction', in *African Philosophy: New and Traditional Perspectives*, ed. by Lee Brown (New York: Oxford University Press, 2004), pp. 3–20.

Brückner, Thomas, 'Across the Borders: Orality Old and New in the African Novel', in *Fusion of Cultures?*, ed. by Peter O. Stummer and Christopher Balme (Amsterdam: Rodopi, 1996), pp. 153–60.

Butler, Judith, *Bodies that Matter: On the Discursive Limits of "Sex"* (London: Routledge, 1993).

———, *Giving an Account of Oneself* (New York: Fordham University Press, 2005).

———, *Precarious Life: The Powers of Mourning and Violence* (London: Verso, 2003).

Casanova, Pascale, *The World Republic of Letters*, trans. by M. B. Debevoise (Cambridge: Harvard University Press, 2004 [1999]).

The Catholic Commission for Justice and Peace in Zimbabwe, *Gukurahundi in Zimbabwe: A Report on the Disturbances in Matabeleland and the Midlands, 1980–1988* (New York: Columbia University Press, 2008).

Césaire, Aimé, *Cahier d'un retour au pays natal* (Paris: Présence Africaine, 1956).

———, *Discour sur le colonialism, Suivi de Discour sur la Négritude* (Paris: Présence Africaine, 2000 [1955]).

Chait, Sandra, '*The Stone Virgins* by Yvonne Vera', *Africa Today*, 50.4 (2004), 132–5.

Chan, Stephen, 'The Memory of Violence: Trauma in the Writings of Alexander Kanengoni and Yvonne Vera and the Idea of Unreconciled Citizenship in Zimbabwe', *Third World Quarterly*, 26.2 (2005), 369–82.

Cheah, Pheng, *Spectral Nationality: Passages of Freedom from Kant to Postcolonial Literatures of Liberation* (New York: Columbia University Press, 2003).

Chikwava, Brian, 'Free Speech in Zimbabwe: The Story of the Blue-Stomached Lizard', *World Literature Today*, 80.5 (2006), 18–21.

———, *Harare North* (London: Vintage, 2009).

Chinweizu, Onwuchekwa Jemie and Ihechukwu Madubuike, *Toward the Decolonization of African Literature* (Enugu: Fourth Dimension, 1980).

———, 'Towards the Decolonization of African Literature', *Transition*, 48 (1975), 29–57.

Chiwome, Emmanuel, 'The Role of Oral Traditions in the War of National Liberation in Zimbabwe: Preliminary Observations', *Journal of Folklore Research*, 27.2 (1990), 241–7.

Cobham, Rhonda, 'Problems of Gender and History in the Teaching of *Things Fall Apart*', in *Chinua Achebe's* Things Fall Apart: *A Casebook*, ed. by Isidore Okpewho (New York: Oxford University Press, 2003), pp. 165–80.

Coetzee, J. M., 'Into the Dark Chamber', in *Doubling the Point*, ed. by David Attwell (Cambridge: Harvard University Press, 1992), pp. 361–8.

Colmeiro, José F., 'Exorcising Exoticism: *Carmen* and the Construction of Oriental Spain', *Comparative Literature*, 54.2 (2002), 127–55.

Colson, Robert L., 'Arresting Time, Resisting Arrest: Narrative Time and the African Dictator in Ngũgĩ wa Thiong'o's *Wizard of the Crow*', *Research in African Literatures*, 42.1 (2011), 133–53.

Cooper, Brenda, *Magical Realism in West African Fiction: Seeing with a Third Eye* (Abingdon: Routledge, 1998).

———, *A New Generation of African Writers: Migration, Material Culture & Language* (Woodbridge: James Currey, 2008).

Coundouriotis, Eleni, 'The Child Soldier Narrative and the Problem of Arrested Historicization', *Journal of Human Rights*, 9.2 (2010), 191–206.

Crenshaw, Kimberlé, 'Mapping the Margins: Intersectionality, Identity Politics and Violence Against Women of Color', in *Identities: Race, Class, Gender, and Nationality*, ed. by Linda Martín Alcoff and Eduardo Mendieta (Malden: Blackwell, 2003), pp. 175–200.

Currey, James, *Africa Writes Back: The African Writers Series and the Launch of African Literature* (Oxford: James Currey, 2008).

Currie, Mark, *Postmodern Narrative Theory* (Basingstoke: Palgrave Macmillan, 1998).

Dalley, Hamish, 'Trauma Theory and Nigerian Civil War Literature: Speaking "Something that was Never in Words" in Chris Abani's *Song for Night*', *Journal of Postcolonial Writing*, 49.4 (2013), 445–57.

Dane, Robyn, 'When Mirror Turns Lamp: Frantz Fanon as Cultural Visionary', *Africa Today*, 41.2 (1994), 70–91.

Dangarembga, Tsitsi, *The Book of Not* (Banbury: Ayebia Clarke Publishing, 2006).

———, *Nervous Conditions* (New York: Seal Press, 1988).

Darah, G. G., 'Introduction', in *Radical Essays on Nigerian Literature*, ed. by G. G. Darah (Lagos: Malthouse Press, 2008), pp. xv–xlvii.

Davis, Caroline, *Creating Postcolonial Literature: African Writers and British Publishers* (Basingstoke: Palgrave Macmillan, 2013).

Davis, Mike, *Planet of Slums* (London: Verso, 2006).

Derrida, Jacques, *Of Grammatology*, trans. by Gayatri Chakravorty Spivak (Baltimore: The Johns Hopkins University Press, 1976).

Dirlik, Arlif, *The Postcolonial Aura: Third World Criticism in the Age of Global Capitalism* (Boulder: Westview Press, 1997).

Driver, Dorothy and Meg Samuelson, 'History's Intimate Invasions: Yvonne Vera's *The Stone Virgins*', *English Studies in Africa*, 50.2 (2007), 101–20.

Dutrion, Marianne, 'A propos d'*Harare North*. Une conversation avec Brian Chikwava', *Malfini: Publication exploratoire des escapes francophones* <http://malfini.ens-lyon.fr/document.php?id=170> [accessed 10 January 2013].

Eagleton, Terry, 'The Ideology of the Aesthetic', *Poetics Today*, 9.2 (1988), 327–38.

Elder, Arlene A., *Narrative Shape-shifting: Myth, Humour and History in the Fiction of Ben Okri, B. Kojo Laing and Yvonne Vera* (Surrey: James Currey, 2009).

English, James, *The Economy of Prestige: Prizes, Awards and the Circulation of Cultural Value* (Cambridge: Harvard University Press, 2005).

Etter-Lewis, Gwendolyn, 'Dark Bodies/White Masks: African Masculinities in *Graceland, The Joys of Motherhood* and *Things Fall Apart*', in *Masculinities in African Literary and Cultural Texts*, ed. by Helen Mugambi and Tuzyline Jita Allen (Banbury: Ayebia Clarke, 2010), pp. 160–77.

Eze, Emmanuel Chukwudi, 'Introduction', in *Postcolonial African Philosophy: A Critical Reader*, ed. by Emmanuel Chukwudi Eze (Oxford: Blackwell, 1997), pp. 1–21.

———, 'Language and Time in Postcolonial Experience', *Research in African Literatures*, 39.1 (2008), 24–47.

Ezikeojiaku, Ichie P. A., 'Towards Understanding *Ndi Igbo* and their Cosmology', in *Radical Essays on Nigerian Literature*, ed. by G. G. Darah (Lagos: Malthouse Press, 2008), pp. 35–48.

Ezzaher, Lahcen E., *Writing and Cultural Influence: Studies in Rhetorical History, Orientalist Discourse, and Post-Colonial Criticism* (New York: Peter Lang, 2003).

Fanon, Frantz, *Black Skin, White Masks*, trans. by Richard Philcox (New York: Grove Press, 2008 [1952]).

———, *The Wretched of the Earth*, trans. by Richard Philcox (New York: Grove Press, 2004 [1961]).

Farah, Nuruddin, *Knots* (London: Penguin, 2007).

———, *Links* (London: Duckworth, 2005).

Forna, Aminatta, *Ancestor Stones* (London: Bloomsbury, 2006).

———, 'Speaking in Tongues', *Washington Post* (10 September 2006) <http://www.washingtonpost.com/wp-dyn/content/article/2006/09/07/AR2006090701167.html> [accessed 19 June 2013].

Fraser, Robert, *Book History Through Postcolonial Eyes* (London: Routledge, 2008), pp. 88–99.

Frow, John, 'The Literary Frame', in *Narrative Dynamics: Essays on Time, Plot, Closure, and Frames*, ed. by Brian Richardson (Columbus: Ohio State University Press, 2002), pp. 333–8.

Furniss, Graham and Abdalla Uba Adamu, '"Go by Appearances at Your Peril": The Raina Kama Writers' Association in Kano, Nigeria, Carving out a Place for the "Popular" in the Hausa Literary Landscape', *Research in African Literatures*, 43.4 (2012), 88–111.

Fuss, Diana, 'Interior Colonies: Frantz Fanon and the Politics of Identification', *Diacritics*, 24.2/3 (1994), 20–42.

Gagiano, Annie, 'Reading *The Stone Virgins* as Vera's Study of the Katabolism of War', *Research in African Literatures*, 38.2 (2007), 64–76.

Gana, Nouri and Heike Härting, 'Introduction: Narrative Violence: Africa and the Middle East', *Comparative Studies of South Asia, Africa and the Middle East*, 28.1 (2008), 1–10.

Gappah, Petina, 'Where Citizenship Went to Die', *New York Times* (22 March 2013) <http://www.nytimes.com/2013/03/23/opinion/where-citizenship-went-to-die-in-zimbabwe.html?pagewanted=all> [accessed 19 July 2013].

Garuba, Harry, 'Explorations in Animist Materialism: Notes on Reading/Writing African Literature, Culture, and Society', *Public Culture*, 15.2 (2003), 261–85.

Gates, Henry Louis, Jr, 'Criticism in the Jungle', in *Black Literature and Literary Theory*, ed. by Henry Louis Gates, Jr (New York: Methuen, 1984), pp. 1–25.

George, Òlakunle, 'The "Native" Missionary, the African Novel, and In-between', *NOVEL: A Forum on Fiction*, 36.1 (Autumn 2002), 5–25.

Gerecke, Megan, 'Explaining Sexual Violence in Conflict Situations', in *Gender, War, and Militarism: Feminist Perspectives*, ed. by Laura Sjoberg and Sandra Via (Santa Barbara: ABC-CLIO, 2010), pp. 138–54.

Gettleman, Jeffrey, 'Kenya, Known for Its Stability, Topples Into Post-Election Chaos', *New York Times* (3 January 2008) <http://www.nytimes.com/2008/01/03/world/africa/03kenya.html?pagewanted=all> [accessed 19 July 2013].

Gibson, Nigel, 'Losing Sight of the Real: Recasting Merleau-Ponty in Fanon's Critique of Mannoni', in *Race and Racism in Continental Philosophy*, ed. by Robert Bernasconi and Sybol Cook (Bloomington: Indiana University Press, 2003), pp. 129–50.

Gikandi, Simon, 'African Literature and the Colonial Factor', in *Cambridge History of African and Caribbean Literature*, vol. 1, ed. by F. Abiola Irele and Simon Gikandi (Cambridge: Cambridge University Press, 2004), pp. 379–97.

——, 'Between Roots and Routes: Cosmopolitanism and the Claims of Locality', in *Rerouting the Postcolonial: New Directions for the New Millennium*, ed. by Janet Wilson, Cristina Şandru and Sarah Lawson Welsh (London: Routledge, 2010), pp. 22–35.

——, 'Cultural Translation and the African Self: A (Post)colonial Case Study', *Interventions: International Journal of Postcolonial Studies*, 3.3 (2001), 355–75.

——, *Ngugi wa Thiong'o* (Cambridge: Cambridge University Press, 2000).

——, 'Nuruddin Farah and Postcolonial Textuality', *World Literature Today*, 72.4 (1998), 753–8.

——, 'The Postcolonial Wizard', *Transition*, 98 (2008), 156–69.

——, *Reading the African Novel* (London: James Currey, 1987).

——, 'Reading the Referent: Postcolonialism and the Writing of Modernity', in *Reading the 'New' Literatures in a Post-Colonial Era*, ed. by Susheila Nastra (Cambridge: D. S. Brewer, 2000), pp. 87–104.

Gilroy, Paul, *The Black Atlantic: Modernity and Double Consciousness* (Cambridge: Harvard University Press, 1993).

——, *Postcolonial Melancholia* (New York: Columbia University Press, 2005).

Granqvist, Raoul J., 'Reflections: Ngugi wa Thiong'o in/and 2006', *Research in African Literatures*, 42.4 (2011), 124–31.

Griffiths, Gareth, *African Literatures in English: East and West* (Harlow: Pearson Education, 2000).

Griswold, Wendy, *Bearing Witness: Readers, Writers and the Novel in Nigeria* (Princeton: Princeton University Press, 2000).

——, 'The Writing on the Mud Wall: Nigerian Novels and the Imaginary Village', *American Sociological Review*, 57.6 (1992), 709–24.

Gugelberger, George M. (ed.), *Marxism and African Literature* (London: James Currey, 1985).

Habila, Helon, 'Introduction', in *The Granta Book of the African Short Story*, ed. by Helon Habila (London: Granta, 2011), pp. vii–xv.

——, 'We Need New Names by NoViolet Bulawayo—review', *Guardian* (20 June 2013) <http://www.guardian.co.uk/books/2013/jun/20/need-new-names-bulawayo-review> [accessed 16 July 2013].

Hale, Sondra, 'Rape as a Marker and Eraser of Difference: Darfur and the Nuba Mountains (Sudan)', in *Gender, War, and Militarism: Feminist Perspectives*, ed. by Laura Sjoberg and Sandra Via (Santa Barbara: ABC-CLIO, 2010), pp. 105–13.

Hall, Stuart, 'Cultural Identity and Diaspora', in *Identity: Community, Culture, Difference*, ed. by Jonathan Rutherford (London: Lawrence & Wishart, 1990), pp. 222–37.

Harneil-Sievers, Axel, Jones O. Ahazuem and Sydney Emezue, *A Social History of the Nigerian Civil War: Perspectives from Below* (Ogete, Enugu: Jemezie Associates, 1997).

Harrison, Sarah, '"Suspended City": Personal, Urban, and National Development in Chris Abani's *GraceLand*', *Research in African Literatures*, 43.2 (2012), 95–114.

Hawley, John C., 'Biafra as Heritage and Symbol: Adichie, Mbachu, and Iweala', *Research in African Literatures*, 39.2 (2008), 15–26.

——, 'The Colonizing Impulse of Postcolonial Theory', *Modern Fiction Studies*, 56.2 (Winter 2010), 769–87.

Hillenbrand, Margaret, 'The National Allegory Revisited: Writing Private and Public in Contemporary Taiwan', *positions: east asia cultures critiques*, 14.3 (2006), 633–62.

Hitchcock, Peter, *The Long Space: Transnationalism and Postcolonial Form* (Stanford: Stanford University Press, 2010).

——, 'They Must Be Represented? Problems in Theories of Working-Class Representation', *PMLA*, 115.1 (2000), 20–32.

hooks, bell, *Yearning: Race, Gender, and Cultural Politics* (Boston: South End Press, 1991).

Huggan, Graham, *The Postcolonial Exotic: Marketing the Margins* (London: Routledge, 2001).

——, 'Postcolonial, Globalization, and the Rise of (Trans)cultural Studies', in *Towards a Transcultural Future: Literature and Society in a 'Post'-Colonial World*, ed. by Geoffrey V. Davis, Peter H. Marsden, Bénédicte Ledent and Marc Delrez (Amsterdam: Rodopi, 2004), pp. 27–36.

Hunt, Katherine, 'Book Review: Abani, Chris. *Graceland*', *Journal of Asian and African Studies*, 43 (2008), 241–3.

Ibitokun, Benedict M., 'The Dynamic of Spatiality in African Fiction', *Modern Fiction Studies*, 37.3 (1991), 409–26.

Ikheloa, Ikhide R., 'The 2011 Caine Prize: How Not to Write About Africa', *Ikhide: Email from America* (11 March 2012) <http://xokigbo.wordpress.com/2012/03/11/the-2011-caine-prize-how-not-to-write-about-africa/> [accessed 16 July 2013].

——, 'The Trials of Chris Abani', *Ikhide: Email from America* (25 November 2011) <http://xokigbo.wordpress.com/2011/11/25/the-trials-of-chris-abani-and-the-power-of-empty-words/> [accessed 1 December 2011].

Imam, Hayat, 'Aftermath of U.S. Invasions: The Anguish of Women in Afghanistan and Iraq', in *Women, War, and Violence: Personal Perspectives and Global Activism*, ed. by Robin M. Chandler, Lihua Wang and Linda K. Fuller (New York: Palgrave Macmillan, 2010), pp. 117–34.

Innes, Lyn, 'Reading Africa', *Interventions: International Journal of Postcolonial Studies*, 3.3 (2001), 317–21.

Irele, F. Abiola, *The African Experience in Literature and Ideology* (Bloomington: University of Indiana Press, 1990).

——, *The African Imagination: Literature in Africa and the Black Diaspora* (New York: Oxford University Press, 2001).

Jackson, Shona N., 'The Economy of Babel or "Can I Buy a Vowel?"', *Callaloo*, 32.2 (Spring 2009), 581–90.

Jameson, Fredric, 'Third World Literature in the Era of Multinational Capitalism', *Social Text*, 15 (1986), 65–88.

JanMohamed, Abdul R., 'The Economy of Manichean Allegory: The Function of Racial Difference in Colonialist Literature', *Critical Inquiry*, 12.1 (1985), 59–87.

Jell-Bahlsen, Sabine, *The Water Goddess in Igbo Cosmology: Ogbuide of Oguta Lake* (Trenton: Africa World Press, 2008).

Jeyifo, Biodun, 'The Nation of Things: Arrested Decolonization and Critical Theory', *Research in African Literatures*, 21.1 (1990), 33–48.

Kandeh, Jimmy D., 'In Search of Legitimacy: The 1996 Elections', in *Between Democracy and Terror: The Sierra Leone Civil War*, ed. by Ibrahim Abdullah (Dakar: Council for the Development of Social Science Research in Africa, 2004), pp. 123–43.

Kanneh, Kadiatu, 'What is African Literature? Ethnography and Criticism', in *Writing and Africa*, ed. by Mpalive-Hangson Msiska and Paul Hyland (Harlow: Addison Wesley Longman, 1997), pp. 69–86.

Kaplan, E. Ann, 'Fanon, Trauma and Cinema', in *Frantz Fanon: Critical Perspectives*, ed. by Anthony C. Alessandrini (London: Routledge, 1999), pp. 146–57.

Karatani, Kojin, 'Use of Aesthetics: After Orientalism', trans. by Sabu Kohso, *boundary 2*, 25.2 (1998), 145–60.

Keenan, Thomas, 'The Push and Pull of Rights and Responsibilities', *Interventions: International Journal of Postcolonial Studies*, 4.2 (2002), 191–7.

Kennedy, Roseanne, 'Mortgaged Futures: Trauma, Subjectivity, and the Legacies of Colonialism in Tsitsi Dangarembga's *The Book of Not*', *Studies in the Novel*, 40.1/2 (2008), 86–107.

Kimber, Charles, 'Interview: Chimamanda Ngozi Adichie', *Socialist Review* (October 2006) <http://www.socialistreview.org.uk/article.php?articlenumber=9845> [accessed 20 March 2011].

ten Kortenaar, Neil, *Postcolonial Literature and the Impact of Literacy: Reading and Writing in African and Caribbean Fiction* (Cambridge: Cambridge University Press, 2011).

Kostelac, Sofia, '"The body is his, pulse and motion": Violence and Desire in Yvonne Vera's *The Stone Virgins*', *Research in African Literatures*, 41.3 (2010), 75–87.

————, '"The Voices of Drowned Men Cannot Be Heard": Writing Subalternity in Yvonne Vera's *Butterfly Burning* and *The Stone Virgins'*, *English Studies in Africa*, 50.2 (2007), 121–32.

Kristeva, Julia, *Powers of Horror: An Essay on Abjection*, trans. by Leon S. Roudiez (New York: Columbia University Press, 1982 [1980]).

Kuria, Mike, 'Speaking in Tongues: Ngũgĩ's Gift to Workers and Peasants through *Mũrogi wa Kagogo'*, *Journal of Literary Studies*, 27.3 (2011), 56–73.

Lacan, Jacques, *Ecrits: A Selection*, trans. by Bruce Fink (New York: W.W. Norton, 2002 [1966]).

Lamas Rodrigues, Angela, 'Beyond Nativism: An Interview with Ngugi wa Thiong'o', *Research in African Literatures*, 35.3 (2004), 161–7.

Lazarus, Neil, 'The Politics of Postcolonial Modernism', in *Postcolonial Studies and Beyond*, ed. by Ania Loomba, Suvir Kaul, Matti Bunzl, Antoinette Burton and Jed Etsy (Durham: Duke University Press, 2005), pp. 423–38.

————, *The Postcolonial Unconscious* (Cambridge: Cambridge University Press, 2011).

————, *Resistance in Postcolonial African Fiction* (New Haven: Yale University Press, 1990).

Lewis, Desiree, 'Biography, Nationalism and Yvonne Vera's *Nehanda'*, *Social Dynamic: A Journal of African Studies*, 30.1 (2004), 28–50.

Low, Gail, *Publishing the Postcolonial: Anglophone West African and Caribbean Writing in the UK 1948–1968* (New York: Routledge, 2011).

Mabura, Lily G. N., 'Black Women Walking Zimbabwe: Refuge and Prospect in the Landscapes of Yvonne Vera's *The Stone Virgins* and Tsitsi Dangarembga's *Nervous Conditions* and Its Sequel, *The Book of Not'*, *Research in African Literatures*, 41.3 (2010), 88–111.

————, 'Breaking Gods: An African Postcolonial Gothic Reading of Chimamanda Ngozi Adichie's *Purple Hibiscus* and *Half of a Yellow Sun'*, *Research in African Literatures*, 39.1 (2008), 203–22.

Makang, Jean Marie, 'Of the Good Use of Tradition: Keeping the Critical Perspective in African Philosophy', in *Postcolonial African Philosophy: A Critical Reader*, ed. by Emmanuel Chukwudi Eze (Oxford: Blackwell, 1997), pp. 324–38.

Martin Shaw, Carolyn, 'Turning Her Back on the Moon: Virginity, Sexuality, and Mothering in the Works of Yvonne Vera', *Africa Today*, 51.2 (2004), 35–51.

Marx, John, 'Failed-State Fiction', *Contemporary Literature*, 49.4 (2008), 597–633.

————, 'The Feminization of Globalization', *Cultural Critique*, 63 (2006), 1–32.

————, 'Fiction and State Crisis', *Novel: A Forum on Fiction*, 42.3 (2009), 524–30.

Masolo, D. A., 'The Concept of the Person in Luo Modes of Thought', in *African Philosophy: New and Traditional Perspectives*, ed. by Lee Brown (New York: Oxford University Press, 2004), pp. 84–106.

Mbembe, Achille, *On the Postcolony* (Berkeley: University of California Press, 2001).

Mbiba, Beacon, 'Zimbabwe's Global Citizens in "Harare North": Some Preliminary Observations', in *Skinning the Skunk—Facing Zimbabwean Futures: Discussion Papers 30*, ed. by Mai Palmberg and Ranka Primorac (Uppsala: Nordska Afrikainstitutet, 2005), pp. 26–38.

McGonegal, Julie, 'Postcolonial Metacritique', *Interventions: International Journal of Postcolonial Studies*, 7.2 (2005), 251–65.

McLaren, Joseph, 'From the National to the Global: Satirical Magical Realism in Ngugi's *Wizard of the Crow*', *The Global South*, 2.2 (2008), 150–8.

Mdika Tembo, Nick, 'Subversion and the Carnivalesque: Images of Resistance in Ngũgĩ wa Thiong'o's *Wizard of the Crow*', in *Spheres Public and Private: Western Genres in African Literature*, ed. by Gordon Collier (Amsterdam: Rodopi, 2011), pp. 337–61.

Memmi, Albert, *Decolonization and the Decolonized* (Minneapolis: University of Minneapolis Press, 2006).

Menkiti, I. A., 'Physical and Metaphysical Understanding', in *African Philosophy: New and Traditional Perspectives*, ed. by Lee Brown (New York: Oxford University Press, 2004), pp. 107–35.

Mercer, Kobena, 'Busy in the Ruins of a Wretched Phantasia', in *Frantz Fanon: Critical Perspectives*, ed. by Anthony C. Alessandrini (London: Routledge, 1999), pp. 195–218.

——, 'Welcome to the Jungle: Identity and Diversity in Postmodern Politics', in *Identity: Community, Culture, Difference*, ed. by Jonathan Rutherford (London: Lawrence & Wishart, 1990), pp. 43–71.

Meredith, Martin, *Mugabe: Power, Plunder and the Struggle for Zimbabwe* (New York: Public Affairs, 2002).

Metscher, Thomas, 'Literature and Art as Ideological Form', trans. by Kiernan Ryan, *New Literary History*, 11.1 (1979), 21–39.

Mignolo, Walter, 'The Many Faces of Cosmo-polis: Border Thinking and Critical Cosmopolitanism', in *Cosmopolitanisms*, ed. by Sheldon Pollock, Homi K. Bhabha, Carol A. Breckenridge and Dipesh Chakrabarty (Durham: Duke University Press, 2002), pp. 157–88.

Miller, Christopher, 'Theories of Africans: The Question of Literary Anthropology', *Critical Inquiry*, 13.1 (1986), 120–39.

Miller, Daniel, *Material Culture and Mass Consumption* (Oxford: Blackwell, 1987).

——, 'Why Some Things Matter', in *Material Cultures: Why Some Things Matter*, ed. by Daniel Miller (London: UCL Press, 1997), pp. 3–21.

Moane, Geraldine, *Gender and Colonialism* (Basingstoke: Macmillan, 1999).

Morton, Stephen, *States of Emergency: Colonialism, Literature and Law* (Liverpool: Liverpool University Press, 2013).

Moss, Stephen, 'Madonna's Not Our Saviour', *Guardian* (8 June 2007) <http://www.guardian.co.uk/books/2007/jun/08/orangeprizeforfiction2007.orangeprizeforfiction> [accessed 20 March 2011].

Mphahlele, Ezekiel, *The African Image*, second edition (London: Faber and Faber, 1974).

Mudimbe, V. Y., *The Idea of Africa* (Bloomington: Indiana University Press, 1994).

———, *The Invention of Africa: Gnosis, Philosophy, and the Order of Knowledge* (Bloomington: Indiana University Press, 1988).

Mzali, Ines, 'Wars of Representation: Metonymy and Nuruddin Farah's *Links*', *College Literature*, 37.3 (2010), 84–105.

Nandy, Ashis, *The Intimate Enemy: Loss and Recovery of Self Under Colonialism* (New Delhi: Oxford University Press, 1983).

Ndlovu-Gatsheni, Sabelo J., *Do 'Zimbabweans' Exist? Trajectories of Nationalism, National Identity Formation and Crisis in a Postcolonial State* (Bern: Peter Lang, 2009).

Newell, Stephanie, *Ghanaian Popular Fiction: 'Thrilling Discoveries in Conjugal Life' and Other Tales* (London: James Currey, 2000).

———, *West African Literatures: Ways of Reading* (Oxford: Oxford University Press, 2006).

Ngara, Emmanuel, *Ideology and Form in African Poetry: Implications for Communication* (London: James Currey, 1990).

Ngũgĩ wa Thiong'o, *Decolonising the Mind: The Politics of Language in African Literature* (London: James Currey, 1986).

———, 'Recovering the Original', *World Literature Today*, 78.3/4 (2004), 13–15.

———, *Wizard of the Crow* (New York: Anchor, 2006).

Niemi, Minna, 'Witnessing Contemporary Somalia from Abroad: An Interview with Nuruddin Farah', *Callaloo*, 35.2 (2012), 330–40.

Nkosi, Lewis, *Home and Exile* (London: Longman, 1965).

———, *Tasks and Masks: Themes and Style of African Literature* (Harlow: Longman, 1981).

Nnodim, Rita, 'City, Identity and Dystopia: Writing Lagos in Contemporary Nigerian Novels', *Journal of Postcolonial Writing*, 44.4 (2008), 321–32.

Norridge, Zoë, 'Sex as Synecdoche: Intimate Languages of Violence in Chimamanda Ngozi Adichie's *Half of a Yellow Sun* and Aminatta Forna's *The Memory of Love*', *Research in African Literatures*, 43.2 (2012), 18–39.

Nossiter, Adam, 'Election Fuels Deadly Clashes in Nigeria', *New York Times* (24 April 2011) <http://www.nytimes.com/2011/04/25/world/africa/25nigeria.html> [accessed 19 July 2013].

Nwakanma, Obi, 'Metonymic Eruptions: Igbo Novelists, the Narrative of the Nation, and New Developments in the Contemporary Nigerian Novel', *Research in African Literatures*, 39.2 (2008), 1–14.

Nyamnjoh, Francis B., *The Disillusioned African*, revised edition (Bamenda: Langaa Research and Publishing Common Initiative Group, 2007 [1995]).

Nzegwu, Nkiri Iwechia, *Family Matters: Feminist Concepts in African Philosophy of Culture* (Albany: State University of New York Press, 2006).

Oates, Nathan, 'Political Stories: The Individual in Contemporary Fiction', *The Missouri Review*, 30.3 (2007), 156–71.

Obonyo Amoko, Apollo, *Postcolonialism in the Wake of the Nairobi Revolution: Ngugi wa Thiong'o and the Idea of African Literature* (Basingstoke: Palgrave Macmillan, 2010).

Ogbuene, Chigekwu, *The Concept of Man in Igbo Myths* (Frankfurt am Main: Peter Lang, 1999).

Ogude, James, *Ngugi's Novels and African History: Narrating the Nation* (London: Pluto Press, 1999).

Ogunyemi, Chikwenye Okonjo, 'An Abiku-Ogbanje Atlas: A Pre-Text for Rereading Soyinka's *Ake* and Morrison's *Beloved*', *African American Review*, 36.4 (2002), 663–8.

Ojaide, Tanure, 'Examining Canonisation in Modern African Literature', *Asiatic*, 3.1 (2009), 1–20.

———, 'Migration, Globalization, and Recent African Literature', *World Literature Today*, 82.2 (2008), 43–6.

Okonkwo, Christopher, 'A Critical Divination: Reading *Sula* as Ogbanje-Abiku', *African American Review*, 38.4 (2004), 651–68.

Okorafor, Nnedi, 'Organic Fantasy', *African Identities*, 7.2 (2009), 275–86.

Okpewho, Isidore, 'Home, Exile, and the Space In Between', *Research in African Literatures*, 37.2 (Summer 2006), 68–83.

Okunyade, Ogaga, 'Weaving Memories of Childhood: The New Nigerian Novel and the Genre of the *Bildungsroman*', *ARIEL: A Review of International English Literature*, 41.3–4 (2011), 137–66.

Oliver, Kelly, *Colonization of Psychic Space: A Psychoanalytic Social Theory of Oppression* (Minneapolis: University of Minnesota Press, 2004).

Ott, Bill, 'review of *GraceLand*', *Booklist* (13 November 2003), 570.

Oyěwùmí, Oyèrónke, *The Invention of Women: Making an African Sense of Western Gender Discourses* (Minneapolis: University of Minnesota Press, 1997).

Pape, Marion, 'Nigerian War Literature by Women: From Civil War to Gender War', in *Body, Sexuality, and Gender: Versions and Subversions in African Literatures 1*, ed. by Flora Veit-Wild and Dirk Naguschewski (Amsterdam: Rodopi, 2005), pp. 231–41.

Park Sorensen, Eli, *Postcolonial Studies and the Literary: Theory, Interpretation and the Novel* (Basingstoke: Palgrave Macmillan, 2010).

Parry, Benita, 'Fanon and the Trauma of Modernity', in *After Fanon* (*New Formations*, 47) (London: Lawrence & Wishart, 2002), pp. 24–9.

———, *Postcolonial Studies: A Materialist Critique* (London: Routledge, 2004).

Peterson, V. Spike, 'Gendered Identities, Ideologies, and Practices in the Context of War and Militarism', in *Gender, War, and Militarism: Feminist Perspectives*, ed. by Laura Sjoberg and Sandra Via (Santa Barbara: ABC-CLIO, 2010), pp. 17–29.

Phelan, James, *Narrative as Rhetoric: Technique, Audiences, Ethics, Ideology* (Columbus: Ohio State University Press, 1996).

———, *Reading People, Reading Plots* (Chicago: The University of Chicago Press, 1989).

———, 'Rhetorical Aesthetics and Other Issues in the Study of Literary Narratives', in *Narrative—State of the Art*, ed. by Michael G. W. Manberg (Philadelphia: John Benjamins, 2007), pp. 103–12.

Phimster, Ian, '"Zimbabwe is Mine": Mugabe, Murder, and Matabeleland', *Safundi: The Journal of South African and American Studies*, 10.4 (2009), 471–8.

Pollock, Sheldon, Homi K. Bhabha, Carol A. Breckenridge and Dipesh Chakrabarty, 'Cosmopolitanisms', in *Cosmopolitanisms*, ed. by Sheldon

Pollock, Homi K. Bhabha, Carol A. Breckenridge and Dipesh Chakrabarty (Durham: Duke University Press, 2002), pp. 1–14.

Prabhu, Anjali, 'Narration in Frantz Fanon's *Peau noire masques blancs*: Some Reconsiderations', *Research in African Literatures*, 37.4 (2006), 189–210.

Primorac, Ranka, 'Legends of Modern Zambia', *Research in African Literatures*, 43.4 (2012), 50–70.

——, *The Place of Tears: The Novel and Politics in Modern Zimbabwe* (London: Tauris Academic Studies, 2006).

——, *Whodunnit in Southern Africa* (London: Africa Research Institute, 2011).

Pucherová, Dobrota, '"A Continent Learns to Tell its Story at Last": Notes on the Caine Prize', *Journal of Postcolonial Writing*, 48.1 (2012), 13–25.

Pyle, Forest, '"By a Certain Subreption": Gayatri Spivak and the "Level" of the Aesthetic', *Interventions: International Journal of Postcolonial Studies*, 4.2 (2002), 186–90.

Quayson, Ato, 'Looking Awry: Tropes of Disability in Postcolonial Writing', in *Relocating Postcolonialism*, ed. by David Goldberg and Ato Quayson (Oxford: Blackwell, 2002), pp. 217–30.

——, *Strategic Transformations in Nigerian Writing* (Oxford: James Currey, 1997).

Rabinowitz, Peter J., *Before Reading: Narrative Conventions and the Politics of Interpretation* (Columbus: Ohio State University Press, 1987).

——, 'Truth in Fiction: A Reexamination of Audiences', *Critical Inquiry*, 4.1 (Autumn 1977), 121–41.

Radhakrishnan, R., 'Culture as Common Ground: Ethnicity and Beyond', *MELUS*, 14.2 (Summer 1987), 5–19.

Ranger, Terrance, 'Nationalist Historiography, Patriotic History and the History of the Nation: The Struggle Over the Past in Zimbabwe', *Journal of Southern African Studies*, 30.2 (2004), 215–34.

Rao, Rahul, *Third World Protest: Between Home and the World* (Oxford: Oxford University Press, 2010).

Richardson, Brian, 'Introduction: Narrative Frames and Embeddings', in *Narrative Dynamics: Essays on Time, Plot, Closure, and Frames*, ed. by Brian Richardson (Columbus: Ohio State University Press, 2002), pp. 329–32.

——, *Unnatural Voices: Extreme Narration in Modern and Contemporary Fiction* (Columbus: Ohio State University Press, 2006).

Robbins, Bruce, 'Comparative Cosmopolitanisms', in *Cosmopolitics: Thinking and Feeling Beyond the Nation*, ed. by Pheng Cheah and Bruce Robbins (Minneapolis: University of Minnesota Press, 1998), pp. 246–64.

——, 'Introduction Part I: Actually Existing Cosmopolitanism' in *Cosmopolitics: Thinking and Feeling Beyond the Nation*, ed. by Pheng Cheah and Bruce Robbins (Minneapolis: University of Minnesota Press, 1998), pp. 1–19.

Rose, Gillian, *Feminism and Geography: The Limits of Geographical Knowledge* (Minneapolis: University of Minnesota Press, 1993).

Rutherford, Jonathan, 'A Place Called Home: Identity and the Cultural Politics of Difference', in *Identity: Community, Culture, Difference*, ed. by Jonathan Rutherford (London: Lawrence & Wishart, 1990), pp. 9–27.

Said, Edward W., 'Beginnings', in *Power, Politics and Culture: Interviews with Edward W. Said*, ed. by Guari Viswanathan (London: Bloomsbury, 2001), pp. 3–38.

———, *Culture and Imperialism* (London: Vintage, 1993).

———, *Orientalism* (London: Penguin, 2003 [1978]).

———, *Representations of the Intellectual* (New York: Vintage, 1994).

———, *The World, the Text, and the Critic* (Cambridge: Harvard University Press, 1983).

Sanders, Mark, 'Representation: Reading-Otherwise', *Interventions: International Journal of Postcolonial Studies*, 4.2 (2002), 198–204.

Sartre, Jean-Paul, *Being and Nothingness: A Phenomenological Essay on Ontology*, trans. by Hazel E. Barnes (New York: Washington Square Press, 1992 [1943]).

Scott, David, *Refashioning Futures: Criticism after Postcoloniality* (Princeton: Princeton University Press, 1999).

Senghor, Léopold Sédar, *Anthologie de la nouvelle poésie nègre et malgache de langue française* (Paris: Presses universitaires de France, 1948).

Sereda, Stefan, 'Riffing on Resistance: Music in Chris Abani's *Graceland*', *ARIEL: A Review of International English*, 39.4 (2008), 31–47.

Serequeberhan, Tsenay, 'The Critique of Eurocentrism and the Practice of African Philosophy', in *Postcolonial African Philosophy: A Critical Reader*, ed. by Emmanuel Chukwudi Eze (Oxford: Blackwell, 1997), pp. 141–61.

Sharpley-Whiting, T. Denean, *Frantz Fanon: Conflicts and Feminisms* (Lanham, MD: Rowman & Littlefield, 1998).

Shepler, Susan, 'Post-war Trajectories for Girls Associated with the Fighting Forces in Sierra Leone', in *Gender, War, and Militarism: Feminist Perspectives*, ed. by Laura Sjoberg and Sandra Via (Santa Barbara: ABC-CLIO, 2010), pp. 91–102.

Shohat, Ella, 'Notes on the "Post-Colonial"', *Social Text*, 31/32 (1992), 99–113.

Siebers, Tobin, 'Ethics ad Nauseam', *American Literary History*, 6.4 (Winter 1994), 756–78.

Sjoberg, Laura and Sandra Via, 'Introduction', in *Gender, War, and Militarism: Feminist Perspectives*, ed. by Laura Sjoberg and Sandra Via (Santa Barbara: ABC-CLIO, 2010), pp. 1–14.

Slaymaker, William, 'Digesting Crow: Reading and Teaching Ngugi's *Wizard of the Crow*', *Research in African Literatures*, 42.4 (2011), 8–19.

Slemon, Stephen, 'Magical Realism as Post-Colonial Discourse', in *Magical Realism: Theory and History*, ed. by Lois Parkinson Zamora and Wendy B. Faris (Durham: Duke University Press, 1995), pp. 407–26.

Smith, David, 'Scores Hacked to Death in Nigerian Sectarian Clash', *Guardian* (7 March 2010) <http://www.guardian.co.uk/world/2010/mar/07/scores-hacked-death-nigerian-sectarian> [accessed 19 July 2013].

Snead, James, 'European Pedigrees/African Contagions: Nationality, Narrative, and Communality in Tutuola, Achebe, and Reed', in *Nation and Narration*, ed. by Homi K. Bhabha (London: Routledge, 1990), pp. 231–49.

Soyinka, Wole, *Myth, Literature and the African World* (Cambridge: Cambridge University Press, 1976).

———, 'The Writer in an African State', *Transition*, 31 (1967), 10–13.

Spencer, Robert, *Cosmopolitan Criticism and Postcolonial Literature* (Basingstoke: Palgrave Macmillan, 2011).

———, 'Cosmopolitan Criticism', in *Rerouting the Postcolonial: New Directions for the New Millennium*, ed. by Janet Wilson, Cristina Şandru and Sarah Lawson Welsh (London: Routledge, 2010), pp. 36–47.

———, 'Ngũgĩ wa Thiong'o and the African Dictator Novel', *Journal of Commonwealth Literature*, 47.2 (2012), 145–58.

Spivak, Gayatri Chakravorty, *A Critique of Postcolonial Reason: Towards a History of the Vanishing Present* (Cambridge: Harvard University Press, 1999).

———, *Other Asias* (Malden: Blackwell, 2008).

———, *Outside in the Teaching Machine* (New York: Routledge, 1993).

———, 'Resident Alien', in *Relocating Postcolonialism*, ed. by David Theo Goldberg and Ato Quayson (Oxford: Blackwell, 2002), pp. 47–65.

———, 'Responsibility', *boundary 2*, 21.3 (Autumn 1994), 19–64.

Steady, Filomina Chioma, *Women and Collective Action in Africa* (New York: Palgrave, 2006).

Stevens, Maurice, 'Public (Re)Memory, Vindicating Narratives, and Troubling Beginnings: Toward a Critical Postcolonial Psychoanalytic Theory', in *Fanon: A Critical Reader*, ed. by Lewis R. Gordon, T. Denean Sharpley-Whiting and Renée T. White (Oxford: Blackwell, 1996), pp. 203–19.

Stratton, Florence, *Contemporary African Literature and the Politics of Gender* (London: Routledge, 2004).

———, '"Periodic Embodiments": A Ubiquitous Trope in African Men's Writing', *Research in African Literatures*, 21.1 (1990), 111–26.

———, 'The Shallow Grave: Archetypes of Female Experience in African Fiction', *Research in African Literatures*, 19.2 (1988), 143–69.

Szeman, Imre, 'Who's Afraid of National Allegory? Jameson, Literary Criticism, Globalization', *The South Atlantic Quarterly*, 100.3 (2001), 803–27.

Tagwira, Valerie, *The Uncertainty of Hope* (Harare: Weaver Press, 2006).

Tiffin, Chris and Alan Lawson, 'Introduction', in *De-Scribing Empire: Post-colonialism and Textuality*, ed. by Chris Tiffin and Alan Lawson (London: Routledge, 1994), pp. 1–11.

Todorov, Tzvetan, *On Human Diversity: Nationalism, Racism and Exoticism in French Thought* (Cambridge: Harvard University Press, 1993).

Trivedi, Harish, 'Ngugi wa Thiong'o in Conversation', *Wasafiri*, 18.40 (2003), 5–10.

Tunca, Daria, Vicki Mortimer and Emmanuelle Del Calzo, 'An Interview with Chika Unigwe', *Wasafiri*, 75 (2013), 54–9.

Uchendu, Egodi, *Women and Conflict in the Nigerian Civil War* (Trenton: Africa World Press, 2007).

Updike, John, 'Extended Performance: Saving the Republic of Aburira', *New Yorker* (31 July 2006) <http://www.newyorker.com/archive/2006/07/31/060731crbo_books> [accessed 19 June 2013].

Vambe, Maurice T., 'Zimbabwe Genocide: Voices and Perceptions from Ordinary People in Matabeleland and the Midlands Provinces, 30 Years on', *African Identities*, 10.3 (2012), 281–300.

Varadharajan, Asha, *Exotic Parodies: Subjectivity in Adorno, Said, and Spivak* (Minneapolis: University of Minnesota Press, 1995).

Vera, Yvonne, *The Stone Virgins* (New York: Farrar, Staus and Giroux, 2002).

Vergès, Françoise, '"I am not the slave of slavery": The Politics of Reparation in (French) Postslavery Communities', in *Frantz Fanon: Critical Perspectives*, ed. by Anthony C. Alessandrini (London: Routledge, 1999), pp. 258–75.

Viswanathan, Guari, 'Introduction', in *Power, Politics and Culture: Interviews with Edward W. Said*, ed. by Guari Viswanathan (London: Bloomsbury, 2001).

de Waal, Alex, 'Getting Somalia Right This Time', *New York Times* (21 February 2012) <http://www.nytimes.com/2012/02/22/opinion/getting-somalia-right-this-time.html?pagewanted=all> [accessed 19 July 2013].

Wainaina, Binyavanga, 'How to Write About Africa', *Granta*, 92 (2005), 92.

Wali, Obiajunwa, 'The Dead End of African Literature?', *Transition*, 10 (1963), 13–16.

Wallace, Maurice O., *Constructing the Black Masculine: Identity and Ideality in African American Men's Literature and Culture 1775–1995* (Durham: Duke University Press, 2002).

Williams, Patrick, 'West African Writing', in *Writing and Africa*, ed. by Mpalive-Hangson Msiska and Paul Hyland (Harlow: Addison Wesley Longman, 1997), pp. 31–45.

Wood, Elisabeth Jean, 'Sexual Violence during War: Toward an Understanding of Variation', in *Gender, War, and Militarism: Feminist Perspectives*, ed. by Laura Sjoberg and Sandra Via (Santa Barbara: ABC-CLIO, 2010), pp. 124–37.

Wood, James, *How Fiction Works* (London: Vintage, 2009).

Wright, Derek, 'African Literature and Post-independence Disillusionment', in *Cambridge History of African and Caribbean Literature*, vol. 1, ed. by F. Abiola Irele and Simon Gikandi (Cambridge: Cambridge University Press, 2004), pp. 797–808.

——, 'Nations as Fictions: Postmodernism in the Novels of Nuruddin Farah', *Critique: Studies in Contemporary Fiction*, 38.3 (1997), 193–204.

Young, Robert J. C., *White Mythologies: Writing History and the West*, second edition (London: Routledge, 2004).

Zabeida, Natalja, 'Not Making Excuses: Functions of Rape as a Tool in Ethno-Nationalist Wars', in *Women, War, and Violence: Personal Perspectives and Global Activism*, ed. by Robin M. Chandler, Lihua Wang and Linda K. Fuller (New York: Palgrave Macmillan, 2010), pp. 17–30.

Zeleza, Paul, 'Colonial Fictions: Memory and History in Yvonne Vera's Imagination', *Research in African Literatures*, 38.2 (2007), 9–21.

# Index